Bottom Dog Press

# Our Working Lives

## Short Stories of People and Work

Edited by
Bonnie Jo Campbell
& Larry Smith

Working Lives Series
Bottom Dog Press
Huron, Ohio

ISBN 0-933087-63-2

Bottom Dog Press
c/o BGSU Firelands College
One University Road
Huron, Ohio 44839
lsmithdog@aol.com

**Cover Art**
Andy Nelson
**Design**
Erin Johnson

**Acknowledgements**

Some of these stories first appeared in the following publications:
Stuart Dybek's "Sauerkraut Soup" in his *Childhood And Other Neighborhoods*
Nancy Zafris' "Death of a Junk Peddler" in *Witness* (1996)
Julie Weston's "Doc" as "Hi Ho" in
*American Jones Building & Maintenance* (1998)
Percical Everett's "Alluvial Deposite" in *Story* (Winter 1998)
Daniel Chacón's "Expression of Our People" as another version in *The New England Review* and in *his Chicano Chicanery* (Arte Publico Press, 2000)
Rachael Perry's "Hawk" as "Hawk and Snake" in *StoryQuarterly*
Gary Eller's "The Habit of Despair" in *Stiller's Pond, Vol. 2* (1991)
Bernadette Murphy's "Clack, Clack, Clack" in *Elipse* (Fall 2000)
R Yañez' "Holy Water" in *Mirrors Beneath the Earth* (Curbstone Press)

We thank the Ohio Arts Council for their continuing support.

## Contents

## Introduction: Writing of Work Today

### Bonnie Jo Campbell (Kalamazoo, Michigan)

"We write too much about love and sex," Stuart Dybek once said after his students discussed a story which took place mostly on a construction site. "We should write more stories like this, about work." The construction site was not only planks, concrete, and power tools—it was a web of interactions among workers, bosses, and customers, all with their own philosophies, temperaments, and frustrations. Such a workplace, it turned out, was rich in everything that made a good story.

When Larry Smith and I put out a call for submissions to this *Working Lives* anthology, we were overwhelmed by the response. Writers across the country sent thoughtful, well-crafted stories in which characters struggle with the challenges and indignities of every sort of job and often found meaning there, often in the camraderie of fellow workers who were similarly angry, exhausted, or somehow resilient and hopeful. It was a privelege to read each submission, and it was a humbling experience to choose, from among them, the small number we could include here.

We hope you enjoy the works of these twenty-one contemporary authors—some new, some established. By writing wisely and beautifully about work, they give us insight into what other people are doing all day (or all night) long. They show us, through these stories, that somebody else's job can be as exotic as a foreign country, as dangerous as a battlefield, as complicated and weird as somebody else's sex life.

"It takes two whole weeks after a routine cleaning for my wife and me to be in love again," a high school teacher says in Brock Clarke's "What We Won't Do." The teacher's wife is a dental hygienist with power issues.

In "Saurkraut Soup," Stuart Dybek's narrator, an ice cream factory custodian, grapples with the meaning of life and work. "Are war wounds different from factory wounds?" he asks, and he doubts whether anyone was ever redeemed by such suffering, outside a Dostoevsky novel.

As Julie Weston's title character in "Doc" travels a quarter mile down into a collapsing Idaho mine to rescue a trapped man, he considers his wartime experience: "Maybe mining underground was like a war, too." In "Miss America," Kaye Longberg's lifeguard must also wrestle life from death's grip, this time in a Detroit swimming pool. Though the plumber in Rich Yañez's "Holy Water" cannot save his wife, he may be able to repair a fountain in front of the nursing home where she lies dying.

Studs Terkel, in his introduction to *Working*, says that those who find work rewarding or even enriching are among a lucky few; he says that our work is more often characterized by violence and humiliation. In Daniel Chacón's

"Expression of Our People," an Apache man has the grisly task of gutting chickens and must explain to the foreman why his Navajo co-worker is freaking out on the job. The greatest humiliation, however, may come as a result of being fired, when a man feels he's lost not only his livelihood but his identity as well—this desperation is palpably rendered in Jeff Vande Zande's "Layoff."

Readers may squirm at the slick cruelty of a store manager on an Alaskan island in Gary Eller's "Habit of Despair," and also at the casual negligence of college-aged painters toward their customers in "Walls of St. Vincent" by Philip Heldrich. A car salesman in "One Version of the Story" by Phillip Sterling can't resist an easy sale but is haunted afterwards when he stops and listens to the buyer's story.

Americans are famous for asking new acquaintances what they do for a living, as a way of making small talk, as a way of getting a quick impression. The conversation then generally passes to other topics. Most fiction treats work the same way—the job becomes an aspect of character, and we move on to adventure, romantic intrigue, or family trouble. Each writer in this collection, however, is like the person who has the nerve to go on and ask, "How the heck can you sort a new piece of mail every second all night long?" Or "What is it really like to amputate a man's arm?"

In Jeanne Bryner's "Turn the Radio to a Gospel Station," we learn what it is like to clean the emergency room night after night, after children "grab their mamas' hot curling irons...and swaller pain pills like baby shower mints." We also learn it's a place where part-time employees without benefits get stuck by dirty needles.

Nancy Zafris's "Death of a Junk Peddler" immerses us in three generations of a world where the scrap metal king is King. Jim Ray Daniels' narrator in "Bonus" begs a job in his uncle's upscale clothing store only to find that work and family can be an uneasy mix.

In Kathleen De Grave's "Cannery Night," a woman in a vegetable processing plant becomes disillusioned with both love and her job when she goes out drinking after the evening shift—but she simultaneously awakens, for the first time, into her own skin.

The community of the workplace is elemental to Jill Hochman's "Stopping in Grace," in which the good-natured narrator explains how three waitresses can have a son together. In "Shrapnel," by John Gilgun, we learn how a job at a movie theater provides one teenager with a sense of belonging that neither his school nor his family could give.

Percival Everett's "Alluvial Deposits" portrays a field researcher determined to simply do his job for the Utah Fish and Game Commission, despite a threat of violence; instead he finds himself moved by what lies beneath that violence. In "Double Shift," Daniel Coshnear presents a frustrated part-time social worker (full-time frustrated blues musician) who finds he just can't help but try again when there's every reason to give up on a particular human soul.

A man accustomed to yanking on pipe wrenches busts his wrist and is advised to take up knitting as physical therapy in "Clack, Clack, Clack," by Bernadette Murphy, and the depth of his healing surprises him. Rachael Perry gives us, in "Hawk," a builder who can "raise a wall by himself" but who resists the hero worship lavished upon him because of a bizarre incident involving a snake.

"We ain't building a fucking piano," says one of the carpenters in Bret Comar's "Square," reminding us that nothing ends up perfect, not a floor tile installation and certainly not a marriage. But often, if we stop worrying, one or the other is good enough.

In this anthology, through a variety of voices and venues, work and the workplace provide setting, metaphor, and meaning. Though we can't claim to have covered the full array of jobs Americans hold—and though we weren't able to include all the stories we loved from the submissions we received—we've got twenty-one fine ones here, so get to work!

## Introduction: The American Short Story of Work—Creating Context

**Larry Smith (Bowling Green State University—Firelands College)**

We all work. Of necessity or will or desire we labor with our hands, our minds, our hearts to make something–all types of labor, all types of jobs. We give of ourselves to provide sustenance and to create choice–for ourselves and others. For a moment, forget money and the struggle it brings. We all work, even the child building a bridge with blocks. We focus, we build, we make, we work.

It's when money comes in, however, that we encounter power and with it, subordination and class, and too often pain and sacrifice. It is a reality we share. Yet, in this post-industrial era, commerce has become not only central but global, and we as workers have been given the primary role of consumer, forced to transform from maker to buyer. This too neat formula denies history and class and thereby keeps us from knowing ourselves as individuals and our culture as community. As Jesse Jackson asserts, "The one thing America hates to talk about, even more than race, is class." Whether conscious or not, the result of this new consumer identity is a denial that leaves us all impoverished. In accepting the name-brand identity of the American consumer, we cannot know each other or ourselves.

The writers assembled here–contemporary American storytellers–reclaim our culture and our identity as working people. They open doors and windows and invite us in. The walls between labor, class, and literature fall before the good 'works' of poets and playwrights, film-makers and fiction writers, essayists and editors. They show us how our work can unite us even as it divides. As part of the whole wave now rising from art and education, and embracing cultural diversity, there flows a healthy acceptance of our identity and complexity. Undeniably Feminist criticism has led the way here in creating a critical context that bridges life and culture to literature. While we need not be confined by the term "working class," we dare not ignore it here. The writings we have assembled are inclusive of class references, though not confined by it. They recognize and celebrate without building trenches. As the term "working class" has broadened and developed, so has the story of work evolved into a post-industrial age.We believe these writings are as much a part of American literature as they are American life; these tales are our roadmaps to America's interior, our working texts.

We can begin by describing a working story or text, then chart the historical development of such writing and finally suggest some of America's chief writers of working lives.

A prime goal of writing of work is to *contextualize lived experience.* Critic Janet Zandy in her study "In the Skin of a Worker" (MLA 1998) rightly poses the question: *What makes this writing a working-class or working text?* Here the emphasis is directly placed on the story's character, its stance, its form and effect, and so an authentic critical dynamic emerges, one that yields a context for understanding writing of work and class within the tradition of American literature.

Such a literature has always existed alongside of our industrial development and decline. Put bluntly, this writing is about people and work–rural, industrial, post-industrial, technological, and including the out-of-work. It goes beyond narrow socio-economic definitions of income and family background to include a majority of Americans who depend 'for a living' on 'wages,' who are closely tied to the immigrant or migrant experiences, people who hold family and neighborhood as central to their lives, who are often first generation high school or college graduates, who work with their hands as well as their brains. Their values are based on a practical and functional use of tools and skills, including language, and usually their history and values are passed along through oral storytelling and direct speech and actions; they are working people who deal with denial and anger as well as sacrifice, cooperation, and persistence. It's a culture marked as much by its wit, ingenuity, and compassion as it is by violence, pain, and alienation. Denial, forced change, and oppression are daily realities of this multi-cultural mix of the out-of-work, the poor, the working poor, and the worker-middle class. This deep and complex system of values demands attention and respect.

Our changing times has seen a splintering of the working family by education and forced migration for jobs as well as through media stereotyping and academic homogenizing, yet, despite all false admonitions to vanish into middle class, the working class still strongly exists. In fact its evolution makes more relevant such a literature that records and expresses contemporary working lives. American writing of work and class integrates our culture by witnessing and revealing it.

To help establish a critical context for this writing we return to Janet Zandy's helpful study of what "makes" a working text by asking: "What space is there for working-class voices, for descriptions of material conditions–the food, clothing, possessions, homes of working-class communities, and between workers and their employers/bosses?" She answers that such a writing or text "invites, cajoles, even insists that the reader step into the skin of a worker." We hold this as a chief criterion for the writing assembled here.

We can mark the values and stance of such writing as containing many (though not all) of these elements: 1) The text centers on the lived experience of working people. The working life is given space and taken seriously by the author. 2) The writing allows space for the working person to represent him or herself, to speak, often as narrators in short fiction. 3) Its consciousness is not wholly individual, but collective in sensibility. "The writer is conscious of his or her ghosts, of the multiple competing, contradictory, and demanding voices that inhabit the 'we' inside the individual writer's 'I'"(Zandy). 4) The working-class culture with its complex of values is revealed with respect, providing an opportunity for recognition. 5) The writings validate the physical experience of the working life, the physicality of suffering and the depth of feeling and thought which exists. 6) The texts are concerned with cultural formation, the historical, personal, and sociological way in which events and circumstances affect a culture. 7) The writing is meant "to be of use" in our culture. Author Toni Cade Bambara clarifies this life-art engagement: "Writing is one of the ways I participate in the struggle–one of the ways I help to keep vibrant and resilient that vision that has kept the Family going on . . . one of the ways I participate in the transformation . . . Writing is one of the ways I do my work in the world." ("What It Is I Think I'm Doing" in *The Writer on Her Work*. NY: Norton 1980). 8) Working-class texts often challenge the dominant assumptions about form and content. Their form is organic, finding its design in the sense of lived experience. That the text feels true is more important than it feel accomplished or polished. 9) The texts are conscious of individual and class oppression. For the writer the engaged consciousness overplays any pretense of aesthetic or critical objectivity; the writer witnesses what is at stake and often takes sides. Finally, I would add, 10) A working story deals with money, family finances, income or the lack thereof as a condition of or an affective force upon the lives of its characters. Often the physical conditions and the accompanying psychological, emotional, and moral demands of the job are conveyed; this latter seems particularly true of our post-industrial age.

Recognizing the short story as particularly an American form and acknowledging working-class fiction's long and interesting past, we can chart its development here. In looking at literary precedents for the American short story of work and class, we note that most short story writers were/are also novelists and many nonfiction writers; virtually all of them have been affected by the fiction that has come before, whether story or novel or creative nonfiction. Certainly the fiction of the later 1800's led many writers to wider views of subject matter and more intimate points of view. American Realists and Regionalists of local color broke ground, as in Hamlin Garland's stark prairie tales in *Main Travelled Roads* (1891) and Stephen Crane's earthy novella *Maggie, A Girl of the Streets* (1893), and so did the intimate portraits of humble people in Sarah Orne Jewett's *A White Heron and Other Stories* (1886) and *A Country of the Pointed Firs* (1896), or Mary Wilkens Freeman's *A New England Nun and Other Stories* (1891). As for opening subject matter and declaring a commitment to working people, it is hard to underestimate the value of Walt Whitman's *Leaves of Grass* (1855) and Mark Twain's *Adventures of Huckleberry Finn* (1884). The truest working-class fiction, however, evolved from Rebecca Harding Davis and her searing novel *Life in the Iron Mills or the Korl Woman* (1861) and her short story collection *Silhouettes of American Life* (1892). Here is writing that meets all the criterion for a working text suggested above: seen from inside the working-class experience, intimate with characters who raise their own voices, conscious of a collective identity, revealing of the working-class family and home-life, validating their physical suffering and economic subjugation, it becomes a text that could be used to awaken social consciousness of class oppression, and one that is daring in its bold originality.

Other important and unexpected 19th century precedents flowed from Russian master storytellers. As their stories came into translation, American authors were astounded. Sherwood Anderson would exclaim, "Until I found the Russian writers of prose, your Tolstoy, Dostoevski, Turgenev, Chekhov, I had never found a prose that satisfied me. . . . In your Russian writers one feels life everywhere, in every page" (*Letters*, 93). Two decades later another American short story writer, James T. Farrell, would declare, "Chekhov raised the portrayal of banality to the level of world literature. . . .[He] encouraged the short story writers of these nations to revolt against the conventional plot story and to see simple and realistic terms to make the story a form that more seriously reflects life . . . Chekhov has not only influenced the form of the short story, but he has also influenced its content" (*Chicago Stories*, "Introduction" xviii). It is easy to see how these American realists were moved by the intimacy of the narrative voice and egalitarian approach of the Russians. They present a non-judgmental, subjective point of view, intimate and often loving with detail, a perspective that welcomed these American sons and daughters of the working class. They also taught a psychological realism, where each of their characters had their story to tell, and each was given respect and space to tell it. They clearly revealed how to break the formulaic definition of the short story as having "a single or a unified impression" and so freed American writers to treat their world and find their own forms.

America entered the Twentieth Century in a wave of change. In the first two decades it would experience an industrial coming of age, a loss of American farm life to urban expansion, a flow of immigration, a rise of feminism, and its first world war. Theodore Dreiser (1871-1945) captured the characters in the midst of this change. His novels *Sister Carrie* (1900) and *Jennie Gerhardt* (1911) brought the age of literary naturalism into the twentieth century, opening censored subject areas and documenting with realistic detail the darker sides of socialization, revealing our base human urge for self-preservation. In his novels and short fiction, Dreiser gives dignity to the human wreckage he portrays, capturing the flow of life with simple sincerity and a bold theme of brotherhood, things that profoundly shaped the American working-class story.

Dreiser was, of course, carrying forward the realism-naturalism of the age from such writers as Jack London (1876-1916) whose stories appeared regularly in magazines ("To Build a Fire" in *Century* 1908) and were subsequently collected in *Brown Wolf and Other Jack London Stories* (1920). He took his readers into the lives of American outcasts. Upton Sinclair (1878-1968), though primarily a novelist, *The Jungle* (1906), *King Coal* (1917), *Oil* (1927), advanced naturalism into a Socialist format, often using his short stories as political tracts, but also revealing the hidden cruelty of a capitalistic society.

Though some short story writers of the Roaring Twenties—F. Scott Fitzgerald, Ernest Hemingway, Ring Lardner–advanced the short story in its form and popularity, creating terse and poetic portraits of individuals, they were little concerned with working characters and themes nor with portraying a collective sensibility. Three writers of the 1920's who sympathetically portray the working life include Sherwood Anderson (1876-1941), Anzia Yezierska (1880-1970), and Margery Latimer (1899-1932). Anderson entered the lives of the small town Midwesterners facing increased industrialization and dislocation of social values, first in his composite novel *Winesburg, Ohio* (1919) and again in his short story collections *The Triumph of the Egg* (1921) and *Horses and Men* (1923). Refusing to falsify their lives by forcing them into slick plotted fictions, Anderson follows his Russian mentors Chekhov and Turgenev, but also Theodore Dreiser and James Joyce, in particular Joyce's composite novel of Ireland, *The Dubliners* (1914). Unlike Sinclair Lewis who uses distance to satirize midwestern life, Anderson collapses the aesthetic distance between his readers, narrators, and characters thereby forcing a deep empathy, a key method of this writing of work.

Margery Latimer shared Anderson's romantic-realism in her *Nellie Bloom and Other Stories* (1929) and *Guardian Angel and Other Stories* (1929; re-issued in 1989). Her refusal to accept the emptiness of literary naturalism is apparent in her impassioned approach, "There's only one possession that's worth having and that is the capacity to feel that life is a privilege and that each person in it is unique and will never appear again."

Anzia Yeziarska, perhaps best known for her immigrant novels set in New York's Lower East Side: *Salome of the Tenements* (1923), *Bread Givers: A Novel* (1925), and *All I Could Never Be* (1932), offers fine examples of working-class writing. It was first collected in the acclaimed *Hungry Hearts* (1920; re-issued 1970, 1997) and finally in *How I Found America* (1991). Heavily autobiographical of her Jewish-American background, these stories are full of crowded street detail and reveal the real poverty and discrimination met by so many immigrants, who struggle for the American Dream, then and now.

What emerged then in the Twenties were new characteristics for the working short story form. Though some writers maintain the flat naturalism of objective narration, we now have the tale told in intimate first person point of view from a working-class person struggling to express his/her life and story, and often yielding to fellow narrators. It joins form and theme, giving space and respect to the teller and the act of telling as we listen closely to the tales of the downtrodden and survivors. It allows the writer to enter the world and locate within a voice, thereby creating a deep and authentic empathy.

The Thirties proved the third heyday for working-class short fiction. Leftist fiction espousing socialist and communist perspectives was openly published in such journals as *The New Masses, Liberator, Partisan Review, Dynamo, The Hammer, Anvil, Blast*, and the *Daily Worker*. Novelists such as Mike Gold (*Jews Without Money*, 1930), Jack Conroy (*The Disinherited*, 1933), Grace Lumpkin (*To Make My Bread*, 1930), Agnes Smedley (*Daughters of the Earth*, 1929), and Edward Dahlberg (*Bottom Dogs*, 1930) were reaching a larger audience. Among the short story writers were the prolific Meridel Le Sueur and Tillie (Olsen) Lerner who published an early segment from her *Yononnindio*. Le Sueur's early stories depict the social struggle in urban and rural settings as in "Harvest" (1929) in which she portrays the travail of midwestern farm life–men and women laboring hard in the fields seeking mutual survival. Her first collection of stories *Salute to Spring* (International Publishers, 1940) was followed by a period of political blacklisting from mainstream magazines during the Forties and Fifties. Her work was issued again in *Corn Village* (1970), was collected in *Harvest and Song for My Time* (1977) and expanded in *Ripening* (1982). Le Sueur is an influence on contemporary writers for her lyrical and terse stories which move the reader by feelings as much as thought.

The Thirties was also a rich period of regional and ethnic writing that treated class. The South was being explored by William Faulkner (1897-1962) in his early stories *These Thirteen* (1931), and his later *Collected Stories* (1948), which included his "Barn Burning" early portrayal of the Southern, "white trash" Snopes family. Erskine Caldwell (1903-1987) had already located his fiction within the Southern poor in the story collections *American Earth* (1931) and *Jackpot* (1940). Both writers give an exaggerated, grotesqued image of the working world and its people. A richer addition to the literature of the working people came from the stories of Zora Neal Hurston (1903-1966), a pioneer African-American author, in her *Eatonville Anthology* (1927) and her *Mules and Men* (1935).

By the late Thirties William Saroyan had emerged as a spokesperson for the immigrant experience in tales of his Armenian-American family as they ventured west. In *The Daring Young Men on the Flying Trapeze* (1934) and *My Name Is Aram* (1940), he writes self-conscious narratives of his writer-self, his family, his people. He was a pioneer in what we are now terming "creative nonfiction," and his stories are full of humorous idiosyncracy and loving kindness.

Like many of these writers who existed outside of Leftist politics, Chicagoan James T. Farrell (1904-1979) produced a rich variety of stories treating the working-class world–its Catholic Church and clergy, schools and universities, unions and laborers, ward and radical politics, street gangs, the often ignored poor of this country. Farrell was outspoken in his opposition to forced models of the popular and the Leftist presses alike. His candid tales are austere and plain, unmarked by exaggeration or caricature. Farrell views his working-class world from the inside, creating solid and memorable characters in their own language. His earliest collection *Calico Shoes and Other Stories* appeared in 1934, and was followed by *Can All This Grandeur Perish? And Other Stories* in 1937 *and $1,000 a Week and Other Stories* in 1942.

The Forties broadened the thrust of working-class writing. John Fante (1909-1979) continued the immigrant story by publishing his Italian-American tales of life in Boulder, Colorado, for his brick-laying father and family. The stories of *Dago Red* (1940) are rich in character and warm humor and were subsequently enlarged in *The Wine of Youth: Selected Stories* (1985). He combines Saroyan's love of the human spirit with the candidness of Farrell. As a first generation American, Fante also depicts the struggle with working-class identity. John Steinbeck was the writing migrant stories in his long novels, such as *The Grapes of Wrath* (1939), but also in his shorter tales of California working people in *The Long Valley* (1938). Farrell's spirit had found a new spokesperson in Nelson Algren (1909-1981) and his gritty tales of Chicago's down-and-out. In *The Neon Wilderness* (1947) his prostitutes, pimps, police and convicts speak their lives bluntly.

In the South Eudora Welty wove tales brilliant and challenging in style and form, yet richly human in their depiction of Southern characters (*Golden Apples*, 1949). Though they may be common, her characters are never ordinary, but richly complex. They lack the grotesque exaggeration of both Caldwell and Faulkner, and the colder tone of another southern writer, Flannery O'Connor.

America's Fifties and Sixties were colored by the repressive atmosphere of McCarthyism, Hollywood blacklisting, and Cold War fears; thus it saw a waning of Leftist writing, though strong tales treating contemporary working-class life could still survive. The strongest of these storytellers were Harvey Swados, Grace Paley, and Tillie Olsen.

Swados' social concerns and education took him into the working-class life where he labored in the aircraft plants of Buffalo and the automotive plants of New Jersey. From this experience he learned "the pity and vanity of American life from the inside" (*On the Line* 1957). Swados' writing witnesses the decline of the American worker and the American Dream as this country moved from production to consumption as its chief concern. "Never mind the machinery, Remember the men!" Swados shouts through his stories which closely detail the growing alienation of modern work. These compassionate monologues of America's forgotten workers prove essential records still.

Grace Paley's delivers delightful and full-voiced storytelling by colorful Jewish-American, working-class women in *Little Disturbances of Man* (1959). Pathos and humor are blended here as her characters speak their lives. All of it is done with great understanding and bold spirit that refuses self-pity. Paley's later stories are collected in *Enormous Changes at the Last Minute* (1974) *Later the Same Day* (1985) and *The Collected Stories* (1994). In the same vein, Tillie Olsen's four-story collection *Tell Me a Riddle* (1961) has become a classic and a model among working-class literature. Less mirthful than Paley, Olsen knew the pains of poverty firsthand and delivers pungent and pointed tales of her characters and their struggles. Olsen has lived the struggle she portrays; her characters have a human scale that demands understanding and empathy.

Other Sixties books focusing on working-class culture include John Updike's early stories of life in coal mining Pennsylvania in *Pigeon Feathers* (1962), and of course his novel trilogy launched with *Rabbit Run* (1960). Philip Roth's novella and New Jersey stories treating his working-class origins and class conflicts were published in *Goodbye, Columbus and Five Stories* (1959). Jack Kerouac's Beat novels from this period *On the Road* (1957), *The Subterraneans* (1958), *The Dharma Bums* (1958) chronicle the working and alternative lifestyles in America.

The Seventies and Eighties saw a host of new short story writers of the working class, most holding close to their working-class roots and themes: John Sayles, Tobias Wolff, Russell Banks, Richard Ford, Raymond Carver, Bobbie Ann Mason, Toni Cade Bambara, chief among them. In John Sayles *The Anarchist's Convention and Other Stories* (1979) all are told in first person monologues, including his "7-10 Split," a characteristic piece, in which the workers from a nursing home gather for a bowling match. Their work and values and struggles are explicit; Sayles is one with working people. Tobias Wolff's *In the Garden of North American Martyrs* (1981) and *The Barracks Thief and Selected Stories* (1984) also portray people in identity and class conflicts.

Russell Banks also began his working-class fiction with *The New World: Tales* (1978) and *Trailerpark* (1981). The latter is a kind of contemporary *Winesburg, Ohio* of intertwining characters set in a Vermont trailerpark. Many of these and *Success Stories* (1986) are semi-autobiographical of what Banks calls his own "scrabbleass" background. Banks has proven himself one of America's most successful writers of the working class, as seen in his award-winning novels *Continental Drift* (1985) and *Affliction* (1989). Richard Ford should be included here for his compelling early stories of the wild and run-down towns of Wyoming in *Rock Springs: Stories* (1983). In dynamic style he delivers close-wrought characters caught in America's post-industrial decline.

Many of these writers, whether in admiration or opposition, were affected by the work of Raymond Carver with his Hemingwayesque, minimalist stories of working people. With his *What We Talk About When We Talk About Love* (1981), *Cathedral* (1984) and his *Fires (*1989) Carver became a major writer of the working class. His stories are not only intimate and terse with the working-class experience, but often grim in their portrayal of lost values.

In the late Seventies and following through the Nineties, America embraced its own rich cultural diversity. Not surprisingly these stories of minority cultures contain a wealth of writing on work and class. This developing interest was pushed along by early and popular writers such as novelist Toni Morrison's *The Bluest Eye* (1970), Alice Walker's *Meridian* (1976) and *The Color Purple* (1982), as well as Gloria Naylor's striking portraits in *The Women of Brewster*

*Place* (1982). Short story writer Toni Cade Bambara's youthful stories of life in New York City and North Carolina first appeared in *Gorilla, My Love* (1972) and again in *The Sea Birds Are Still Alive* (1977). Using monologue, Bambara bases her musical style on urban and African-American speech and creates spirited tales of individuals within a community. Working, class, and racial values blend in her engaged and engaging work.

During the Eighties we also witness the development of a loose regional group of writers dealing with the history and hazards of contemporary life in Appalachia. Chief among them is Bobbie Ann Mason whose *Shiloh and Other Stories* (1982). Breece D'J Pancake's stunning work of Kentucky life appeared in the post-humus *The Stories of Breece D'J Pancake* (1983). Other writers who capture the hardships and beauty of this world are: Mike Henson in *A Small Room with Trouble on My Mind* (1983) capturing impressionistic sketches of his broken hearted characters, Annabel Thomas' portraits of women and families in *The Phototropic Woman* (1981), and Robert Fox's *Destiny News* collection (1977) which often rocks from social to magic realism. Poet-fiction writer Wendell Berry has also provided agrarian tales of families struggling to keep their Kentucky farms going in *Wild Birds and Other Stories* (1986).

Dorothy Allison, famed for her novel of family and abuse, *Bastard Out of Carolina* (1992) actually began as a short story writer with her 1988 *Trash: Stories*. Unabashedly she delivers her world for what it is. Her characters are round, loving and violent, bonded to family and alienated from much of the dominant culture. There is great commitment in her writing, as she tells in the book's preface, "But the desire to live was desperate in my belly, and the stories I had hidden all those years were the blood and bone of it. To get it down, to tell it again, to make sense of something–by god just once–to be real in the world, without lies and evasions or sweet-talking nonsense" (*Trash* 11-12).

Mexican-American culture has been shared and celebrated in the fine work of Sandra Cisneros through her episodic novel *The House on Mango Street* (1989) and the short stories of *Woman Hollering Creek and Other Stories* (1991). In both books, she uses the intimate monologue voice of children and women trying to understand their world by telling of it. They are colored by rich ethnic detail and humor and reveal a story of cultural oppression from without and within. Cisneros deals with poverty, work, family and cultural values with great compassion and wit.

The close of the century saw this flow of working and multi-cultural writing into many young writers. Sherman Alexie's *The Lone Ranger and Tonto Fistfight in Heaven* (1993) reveals life inside the Spokane reservation for his Coeur d'Alene native tribe. His comic-tragic tales combine social and magic realism in a way Native American storytellers might. Bonnie Jo Campbell and Jim Ray Daniels have each created worlds drawn from today's working world of Michigan. Campbell's *Women and Other Animals* (1999) revisits the grotesque themes of Anderson's midwestern smalltown. Daniels' *No Pets: Stories* (1999) captures the pain of auto workers in post-industrial Detroit. Both call us to recognize a present that encompasses past struggles and present travail.

Two fine recent writers of Appalachia are Chris Offutt and Barbara Kingsolver. Both use a contemporary Kentucky setting in their short stories and novels to convey the rich bonding of family and the pressures of economic change and forced migration of the young. In Offutt's two books of stories *Kentucky Straight* (1992) and *Out of the Woods* (1999) he first weaves family legend with the voices of youth, then follows his characters' painful and forced migrations from home. "Sawdust" produces an enigmatic portrait of an Appalachian youth caught in this change. In Kingsolver's novels *Bean Tree* (1988) and *Pigs in Heaven* (1993), and in her *Homeland and Other Stories* (1989) she brings together her two worlds: the working-class people of Kentucky and those of Arizona. Kingsolver had begun her serious writing with a nonfiction study of the mining strikes of Arizona entitled *Holding the Line: Women in the Great Arizona Mine Strike of 1983.* In doing worker interviews and listening close to their stories and their telling, Kingsolver moved from objective reporting to an impassioned advocacy. Her "Why I Am a Danger to the Public" allows Vicki Morales, a striker, to tell her own story of dealing with scabs and neighbors' betrayal with a vigor and an endearing resilience. "I was raised up to believe in God and the union, but listen, if it comes to pushing or shoving I know which one of the two is going to keep tires on my car" (*Homeland*, 228).

In most ways this last story is a perfect model of the American short story of work: intimate with the working experience, its work and culture, giving respect and space for the worker to speak her grief and joy within a collective sensibility, creating a form that exposes the effects of oppression and how character can be molded in resistance. It relies on a vibrant intimacy of voice through an oral, first-person narration, and it includes memoir to allow the life experience to find its organic form. These are the qualities you'll find in this collection of contemporary story writers. They carry on a tradition of writing deeply human and engaging stories—as texts of our working lives.

(Labor Day 2000)

# Our Working Lives

# Sauerkraut Soup

## Stuart Dybek

I couldn't eat. Puking felt like crying. At first, I almost enjoyed it the way people do who say they had a good cry. I had a good puke or two. But I was getting tired of sleeping in a crouch.

"It's not cancer; it's not even flu," the doctor told me.

"What is it?"

"Are you nervous?"

"Puking makes me nervous."

"It's not nerves. It's lack of nerve," Harry, my best friend, a psych major, told me.

He'd come over to try exorcising it—whatever it was—with a gallon of Pisano. Like all *its*, it swam in the subconscious, that flooded sewer pipe phosphorescent with jellyfish. We believed in drink the way saints believed in angels. It took till four in the morning to kill the Pisano, listening to Harry's current favorites, the "Moonlight Sonata" and "Ghost Trio," over and over on the little Admiral stereo with speakers unfolded like wings. We were composing a letter to a girl Harry had met at a parapsychology convention. All he'd say about her is that she lived in Ohio and had told him, "Ectoplasm is the come of the dead." He opened the letter: "In your hair the midnight hovers . . . . "

"Take 'the' out, at least," I said.

"Why? It sounds more poetic."

"It's melodramatic."

"She's from Ohio, man. She craves melodrama."

Working on that theory, we wrote he was alone, listening to the "Moonlight Sonata," sipping wine, waiting for dawn, thinking of her far away across the prairie in Ohio, thinking of the moonlight entering her bedroom window and stealing across her body, her breasts, her thighs. We ended with the line "My dick is a moonbeam."

I watched him lick the envelope and suddenly my mouth seemed full of glue and the taste of stamps. My tongue was pasted to the roof of my mouth. I gagged. From dawn till noon I heaved up wine while Harry lay passed out on the floor, the needle clicking at the end of the record. It felt like weeping.

After a week's hunger strike against myself I still didn't know what I was protesting. Nothing like this had ever happened to me before. I did remember my father telling me he'd had an ulcer in his twenties. It was during the war. He'd just been married and was trying to get his high-school diploma in night school, working at a factory all day. Once, climbing the stairs to the El, the pain hit him so hard he doubled up and couldn't make it to the platform. He sat on the stairs groaning, listening to the trains roar overhead while rush-hour crowds shoved by him. Nobody tried to help.

"Must have figured me for a drunk," he said.

It was one of his few good stories, the only one except for the time he'd ridden a freight to Montana during the Depression, when I could imagine him young.

You're getting melodramatic, I told myself. I had begun lecturing myself, addressing myself by name. Take it easy, Frank, old boy. I would have rather said, Tony, old boy. Tony was my middle name, after a favorite uncle, a war hero at nineteen, shot up during a high-altitude bombing mission over Germany. He'd returned from the war half deaf and crazy. He'd perfected a whistle as piercing as a siren and all he did for three years was whistle and drink. He had hooded, melancholy eyes like Robert Mitchum's. His name was Anthony, but everybody called him Casey. Franklin is a name I'd never especially liked. My father said he'd given it to me because it sounded like a good business name. I'd never been successful in getting people to call me Tony. You're a Frankie, not a Tony, they'd say. Finally, I regressed to what they'd called me in the neighborhood: Marzek. Nobody used first names there, where every last name could be spit out like an insult. There was no melodrama in a last name. People are starving in this world, Marzek, and you aren't eating. Famine. War. Madness. What right do you have to suffer? Trying to hold your guts together on the Western Avenue bus riding to work. At your age Casey was taking flak over Germany.

I worked part time for an ice-cream company on Forty-seventh. Supposedly, I was going to school during the day and so I didn't get to the factory till after three, when the lines were already shut down. It was October. The lines that ran overtime in summer shut down early in fall.

A few of the production crew were usually still around, the ones who'd gotten too sticky to go home without showering, and the Greeks who'd worked in the freezers since seven A.M. still trying to thaw dry ice from their lungs and marrow. The locker room stank of piled coveralls marinating in sweat, sour milk, and the sweet ingredients of ice cream. I opened my locker and unhooked my coveralls from the handle of the push broom. That terrible lack of sympathy pervading all locker rooms hung in the air.

"Look how awful he looks," Nick said to Yorgo. "Skin and bones."

I quickly tugged on my coveralls.

"Moves like he got a popsicle up the ass," Yorgo said.

"It's a fudgsicle. Greek cure for hemorrhoids."

"He got morning sickness," Nick said.

"It's punishment for being a smartass. God is punishing you. You think you don't pay sooner or later," Yorgo said.

"I'm paying."

"You only *think* you're paying. Just wait. You won't believe how much more expensive it gets."

I pushed my broom along the darkened corridors, a dune of dust and green floor—cleaning compound forming before me. The floor compound reminded me of nuns. They'd sprinkle it on vomit whenever someone got sick in class. Vomit filled my thoughts and memories.

*Has it come to this, Marzek?*

It's what Harry had kept mumbling as I barfed up Pisano. It was his favorite expression. *Has it come to this,* he'd ask at the subway window as he paid his fare, at restaurants when they brought the check, at the end of the first movement of the "Moonlight Sonata," in letters to Ohio.

A month ago it had been summer. I'd worked production, overtime till six p.m., saving money for school. At night I'd played softball—shortstop for a team called the Jokers. I hadn't played softball since early in high school. This was different, the city softball league. Most of the guys were older, playing after work. The park was crowded with girlfriends, wives, and kids. They spread beach blankets behind the backstop, grilled hotdogs, set out potato salad, jugs of lemonade. Sometimes, in a tight game with runners on, digging in at short, ready to break with the ball, a peace I'd never felt before would paralyze the diamond. For a moment of eternal stillness I felt as if I were cocked at the very heart of the Midwest.

We played for keggers and after the game, chaperoned by the black guys on the team, we made the rounds of the blues bars on the South Side, still wearing our black-and-gold-satin Joker jerseys. We ate slabs of barbecued ribs with slaw from smoky little storefront rib houses or stopped at takeout places along the river for shrimp. Life at its most ordinary seemed rich with possibility.

In September we played for the division championship and lost 10-9. Afterward there was a party that went on all night. We hugged and laughed and replayed the season. Two of the wives stripped their blouses off and danced in bras. The first baseman got into a fist fight with the left fielder.

When I woke hung over it was Monday. I knew I'd never see any Jokers again. I lay in bed feeling more guilty than free about not going to work. I'd worked full time all summer and had decided to take the last week off before school began. I wanted to do nothing but lie around for a solid week. My tiny apartment was crammed with books I'd been wanting to read and wouldn't have a chance to read once school started. I'd been reading Russians all summer and wanted now to concentrate on Dostoevsky.

"Anybody who spells his name so many different ways has got to be great," Harry said.

I started with *Notes from the Underground*, then read *The Possessed* and *The Idiot.* The night before school reopened I read *Crime and Punishment* in a single sitting. It was early in the morning when I closed the book, went straight to the bathroom, and threw up. That was the first time it felt like crying.

In high school the priests had cautioned us about the danger of books.

"The wrong ones will warp your mind more than it is already, Marzek."

I tried to find out what the wrong ones were so I could read them. I had already developed my basic principle of Catholic education—the Double Reverse: *(1) suspect what they teach you; (2) study what they condemn.*

My father had inadvertently helped lay the foundation of the Double Reverse. Like the priests, he'd tried to save me.

"Math," he'd say. "Learn your tables. Learn square roots!"

On Christmas and birthdays he'd shower me with slide rules, T squares, drafting kits, erector sets. Each Sunday he pored over the want ads while I read the comics. He was resigned to his job at the factory, but he was looking for jobs for me—following trends, guiding my life by the help-wanteds the way some parents relied on Dr. Spock. By the time I was in sixth grade he'd begun keeping tally sheets, statistics, plotting graphs.

"Engineers! They are always looking for engineers—electrical engineers, chemical engineers, mechanical engineers."

It was what he'd wanted to be, but he'd never had the chance to go to college.

I enrolled in drafting class, machine shop, wood shop, math. When I became the first person in the history of Holy Angels High to fail wood shop without even completing the first project, a sanding block, he became seriously concerned.

"You gotta be more practical. Get your mind on what's real. I used to read Nick Carter mysteries all the time when I was a kid. I read hundreds. Then, one day I asked myself, Is this practical or just another way they make a sucker out of you? Who's it helping? Me or Nick Carter? I never read another."

"But Shakespeare," I said.

"Shakespeare? Don't you see that one well-designed bridge is worth more than everything Shakespeare ever wrote?"

I swept my broom past the lunchroom. I thought about my first day working the production line. When they relieved me I got my lunch, thinking it was noon. It was only the ten-fifteen break. Sweeping floors seemed like relaxation after production. But people endured the line year after year. Except in Dostoevsky's novels I couldn't think of having ever met anyone purified by suffering. I didn't want Siberia. The freezers were bad enough. People were condemned to them every day—without plotting against the czar.

The cleanup shift was in the lunchroom taking one of several breaks. The men worked after the bosses had gone and were pretty much on their own so long as the machines were clean in the morning. Unlike for the production crew, a break for cleanup didn't mean a ten-cent machine coffee. It meant feasting. Most of them were Slavs, missing parts of hands and arms that had been chewed off while trying to clean machines that hadn't been properly disconnected. I could never exactly identify where in Eastern Europe any of them were from.

"Russian?" I'd ask.

No, no-vigorous denial.

"Polish?"

No. They'd smile, shaking their heads in amusement.

"Lithuanian?"

Ho, ho, ho. Much laughter and poking one another.

"Bohemian?"

Stunned amazement that I could suggest such a thing.

The lunch table was spread as for a buffet. Swollen gray sausages steaming garlic, raw onions, dark bread, horseradish, fish roe.

Still, despite the banquet, a sullen, suspicious air pervaded the room. Next to the cleanup crew, the Greeks from the freezer were cheerful. Not that they weren't always friendly toward me, though they were distressed that I was sweeping floors, as that had previously been "a colored's job."

"Want *y'et*?" the burly, red-bearded man missing the index fingers of both hands asked, offering rye bread spread with pigs' brains from the communal can.

Cleanup always offered me food, urging *y'et*, *y'et*. It rhymed with *Nyet*, but I suspected it was one of those foreign words actually manufactured out of English some contraction of "you" and "cat." They'd been concerned with my eating habits since the time they'd seen me plunge my arm up to the elbow into the whey and scoop out a handful of feta cheese from the barrel the Greeks kept in the fruit cooler.

"*Nyet*, *Nyet*," they'd groaned then, screwing up their faces in disgust.

"*Nyet*, *Nyet*," I said apologetically now, declining the brains, pointing to my stomach and miming the heaves. "Can't eat . . . sick . . . stomach . . ." I explained, lapsing into broken English as if they'd understand me better.

"Have to *y'et*. No *y'et*, no live."

"That's true."

"*Y'et* ice cream? Dixie cup? Creamsicle?"

"*Y'et* ice cream!" The idea startled me. After a summer of production, ice cream seemed no more edible than machinery. I wanted to sit down at this cleanup banquet table and discuss it. To find out how it had remained food for them; what it was like to work in after-hours America. They knew something they were hiding. I wanted to explore paradox with them: how was vomiting the same as crying? Dostoevsky like softball? Were factory wounds different from war wounds? We could discuss ice cream. How did working transmute it from that delight of childhood into a product as appetizing as lead? But my broom seemed to be drawing me away as if on gliders, down unswept, dark, waxed corridors.

Besides, the engineering of ice cream is another problem. This is about soup. Or *zupa*, as cleanup called it. They called it after me, the words echoing down the corridor like their final pronouncement as I glided away: *y'et zupa ... zupa. . . zupa ...*

I stood before my locker stripping off my coveralls, gagging on the sweaty-sweet effluvia of flavors hovering around the laundry bin—strawberry, burgundy cherry, black walnut, butter brickle. *Zupa* chicken broth, beef barley, cream of celery—sounded like an antidote, the way black olives and goat cheese could counterbalance a morning of working with chocolate marshmallow, or pigs' brains on rye neutralize tutti-frutti.

It was six when I punched out; the deceptive light of Indian summer was still pink on the sidewalks. I walked, paycheck in my pocket, along the grassy median of Western Boulevard, traffic whizzing on both sides like sliding, computerized walls of metal and glass. Workers were racing away from the factories that lined Western, down streets that resembled nothing so much as production lines, returning to resume real lives, trailing the dreams they survived by like exhaust fumes—promotions, lotteries, jackpots, daily doubles, sex, being discovered by Hollywood, by New York, by Nashville, sex, going back to school, going into real estate, stocks, parents, sex, embezzlements, extortions, hijackings, kidnappings, wills of distant millionaire uncles, sex ...

These were things we'd talked about all summer while the ice cream filed by. Now I was free of it, weaving slightly as I followed the wavy trails of strawlike cuttings the mowers had left. I could still feel the envy I'd had all summer for the guys riding the mowers over the boulevards, shirts off, tanning, ogling sunbathing girls while grass tossed through the almost musical rotary blades. It had seemed like freedom next to working in a factory, but those were city jobs and you had to know somebody to get one.

The factory had changed my way of thinking more in one summer than my entire education had. Beneath the who-gives-a-shit attitude there was something serious about it I couldn't articulate even to myself, something everyone seemed to accept, to take for granted, finally to ignore. It had to do with the way time was surrendered—I knew that, and also knew it was what my father, who'd worked in a factory all his life, had wanted to tell me. But he'd never been able to find the words either, had never heard them or read them anywhere, and so distrusted language.

My stomach was knotted. I was feeling dizzy and for a moment thought it might be because the line of grass cuttings I was following was crooked. When

I stood still the colors of the trees looked ready to fly apart like the points of unmixed pigment in the van Gogh self-portrait I'd stare at every time I went to the Art Institute trying to provoke that very sensation. It wasn't a sensation I wanted to be feeling now. I sat down in the grass and lowered my head, trying to clear the spots from my eyes. I tried breathing rhythmically, looking away from the trees to the buildings across the street. The flaring light slanted orange along the brick walls in a way that made them appear two-dimensional, faked. The sky looked phony too, flat clouds like cutouts pasted on rather than floating. It looked possible to reach up and touch the sky, and poke a finger through.

I was starting to go nuts. It was one of those moments when the ordinariness is suddenly stripped away and you feel yourself teetering between futures. Then, at a restaurant across the street, under a Coca-Cola sign, I ate a bowl of soup and was reprieved.

A week later I doubt if I thought much about any of it—the weepy, wrenching heaves that felt like spitting out the name Raskolnikov, the involuntary fast, the universe turning to tissue on Western Boulevard. It was a near-miss and near-misses are easy to forget if we notice them at all. In America one takes a charmed life for granted.

Casey once told me that's what had seemed strange to him when he first got back from the war. People seemed unaware they were about to die. It took him the next three years of whistling like a siren to readjust. By then he'd drunk himself into an enlarged liver, having settled back into the old neighborhood, where the railroad viaduct separated the houses from the factories and every corner was a tavern. His entire life had become a near-miss at nineteen.

When I try to recall the times I almost died I get bogged down in childhood—repeated incidents like Swantek (who at age twelve was more psychotic than any other person I've ever met) demonstrating a new switchblade by flinging it at my head, grazing an ear as it twanged into a door. But my closest call would come a few years after that day I opted for *zupa* on Western Boulevard. It was as Casey had observed—I had no awareness of death at the time, though certainly there were strong hints.

By then the ice-cream factory was only a memory. I'd finished college and was working for the Cook County Department of Public Aid on the South Side. I was living on the North Side in an efficiency apartment half a block from the lake. It was August, hot, and for the last few days there'd been a faint, sweetly putrid smell around the refrigerator. For the first time since I'd lived there I stripped the shelves and scrubbed everything with Kitchen Klenzer. While I was at it I even cleaned under the burners on the stove.

The smell only got stronger, except now it was tinged with bleach. I tried moving the refrigerator, but it was one of those types in a recess in the wall and I couldn't budge it.

I went downstairs and rang the manager's bell. No answer. By the time I got back to my apartment the smell had permeated the entire room. I got a towel and blanket and left to sleep the night out on the beach.

As soon as I hit the street I knew something was wrong. Police and ambulance flashers whirled blue and scarlet at the end of the block, fusing into a violet throb. Shadows hurried away from the beach in the dark, cutting across lawns where sprinklers whipped under streetlights. At the end of the sidewalk a couple of cops had a kid pinned down, his face grinding in sand, eyes rolling as if he were having a fit. Flashlights moved slowly across the dark beach and groans and crying echoed over the hollow lapping of water. I hung around long enough to find out what had happened. A local gang, ripped on drugs, had made a lightning raid with bats, knives, and chains. Apparently they were after a rival gang, but anyone out on the beach had been attacked.

Back in my apartment I smoked an old cigar, trying to smother the smell long enough to fall asleep. I was still tossing, half awake, sweating, trying to suck breath through a cold towel without smelling, when the buzzer rang around two A.M. It was Harry with a fifth of old Guckenheiiner.

"What the hell's the stench in here?" he asked.

"BO?

"No." He sniffed. "I know that smell. It's death! Yeah, death, all right—rotting, decomposing flesh . . . decay, rot, putrescence . . . maggots, worms . . . that's it, all right, the real stuff. Where'd you hide the body?"

"Behind the fridge."

"Don't worry. You can cop an insanity plea. I'll get you a nice wing. Something quiet with the seniles—take a lot of naps. No, it gets too petty there. Maybe the hydrocephalics. You'd have to drink a lot more water to fit in. Aaaiiiyyyeee!" he suddenly screamed. "See them? There! Giant, swollen heads!" He was pointing at the window, eyes wild. "Whiskey, I need whiskey," he rasped, slugging from the bottle, then wiping his mouth with the back of his hand. "Aaaiiiyyyeee." He shuddered quietly.

*Aaaiiiyyyeee* had replaced *Has it come to this* in his lexicon since he'd been working at Dunning, the state mental hospital. He claimed to see hydrocephalics everywhere.

We walked out along the cooling streets, away from the lake, into a deserted neighborhood where blue neon Stars of David glowed behind grated shop windows. We were passing the old Guckenheimer, washing it down at water fountains, trading stories on our usual subjects—poverty, madness, slums, asylums—laughing like crazy. Harry kept breaking into the childhood song he'd started singing in my apartment:

*"The worms crawl in,*
*The worms crawl out,*
*They turn your guts*
*To sauerkraut......"*

About four in the morning we found an open liquor store and bought another bottle. We sat drinking on a bench on the Howard Street El platform. Howard was the end of the line. El cars were stacked on the tracks, paralyzed, darkened, in lines that crossed the border into Evanston.

"We could probably walk to the next station before the train comes," Harry said.

We jumped down on the tracks and started walking, stepping carefully along the ties. The tracks looked down on the streetlights. We were even with roofs and windows reflecting moonlight. It was lovely, but we kept checking behind us for the single headlight that meant the train was coming. Then we'd have to jump the electric rail to the next set of tracks. The only danger was if we caught trains coming in both directions. We weren't saying much, our ears straining to hear the distant roar of the El, but it was perfectly still.

"This is the feeling I sometimes get in flying dreams," I said.

It was in that mood of ecstasy that I decided to piss on the third rail. It suddenly seemed like something I'd always wanted to do. I straddled it carefully and unzipped my fly. I was just ready to let go when Harry split the silence with an *Aaaiiiyyyeee.*

"What's the matter—train coming—"

"Aaaiiiyyyeee!" he repeated.

"Hydrocephalics?"

"Suppose the current goes upstream and zaps you in the dick?"

I carefully unstraddled the rail, zipping up my pants.

We were staggering now, which made it hard walking on ties, but made it to Fargo, the next station, with time to spare. When the train came we rode it three more stops, then walked east to the beach. By then a metallic sheen had spread from the auras of streetlights to the sky. In the faint blue light over the lake we were amazed at how filthy the beach was before the early crews arrived to clean it. Wire baskets overflowed. Piles of smashed cartons, cans, and bags littered the sand. It looked like the aftermath of a battle.

We began mounding garbage at the lapping edge of water the way kids mound sand for castles. A disk of new sun was rising across the lake from the general direction of Indiana. Two nuns, dressed in white with wimples like wings sprouting from their heads, glided past us and smiled.

*"And the dawn comes up like thunder,"* Harry was singing.

We took our clothes off and lit the pyre of paper and cartons. Its flames flicked pale and fragile-looking against the sun and foil of water. We sprinkled on the last swallow of whiskey and danced around the fire, then took turns starting back in the sand and running through the blazing paper into the lake.

The squad car came jouncing over the sand just as I was digging in for another sprint. One of the cops was out before the car even stopped. He missed a tackle as I raced by him into the flames, splashing out into the water. I stayed under as long as I could, then just kept stroking out. They followed me in the car along the breakwater, loudspeaker announcing that if I would come back we could talk it over.

When I woke it was noon. I was on my bathroom floor with the mat tucked over me. In the next room Harry was saying to the landlord, "Death ... It stinks of death in here ... corruption ... putrescence ... rotting flesh . . . abandoned bones .... What kind of charnel house-are you running here anyway?"

The janitor arrived and removed a mouse from behind the refrigerator. And sometime later a coroner told me one of the most awful deaths he'd seen was that of a man who'd urinated on the third rail.

As far as I could see, the restaurant didn't have a name except maybe Drink Coca-Cola. I went in because it had an awning—forest green with faded silver stripes. It was cranked down, shading the plate-glass window from the corona of setting sun. Forty-seventh had a number of places like it, mostly family-owned, bars that served hot lunches, little restaurants different ethnics ran, almost invisible amid McDonald's arches and Burger King driveways.

I sat on the padded stool, revolving slightly, watching the traffic go by on Western, knowing if I could eat I'd get my rhythm back and things would be all right. I picked the mimeographed menu from between the napkin dispenser and catsup bottle. Nothing unusual: hamburgers, hot beef sandwich and mashed potatoes, pork chops. Handwritten under soups was *Homemade Sauerkraut Soup.*

I'd never had sauerkraut soup before. I'd been thinking of *zupa*, but of something more medicinal, like chicken rice. "Homemade" sounded good. How could sauerkraut soup be otherwise, I thought. Who would can it?

"Yeah, ready?" the waitress asked. She was too buxom to be grandmotherly.

"Sauerkraut soup."

She brought it fast, brimming to the lip of the heavy bowl, slopping a little onto the plate beneath it. It was thick and reddish, not the blond color of sauerkraut I'd expected. The kind of soup one cuts into with the edge of the spoon. Steaming. The spoon fogging as if with breath. The peppery smell of soup rising like vapor to open the bronchial tubes. I could smell the scalded pepper and also another spice and then realized what colored the soup: paprika.

After a few sipped spoonfuls I sprinkled in more salt and oyster crackers for added nourishment. The waitress brought them in a separate bowl.

Sometimes I wonder if that place is still there on the corner of Forty-seventh. I like to think it is—hidden away like a hole card. I daydream I could go back. Drive all night, then take the bus to the factory. Open my old locker and my coveralls with *STEVE* stitched over the pocket would be hanging on the handle of the push broom. Walk in the grass down Western Boulevard. Sit at the counter sipping soup.

Outside, the crepe-paper colors were fading into a normal darkness. A man with a hussar's mustache, wearing a cook's apron, was cranking up the awning with a long metal rod. Neon lights were blinking on. I ordered a second bowl. I was never happier than in the next two years after I'd eaten those bowls of soup. Perhaps I was receiving a year of happiness per bowl. There are certain mystical connections to these things. Only forty cents a bowl. With my paycheck in my pocket, I could have ordered more, maybe enough for years, for a lifetime perhaps, but I thought I'd better stop while I was feeling good.

# Death of a Junk Peddler

## Nancy Zafris

Metal Shredder funerals are the worst. By far.

This knowledge creates dread, and the dread starts creeping in where it shouldn't. Breathing, just floating to the next moment, that's what this day is about. But now there's dread and it's put your rational systems on alert. The brief comatose luxury of grief—gone.

It's not your fault. Look what you have to contend with. After all, the other metal shredders will be here from the tri-state area and even beyond, and they are strange wealthy men with magnet key chains, men for whom the wide world is either ferrous or non-ferrous. Like the man they've come to honor, they're prone to acting up.

Your dad is sitting beside you. You and he are left to run the business. He's a man of charm and power, son of the deceased—he won't mean any disrespect but his need to rule could cause some problems. Then there's your mom who hated your grandfather with the purity of #1 copper. Your family embarrassment, Aunt Rhonda, an alloy of barfly and upper crust, might stop by since she's the daughter. Also in attendance, your quiet sister, modest and underrated as the vagus nerve. *She's nice* has been the tag attached to her since the eighth grade. Her ambitious husband, your brother-in-law, can look forward from this day to being comptroller at the scrapyard without a very old man pecking out misery on his shoulder.

Your grandfather was eighty-seven years old and he was at the yard every day by 7:30 a.m. You had to get up by 5:30 to get in a jog and beat him in, and in the winter it wasn't pleasant (Elise always promised a treadmill but it never materialized). He always dressed in a suit. The tie was tucked in between shirt buttons to protect it from the machinery, and the suits came from those secretly located clothing stores that cater to old men and their need for flammable blends in gargoyle plaids.

Your grandfather's jacket stopped changing seasons the last couple years—wool cloth even in the summer heat. That's when his frailty began beating like a heart.

You caught him spending more and more time at the non-ferrous bins, helping the minimum-wage grader to sort the brass fittings from copper pipes. Or teaching him how to salvage a joint of No. 1 copper from No. 2 copper tubing, a trick that could boost earnings by 45 cents. It was back to basics. Back to the scrap heap where he had started, knocking on the back doors of people's houses, throwing it all on a horse-drawn cart. He was strong as a horse, too, legendary for his strength. He could carry a barrel of water a city block, was knocked down by a train once and got back up. But now he worked with a shuffle. He worked at the speed of an iceberg.

The back hem of his wool jacket grew a frown as his shoulders aged into a hump. The tie, tucked in military style close to the belt, began ascending until it was almost as high as a bow tie. Somehow this ascent tugged at you in no small way. You remembered *mortal coil* at the sight of the tie's long shadow snaking inside the shirt. You thought *seven stages of man* at the way the tie climbed the rungs of the buttons. You knew he was going to die, that he had started his journey, and you wished you could talk to Elise about it and also maybe offer an apology. Your ex-wife had been a high-school English teacher, cramming poetry down your throat as if you were one of her ninth-graders, but then you finally began to appreciate what she was trying to tell you. Too late: she's in Telluride, Colorado, now with another man. Telluride—one of the essential elements but it's nonmetallic—even her newly chosen place to live is a careful poetry aimed at telling you something.

She won't be at the funeral. It's nothing malicious. It's just nothing, like the rest of the world's regard. Funny, those last two years as you watched him fail—and this is something she would understand—without those two years, this odd unlikable man would have been to you what he was to the world: another so-what who had lived, another so-what who had died.

> *Everything made of metal contains scrap.*
> *And everything made of metal eventually becomes scrap.*
> *-from* Don't Ignore Scrap, It Won't Ignore You,
> *written by your grandfather*

Who's going to pass out his pamphlets now that he's gone? He was working the grocery stores during Recycling for the Homeless Day and the high schools during Scrap Art Day. He was convinced that scrap was the yoga of life and he was the yogi. He thought his knowledge was infinite, in fact he knew it was. He insisted on being the judge during the Scrap Art competition, picking winners of no artistic merit but with the highest gross junk value. He was a man without doubt. He had your father's arrogance but not his charm. It was true that he could spot-grade 100 varieties of non-ferrous—light copper, refinery brass, cocks and faucets, curpo—but he tried to teach Elise about poetry. He would say things to her like *A good man is made of bronze, the calm surface is his essence* and expect her to write it down. He'd force her to write it down, the jungly yellow growths of his fingernails tapping on her hand till she put pen to paper. And you did nothing to stop him.

It's starting to come back, all the bad things about him, though you try to push them away. You wish to preserve his good memory on this day. His friends are here, friends and colleagues, the people who worked for him, the people he helped.

Murray Kempleton has just arrived you notice, all the way from Lebanon, Pennsylvania, home of the first gas cutting-torch. In the world of scrap the gas cutting-torch was an invention the equivalent of talking movies. Murray probably tries to take the credit for it. He's even older than your grandfather. He comes up to your dad and says something like *Thought he'd never die.* His daughter holds him along his forearm and guides him toward a pew. The daughter seems nice enough but you can see from the ironing lines that Murray's shirt has been sent to the dry cleaners. Your mother wouldn't wash your grandfather's shirts either. Nor would she pick them up off the floor for him. It's true, he smelled. Although he dressed neatly, the clothes didn't necessarily have to be clean. Your grandfather was a man who tried to turn his scrapyard into an obsessively organized and disinfected medical tent. He would stand under the wet scrubber and watch the iron drop into a bin until he spied a small piece of magnesium tangled in with the ferrous. He'd yell, There's sixty cents in here, get it out! But he was also a man who would stand in his bedroom among a sea of dirty socks, and a pair from the floor was the same to him as a pair from the dresser.

He moved in with your parents five years ago after your grandmother died. That's when it really started. The scrap man meets the scrappy daughter-in-law, even though your mother under normal circumstances would hardly be characterized that way. She's someone who usually wears a mask of royal imperturbability. Looking at her now in church, the hair drawn back in a French knot, one could interpret her expression as the lacquered beauty of grief. One could, but not you. You know it for just lacquered hardness. Later you'll see her standing at the reception following the service—the scrap dealers digging into the cold cuts with hearty abandon, their appetites wakened by the trouble they'd caused-and for a surreal split second you'll think she's a mannequin. Two weeks from now you'll happen to glance at the window of a used clothing store while waiting out a red light, and you'll be shocked to see a real mannequin displaying the dress she wore to the funeral, discarded as quickly as your grandfather's effects. You won't come to any new conclusions about your mother. More than anything it will make you feel that Siamese connection to Elise, a lifeline you cannot sever or you might die. It's a moment you need to share with her. Maybe you'll even pick up the phone and dial.

Your mother's royal mask comes off if you step into her domain and get things dirty, and your grandfather certainly did that. Elise called your parents' two-story the Greta Garbo house—the house that just wanted to be left alone. Putting something on the kitchen counter or walking across the carpet was at all costs to be avoided. Your mother took the "living" in "living room carpet" at serious face value. The wool was alive, it was cryptobiotic soil, every step was killing it. If you were a Sierra Club backpacker you maybe could understand. The "leave no trace" philosophy applied more strongly to this house than any protected wilderness. Your father had a shower installed in the garage and there he cleaned up and changed into his indoor clothes after a day at the scrapyard.

But not your grandfather. He trailed in his pelt of fine metallic dust and poured himself a shot of Johnny Walker Black right on the polished kitchen counter. Unfortunately he didn't take his drink neat, causing further damage as he rummaged for ice cubes, apparently believing ice trays might be stored in the designer white cabinets next to the plateware. He left the refrigerator finger-painted with dusty oxide. The freezer's rim of frost bled a liver maroon after he had foraged through to the cubes. The pleased shudder that ran through him when the Johnny Walker hit its spot whisked off more iron flakes. It didn't help that he badmouthed your mother's dream house as useless scrap. He pulled out his magnet key chain and tested the silverware for any ferrous pull. This is 301 stainless! came his scoff, and your mother's silver-plate utensils in Trillia pattern were gleefully denounced. His magnet also discovered yellow brass light fixtures contaminated with iron. What a ruthless scholar he could be. He *reduced* your mother's house, almost as though working himself through the mobius verity of *Reduce, Reuse, Recycle*. If your mother had understood this, she might not have left him alone. Because then came the Reuse and Recycle part, in the form of his home improvement ideas.

Your mother went away for three days to a holistic spa in Arizona, then met your father in Sedona for another three, and when they came back the old man had knocked down the wall between living room and dining room and replaced it with a gigantic ant farm. It was framed by glass block and landscaped with sand and little trees and logs. He'd hired the architect Judge Cotter had used for designing an indoor Palm Beach, with chipping green for him and handicapped lap pool for his partially disabled wife. The judge had been immensely pleased with the result and sent him over to your grandfather. And you had to admit, the man did good work. It was a nice ant farm. If he's smart, the architect will attend your grandfather's funeral and pass out business cards. Scrap dealers are always coming up with peculiar notions, and they need architects to prevent disaster.

Your grandfather was starting to fall asleep during meals. The odor that no one acknowledged wafted from him in ovenish waves. It was your mother who got to watch the ant farm while she sat there, unable to eat. She could see through to the other side to the ruined living room carpet, its once golden field now tarring the floor in geological upheaval. The ant farm took up the whole wall, but your grandfather had to press his face to the glass before he could see any of the little workers. His mouth marks were ping-ponged all over the glass. You could read the graph of his desperation as the mouth marks pulsed high and low. Your mother might not understand, but you knew what he was searching for. After all, you're a metal shredder yourself. It's in your blood. Your grandfather was trying to peel back the world and examine its stitching. He was watching the world built from the bottom up. He was waiting for the ants to explain it to him. You've had the same feeling yourself standing at a topographical globe. You spin it, feeling its bumpy surface. Your stomach tightens. What is it you want to do? You want to dig your fingers into the earth's topography and lift it away. You want to pull out the continents floating on the oceans and take a look. It's all scrap inside, guard rails and piping and nothing else. Except one other thing—poetry—and this you've learned too late. But at least you've learned it, and this is what you want to tell her.

*Count sheep, one little lamb, two little lambs.*
*Count scrap, one elder brass, two malic nickel.*
*Easy, and it works just as well.*
*-from your grandfather's* Homey Bits of Scrap Wisdom,
*passed out free at the weighmaster's station.*

The last of the old guard, Happy Lazar and Jacob Kolski, find their way to Murray Kempleton's pew, their suits obviously bought at that same place your grandfather shopped. Happy Lazar is down from Cleveland; he's looking poorly since the last time you saw him, having developed the turtle-ish slouch, shoulders high, head low, that you recognize from your grandfather's last months.

The old guard, down to three.

How much trouble they used to cause at these events. Clasping Happy's hand, now thin as a girl's, you feel sadness at the fan of finger bones plucking through his palm like four sharp piano keys, but major relief as well: *Finally too old to raise a stink*, you whisper to your father. In twenty minutes you'll eat your words. You'll forget the pang you feel for these three old men mortally wounded by age, and you'll want to throttle them. You'll want to throw them in the baler and string them up.

*Battery lugs are coded as* Rakes *in the business.*
*Aluminum grindings are called* Twitch.

This year marks the year your dad is old enough to get his Golden Buckeye card. Not to worry—that's hardly old these days, fifty-five, and your dad has lost none of his vigor or strength. You have this thought about him that you've kept secret; it started the day of the infamous Bronco chase and grew and nagged at you. It's that O. J. Simpson somehow reminds you of your father—the charisma, the smile, the noble profile and intelligent eyes, but underneath ...

Not that your father would ever commit murder, but now and again a murderous temper surfaces. It happens when his authority is threatened, which is not that often since he's an imposing man. But Tommy Landers from Indianapolis has just made his entrance in Olympian fashion and he could be a clone of your father: good looks, big body, eyes that can ripple with emotional depth or cut like a shredder. As if hearing you think, Tommy poses at the back of the church to let the sun's rays beam off him in a holy crown.

Tommy's been after your dad to buy his shear; he wants to redirect his scrap business into white goods. Your scrapyard won't take refrigerators or washers or dryers any more, too many fluorocarbons and PCBs, so there's a market out there that Tommy wants to exploit. There's no reason your dad can't buy the shear; after all, you need a new shear and you're in charge of the daily operations anyway, but it's something personal between them. You see that dark side rising to the surface when Tommy and he are in the same room; it actually rises to the surface like a tan. If *Time* magazine did a mug shot of your father, they'd have to darken him up just like they did O.J. He turns the color of jealousy and you can actually see it. It ambushes him with a vehemence when it strikes because he's never had to get used to it. The daily feedings of crow or envy are for the rest of the plodding world, not him.

Tommy Landers comes up to offer his condolences. His mouth is aimed only at you with a bit of an Elvis twitch to include your mother. Your dad is shut out. Shredder etiquette demands at least a handshake, but they look elsewhere as their fingers intertwine, so that their nods appear directed toward Jesus on the cross, on the one hand, and toward Wanda the weighmaster cashier, on the other.

Pekoe *is the 200 series of stainless steel.*
*Yellow brass is* Honey.

An invisible force is at work. The mourners have classified themselves in their seating choices. The church has turned into a scrapyard with the mourners ranked like grades of metal, best to worst. The purest grade, the family, is here in front. The finest alloys come next, his peers in the business, then colleagues in other fields, Judge Cotter among them.

Iron, the scrapyard's tumbleweed, sturdy but rusty, takes up the middle ground of pews: Wanda the cashier sits here, as does the weighmaster, the many graders and their foreman, the yard boss, the Linkbelt and shredder operators, the welder, the truckers and freight loaders; and the private haulers, entrepreneurs of the blue highways, who scavenge the roads for bumpers and radiators. They sit with sour blank looks and arms folded across the perch of their iron-hard pot bellies. You can't tell it by looking at them, but they loved your grandfather. They respected how he'd worked his way to the top, not inherited it like *some others.* Well, it was impossible for you to work your way to the top when you woke up already there. Your grandfather gets to go to his grave hoarding the secret gloat of all pioneers: that it happens only once and he's the man who did it. Everyone else is just following his trail. He knew it, and coveted it. It was his secret weapon against your awesome father. You he never cared about impressing. Not that he didn't like you, you just weren't in his league.

The self-classification continues all the way to the rear where, hiding behind the iron middle, sit the contaminants. Here begins the sprinkling of lead, the Hispanics and the Vietnamese who are paid in cash; some stragglers you might have recognized had they not gone further downhill from the last time you barely recognized them—in fact, if you knew who they were you'd be surprised they weren't dead; and now some older folks, black men and women, whom you definitely don't know, people from a bygone era. These are shadows striding toward you from a dark rainstorm. The memories attached to them have so long been stored as dried seed that this flood is too much nourishment. You've got to back off, let the memories either blow away or thrive on their own. Who are they? Are you sure you've seen them before?

> *The question is often asked. What is a fair price for scrap?*
> *The question is irrelevant.*
> *-from his* The Common Man's Guide to Getting Your Money's Worth From Scrap.

What your grandfather meant is that scrap is worth whatever people pay for it. Ten years ago zinc was worthless; now it sells for eighty cents a pound. You see the unfamiliar mourners fringing the back pews and wonder who they are. Are memories just scrap? The question is also irrelevant. Because they will continue to have whatever worth you assign to them.

Who are they? You haven't decided if it's worth remembering.

> *No. 1 copper is known as* Barley.
> *No. 2 copper is called* Birch.

You can't help smiling at Wanda's addled good nature. She's waving enthusiastically to Tommy Landers after she mistakes his avoidance of your father's eyes as a nod to her. She's a woman of remarkably few preferences as far as human beings go. She likes everyone a little too much. Maybe she's just desperate for flesh and blood after fifteen years of being locked inside a bulletproof glass cage, communicating through a mouthpiece drilled above the coin well. She's the only female in the scrapyard. Women in the scrap business has always been a dicey proposition. They tend to run toward ruination. That's certainly been true of Rhonda, your father's sister. Thank god your own sister teaches the third grade.

You're not sure Rhonda will be here—you don't keep in touch, haven't even seen her in two years—but you're certain her children won't. Boys all of them, scattered in Orlando, Naples, and Ft. Worth. The last you heard her ex-husband was managing a public golf course in Knoxville, but Rhonda hasn't seen him in over a decade though she's been dating versions of him for twenty-five years—operators itching to score who are bound to say something ridiculous before the day is through. *Visiting hours at my mother's nursing home close at six today* is a favorite early exit line.

Vernon is the name of her ex-husband. You were still a kid when he was last around, but you remember him. He was always nice to you, gave you Juicy Fruit gum and dollar bills like you were one of his pals. Your grandfather despised the guy and his hatred was always a dangerous thing. Your brain detours for a moment. A limbic misfire reminds you of the visits with your grandfather to that other part of the city—a whisper tells you he was hiring someone to beat his son-in-law to a pulp. Remember the hospital stay? Then your brain is back to Juicy Fruit gum, the fruity spray of aroma as Vernon peeled off the wrapper and folded the stick as he handed it to you. It's still how you eat gum to this day, folding it on the way to your mouth.

Given Rhonda's past history, you expect her to strut into church in black leggings and high-top hair, her spike heels nailing out a cigarette by the back pew. But the moment of shock her arrival causes is of a different sort. Her black dress is subdued, her manner limp, but it's her face. My god, she looks like your grandfather. Your grandfather with a Supremes wig on. Drinking and eye tucks have skimmed her face down to a spear point, and the features that peer out under the hair are tiny and bitten. She's all alone. Where's the boyfriend, jail? a cockfight? visiting Mother in the nursing home?

Stop it. You're acting like your father and mother. No wonder Elise got sick of you.

Rhonda offers you a gentle kiss and sits down beside your sister and clasps her hand. Then she bows her head and begins to cry, as quietly as she can, but soon everyone is hearing it. Like your father, whose deep breaths try to smother his agitation, you focus your attention on something else.

Rhonda Fleming, for example, your grandfather's favorite actress. She starred in lots of pirate movies but that's all you know about her. Your grandfather was watching one of her films when he died, a bit of funny symbolism you didn't realize until now.

Another phantom speaks to you. For some reason you and your sister are alone in Rhonda's house. The TV turns on in the kitchen and between gunshots and horses neighing erupts a convulsive panting. The two of you sneak up from the basement romper room where you have been setting up empty soda bottles as bowling pins. A blackness runs liquid through your scared six-year-old body. Somehow you understand that something awful will be there to meet you at the top of the stairs. This is something you really don't want to know about. You'll be part of that world soon enough.

In the kitchen Rhonda has collapsed in your grandfather's arms, trying to catch her breath between sobs. Your grandfather is saying, *He needs the shinola wiped off his behind.* He's patting her back, kissing her forehead. Nobody treats *Daddy's little girl like that and gets away with it.*

*Don't hurt him, Daddy*, she weeps.

*You don't worry. Daddy's going to take care of his little girl. He'll take care of it. You just let Daddy take out his old shinola remover kit.*

Shinola ... No way. Was your grandfather ever that obvious? Yet something makes you turn around. Way in the rear, a black man, twenty-five years older than when you saw him last, catches your eye. Your grandfather unloaded turkeys, steaks, lamb chops, and a new battery from his trunk and brought them inside the man's house. hey went into the kitchen to talk. You sat with the wife and a boy as small as you who wouldn't come out from behind the easy chair. In the car your grandfather said, No one has to know you were late for Little League. When you didn't answer he said, Isn't that right? A few days later, Vernon was in one hospital and Rhonda, with a nervous collapse, was in another.

Your father is still redirecting his agitation into his lungs as Rhonda's weeping continues. It's not sympathy he feels, nor love or obligation. He is her brother. He needs to offer comfort. Only he is in the position to do this. Instead he sucks air. It's the same comfort you'll one day be called upon to offer to your sister. Already you sense you won't rise to the occasion, not without Elise by your side. Will she come back? You know she won't. But you could be wrong. You're so often wrong these days. There could be a message on your machine for you to call. She could come back tomorrow.

Elise's message plays in your head. *Call me, okay*. You'll have to stifle a laugh at that one. *Call me, okay*—the poetess, not so good at speeches. *Look, there's a letter in the mail explains it all.* You knew the message would end with that. She's lost without her pen. Plus she's got to get in the last word. You study your watch. It's noon right now. That means it's ten a.m. in Telluride. She'll probably call a little after five, which is perfect because you'll be home around seven.

When you look up you realize you've been talking to yourself. It's okay; no one has heard you. Your muttering has been drowned out by the argument taking place at the coffin. You can't believe it. It's the old guard, still up to their tricks. Who helped them up there? You were sure rheumatism would keep their spines soldered to the seat this time. Your father is fighting through your mother's knees to get to the aisle, but it's too late and besides, nothing will stop them now. The magnets attached to their key chains are already out and testing the coffin for any pull. Happy Lazar slaps the coffin with his thin, bony palm and shouts, "This is yellow brass!

"Sit down," your father says, setting his hands on Happy's shoulders.

"Let him have his say." Tommy Landers pushes him aside, pleased to order your dad around.

Your dad is quickly roused and squares off against Tommy, but you're there to step between them.

"There's a five-percent pull on this," Murray Kempleton croaks.

"Let it go. Let it go," your father says.

This time Jacob Kolski pounds the coffin. He's hale and strong at eighty-two. With a nauseating surge in your stomach, you watch your grandfather's corpse rock and settle with each of Jacob's punches, the strong stitching keeping the folded hands in place.

Jacob declares, "Your grandfather wanted copper, not yellow brass, and what a metal shredder wants for his coffin a metal shredder gets."

He has a point.

*Light copper is called* Dream.

It could have been a lot worse, you think later. Your grandfather could have tumbled out onto the floor. The old guard didn't behave that badly; they were just protecting their friend's interests, and they were only as obnoxious as their old bones would allow. In their younger days they would have keelhauled the mortician in the baptistery and flown him from a flying buttress. Having Judge Cotter officiate a quick I.O.U. for a copper coffin didn't take too much time—people hardly noticed, and afterward the funeral continued without a hitch. You know in your heart the old man would have been pleased at the fuss. His only disappointment would have been that your dad didn't floor Tommy Landers with a haymaker.

You pour a Johnny Walker Black on him. It's ten p.m. and the answering machine blinks zero. There's still time. It's only eight o'clock in Telluride.

She's taught you the burden of life's major platitude, that love can save your soul or break your heart and you want to repeat the one cliché that rises above all others, *I love you, I love you, I love you, please come back.* You want to dial her up and tell her that it's all right, she doesn't have to call tonight. You understand. You know what she wants to tell you. You know it's hard for her to say it. You sit on the couch until midnight and fall asleep to her benediction: sweet dreams. To the old man in his copper coffin, sweet dreams. Sweet untarnished dreams.

# Cannery Night

## Kathleen De Grave

Dear Davy,

Probaly you don't even think about me. Probaly you got some belly-dancer woman to keep you company and all those promises you told me about how you'd write every midnight from your hammock and how you'd love me forever just never was true.

But I decided I was going to write you this letter just in case you come back and find out I'm not where you left me.

It's hot as heck already this morning and I been up all night. Even now when the trucks go by my little apartment I can hear the tar sucking under their tires. The morning isn't hardly started, just some pale light behind the trees I can see out my window. Everything's quiet in between the crickets and the trucks. So this is the right time for me to write you this letter, when I'm all alone and you are out on the blue waves somewhere.

I'll start at the beginning.

It was so hot yesterday we maybe thought they was going to close the canning factory. The ladies up in beans was getting dizzy watching them little green beans go by and by, and some, so I heard, fell off their high stools and was sick right there on the floor.

But no. The corn was just coming in and there's always somebody waiting to take an empty spot, so Tilsen's didn't close and I had to go to work like usual.

We must of put through twenty thousand cans last night. You should have seen them cans go flashing by high up near the ceiling. They come off the machines Indian file onto this big belt that carries them almost straight up to that skinny belt that runs along the ceiling, so high a person can't hardly see them except for their sparkle. All the belts and all the different shapes of cans is like a spider web, just catching the sunlight. Only this is electric.

It's not so hot and wet in cans as in the rest of the factory, but it's noisier. There's maybe a thousand empty cans clicking together all at one time and unless the lines stop, the rattle don't. We're the beginning of everything. Without cans there's no place for the vegetables to go.

What I'm wanting to tell you is this. Last night . . . But no. First I gotta let you know all the steps that led here. I don't want you to misunderstand.

Yesterday afternoon, just before my shift started at 3:00, for the first time I got to go up to the third floor in Veg-all. Virga took me, because I was afraid to go alone up them steps. There's no light and the steps is just wide enough for one person at a time, and I always been wondering what was at the top—it seemed like a little mystery. So I asked Virga if she would. Virga is a Norway woman with freckles all over her arms and two long red braids down her back. She wears her shirt sleeves rolled up to show her muscles. I can count on her.

Veg-all is so different from cans, I thought I was in another world. It's quiet, just the hum of the vats. Corn and carrots and cubes of potatoes and olive-skinned beans all rush down from nowhere like different colored paints, sliding and tumbling downhill faster then the belt can move, spilling over the sides all along. Wherever I would put my foot I'd mash vegetables under my shoe and there was the smell and the wetness of hot broth and spices. You could hear the broth boiling and the vegetables sliding down. Oneida women spoon the froth off onto the floor, their faces shining with sweat. Another woman stirs and stirs.

All night long I couldn't get the vision of that room out of my head. It kept coming back when I didn't expect.

You don't know about this job unless you been reading my letters, which I'm betting you ain't. I been sending them anyway, even if that makes me a fool—just a little foolish girl, because, Davy, I want you to know, you always been right there at the core of my heart.

Well, normally nothing is different at work. I go in at 3:00, work my rear end off till 11, and go back home to this little apartment I been in for two months now. But things was different last night. Not just because I got the guts to go upstairs but also because a new guy come on the floor. Most of us in cans is women, except for the foreman, so we get to do the good jobs like being handyman and driving forklift too. You can figure out what happened when a guy showed up.

Nobody likes to work the machines, except Anne who's an expert, because they're tall, maybe 13 feet, and up that high it's hot. And too the machines is always going. A flat of cans comes up and the cans start moving right off onto the belt. You gotta be quick the way Anne is to see the dent and grab the can before it gets away. And the cans just keep coming. When one stack of cans is done, and there's probaly 500 cans in a stack, the handyman pulls out the empty pallet and pushes in a full one. It's got to all work smooth and fast or you watch those last cans move out of sight and pretty soon the whole place shuts down and the foreman comes to see why.

Besides you get a lot bigger check come Friday driving forklift.

So when the foreman takes Virga off bug and puts the new guy on, someone's gotta pay.

I want to make you understand about this. About Clyde and all—that's the new guy. I'm going to try to tell it step by step.

Ok, this Clyde guy is a college boy, but he ain't half as sharp as he thinks he is. Short, and skinny legs. Not like you. He wears a dirty blue cap he pulls down as far as it'll go so he has to keep his chin in the air to see. His skin looks dirty too, and his hair.

First thing he does is drive over by me. I was helping Shirley be handyman last night, so I was sitting on a half stack of 609's, taking it easy. He probaly picked me out because I'm the youngest one there and everybody else looks married.

"What's everybody so hot about?" he asks me. I didn't answer him right away.

"Hey, I'm talking to you." But I don't say nothing.

He puts his foot up on the steering wheel and leans back, like he owns the place. "How old are you anyway?"

"You took Virga's bug," I tell him.

"Which one's she?" He throws his head back so's he could see where I'm pointing, way up on top of the eight-ounce, finally has to push his hat out of the way.

There was Virga and Anne, Anne with her long tongs picking cans like a bird pecks seed and Virga pulling cans off with her bare hands, her muscles rolling under her skin every time she slaps a dented can into the waste box. She was watching us right now, her eyes on Clyde. The heat was so bad up there her face was red.

"What's she so pissed off about?"

"You're earning a dollar and a half more an hour then she is—right now, sitting here doing nothing."

Clyde scratches his belly, his T-shirt and jeans as dirty as the rest of him. He looks at me with a little smile. "I bet she can't drive anyhow," he says. He's flirting with me. Thinks he's hot stuff. I'm sitting there confused.

Just then I seen Shirley sweeping cans out from under the eight-ounce machine like she's frantic and every little while she looks up and yells, "Where is he?" Then it comes to me that the eight-ounce is almost empty, no new stack waiting to go in. And there sits Clyde with his foot up.

"If I was you," I says to him, jumping down because I was suppose to be over by Shirley too, "I'd get moving."

Clyde looks around, caught by surprise, then roars off as fast as that bug can go, weaving back and forth all the way. Meanwhile the last stack of cans is raising up higher and higher. When the pallet gets to the top, they'll clear off the last cans and send the pallet down. You should have seen the way Virga watched Clyde drive off while she picked those cans faster then ever. The new stack better be there on time.

Shirley was going just about crazy. She was pulling levers and kicking rollers in a fury, but nothing she could do would get the stack there any faster. She had me over there crawling under and through and around the machine to find stray cans, and every once in a while she'd get hold of the broom again and swish it around. When she bent over, I could see the outline of her bikini pants showing under her shorts.

Did I tell you how I got a kind of sixth sense for underwear? Inherited from my mother. Somehow, I know what kind of underwear certain people are wearing. I can't do it for strangers, but if I know you a little bit I know what you got on, see it in my mind's eye.

Shirley has a whole set of undies with the months on them. But last night I could tell she was wearing something special, probaly some silk bikini pants with a green and gold Green Bay Packer football helmet front and center, with that big white G. Right then I knew she had plans.

But then Clyde came into view with the cans. He had the stack lifted just high enough on the forks to make it so he couldn't see where he was going. And it being his first night, he of course didn't think of going backwards. When he got to the eight-ounce, he started backing up and roaring forward, gunning the motor, the whole stack teeter-tottering a little further off the forks each time.

Virga and Anne up top was finishing off the last layer when he ends up spilling the six foot stack of half a thousand cans all over the concrete floor, putting a good size dent in most of them. The crash comes just as Anne pushes the button to bring the empty pallet down.

Clyde starts swearing at the cans like it's their fault and backs up in little jerks, trying to make the pallet fall off, crushing cans under his wheels. But the pallet just hangs on, dragging its metal bands.

Virga slides down the eight-ounce ladder straightlegged, then stands next to Shirley, her arms folded. She don't say a word. Finally Clyde shuts the motor off and looks at her from under his hat. The eight-ounce is humming as the empty pallet comes down and the noise from the cans on the line gets quieter and quieter the further they move out of sight. So Clyde at last jumps out of the forklift, kicks the pallet off the prongs, and just stomps off.

Virga climbs into her old place on the bug like she's coming home. She flips the engine on and steers her way backwards out of the maze of cans, just taking her time. She goes to the nearest stack of cans, runs the forks under the pallet, smooth as you please, and picks the stack up like you would a forkful of mashed potatoes, then drives back smooth and straight and sets the stack square on the rollers with one try.

In an instant, Shirley cuts the bands that hold the cans straight then pushes the button that will pull the stack in, and Virga swings off the bug and back up the ladder to the top of the machine. I can see the elastic band of her plain white cotton underwear flashing between her jeans and her T-shirt.

After Shirley and me picked up all the cans Clyde dropped, I went over to the big doors where the railroad cars pull up for loading and leaned back against the doorsill. As long as one leg is hanging over the edge, we're counted as outside the building and so we can smoke. Not that I do—well, maybe just a little. When I started this job maybe three months ago, I thought I'd try an experiment. This was going to be the new me, tough and not taking nothing from nobody. I'd wait till I was in the car driving down the highway to work, Mom's house a good mile behind me just in case, and I'd pull out this carton of Winstons I bought from the gas station. I'd light up, using the car's cigarette lighter—that still works even if the radio don't—and put my elbow out the window. That pack lasted me three weeks, because I'd miss days, you know. The last one or two was pretty stale. But I been carrying a pack around with me since then just supposing I want to try starting again.

Anyhow, this loading dock is where me and Shirley take our breaks. So I was leaning back, thinking about you out on the ocean, wondering if it ever gets as hot there as it does at the factory. I could imagine you leaning on the ship's railing, looking at the colors in the water, and I sort of dreamed, sitting there in the doorway, until the sun on the water seemed like the vegetables coming down and then that turned into the leaves on the trees last fall when you and I was in the park laying down and looking up at the sky through the yellow and orange, listening to the branches creaking over what you called wind waves. Your eyelashes brushed my cheek and you told me to wait for you. Do you remember, Davy? You said that you'd come back some day, for only me.

I woke up when Clyde came over. He stood right by me, one arm up on the doorsill, closing me in.

"You know what's wrong with you?" he says. I stand up, meaning to get away, but he don't move his arm, "You need a good fuck." And he moves his hips.

I just sorta stand there. A lot of the guys at the factory talk that way and I'm almost use to it. But this was personal. The problem is, he was looking at me with that smile again, like he was saying something nice to me, a little invitation. I'm so confused I don't even make a move when he puts his other arm up to block me in completely. I guess it was lucky for me that Virga came up behind him.

"Hey, fella. You," she says, clamping her hand on his shoulder till I could see it hurt. "You let her go, ya?"

When he turns, I break past him to stand next to Virga. They glare at each other, neither one able to stare the other down.

After work, about 1:30 in the morning (It was a long shift. They made us do overtime), I said ok when Shirley and Virga asked me to go across the street with them to get some beer. That was the first time I ever done that because you know I'm not old enough, but they didn't care, and Virga said she'd take responsibility. Sometimes I think about what my mother would say about all this. You know how at home nobody never drinks, nobody says swear words, we just don't break the rules. I always thought that was my dad's way of running things, because he read the Bible all the time and thought the devil was most everywhere, but mainly in us kids. After he died I thought Mom would ease up, but things just got tighter. I had to wear skirts that came below my knee and couldn't have no boys over or on the phone. I never told you this in case you would get scared off. When I met you in the park those afternoons, I had to sneak out. If Mom would of seen us laying like that side by side—!

And then you left and then the letters stopped coming—I thought at first Mom was stealing them, but I always got to the mail first, so she couldn't be. A month or two ago I just moved out. I couldn't see myself tied up in the house like that and me almost 19. I had my mail forwarded here, and every day, the first thing I do when I hear the mailman at the door, is run to get the mail put right in my hands, so if there's a letter from you I won't miss it.

But there never is.

Anyway, it's 1:30 in the morning and the factory is still going strong trying to fill and cook and box up all those cans we sent through. To get to the punch clock, Shirley and me and Virga had to walk through the cooling room. The men in there walk along the edge of a concrete bath where they dip the baskets of cans 400 degrees hot. The men sweat, everything is wet and slippery. One wrong move! Heavy wooden baskets on iron hooks run on coasters near the ceiling. Dip in the bath, then into the cool air—baskets filled with silver cans. Everything steaming. Too hot to touch. The men breathe in that steam all night. During supper in the cafeteria when their shirts dry, you can see the white outline of sweated salt on their backs.

We duck beneath a few rows of hanging, cooling baskets to an open space. When she straightens up, Shirley pulls her shoulders back to show her big breasts. The men stare at us.

They dress alike—leather boots, shirts hanging open to show dirty T-shirts, pants low on the hips. Most of the men on the bath are Indian. Mexicans are below, sweeping the floor dry.

Sometimes I wonder about that.

So we're walking though, ducking our heads, when a basket comes swinging, dripping, from a man's hand and coasts down the line, just missing us. Soft plop against the basket it hits sets the whole line trembling. My heart starts going like nothing.

We punch out at the clock there and, as I turn to go upstairs, I see Clyde leaning his elbow on the edge of the bath at the far end, watching us as he talks to one of the men.

It was still hot outside even that late, no wind. The streets was empty. In fact, we just had time to get to the bar before it closed. I felt strange on that street—out so late, cutting across in the middle of the block, 5 or 6 migrant guys squatting along the factory wall, watching us as we scoot across under the street light.

Inside the bar it wasn't much cooler then on the street—just a fan blowing high up on the wall. Some fellows from the warehouse was already there, sitting at the end of the bar nearest the door.

"Hey Virga!" they yell, as soon as we come in. "Come over here!"

She goes over by them and Shirley and me sit a ways down the bar. The warehouse men like Virga—they like to hear her talk. "I'm strong, ya?"she'd say. When she's a bug driver, she helps them out if she has time. Shirley buys me a beer and we turn around on our stools to watch Virga.

I take my first drink and get confused again. The beer is pretty—I like the foam and the golden color and the way the glass sweats when I pour it in, but it sure is bitter. And it burns. But the funny thing was, there was something I liked about that bitterness and that burn. It's as if my throat needed just that after 10 hours of breathing in that factory air.

Nobody said nothing about me being too young, didn't ask for my driver's license or nothing, so I started to ease up and enjoy it.

The bar was noisy. Virga and her bunch was laughing over something, our foreman and some other fellow, both drunk already, was playing pool at the far side of the bar, yelling at each other about a cue stick, and the one little fan rattled over our heads. Shirley had a hard time staying by me, even though I knew she was trying to be nice. When one of the warehouse men cracked a joke, she'd shout something at him. So I told her to go on ahead, I was just happy to watch. She slid off the stool and as she walked over by them she pulled her shoulders back again and tucked her shirt tighter into her jeans.

I saw Clyde come in before he saw me, so I turned back to the bar, hoping he wouldn't know who I was. But he comes right over and sits down next to me and orders a beer of his own.

Virga is standing in front of everybody in her group, telling a story about a gong she rigged up to call the kids home to eat. Everybody laughs when she shows them how she swings the mallot to hit the gong. I pretend to ignore Clyde, turn around again to watch Virga, ready to run if I have to. Clyde turns around too. Like I said, Virga's arms are big—we could see that when she pretended to swing the mallot. She's strong enough to lift full boxes of cans into a boxcar for a half hour straight.

Clyde mumbles so I can hardly hear him, "I'll bet she's a dyke." I think I must be imagining this. Even he couldn't be that stupid. Then he says it again, so everyone can hear. "I'll bet she's a dyke."

It gets real quiet. Everybody just looks at him. Virga has her arms up, in mid-swing, and she looks at Clyde too, like she can't believe what he said. Clyde turns back to the bar and hunches over his beer. I don't know if he knew Virga was coming up behind him, but she put her two hands on his shoulders and pulled him over backwards, beer and all. I could hear his knees scraping the bottom of the bar edge. And then he was on the floor, beer all over him, his feet tangled in the bar stools legs, his head cracking on the floor, making his cap fall off.

For a little bit everything hangs like that, Virga standing over Clyde, the bar quiet except for the fan.

Then Shirley cheers and everybody else joins in. I decide this is pretty funny. Maybe the beer was getting to me.

The bartender, though, tells us to leave. He must of called the cops because pretty soon we could hear the sirens coming.

Everybody goes back to their beers to finish them quick, except for the foreman over by the pool table. He just sits down on the floor, too drunk to move. Virga reaches out her hand to help Clyde up. He rubs his head, but takes her hand anyway. Then when he's standing, he tries to wipe the beer off himself.

Only because he looks so pitiful, not cocky at all anymore, I hold out some bar rags. Virga takes one. She wipes his face and neck real slow, looking him straight in the eye all the time, then she kisses him, gentle, holding the rag under his chin.

I'm confused again. The whole night was like that. First Veg-all, then Clyde, then the beer and this kiss. My stomach just sort of dropped. I drank my third beer fast, even knowing it would hurt my throat. I was feeling—something. Maybe I remembered those long kisses with you when nobody was looking. All I know is I hurt and wanted to cry.

But the sirens was getting closer, so I didn't have time to think about it. I stood up and had to catch myself from falling. And my lips were numb. Someone lifted the foreman to his feet and everybody headed out the door to their cars. Before I knew it I ended up with Shirley and Virga and Clyde and one of the warehouse men in Shirley's car, racing in the opposite direction from the police and from where I live.

Davy, the truth is, I was very drunk. I just went along because I didn't even think. Shirley said we should have a swim party at the park after she stopped at home to get a couple six packs, and they all said yes.

I just let myself sway with the car, speeding around curves, the cool air blowing in my face. It was like I was going somewhere I never been and once I got there I'd never come back. I tried to think about how I felt, and kept remembering how it was when you kissed me that way out in the park, so long I lost my breath. I wanted—I don't know what. But it was strong on me, just wanting. Virga's kissing that guy when he was so mean to her—I don't know. I guess I just wanted someone to lift up my face that way.

When the moon went under, the night was blacker than black, but when it came back out, I could see everything clear, like in a lightning flash. Clyde was sitting up front with Shirley and the warehouse man. He took his sticky shirt off and the next time the moon came out, one shoulder gleamed.

Shirley drove up right next to the crick. We was the only ones there except for some dogs barking down near the dance hall building. There was just one light over in the parking lot. Shirley handed round some beers after we piled out. Because my feet was so hot, I took off my shoes and socks and rubbed my feet on the wet grass. Then I sat down—dizzy.

When Shirley started to take her clothes off and yell for us to come swim, I found out I was right about the Packer helmet. The moon came out and it was beautiful, all those bodies in underwear I'd only guessed. The warehouse man had boxer shorts covered with Budweiser labels and Clyde wore leopardskin BVD's. Virga had on the cotton underpants I already knew about and a sleeveless undershirt instead of a bra.

In that same moment I saw trees and bushes a dark green and grass covered with dandelions and clover. I read in one of my dad's Bible books somewhere that the Garden of Eden use to be all trees and flowers—"lush" the book said. I didn't know what that meant, so I looked it up and when I did I found out it meant "drunk." That's how it was here, drunken like that, reminding me of the vegetables and colors and the steam in Veg-all. The colors was all there in my mind again, and I ached so bad.

Everybody was in the water, splashing, except me, so Virga stands up out of the crick, her braids dripping, and motions me in. The moon went back under, but while I was taking off my things, I could feel the flowers with my toes. By the time I got into the water, everybody else was swimming off toward the dance hall and the dogs. I watched the dogs run down the bank and jump in to swim with us, but I was too dizzy to swim far, and so just laid back and let myself go with the current. Above me the moon was white, like the inside of an apple.

Then Clyde is there on the bank, his hair slicked back because it was wet, and drops of water are running down his shoulders and chest.

He seemed to be washed clean and new. This time when he said something, his voice was soft, and he had that little smile again. "How about it?" he says.

I stand up, the water coming up to my waist, the gravel sharp on my feet.

This is what I had to tell you, Davy. About how his eyes looked right at me, him standing there in his BVDs, and how the colors was swirling in my head. Shirley and the warehouse man was off in the shadows somewhere and I could see Virga swimming towards us, still far down the crick, and I wondered what she would tell me to do, and what you would.

I get out of the water, just dizzy and shivering. I hear the splash of Virga's arms and feet swimming with the current, fast. Clyde is looking at her.

When I climb up the bank and turn back to look, the moon comes out and I see Virga come up out of the crick, the water dripping off her. Beautiful. Clyde seems kind of overdone by her. He stumbles and sits down on the bank. Virga comes over by him and sits down, then puts her white leg over his and runs her foot down the inside of his calf.

It was too much for me, Davy. Everything just got to be too much. I didn't know what was what. Everything seemed to be wrong, backwards. And it was like the moon coming out in my mind. I saw all the wrongness, all the lies. Everything. What I said about the canning factory being almost magic with those vegetables and those colors—that was a lie. It's Indian women and poor women standing at worm tables all night picking out bugs and hacking corn cobs with knives. And it's slop on the floor and scars on your hands and strained backs. And you, Davy. You're a lie. A goddam terrible lie. Because I knew then you was never coming back. And I was a lie too—all my wanting and saving myself just came down to nothing.

I held that thought in my mind, looking at the two of them and me. It burned so much it was bitter. My throat felt it. It was that wanting again. And I didn't know which one I wanted more—him with that little smile and his wet BVDs or her with that leg thrown over him like that, leaning back on her arms, her breasts clear through her undershirt, her braids streaming down behind her. I wanted it all. Both of them and the trees and the water and the clover and the devil too. I ached for all of it.

You know, I never felt that before. Not with you. All that kissing made me happy because I thought I was loved, but I never felt that burn.

I could have Clyde. I knew it. Virga would give him to me—she had him captured already. But that idea just bothered me because it wasn't enough. It's like getting that present you been wanting and wanting and it's exactly like you wanted but it makes you feel awful because now it's yours.

It was clear to me what I'd be giving up, too. And that seemed big—as big as what I wanted. Virga moved her leg away from Clyde and stood up, tall and graceful. "Do you want him?" she asks me.

He gives me that smile. "Come on," he says. But he don't move, just leans back. I'm standing there in my underwear thinking about how I saved myself for you and wondering if you knew that or cared.

And that's when I knew—part of that lightning flash—that I was beautiful too, and the wanting included—me. I was drunk on everything. I was lush.

So, that's why I'm writing this letter, what I'm wanting you to understand. I won't be here when you get back. Wisconsin is just too little for me—I need something big, someplace I can figure out what this ache is all about. California maybe. Or Alaska. Or Arkansas.

I want you to know you're still in the core of my heart, but there's a lot more heart to go around and I can't save it all for you anymore.

Only yours—no longer

# Doc

## Julie Weston

Doc Dahlman swung his 1959 Ford stationwagon alongside the pickups with frosted windows parked by the Gem Mining Company office. In his headlights, two miners in yellow slickers quarreled. One man poked his finger at the other to make a point. The second man raised his fist and pounded air. Their headlamps stabbed the chilly dark with spears of light, and behind them, an electric locomotive hauling ore rattled out of the mine tunnel. Doc grabbed his medical bag. He wasn't one of Snow White's dwarves; he wouldn't need a pick to find his treasure.

The taller miner turned from the argument as Doc approached. "You got here fast, Doc. How's it going?"

"Fine. Tell me what to do." He raised his voice to be heard over the noise, and then worried that he had been too abrupt, advertising his nervousness.

"We need to outfit you first. I'm Les Cleveland. You delivered our son a few years back. This here's Curly, the foreman on duty tonight."

After Les said his name, Doc Dahlman recognized him as a company supervisor. Curly, whose round face had a tricky smile, led Doc to the dry room. Overalls, boots, a set of slickers, hardhat and lamp had been set aside for him. He shrugged off his old khaki long coat, the one he'd worn since medical school, not out of necessity but more as a badge of pride, and pulled on the "diggers," as Curly named them, over his clinic whites. He hoped the extra layers would warm him up.

"Curly, have you seen our man?"

"Nope. Just heard from one of his partners. He's hung up in a stope off 18. He was settin' timber, and it all come crashin' down. They tried to get him out, but so far, he's stuck tight." Curly helped Doc fasten the belt with a battery pack for the lamp around his waist. It had to be let out two or three notches.

"Anyone know first aid down there?"

"Yeah. There's a kit at the man-skip station. They done what they can, accordin' to the guy I talked with, but—" Curly said and raised his eyebrows, "—they figgered you'd know better what to do."

Doc settled the hardhat on his head, then adjusted the battery coil so it wouldn't catch on his arm. "The dispatcher said he was still alive, but probably has some broken bones and needs a shot of morphine before they can move him." Doc felt as if he were suiting up for battle. In a sterile operating room, he knew what to do. He got used to a tent hospital on the French front and knew what to do. But in a hole in the ground?

Outside, another engine, this one pulling small cars to carry miners, idled on the track. Doc and Curly climbed into the lead car and sat down. Les sat across, his knees brushing theirs. Doc settled his bag on his lap. A man-train, Curly had called it. All three were crammed into a space half the size of an elevator car.

The dark night deepened when the train pulled into the tunnel and left the office lights behind. Wheels rumbled on a track, and the sound echoed off walls in a deafening clamor. Les pulled a pair of ear plugs out of his pocket and handed them to Doc, motioning with his thumb and index finger to twist the ends before putting them in his ears.

Les leaned over and shouted. "Ride takes about twenty minutes to the main shaft. We'll switch and go down there." Again he gestured, making a diving motion with his hand.

Doc's stomach dove with it. He swallowed hard and nodded, already feeling sweat break out on his head. It wasn't from heat in the tunnel, although the temperature seemed faintly warm. When he realized he couldn't see how close the walls were unless he aimed his light outside the car, Doc faced straight ahead. He would pretend this was a night train in France on its way to a medical station, and not a narrow rock tunnel knifing into the middle of an Idaho mountain. He'd never been inside the mine.

Curly smoked a cigarette. Les shouted information from time to time. Doc made out occasional words, but he didn't answer. All of his concentration was focused on not throwing up in someone's lap. He thought about the White Horse scotch in his office. The amber liquor had lapped back and forth in the bottle when he pulled out the drawer of his desk, looking for morphine ampules. He wished he'd taken at least one swig—it might have settled his fear. But it would have broken his rule: no drinking on call. The bottle was his safety valve. As long as he knew it was there, he told himself, he didn't need it.

The man-train moved from pitch black to a lighted cavern as big as the Corner Club's bar. This isn't so bad, Doc thought. The nausea left him. When the train stopped and the three climbed out, he was able to smile. Several miners, dressed in jeans, boots, work shirts and hardhats, waved to him. They carried coffee cups or smoked cigarettes and were lounging around. One man squatting against the wall called out, "What's up, Doc? Get bored at the hospital?"

Doc waved. He recognized a patient, someone he'd sewn up at least once and treated for broken bones twice. Before he could answer, Curly did."They said, 'get a sawbones.' That's what we got."

"Hey, Curly." One of the miners lifted his cup in a toasting motion. "How's the negotiatin' going? You gonna get us a new contract one of these here years?"

"Hold your shorts, Obin," Curly answered back. He glanced over at Les and continued, "We've got the Company backed into a corner. Shouldn't be too long, now."

Another man who had walked in from a tunnel at the other end of the room said: "Hell, Curly. I thought mebbe we'd strike. I been needin' a vacation!" Several of the men laughed and someone else said, "All you do is sit on your butt. What you need a vacation for?"

Les pointed off to Doc's left. "We're heading down that drift there to the #2 hoist. It's the main shaft down the mine. Too bad we're in such a hurry. I'd like to show you around a little. You should see the cable." Les's glasses reflected the light. "It's that big." His thumb and forefinger were almost two inches apart. "Big sucker."

Doc walked between the two men as they followed railroad tracks down a tunnel and around a curve. He wondered why Les hadn't said anything when Curly talked about the Company. Then he remembered Les was probably one of the men around the bargaining table. No strike would be good news to everyone. Dark closed in again, but Doc's claustrophobia had diminished. The tunnel was wider than his arms could stretch and a couple feet over his head.

"Don't touch the wire, Doc. It'll fry ya."

A cable ran above his head. He hadn't noticed it until Curly warned him. He imagined electric death and made sure his hands were at his sides. As in high places where he wanted to step off to see if he could fly, he had to resist the compulsion to reach up. He forgot about the union contract.

"Why didn't the first aid crew just bring the man in?" Doc asked. "By the way, what's his name?"

Les answered. "Rocky Belanich. Usually we would. We hardly ever have to get you docs out of the hospital, you know. Rocky's stuck tight and his partner in the hole says he needs help bad. Didn't the dispatcher tell you?"

"He said a load fell on him—sounded like a bunch of lumber—and that they were having a hard time getting him out. He thought the man needed some treatment while they pried him loose. Otherwise, he might not make it." Doc shifted his medical bag from one hand to the other. Already, it felt heavy. "I'm used to treating them after you've carted them out."

Les took the bag from Doc when they reached the hoist station. A man-skip was waiting. "Here, I'll take this. You just follow Curly there. Do what he does."

Doc stepped onto the skip. He had expected an elevator of some sort—one of those kind he'd seen in pictures, where the miner balanced on a small step and a wire cable dropped him straight down, like a vertical conveyor belt. This was something else entirely. It looked like a metal sled with notched seats. He remembered Les's diving hand. The sled aimed at the same angle down a narrow, black hole.

"We sometimes call this man-skip a pickle barrel. We all get lined up like pickles on these here seats, and the hoist man lets 'er go." Curly laughed and gave Doc a hand to help him settle in. Doc squeezed his butt to get some purchase on the narrow wood seat. "We warned him to slow down a bit tonight. Just in case you ain't been in here before."

Les pulled a cord hanging from the ceiling of the shaft station, then climbed in and sat below Curly and Doc. Slowly, the sled began its descent. Doc's heart sank faster. He reached out to hold onto the metal railing on the side and scrunched his shoulders down. The huge beams holding back the mountain were so close, he was afraid they would brush his hardhat off, maybe his head too. He hoped two inches of cable was strong enough.

"Don't put your hand out!" Curly grabbed Doc's arm. "It'll get chopped off quicker'n a Frenchie's head."

Doc breathed in as deeply as he could. With air coming in, he could hardly scream out. Les and Curly were as comfortable as if they were sitting on bar stools. Doc thought longingly of the red leather stools at the Corner Club. How many hours before he'd be there?

"You weren't here the year of the fire, were you?" Les turned his face up. He was careful not to let his beam shine in Doc's eyes.

"No, that was before my time. I've been here about thirteen years. Almost fourteen. After the war." Doc watched the rock slide by. From time to time, drops of water splashed on him. He couldn't help asking, "How deep are we going?"

"Not far. We come in on the 900 level. Rocky's at 18. That's 1800 level, 1500 feet or so below 9. He's been workin' on the Quill vein."

That's a quarter mile, Doc thought, the distance from his house to the turn-off from Main onto Division. He closed his eyes and reviewed the contents of his medical bag—bandages, scalpels, sutures, needles, tools and medicine. The mental activity helped calm the flip-tripping of his heart. If he were an older man, he might have worried about his own health. He knew he was too heavy and smoked and drank too much, but forty-five years didn't seem old next to some of his patients.

"You OK, Doc?"

"Yeah. Just going over what's in my case. That dispatcher wasn't very specific, based on what you guys have been telling me."

Les and Curly exchanged glances. Neither said anything. The skip slid down the hole to another station, similar to the one where they loaded, and stopped. They had passed a series of levels with flashes of loading stations, not unlike the floors in a store from behind the bars of an elevator, too quickly to see much except large black and white numbers—10, 13, 15, now 18.

Les helped Doc climb out. “Follow me. We’ve got to slog down the drift here,” he said, pointing to a dark tunnel that led away from the station lights, “until we reach the stope. This one isn’t too deep. We’ll climb down a couple ladders and have you at your patient in no time.”

The tunnel was just like the one on Level 9. They followed metal tracks, and a wire led the way above their heads. Doc concentrated on pulling one boot from the mud and taking the next step, on staying upright. Diamonds didn’t light their way as in the only other mine tunnel he’d seen—in the Snow White movie with his kids. When they turned off the tunnel and stopped at a black hole in the ground, he thought, oh fuck. I can’t do this. His headlamp showed a ladder descending into the gloom.

“I’ll go first, Doc,” Curly said. “Then you and then Les will come last. Here, gimme your bag.”

Doc did as he was told, concentrating on the gritty feel of the rungs under his hands and the careful placement of his boots and the dirt and rock wall in front of his face and a smell not unlike cordite, only this wasn’t a war. After thirty or forty rungs on the ladder, he found himself in a room hollowed out from rock. The stope. At the other end, twenty feet or so from the ladder, he saw in the ambient light of headlamps two men who guarded another, lying almost four feet off the ground on a stretcher propped up with wood posts.

When Doc reached them, he saw why the prone man was so high. His right arm disappeared at the elbow into a pile of timbers, rock and mud. Shirtless, he lay on his side, but Doc saw dried blood and a scrape along the side of the man’s face. His back was scratched and dirty, his breath shallow. Doc checked him over. The men had rested the stretcher so the feet were higher than the head, a preventive measure for shock. Through a stethoscope, Doc heard an irregular and thready heart-beat with a syncopated feel to it, like a drum. Although the miner needed attention fast, in the position he lay, it would be difficult to treat him. Doc checked the arm. It was probably smashed almost flat in the debris.

“Slight shock. Heart arrythmia. Possible heart attack. Arm looks lost. We need to get this man, Rocky’s his name? to the hospital now.”

One of the men sitting below the body said, “We know that, Doc. We can’t get his arm out. We tried crow bars, a hydraulic pump, everything we could think of. We need equipment too big to get down here without takin’ it apart. Someone’s workin’ on that, but it’ll be mornin’ before it gets here.”

“We can’t wait that long, fellows.” Doc had already concluded there was only one answer. Curly had pegged it. Sawbones was what they needed all right. “Les, can we talk a minute?” The two men stepped back toward the ladder. “The man’s arm has to go if you can’t move the rocks and wood crushing it. Has everything been tried?”

Les shrugged. “They’ve been at it since about four this afternoon. The load fell just at quitting time.” He motioned with his hand to the roof of the stope.

"Not only that, it shifted a while back. We've been afraid to apply any more pressure, either on Rocky or on the timbers and muck."

Water dripped along the walls. One miner talked in low tones to Rocky. Doc doubted if the injured man heard. "I'm going to need some help. We'll use ether to make sure he's out. I'll inject some 'dig', digoxin, to try and straighten out that heartbeat, but it takes a while to work. Then I'll start cutting. Can you and Curly assist me? I'll tell you what to do." Doc studied the other man's long face. "He may die. The odds are pretty stacked against him."

Les didn't hesitate. "Curly and me are both old hands down here—seen lots of blood. Seen a few dead men, too, in our time." Les turned to walk back to the others, then stopped. "Doc, there may not be a hell of a lot of time. Once one load goes, others sometimes follow. The men propped up a few timbers," he said, pointing to five wood posts jammed in between the floor and the rock ceiling, "but those may not be enough. I don't want to scare you, but you need to know."

The news didn't surprise Doc, nor even raise the level of his fear. He was more frightened of panicking at the close spaces than rocks falling. Artillery around the field hospital during the war had scared him at first, but he had finally forced himself to ignore it. That was when Scotch whiskey became one of his companions.

Maybe mining underground was like a war, too. Man against nature, or vice versa. Over the years, his initial shock at the brutality of mining as a way of life had worn down to resignation. Mining was hard, dangerous work. The men knew it; so did their families. All Doc could do was treat the miners—patch them up when he could, console the survivors when he couldn't. After a number of late night drunks with company men and early morning meetings with union safety committees, he had figured out this mine was no worse than most and maybe better than some.

Les sent one of the miners to alert the hoist operator and arrange for transport out. Rocky would be coming up soon, one way or the other. Curly found a piece of lagging and rigged up a small table next to Rocky. Doc placed his bag on it and got to work. After pulling rubber gloves on over his hands, he passed gauze pads and a bottle of alcohol to Les to clean off the man's upper arm, while he prepared the injection to stabilize the heartbeat. When Doc inserted a needle into the rubber-tipped bottle and drew out the fluid, he sensed that Les, Curly and the remaining miner watched his shaking hands. Ignore it, he told himself. They aren't the patient. He found a vein in the free arm and inserted the needle. He felt rather than saw the third man flinch.

"Curly, you're the ether man." Doc tied a mask across Rocky's face. Because he lay sideways on the stretcher, Doc was worried the anesthetic wouldn't drip right. He also needed more room to maneuver next to Rocky's arm. He explained the problem to Curly, who suggested the stretcher be tilted away from the wall. Rocky's arm restricted much movement, but Curly managed to get Rocky's face turned up and narrowed the gap between Doc and Rocky's arm where it disappeared in the wall. From the small bottle Doc handed him, Curly released drops of ether onto the face mask. Rocky's breathing slowed and deepened. Doc checked his pulse. It hadn't changed much, but he couldn't wait.

"All right, Les. I'm going to tie a tourniquet onto his arm here. You take another gauze pad and paint Rocky's arm with betadine between here and here." He marked off a three inch area a scant half inch from the entrapping earth, and then pulled out a flat rubber tube from the bag. Les leaned from the other side of the stretcher and swabbed the yellow-brown liquid on Rocky's skin.

"You, what's your name?" Doc looked over at the other miner, who still hovered, waiting for directions or afraid to move.

"Dominick." His voice seemed to come out of his knees. This miner had thick shoulders and a greasy beard. Deep bags under his eyes gave him a hollow look. He stared at Doc's hands.

Doc handed him a white cloth from his bag. "Pin this surgical cloth and drape it so as little dirt as possible gets into the cut." Thank god he had prepared the bag for surgery, he thought. "See these clamps? They look like scissors. They'll hold the cloth together or onto something else. I only have two to spare for this. Les, help him."

Doc lifted one of Rocky's eyelids, felt a pulse in the man's neck, and watched him breathe. "OK, Curly. You can stop for now. Check his pulse for me every two minutes. If it changes, let me know. Here." He placed one of Curly's hands on Rocky's neck. "Got the count?" Curly nodded. He could have been checking a hand of cards. Les was perspiring. Dominick twitched, fussed with his face, shifted his hardhat, rubbed his neck, but he made no move to leave.

"All right, here we go." Doc had pulled two scalpels from his bag. The knives looked almost delicate in the light beam. He selected the smaller one. "Dominick, I need your light. Keep it focused right on the brown patch. Les, you too. Curly, if you can do two things at once, shine your light over this way." All the beams aimed directly at Doc's right hand. It still shook. Then, when he placed the knife in the center of the cleaned section and carved from the back side around to the top of Rocky's arm, his hand held steady and firm. The slice was clean. A thin line of blood welled up, marking the cut, and yellow fat, like the globs under a chicken's skin, swelled into the wound.

"OK Dominick. You saw how to use the clamps. There are a mess more in the bag. Take one at a time and clamp off any bleeding veins on that side of the incision while I do it here. There won't be too many on account of the tourniquet. Watch me first." Doc reached into his bag, drew out one of the scissors-like instruments, opened the handle, placed a pincer end against a bleeding tube and let the handle close. "Like this." The pincers stopped the small stream of blood. "Les, hand me those rake-like instruments, the retractors. I have to finish the cut around the underside and clamp back the flesh." He sliced with his knife through tissue and muscle to the bone. "Curly, how's he doing?"

"Fine, Doc. No change."

A timber groaned over Dominick's head. The earth seemed to settle in tighter on Rocky's arm. All the lights except Doc's swiveled up. "Goddammit! Keep those lights on this arm!"

With his knife, Doc exposed the arm bone, the humerus. It was pale white, and to Doc, unrelated to the man on the stretcher or the black hole in which it lay, exposed to dust, dripping water, fumes and poisons from the mine. "Les, reach into the bag and hand me the saw. Looks like a keyhole saw. Wipe it off with the alcohol, first.

"Dominick, you and Les have to hold his body as still as you can, but give Curly enough room to check his pulse and breathing." Doc placed the saw against the bone in the opened wound. "This'll sound like a dentist grinding away on a tooth. He can't feel it." Doc risked a look up. "Ready? Here we go."

With the instrument held in both hands, Doc braced his feet apart. He sawed back and forth. The rasping made him grit his own teeth. On the first back grate, Rocky's body moved slightly. He felt Les take a firmer hold and after that the body did not move. Sweat poured off Doc's face. "Les, I need you to wipe off my forehead. Quickly."

Les took a gauze pad from the bag and wiped across Doc's face. Then he again gripped Rocky.

"Curly?"

"No change, Doc."

When the bone was severed, the body almost fell. Dominick took up the slack with a swift movement. His lamp glanced off the saw, onto the pulpy end of arm sticking out from the wall and back again, so fast Doc hardly missed the light. "Get the clamps off the stump in the wall, Dominick. I'll get this end finished off." Doc removed the retractors, applied a piece of gauze to the end of the bone and clamped the gauze to a flap of skin.

"Les, I need more gauze and tape. I'm not going to try anything fancy down here. We'll leave the tourniquet and clamps on, plaster the gauze around the end and get the hell out of here."

Les stripped open more gauze packets and handed them over. He found a round tape and scissors and cut off pieces when Doc's hand came up.

A heavy breath, almost a moan, escaped from Rocky.

"Curly—" Doc began.

An echoing moan came from the timbers beside the men, as if the mountain wanted its victim back. Dirt and a few rocks fell behind them, in the direction of the ladder leading out of the stope.

"Yeah, Doc?" Curly's voice had the same seeming lack of interest Doc had heard all along. His tone almost mimicked the nurses in surgery at the hospital—waiting for instructions and ready to follow them.

"Never mind. If he comes to, he comes to. Strap his body on this stretcher as tight as possible to get him up the ladder. Then you can drop a little more ether."

Dominick held Rocky's body close while Les and Curly wrapped a length of thin rope around Rocky's thick legs and the bottom half of the stretcher. Doc anchored Rocky's stump to the side handle with more tape. A clamp loosened and blood spattered Doc's already bloody hands. He tightened the clamp.

"Doc, you go first. We need you on top so we can maneuver Rocky up without worrying."

There wasn't room in the ladder shaft for Doc to stay beside his patient, so he began the climb. When his head poked into the tunnel on Level 18, he gulped in the air, fresh by comparison to the stope. Curly followed with Doc's medical bag. Les came up backwards, his body straining with the load behind him and the effort to relieve Dominick of some of Rocky's weight. Slowly, the unconscious man on the stretcher rose out of the ground. Dominick was last. The two ends of the stretcher rested on his broad shoulders. He moved as gently and carefully as if it were a small child he handled.

Doc hadn't been aware of Dominick's bulk in the stope. His attention had been too narrowly focused. The huge miner stood head and shoulders above him. His knees were mud-soaked and his pants were torn. The man had been kneeling the whole time.

At a motion from Doc, Curly dragged the ether bottle from his slicker pocket. He stooped over Rocky and slowly dripped the liquid onto the gauze mask. Les and Dominick had pulled the stretcher to the top of the ladders without soaking Rocky in mud. He looked no worse than he had below.

A hand cart was waiting. The driver helped situate the stretcher so it lay flat. Then the group followed it down the tracks to the hoist station. There, the stretcher had to be lashed to the man-skip. Doc checked Rocky's pulse again, and, with Curly's help, climbed in. The others had to wait for the skip to come back for them.

"See ya, Doc." Curly patted Doc's leg. "Thanks. If he don't make it, it won't be your fault." He rang a signal to the hoist man.

As the man-skip pulled up and the men disappeared from sight, Doc heard Dominick say, "Did you see how his hand shook? Stopped the second that bitty knife touched Rocky's skin."

"Good ole Doc," Curly answered.

Doc's fear had disappeared some time between the dig shot and the first slice. He didn't think he'd stop for a Scotch after all. Just go home after he settled Rocky at the hospital. Were the men ever scared? He supposed the answer was both yes and no. But he knew if he were a miner, he'd vote to strike in order to stay above ground for a while.

*Hi ho, hi ho* sang in Doc's head. No diamonds in this mine—just lead, silver, zinc, and half a man's arm.

—*John Gilgun*

# Shrapnel

## John Gilgun

There's an intercom on the wall over Miss Quimby's desk in homeroom that connects us to the principal's office. Every day after lunch, we get messages about contributing to United Way or buying tickets for the Harvest Moon Hop or going to an assembly where Mr. Seltzer of Seltzer Jewelry will talk to us about buying class rings.

I worked for Mr. Seltzer and I know the mark-up in those class rings. I wouldn't buy one if you did Chinese water torture on me. I not only worked for Mr. Seltzer, I got fired by Mr. Seltzer, because I came in late one afternoon.

I'm keeping this from my mother. I still pretend to go to work after school but I hide out in the public library. Then I go home at five-thirty and bullshit my mother about the hard work I did that afternoon for Seltzer, down in the basement of his jewelry store wrapping packages.

"I wrapped twenty packages this afternoon. Phew. I'm bushed."

"That's good. You're workin'," my mother says.

"Yeah. Workin'."

"Well, workin'. That's what it's all about, y'know."

All bullshit. Seltzer canned me. I'm looking for another after-school job. If I get one, I'll tell my mother I quit Seltzer and took this one because it pays more.

So I'm listening to the intercom and I'm listening hard because after the Harvest Moon Hop stuff, which doesn't apply to me, the principal announces the job openings for the day. Job openings apply to me big time because it's been two weeks since Seltzer fired me and I can't keep lying to my mother. I don't have any money and pretty soon the fact that I don't have any money is going to come out. Because I'm going to have to ask my mother for carfare. I won't even have a dime to ride the city bus to school in the morning. Then she'll know. She'll say, "What about the money you earn at Seltzer's?" Then it'll be out in the open—not only that I got fired but that I lied about it—and my ass will be grass.

The principal says there's one job opening today. If you want to apply for it, you need to go up to the city hospital and talk to a Mr. Brendan Kirby in the Specimen Lab in the basement of the west wing, Room B-12. So I write that down and after school lets out I hustle my ass right up there.

Mr. Kirby has a splotchy boozer's nose and a beer belly. He's wearing a dirty smock and his shoelaces are untied and I think he's half in the bag though it's only two in the afternoon. But he's nice enough to me. He explains that specimens have to be kept in jars for a certain number of days after an operation, it's state law, and then the jars have to be emptied out. He takes me in a room and shows me the jars. Here's someone's gall bladder and here's someone's appendix and here's someone's something else floating in fluid in these jars.

"You just empty them in this metal container over here and when it's full another guy takes them out and burns them in the incinerator," Mr. Kirby says. "It pays sixty cents an hour."

That's what Seltzer paid me. So I can't tell my mother that I quit Selzer to work here because this place paid more. They don't pay more. They pay exactly the same.

But at least I'll be working.

"I'll take it," I say.

"We need for you to get this signed," Kirby tells me, handing me a piece of paper. "Your father or mother can sign this. Bring this back and you can start then."

"What's this?"

"Well, it's a permission. Because you're...How old are you?"

"I was sixteen last month."

"Well, so we need your father or mother to sign. Because of your age. You understand."

My mother's ironing her pink waitress uniform in the kitchen. I tell her I got this new job emptying people's organs into a metal container. "It's in the hospital. It's good training in case some day I want to go to medical school and become a doctor. You have to sign this paper. Because I'm only sixteen."

She says right away, without a second's hesitation, "You got fired, didn't you?"

How did she know that? "Yes," I answer. "I came in late. It wasn't my fault."

"Well, you're not going to take any job emptying people's guts into a container. We're bad off, but we're not that bad off, not yet anyway. Tell the guy at the hospital I wouldn't sign the paper. And don't tell your father you got fired."

Then the miracle happens. Two days later the intercom comes on and the principal says there's a job at the Alhambra Theater for an usher. If you want it, you need to get over there and blah, blah.

As soon as school is out, I run to the Alhambra, which is a block from the school, and talk to the manager and I get the job. I'm introduced to the head usher, Jim Bolton, and he gives me a red and black uniform and a flashlight and I'm on. All I have to do is show people to their seats. Plus I get to see all the movies for free. I could be emptying out people's diseased organs into a metal container. Instead I'm watching a movie about two guys on the rodeo circuit both in love with the same woman, starring Kirk Douglas.

Mildred Hagenlocker is hiding out at our house. Her husband beat her up and when she was lying helpless in the driveway he tried to drive over her in his Desoto convertible. Her daughter Kathleen was there and pulled her away seconds before the wheels of the car would have rolled over her, crushing her to death. Mildred is sleeping on the couch in the parlor. I get up to pee in the middle of the night and I hear her yelling in there. She's having nightmares. When she's awake, she cries. She looks awful. Her eyes are swollen up and black. She has big ugly bruises all over her arms. She works as a waitress with my mother but she can't go to work looking like that.

The movie this week is One Minute to Zero with Robert Mitchum and Ann Blyth. It takes place in Korea and it's about how Robert Mitchum has to bomb lines of refugees because North Koreans are hiding with the refugees and crossing the border into the south. Ann Blyth doesn't think it's right to bomb innocent refugees but in the end Robert Mitchum proves it is and she agrees to marry him and the movie ends. The song that goes with the movie is called "When I Fall In Love."

And I am in love with John Hirshler who's only a sophomore.

With the money I'm earning as an usher, I buy a used typewriter for $13.95. I want to write about how I feel about John Hirshler but I know that's not smart because my mother might read it. To type "I love John Hirshler" would be stupid so I don't do it.

Instead I type all the things I love about him and leave it at that, like his hair, his eyes, his lips. I type "hair, eyes, lips" right down the page and leave it at that. It's not enough because I feel much more than *hair eyes lips* but typing anything more isn't safe.

There's no privacy in our house. I can't even type "John Hirshler came into the theater Sunday afternoon" because that would give me away. I put what I typed in a folder and put the folder in a cardboard box and shove it under my bed and hope for the best though I know my mother will find it and read it. She gets into everything.

I'm a homo. I'm always falling in love with guys like John Hirshler. I can't help it. It's the way I am. You can't talk about it and it's not smart to write about it but I have to admit it to myself.

Still, I want to be friends with John Hirshler. I want to eat lunch with him and talk to him and walk around the halls with him. I really want to *be* him, see the world through his eyes, run around in his body, have his parents instead of my own, live in his house, wake up in his bed as *him* not *me.*

But instead I can't even talk to him because the word's out that I'm a homo, the guys spread it around, so anybody who's seen talking to me must be a homo, too. So no one talks to me.

The movie this week is called *Plymouth Adventure* . It's about The Mayflower. Spencer Tracy is the captain and he's trying to get the Pilgrims across the Atlantic to Plymouth Rock and they have to face storms and sickness but he's a great captain and he gets them through. The wife of one of the Pilgrims falls in love with him and her husband is jealous but they work it out—Spencer Tracy is more into being the captain of a ship than falling in love—and they get to America.

We're showing this because it's Thanksgiving.

I want to be in John Hirshler's body eating Thanksgiving dinner in his house with his relatives. I see myself as John Hirshler, opening his/my mouth and saying through his/my beautiful teeth and using his/my tongue, "Hand me the cranberry sauce, please, Mother."

In the drugstore I find a paperback novel called *The Well of Loneliness* and it says on the back cover in red letters WHY CAN'T I BE NORMAL?

I'm not normal. So I figure this book will give me some answers. I buy it for 35 cents and take it home and hide it with my writing in the cardboard box. I find out I can't even read the book. It's so badly written. I'm disappointed but what can I do? I'm finding other things to read in the library which are well written but none of them tells me why I'm not normal. What made me abnormal? I need to know.

Sometimes everything happens at once. Within a two day period, my mother's friend Allison Winograd gets murdered in Chinatown, my mother has a fight with her boss and the people who own our house say they want the French doors.

Allison Winograd was stabbed to death in an alley outside a restaurant in Chinatown. What was she doing in Chinatown? Who stabbed her? Why did he stab her? No one knows the answers to these questions. My mother is upset. Her girlfriends gather in our kitchen and they talk about it and they have different theories. I walk in and they shut up and wait for me to leave. But I can get in the pantry and put my ear to the door and listen. My mother's girlfriends agree that it doesn't make sense. Allison wasn't a prostitute and she wasn't an alkie and she wasn't a junkie and why Chinatown? She'd never been to Chinatown in her entire life. Did someone kidnap her and bring her there and then stab her there?

My mother's nerves are on edge because of the murder and she gets in a fight with her boss at work and he pushes her. She comes home and cries and says my father has to phone her boss and tell him he can't lay his hands on her that way. I can tell my father doesn't want to do it but is he a man or a mouse? So he phones and the boss yells at him. I can hear the boss yelling over the phone. It's that loud. So my father becomes humble and conciliatory. So he's a mouse and the next day my mother goes back to work as usual.

The people who rent our flat also own the house. They live upstairs. The only thing we have in our flat that has any class is a French door between the parlor and the hall. The people upstairs say they want it for their flat. My mother says, "It's the only decent thing in the house." But in the end they come down and unscrew it and take it upstairs and my mother sits in a chair and cries. There's nothing we can do to stop her. My father can't stand it and leaves the house. He goes to a bar. I'm too young to go to a bar so I have to sit there and listen to it.

My father comes back an hour later and she's still crying.

"Why doesn't she stop?" I ask. "It's driving me crazy."

"Shut up," he says. "You don't know how a woman feels."

"Neither do you," I answer.

The movie this week is *Blackbeard the Pirate.* In the last three minutes of the movie, they bury him up to his neck in sand and the tide comes in and you see him drowning. Bubbles go up from his mouth and his eyes roll back and he dies a terrible death. But it's all right because he's a pirate which means he deserved to die. The End.

My mother doesn't work on Tuesdays so on Tuesdays she drinks. Drinking kills the pain. I come home after work at the theater. It's five-thirty. I put the key in the lock of the front door and turn the key. But she opens it herself from the inside. Her face is distorted and there's something wrong with her. My heart races.

She says, "You don't live here. Go away." She's blocking the door, which is only open part way.

I say, "Hey. Where else do I live if I don't live here? Ha ha."

But it's no joke. "This isn't your house. Go away."

"Where am I supposed to go?"

"You can't come in here," she says. Then she closes the door in my face.

I hang out for an hour in a drugstore nursing a Coke and then come home. She's not home. Where's she gone? Who knows?

The movie this week is *Our Lady of Fatima* which the manager booked because he thinks Catholics will come to it. Like maybe the priest will tell them at Mass that they should go to it. A Jesuit is sitting at a card table in the lobby selling a book called *The Miracle of the Catholic Life* for $2.98. The movie's a piece of shit and I ask to be allowed to take tickets in the lobby so I don't have to look at it. They let me do this. So I'm out there with the Jesuit and the card table and the books. I don't talk to him. He doesn't talk to me. He sells one book all afternoon. Even with God on your side, life's grim.

New Year's Eve the ushers who are on duty get together in the usher's room and Jim Bolton, the head usher, gives each of us some whiskey.

I hang back the way I've been conditioned to do by the guys at school, but Jim says, "You're an usher, too." So I come forward and I get to drink some whiskey. It warms my stomach and relaxes me. I don't say anything because I'm so used to being put down by the guys at school every time I open my mouth but I feel like I'm a part of the group here. And it's true, I am a part of the group. I'm an usher, too. I work here. I'm one of them. It feels good to belong.

After work I go outside to wait for a city bus to take me home and it's so cold and it looks like there are no busses this time of night so I go up the street and wait on the corner and when a car approaches I put out my thumb. Two cars don't stop and then one does. I get in the back and tell them where I'm going and the driver says he can drop me off two blocks from my house. I say fine.

These guys are two sailors in uniform and they're in town because their buddy died and they had to go to his funeral. The one sitting in the passenger seat is bitter and angry. He hates the government, his hates the military, he hates war. The driver keeps agreeing with him but he's not as vocal about it. I'm excited because I hate war, too, but I never express my hatred and I certainly never hear anyone else say they hate it.

Before they let me off, the guy who's so bitter says to his buddy, "Fuck. If it isn't the fuckin' shoe factory, it's fuckin' Korea. What chance do we have? In the end, what's it come to? A piece of shrapnel in the ass."

I get out and thank them and they drive off. When I get home to an empty house I'm so excited I type "Life's a piece of shrapnel in the ass" and I put it in the folder and put the folder in the cardboard box and shove it under the bunk bed.

But that night I dream I'm lying in my bed and there's another kid lying naked in another bed across from me. He says, "Have you seen the rays shooting from the holy cross?" I say, 'No, not yet." He says, "You will." I can see his naked stomach and his belly button and his cock. Then I see a black box tied with ribbons on his leg. I ask him about it and he says it's something that's always been there. I tell him I want one for myself. He unties the box and hands it to me. I wake up, feeling happy.

I'm standing in the back of the theater talking to Tom Rhatican. We can talk because the movie's a big noisy musical with Marge and Gower Champion and they're doing one of their tap dance numbers.

I say, "So this sailor says that life's a hunk of shrapnel up the ass."

Tom says, "*Up* the ass?"

I say, "No, I mean, *in* the ass. He said in the ass. But in or up, it's the same."

"No, it's not the same."

"Yes, it is. He meant that you get fucked over by life. What's the difference?"

"When you grow up I'll tell you."

Tom laughs and walks away. The thing is, he isn't laughing at me, the way the guys at school would laugh at me. He's laughing because it's funny and he's enjoying himself. That's the difference between beingan usher here and being in school. You can enjoy yourself in here. It's dark in here so you can relax and enjoy yourself. No one puts you down for feeling good. Because who can even see you, right? If you got a smile on your puss, who can see it?

*Wipe that smile off your puss!*

No one ever says that in here. I like this job and I want to do this for the rest of my life. Which I know is impossible because it's just a job for high school kids.

Tom asks me to go swimming with him at the Y and I tell him that's great and we go. I remembered that you swim naked in the pool but that's changed. You have to wear a suit now. That's the new rule. And I don't have a suit. The guy at the front desk says there are suits in the cardboard box and he tells me to pick one out. I pick one out and it's way too big but I pull the strings tight and it'll do fine.

While we're changing, I sneak a peak at Tom's cock and it's beautiful. Tom rubs the black hairs on his belly and says he's got a lot of them because he jerks off all the time. He's also got black hairs in the center of his chest and they're sexy after he comes out of the water and they're flattened out because they're wet.

It's fun to swim with him and afterwards we hang out in a drugstore and have Cokes and talk. It's vacation and I don't have to think about school. I lower my guard and relax and enjoy myself bullshitting with Tom Rhatican. He's not mean or hostile or cynical. He's just a kid who enjoys life.

When I get home, feeling good for once, my father's there and he says my mother's in the hospital. It's the change. She's going through the change. It's her hormones.

"They're giving her some tests," my father says. "Try to be nice to her when she gets home. She's going through the change."

I go in the bedroom and type out something about swimming with Tom and try to forget about my mother's hormones. I'm glad I'm a guy. My hormones are fine. They'll always be fine. Thank you God for making me a man.

My mother comes home from the hospital. She's got medication but sometimes she doesn't take it. Also, she's not supposed to mix the medication with alcohol and she forgets and mixes the two. Sometimes she's nice and sometimes she acts crazy and sometimes she cries and sometimes she just sits at the kitchen table staring out the window at the snow.

Of course she still works five days a week as a waitress. Her friends are in and out giving her comfort. Women can have friends who come in and out and offer comfort. Men can't. It's the only thing that might make me want to be a woman, having friends who are in and out offering comfort.

Typing is a comfort. So I find myself typing more and more. I sit on a hassock I bought at Woolworth's. The typewriter is on a metal drum that used to hold soap chips. I get so into writing, I forget that my back hurts from bending over the typewriter. I just write and write. I can't stop. I've forgotten about caution now and I write down everything I feel.

My mother comes in, "What's that gonna get you?" she asks.

"'What's that going to get you?'" I type.

"It's a waste of time," she says.

"'Waste of time,'" I type.

"How many bags of potatoes will typing buy?" she asks.

"'Potatoes,'" I type.

"That's not payin' any rent."

"'Rent,'" I type.

"Some day you'll learn," she says.

I type "Learn what?"

It's February, the bleakest time of the year. It's been months since I bought *The Well of Loneliness* and I'd forgotten it was in the box under the bed. Then something reminds me. I keep hearing *normal normal normal* all the time, on the radio, at school, on television. So I remember what was on the back of the novel in big red letters: WHY CAN'T I BE NORMAL? The book's so badly written, I couldn't read it. But I decide to give it another try. I want to know the answer to that question so bad. *Why can't I be normal?* If the answer is buried in this book, I'm going to find it.

I get under the bed and get the box and go down through all that I've written, maybe forty pages. And then I go cold all over and then I start to sweat. Because... Because the book isn't there.

I go over the whole house in the afternoon. It's a Tuesday and my mother isn't working. My father has taken her to the bar on the corner. He's being nice to her because she's going through the change. I go through every cabinet, every closet, every cupboard, every bureau drawer. I look behind and under everything—the sofa, the refrigerator, the day bed in the dining room. It's nowhere in the house. I sit down on my bed and hold my head in my hands knowing where it is. My mother's put it in her pocketbook and that pocketbook's beside her in the booth in the bar at this very minute. If she took the book out of the box, she's read what I typed. What have I typed? Did I say I was in love? Did I write about the dream about a naked guy lying in the other bed? Did I type out that Tom said he had black hairs on his stomach from jerking off? Did I write about sneaking a peak at his cock? Did I write about drinking whiskey in the usher's room?

Whatever I wrote, she's read it. But I knew she'd read it. I knew this as I was typing. Why did I do it?

*—John Gilgun*

They come in at nine that night. They go into the kitchen and sit at the kitchen table. I'm in my room. They don't know I'm home. I walk softly in my stocking feet up the hall and through the dining room and into the pantry. The door is open a crack and I can look through the crack at them. He has a bottle of beer in front of him and she has a highball.

They're talking about me.

My mother says, "He bought the typewriter with his own money. He earned it by workin'. I'd take it away from him but he paid for it with his own money. He's not a bad kid. He goes to work every day. He never misses a day. He works like a trooper. He loves it."

My father says, "The kid hasn't got a friend in the world. He can't get along with anybody. He's never been on a single team. Nobody will have him. So what else can he do but work? He's got no friends to hang out with."

My mother says, "The clickety-clack, it drives me crazy. My nerves. He sits in there all the time when he's not in school or working, clackin' away. It's not normal. He's not normal. Why can't he act like a normal kid? What normal kid would clackety-clack like that all day? And the things he writes. I don't even want to talk about it. Sometimes I think he's a mental case."

My father says, "What's he going to do when he grows up? I can't see him workin' at the plant. A guy needs friends on the job. And he's a queer. What are we going to do with him, a kid like that? He's useless. What did I do to deserve a kid like that? A *queer*. "

My mother says, "Yeah."

My father says, "Yeah."

He takes a sip of his beer. She takes a sip of her highball. I crawl on my hands and knees out of the pantry, through the dining room, down the hall and into my bedroom.

Twenty-two days pass before I speak to either of them again.

For twenty-two days I come home from work and go right into my room. If I eat, it's food I've scrounged on my own from the pantry. If they're in one room, I make sure I'm in another.

I hate them more than any other two people on the face of God's green earth. I am in such a rage against them, I know if it ever comes out I'll start screaming and I'll never stop. So as soon as I come home I clench my teeth and refuse to speak.

The problem began with the typewriter. Without the typewriter, I wouldn't be writing. If I wasn't writing about my life, my mother wouldn't be reading about it. If she wasn't reading it they wouldn't be calling me a useless queer.

I decide to get rid of the typewriter. Useless, fuckin' typewriter. Waste of time. What'll it ever get me anyhow?

On trash day, I make a decision to put it out by the ash barrels on the sidewalk. Let the trashmen take it. That'll solve the problem. But I don't even get it to the door of my bedroom before I know I can't do it. I love the typewriter too much. I put it back on the metal drum that once held soap chips.

But I can burn what I've written. So I take everything I've written down cellar and open the door of the furnace. I can throw it in and that's the end of it. There's a roaring fire in there because the flue is open and there's a hard wind blowing outside pulling the air up through the chimney. I throw in a page and watch it turn to ash immediately on the hot coals. Whoosh. Gone.

But I regret the loss of that page. I want it back. Well, it's gone. And here goes the second page. And I watch this one go up in smoke. And I feel twice as much loss as I felt with the first one. It's awful. It makes me want to cry.

That's it. I close the door of the furnace and kneel there, holding the remaining pages.

"Fuck 'em," I tell myself. "Fuck 'em all t' hell."

And I go back upstairs, holding the pages to my chest.

# Bonus

## Jim Ray Daniels

It's humiliating, sucking up to relatives for jobs. Not a lot of folks in my family can do much about getting anybody a job, but I've hit them all up: Cousin Larry got me in at the grocery store as a bagger (a pretty good gig till we went out on strike and they fired us all and got away with it), Aunt Fiona let me work at her Dairy Queen one summer and paid me more than she had to, Uncle Stan got me in at the Ford plant (laid off in six months).

My family, it's good family, though alcohol wiped out my dad and two uncles, and one cousin, beautiful Debbie. We know how to throw a good party, even if it kills us, and Cousin Freddy's annual pig roast at his place out in the country was no exception. Some of the young bucks were already drunk and couldn't wait, ripping half-cooked meat off the damn pig.

I wasn't a young buck anymore, and my prospects, as they say, weren't looking up. I was twenty-six and had just moved back into my mother's house. Earlier that afternoon, I'd exchanged punches with my older brother Terry because he said I was hiding under my mom's skirts. We didn't draw blood or nothing. Just like when we were kids.

Last year after our dad died, Terry had his stomach stapled up and lost all this weight, got married, so he'd been thinking he's hot shit. Since my dad died, I haven't been able to focus on much of anything. It didn't seem to bother Terry none, though my mother claimed he kept it all inside. We all knew it was coming—doctor told my dad flat out if he didn't quit drinking, he'd be dead in a year, and he was right. But I've always been good at putting off the truth—trying to cheat another 1000 miles out of bald tires, getting a blowout on the freeway.

Fighting with Terry got me going. I had to get a job soon, or I really would be a momma's boy. Uncle Lester was my last shot. I swallowed the warm backwash of my fourth beer and edged over next to him.

"Uncle Les?"

He was sipping wine. Something he picked up from his new wife. He sighed, "Yes, Bobby."

He was still calling me Bobby. Not a good sign. I've been trying to change to Rob for years.

"Uncle Les, I'm not gonna shit you, I need a job. You got anything at the store for me?"

I'd resisted Uncle Les. He owned a large clothing store in West Bloomfield —one of Detroit's snooty suburbs—and I did not want to be trying to sell shit to rich people.

He looked me over and sipped at his wine. "You ready for sales, Bobby? Commission work?"

My stomach growled. I wanted to be over with the young cousins eating raw meat—anything but this.

"Sure am, yes, I really am." I tried my best, but I was staring at the ground when I said it.

"Listen, Bobby." He put his hand on my shoulder. "You couldn't sell me a new suit. You're just like your dad." I winced. I never drank more than six beers anymore, and no hard stuff. I was melting into a warm piece of shit underneath his shoulder.

"Just give me a chance," I said. Damn it, I was almost crying.

He paused and sighed again. "I can get you in the stockroom, but you know it doesn't pay much."

I knew Uncle Les was no Aunt Fiona, and he wouldn't be paying me anything more than a—than a stockboy. My unemployment from the factory job had run out months ago. "I'd like that, Uncle Les," I said.

"No experience necessary," he laughed.

"But I have experience," I said.

"I'm sure you do." He laughed again. I looked around at the pig carcass, half charred, half raw meat. Cousin Tim was puking off to the side. Uncle Les's new wife Cindy came up and grabbed his arm. Uncle Les had been married so many times, we didn't call his wives "aunt" anymore.

"Come by the store on Monday. I just fired this kid last week." Kid. I was about to ask him exactly how much it paid, but thought better of it. I didn't even have gas money for my old rust bucket. I swore I wasn't going to live with my mother more than a year. I promised myself the job would just be temporary.

I walked off and stood by myself on a hill on the edge of Freddy's property overlooking his neighbor's Christmas tree farm. Freddy'd done alright. Since he drove trucks cross country, it really didn't matter where the hell he lived, so he bought himself this nice property—out near Brighton, about an hour north of Detroit. He had his own rig and was his own boss, kept his own hours. He'd been my drug source for many years. Truck drivers have access to the best speed. Though I had no desire to do speed anymore—if anything, I wanted to slow things down.

I looked out at all those green trees swaying in the warm wind. They reminded me of my father dancing at family weddings. He didn't move much. Just this gentle sway, his drunken arms draped over my mother's shoulders, his eyes closed, the wisp of a grin on his lips. I think I loved him the most when I was watching him dance.

* * *

Uncle Les was true to his word, and by Monday afternoon, I was wearing a name tag which I'd had them type "Rob" on, and I was unloading a UPS truck full of boxes, getting advice from Byron, the other stockboy, on the finer points of dolly maneuvering.

I didn't see much of Uncle Les around the store, and he barely acknowledged my presence when I did bump into him. Some days, I never even saw him. The other employees kidded me as soon as they found out I was Uncle Les's nephew. They started calling me Baby Huey because I was a little chubby. Byron had been there for years, but he was still years younger than me. He was the pet of all the saleswomen. He was going to college at night, and was nearly through with his engineering degree. "Two more semesters," he said, "and I'm out of here."

I looked like a real loser compared to him—and being Uncle Les's nephew to boot. Byron, to give him credit, sat with me at lunch and brought me into the circle, so that after a couple of months, I felt like a part of the Lester's Best family, even if I was Baby Huey.

Byron and I often stayed late to restock the shelves so everything would be ready when the store opened the next morning. The sales people took off at six o'clock, on the dot. When it got close to Christmas, the store stayed open till nine, and we often worked until eleven restocking. Uncle Les stayed late too. He liked to be the one to lock the doors.

* * *

I'd had a crush on my beautiful cousin Debbie. My family might seem a little nuts, eating raw meat and all, but we were civilized most of the time, and we didn't go around hitting on our own cousins. I think she liked me too, though, back when we were fourteen, fifteen. I held her hand once behind the garage at my brother Terry's high school graduation party. She had found me back there chewing on weeds and feeling sorry for myself. I could only handle so much of the family drinking and bullshitting. My father was really tanked that afternoon. And hell, I was a teenager and hated being around my parents anyway.

I half-enjoyed being lonely back there, the voices and laughter quiet in the distance, the setting sun squeezing in between two garages just to find my pimply little face. But when Debbie rounded the corner, my heart did what hearts do when they're surprised by love.

"Hey stranger," she said.

"Hey," I said, smiling and squinting up at her.

"Is this seat taken?" she asked, and sat down in the weeds next to me without waiting for a reply. My father didn't believe in worrying about growing grass where no one could see. He stored rusty junk back there, stuff that didn't fit in the garage—a shovel with a broken handle, the frame for a go-kart, remnants of a couple of lawn mowers.

"Man, your dad's really loaded today," she said, blowing imaginary smoke rings.

"What else is new," I said.

"He's really giving my dad some shit." She emphasized shit with an edge that made me feel somehow responsible.

I shook my head. Uncle Les was Debbie's father. Debbie was from his first marriage, to Aunt Tracy. Back then, Tracy was in and out of institutions for schizophrenia, and Uncle Les was busy with Sally, wife number three, so Debbie grew wild like one of those weeds.

"How's your mom?" I asked.

"Okay," she said without expression. Then, "I guess," which meant "no."

My father, who worked on the line at Union Carbide, gave Uncle Les a hard time for having an easy job, not getting his hands dirty, and he always quizzed Uncle Les on how he was treating his employees, what benefits they got, etc. My dad was only a union man when it suited his own purposes. When it came to Uncle Les, my dad was Mr. Rank-and-File. They were brothers with ten years between them. My father was the older one. They'd never been close. With family, I didn't have to apologize for my father. They knew what to expect.

"Listening to any good tunes lately?" I asked. Debbie and I always talked rock 'n roll. We listened to the same radio stations and exchanged albums to tape. Neither of us was doing well in school, and we shared the bond of failure—though I'd never been held back a year like she had. For a girl to be held back was a scandal, but she seemed oblivious to it, more determined than ever not to succeed.

"Nah. Nothing sounds good lately," she said softly. "Nothing." I nodded silently, then reached out and put my hands on top of hers in the grass between us. She turned her hand palm up and squeezed mine. I wanted to pull her to me and give her a hug, but we had just reached the age where we'd stopped hugging and kissing our cousins, and I wasn't brave enough to hug somebody when it might mean something else—particularly my own cousin. I confess, while she sat there in her pretty white blouse confessing her sadness, I was studying how the sun shone to reveal her white bra underneath. Her long dirty-blonde hair hung straight over her shoulders and down her back, and her herbal shampoo cast a spell over me like incense in church.

It felt good to just sit there alone together—the simple comfort of it, her warm moist hand in mine, the drunken party fading behind us. She didn't have to tell me why she was sad. It was how I felt too. It wasn't any one thing. It was everything, the big rainy world out there, and the leaky roofs of our family.

Then Terry came back, a little drunk himself, because "wasn't he eighteen years old after all, and a high school graduate," my father'd told my mother as he opened beers for himself and Terry before the party even started.

"So what have we here? Kissing cousins?" Our hands separated instantly, and we looked at each other with a frantic mixture of fear and love. Terry turned and rushed back to the party. We hurried behind him, but there was nothing we could do. The old brown paint had turned to dust on the back of the garage, and both our backs were stained with it. Debbie slipped out the gate and down the street while I watched Terry tell our father God knows what. They were across the cracked driveway from me, and I could not hear their voices above the screaming little cousins and the ball game on the radio. Next thing I knew, my father was backhanding me across the face and shoving me into the house, where he could whale on me in private. I fell into tears, face down on my bed. Angry voices raged on outside. My parents, Uncle Les, then cars quickly pulling away. Terry came in and yelled at me for ruining his party, then he fell on his bed, face down like me, and passed out.

I know Terry sounds like a shit, but while I was a little chubby, he was enormous and hadn't had a date all through high school, and he was, I think, a little in love with Debbie himself. Maybe he thought acting like my dad was the way to get approval. It took a staple in the stomach and being "born again" for him to get his act together. "Born again." My mother and I shared a laugh about that when he did it. "Who gave birth to him this time?" she wondered.

Debbie OD'd at age twenty in her dorm room at the end of exam week. Uncle Les had insisted she go to college. She got in Central, one of the easier state schools, but she was partying all the time—flunking out, she'd confided to me at Thanksgiving, the last time I saw her. In the official Uncle Les version, it was an accidental overdose, but she knew what she was doing.

Since I moved back home, I've started sitting behind the garage again, even though it's just my mother and me now, and I can be alone all I want.

* * *

My father had a point about how Uncle Les treated his employees. Seems like he fired somebody every so often just for the hell of it. Right before Christmas, he'd fired this poor girl just because she took some gift boxes home to wrap her own presents in. I mean, the boxes were empty.

I kept quiet and kept those shelves stocked. Uncle Les started calling me Rob, and I was grateful for that small gift. The money wasn't much, but since I was living at home and not paying rent, I was actually building up a little savings, though every morning I prayed my car would start, that it would hang on at least one more year. With Byron's encouragement, I'd signed up for a computer science class at the community college. I was enjoying it, working hard. A lot of the other students were older, so I didn't feel like a loser. We were all in it together, trying to figure things out a little late, but maybe not too late. I was losing weight, and doing sit-ups before I went to bed. Up to one hundred. I'd had coffee twice after class with a cute blonde divorcee with two kids who was telling me every little secret of her life. It seemed like she had a lot more to tell, and I was hoping she did. For a few hours every week, I felt like I was doing high school over again, doing it right.

The store was making a ton of money during the Christmas rush, and Uncle Les was in a good mood most of the time. One day when we were tag-teaming a big delivery truck with our two wheelers, I asked Byron whether there'd be Christmas bonuses.

"Just for the sales people. Sometimes," Byron said, and winked. "Your uncle likes the cute ones." Then he moved uncomfortably close to me as I bent over a stack of boxes. "Unless you want to take your own bonus," he said. He hesitated, like there was more, but then he walked away, wheeling a high load of boxes out of the truck so I could not see his face.

Another night when we were working late, restocking, I grabbed him over by Men's Shirts. "Byron," I said, "How do you take your own bonus?"

"Hey, you're not narcking for your uncle, are you?"

I stood behind a stack of boxes loaded with Arrow shirts in all colors and sizes. I pulled at the collar of my T-shirt. We didn't have to wear ties like the sales people. Was I? Was I gonna be a narc for Uncle Les? Did it depend on what Byron was going to tell me? Byron had heard me badmouth Uncle Les often enough to know I had no great love for him. Maybe I'd laid it on a little thick just to get accepted. I already felt like I was betraying family, but I hadn't done anything except complain.

I sighed deeply. He didn't seem worried. "Hey, I'm out of here in a few months anyway," he said. "This is my last Christmas. I'm trying to show you something, do you a favor. Help you get out and get your own place." Byron was living at home too, but the whole college thing put a different spin on it. And he was younger. "It's for a good cause. I call it the Byron Murphy College Fund," he laughed.

When we'd work late, Byron would slip some things out on the loading dock, then hide them behind the dumpster. In the darkness, he could easily retrieve the stuff later.

"Hey, Uncle Les is pretty sharp. How come he hasn't caught you?" I asked. My stomach was sloshing with what Debbie and I used to call "bad karma," though I never exactly knew what karma meant.

"It's simple. He trusts me."

It wasn't that simple. Byron had partners. But the trust, that was a big part of it. After Christmas, when all the returns came in, his friends returned the stuff he'd stolen. We catered to a clientele with bucks, and I guess it was considered unseemly to ask for a receipt if the customer didn't have one. If it was an item the store sold, you could get cash back, no questions asked. Christmas bonus.

Byron either liked me or felt sorry for me, or both. He had an upbeat take on everything. He was going places, and I wanted to follow him, at least part of the way. I'd felt defeated when I'd started there, ripe for being taken in by Byron's charm. Hell, even Uncle Les liked him. Though he was years younger, I tended to look at him like an older brother. Terry? I couldn't say a word to him about anything. "When are you going to grow up?" Terry always said. I didn't have an answer for that, and if I did, I wasn't going to give it to my big brother.

I thought our dad's death or Terry getting his stomach stapled might change something between us, but we were still ended up at each other's throats at every family gathering. It was like we were locked in stone and could only crash into each other, and bounce off.

"It's only a few hundred a year," Byron said.

"Hey, that's probably more than any bonus Uncle Les gives out."

"Well, there you go," was all he said to that, and shrugged.

But still, it was Uncle Les. I wished immediately that Byron hadn't told me, though I couldn't blame him. I was the one who'd brought it up again. Just then, Uncle Les came by, banging a clipboard against his thigh.

"You guys almost ready to go? Ten minutes," he said, and kept moving past us.

"We gotta hustle these shirts," Byron said, and that's what we did.

Once Byron told me what he was doing, I tried to avoid him once the store closed. I didn't want to witness anything. Byron seemed sure I wouldn't tell, even though I'd told him I didn't want any part of the action myself. Part of me wanted in, and part of me wanted to tell Uncle Les.

* * *

After Debbie died, Uncle Les gave me all of her record albums. They were sitting on the porch one day when I got home from school. I brought them in, took them to my room and stacked them alphabetically, mixing them with my own. I even saved the doubles, twinning them.

I don't remember much of what Debbie and I said to each other back when we were favorite cousins. It's like those records. I can't remember why we liked a lot of them—I stare at the album covers and shake my head. I don't even have a turntable that works. I listen to tapes and CDs, if anything. The records anchor one corner of my room, their frayed, dusty jackets holding each other up.

The week before Christmas. December 21, the date Debbie died. I'd never seen Uncle Les on the anniversary, and I was curious to see how it affected him. After closing time, I went back to his office, where he was shuffling stacks of inventory reports.

He looked up. "Rob. What's up?"

"Hi, Uncle Les," I started. Even then, I didn't know what I was doing there. I wasn't ready to talk, but he was waiting. I tried to study him for traces of grief.

"Uncle Les, do you give out Christmas bonuses?" I asked.

He laughed. "Not to someone who's only been here a few months. Even if you are family."

"You mean, like, Byron gets one."

"Sure, Byron's proven himself here."

Oh, shit, I thought. Everything was tilting on me. Where was I going now? "You know, today's the day. The day Debbie died."

He quickly turned and lashed out. "Of course I know. What do you expect me to do, close the store? Wear black? I mean...."

"I still miss her," I interrupted. In our family, you didn't talk about dying or loving. You grabbed another beer, you playfully punched each other in the gut and said, "You're not getting serious on me, are you?" No wonder Terry bailed out on us and started talking to Jesus.

Uncle Les sighed. "Listen. Do you doubt that I do? Every year, I try to keep as busy as I can just to get through the fucking day," he said, his voice rising again. He looked tired. "Is that all you came to say, 'can you give me more money and don't you miss your dead daughter?'"

"I was never good with words, you know that. That's why you made me a stockboy," I said, trying to smile, though tears were finding their crooked way down my cheeks.

Uncle Les smiled tightly. He stood up, came around the desk, and put his arm around me. "We can't have our friend Byron walking by and seeing us bawling like a couple of...."

He didn't finish, and I couldn't finish for him. A couple of what? And what about Byron, who had lied to me, who now had made it easy for me to betray him? I said nothing. I did nothing. It was the kind of compromise I knew I would have to make to get on my with life.

His arm fell off my shoulder as he led me back into the store. Our little moment was over. I was a stockboy.

"Do you ever listen to those records?" he asked, stopping in the aisle. "Her records?"

I turned back toward him. "No," I said, though I sometimes fingered the album jackets and traced the letters where she'd scrawled her name.

It doesn't matter if I took anything or not, and I might have taken a few things after all. It doesn't matter if I happened to have given her the drugs she took to kill herself, and maybe I did. What matters is that I went home and tossed those records. It cleared out a lot of room. Kind of like getting your stomach stapled shut and watching the weight disappear. What I was gonna do with that room, I had no idea.

— *Kaye Longberg*

# Miss America

## Kaye Longberg

Come and open the steamy white door of the Detroit Aquatic Center. You'll wonder if you're still in America. Inside, it's full of Arabs. They're from everywhere: pick a country, pick a war. Here they're all cousins, linked by Islam and by language. They gather at the pool and make it theirs. Dark heads bob in the water; the humid air resounds with Arabic. Wives and mothers sit watching from a low set of bleachers. The women are darkly veiled, fully dressed, and noisy. Only the children use English. It slips out when they're excited.

The whitest skin belongs to the lifeguards on opposite sides of the pool. Slight Kurt Nederveld is watching the shallows. He's in the low chair with the veiled women at his back. He can sense their sweat, their lust for the pool. They just don't shut up, these dark-eyed women who can't or won't swim. Their daughters swim. He sees pretty girls with pretty bodies, swimming in veils. They splash around in a tight little group, smiling as they adjust one another's veils, which stick to their heads like soggy black hoods, oddly enhancing their faces, their eyes. He's charmed by the girls' shy glances.

Across the pool, beside the diving pond, is Amber Crawley. She's in the tall chair, a throne of a chair, wearing her favorite suit: red, with white stars across her breasts. The whistle riding her chest glints as she breathes. Kurt used to compare Amber to the girls on *Baywatch*, but after he asked her out and she turned him down, the compliments stopped. Now he ignores her, just as the Arab men do, though none of them has ever asked her out. She's noticed that just the boys look at her, and the men scold them for it. She doesn't need to know Arabic to understand that she's taboo, but she'd rather feel amused and flattered than hurt.

She avoids looking at the veiled women. Her attention belongs on the swimmers, and she tries to think of them as bricks. She was trained this way, with actual bricks. You saw the brick wavery on the bottom, you dove in and pulled it to the surface. It was the same easy rescue every time. She has saved two kids and a retarded guy, and their panic made her afraid for her own life. She tells herself that if there's trouble, she'll stay as calm as she was when retrieving bricks.

Trouble in a pool often resembles fun. Especially with the kids. Their squeals of laughter sound the same as fright. A frothy, frantic struggle to stay afloat can just be play. They shove and dunk each other as if there were no rules.

From her tall chair Amber can see the whole pool, and between divers she watches the two Ahmeds, Big and Little, who are outside of the diving pond but closer to her side of the pool than to Kurt's. The boys are chest-deep, playing underwater catch with a rubber missile.

They call her Miss America, and they have intimate memories of her from their dreams. She appears on a cloudy chalkboard at school when the teacher drones and division takes no thought. She's in the rubbery nub of an eraser, the smell of it shedding, the feel of it pink and hard. She interrupts prayer at the Mosque where she must never ever be. She must be punished for that. Big Ahmed, glancing for veils to be sure they won't see, grips the missile to his groin and thrusts his hips with an "Uff, uff, uff," that is easily understood, along with Little Ahmed's lewd laugh, by people like Kurt Nederveld across the pool and their uncle on the high dive.

Mohammed Towfiq is up there where the air is sultriest, having just mounted the board. It's cold and rough on the soles of his feet, and still vibrating from the last diver's jump. He leans to the side, sees through the chrome railing his nephews, the two Ahmeds, behaving shamefully. He looks around angrily for his brothers. One is swimming laps and the other has become the white whirl the pool spit up at the board's last thump. A sharp whistle would stop the boys without telling a mother who was doing what, but his mouth is so dry he can't make a sound. It's the holy month of Ramadan, and he's been fasting. He coughs and feels his head swim, the board trembling under him like the ground in Beirut the day he pulled a cold female leg out of rubble that had been an apartment building.

Back home in Lebanon he could want Big Ahmed for his daughter Halla, but here the boy has too much McDonald's in him, too much toy missile and not enough *hajj.* Let the cough wet his mouth and the board go still, let the platform stop rising and he'll whistle some respect into them. Not for *her*, her body all bare and taking that pose of authority. For *themselves* in Ramadan.

Little Ahmed's laugh, though, has gone reckless and has caught her attention. He's been fighting Big Ahmed for the missile and getting dunked for his trouble. The woman, breasts and thighs and milky skin, sits tall in the chair and calls, "No dunking." Big Ahmed says what sounds like, "No funking." He dunks Little Ahmed again.

Mohammed Towfiq holds both railings, trying to balance himself between them. Below, in the dimming blue square, he sees his brother surface and start for the side. He sees Big Ahmed and Little Ahmed blend into one. The woman stands up. She has a whistle between her breasts. But something's happening to the light. It's dim like the room in Miami where a woman, gritty with sand, salty with sea, defiled him. She was dark as his wife but hot with sun that outlined her breasts: a sumptuous pair of stark white triangles cold to the touch. And below, strange to him, the dark tuft she hadn't shaved.

To escape the memory he can jump off the board. He squints his eyes and starts to run. That's the board bouncing, not weakness in his legs. He feels the board dip with his weight and fling him up.

He's out of Miami but still in America, his safety and ruin. He arcs head-first into a fall from consciousness that breaks his form, peeling back his arms. As his head hits the surface he enters a dream, a lulling, muffled warmth.

At ten seconds the shadow in the pool hasn't risen. Or has it been more than ten seconds? Twenty? The water's so rippled she can't see a thing. She wants to be sure, but there's Kurt Nederveld, that runt, jumping out of his chair as if she can't manage. *She's* the deep end. She stops him with a toot of her whistle. The sound brings a hush. People stare in alarm as she dives into the pool. Kurt carefully sprints for the deep end. A few of the children are foolish enough to keep staring; everyone else looks away. Little Ahmed looks for his father and sees him back slowly down the ladder of the diving platform. His father sees him looking and makes a face that says, "Don't."

"Who is it?" Little Ahmed whispers, drifting up close to Big Ahmed.

"No, don't look. It's *Amu* Mohammed Towfiq."

"*Ensha Allah*, it's not!"

"It is! Don't look, just swim. It's nothing at all."

He's a big blue-skinned guy with his arms out front like a sleep-walker. She swims in from behind, grabs him by the armpits and pushes off the floor. Instead of a brick he's a whole sack of them. Her push, sluggish with his weight, presses her body against his. She starts to kick but his legs are in the way and already he's sinking back to the floor. Her heart is racing, pulsing in her ears. She takes a closer hold, wrapping her arms around him, spooning his body in hers. She goes into a squat for a better push off the bottom.

Kurt watches anxiously through twenty feet of water that plays with their joined shape at the bottom. He lifts his eyes for an instant and glances around, expecting to tell people to stay back, but people aren't gathering. They swim and talk as before, as if the alarm of her whistle weren't still ringing in their ears. Kurt's been counting seconds since the whistle blew. He stares into the water, feeling pressed for air. They look short as dwarves down there. They're still joined, and creeping along the floor instead of rising.

When he feels her arms around him, Mohammed Towfiq blinks his sting-ing eyes and understands why his lungs are burning. He sees the blurry distance between himself and the surface. Her breasts are pressing against his back and her hair sweeps his cheek, and he knows he has to resist her. He thinks of his family at the surface and the shame, more crushing than his need for air, if he lets her take him up. And yet he can't just die.

He grips one of her wrists and leans his weight on her as he grabs for the other. She pries at his fingers and tries to wrench free. She goes for his arm with her teeth. He spreads his hand over her face and shoves her head back. He sees a glint of the whistle between her breasts, slips his hand under her jaw and clenches the cord at her throat.

Kurt dives in and kicks toward them. They look to be in a death-lock, which means the guy could actually live. But will they separate? Obviously her approach was all fucking wrong. She's arched under the guy, too weak to lift him, one arm not even pushing but flailing. Her boobs are billowy in her star-spangled suit. She's never looked so pathetic, and there's something good about that that holds Kurt's eye.

Tugged by the arm, Mohammed Towfiq swirls into the pull of a miraculous man. He goes numb, releasing Amber. Amber shoots to the surface, bursting for air. She's holding the side of the pool, gasping, when Kurt breaks the top. Kurt gulps air through his mouth; the Arab doesn't. Kurt pulls him to the side, where a few people casually help with getting him out of the water. Kurt wonders about his chances, but immediately the guy makes gurgling sounds and starts to heave.

Mohammed Towfiq rolls onto his side and lets the water out, the air in. His brothers' voices sound close, but muffled. He sits up, stands with their help, and without so much as a glance at Kurt, walks away.

Kurt watches in disbelief. His thanks'll have to come from her. He goes to the side, stubbing his toe on the ledge. She gives him a trembling hand and he pulls her out.

"You dropped the ball down there," he says. "That guy could've died."

He stares at her expectantly. She doesn't answer, doesn't look at him. Her eyes are bloodshot, her lips are blue. She's pale as the towel she wraps herself in.

She gazes across the pool at the women in veils, feeling an eerie affinity to them. She dabs at water rolling down her face; they dab at sweat. They speak a fervid gibberish she understands. She could speak it herself. Anything she tried to say right now would sound like babble.

# The Walls of St. Vincent

## Philip Heldrich

We were the worst in all of Wichita.

We showed up late for work, took long lunches while the paint dried, and left early for the lake. Sometimes after starting a job, we never returned. We made barely enough to pay our rent, let alone go back to the state college across town in the fall. We survived on bologna sandwiches, Ramen noodles, and Pabst beer. When I spoke with my father in Topeka, I told him we were doing well, fast becoming some of the city's most wanted painters, that money was no problem for the first time in my life. Truth was, between jobs we might wait weeks for another offer. We made promises we didn't keep. It seemed no different with Mrs. Vincent.

On the day she called us in mid-June, we had been out of school for nearly a month without a single lead, past due on all our bills. When I spoke with her, I tried hard not to sound desperate, tried to hide that we were sinking, just as my father had predicted. "We'll paint the window frames and clean your gutters for free," I told her. "It'll only take a couple of weeks." When we met to do the estimate, Dave convinced her to give us half the money up front, which anybody who knew us would have seen was a big mistake.

The work should have been easy, a simple exterior a few streets away from the Boeing plant, where they built the big birds. It was a good neighborhood similar to my old neighborhood in Topeka where my mother still lived. After my father left to move across town with another woman, my mom couldn't afford to leave. Mrs. Vincent's neighbors, like my own, were people who worked hard, most of them at Boeing. It was a place where going to work and raising a family still meant something respectable. There was an unspoken bond between us. We were all in it together, that's what I felt.

On our first morning, I welcomed the rhythms of a new job—waking early, putting on our dirty overalls, fixing our lunches with stale bread and week-old ham. "We're going to make it," Dave assured me. More than anything, I wanted to believe him to prove my father wrong. I thought about my return to college in September, the easy days of late morning classes, the all-night parties, how I would be reunited with Sarah Birdsol, who had a position as a summer intern with a design company in Kansas City.

When we arrived in our paintmobile, my rusted, twelve-year-old Plymouth Horizon with doors that didn't open—once a high school graduation gift from my father—we unloaded our ladders from the roof, then fixed them against the front wall of the house. We wasted no time setting up our buckets and brushes. On a fold-out card table near the front door, Mrs.Vincent had laid out for us a platter of doughnuts and cookies along with a steaming pot of coffee—the job was like none before. Next to the table, she set up a lawn chair with an umbrella facing the front of her home, where she would sit most of the morning in the hot Kansas sun to supervise our work. The widow, dressed in overalls and a ball cap, seemed shortened by age. She appeared slightly withered, as if any day she could keel over and be gone, perhaps lifted away in a tornado. Her gray hair had a purplish tint, the wrinkles in her face set deeply in her weathered skin. Her fingers were thin and bony, slightly crooked from arthritis. Although she wore glasses, most of the time they hung from her neck on a silver chain. "You can begin here," she told us, as if we were neighborhood boys working for our allowance.

Even with Mrs. Vincent overseeing our efforts, we painted that morning better than we had ever painted, as if somehow a curse had been lifted. Every brushful seemed to go on easy, as if after all our past botched jobs, we had finally acquired some technique. No edge seemed too difficult. Dave, a lanky fellow with long arms, was able to push paint into every nook. Having a stocky frame and short legs, I covered all the low spots. In places where the walls needed scraping, chips flaked off like powdered sugar. We worked out a system for smoking, too, since Mrs. Vincent had made it clear that no smoking was allowed on her property, being that her husband had died of emphysema. One at a time, we went to her backyard, while the other covered in front where Mrs. Vincent sat reading her morning paper, refilling our coffee mugs, or dozing in her chair. All morning, as we glided our brushes across the wall, I pictured Sarah with her blond curls and tanned belly, the way we liked to take long drives in the country on a Sunday afternoon in her father's Roadster. Since our semester had ended, we talked a few times a week by phone, and because I could not afford to call her, I waited for her to call me. Sometimes we talked until late at night, making plans about the fall semester. One night, I proposed the possibility that we might live together, maybe even get a cat. When times were bad and I was without work for weeks at a time, I never let on about my situation, explaining how I couldn't visit on weekends because we were always so busy.

As we spackled cracks in the boards and sanded rough edges, Dave enjoyed ribbing me about Sarah, but he too had his plans. The youngest of six raised in Dodge City, he told me about saving for a ticket to take his mother to a Kansas City musical in the fall. "It's something she's always wanted to do," he told me. I tried hard not to laugh, but the big guy was serious. He was only the second child in his family to attempt college, an older brother having tried but failed. "I'll do better next semester," Dave had said after barely passing his first year's composition courses.

"Either of you two would have made a good man for my daughter," Mrs. Vincent said to us that morning. I tried to boast how we ran a successful painting company, made good grades, and always called our folks for holidays and birthdays. If I thought about it long enough, I could begin to believe my own lies—like the stories I told my father to explain my continually impoverished condition—as if somehow they passed over into truth. That first morning, Mrs. Vincent told us how years ago her daughter, who now lived in Kansas City, had married at college against her best advice. For their honeymoon, the couple had planned to drive to the East Coast, but somewhere in the middle of Ohio they split-up. According to Mrs. Vincent, the man was not the fellow he had claimed to be, his "experiences," as she put it, more vast than even her daughter was led to believe. "She never remarried," Mrs. Vincent said, the regret heavy in her voice. "No husband, no children." I pictured the couple somewhere outside Columbus, she driving off in the car, he left standing along the roadway. "Since then, we've hardly spoken," Mrs. Vincent confessed. Listening to her made me think about my father, how we only talked when I needed money, how his step-son attended a private college in Pennsylvania at my father's expense while I struggled to save for my fall tuition. I felt sorry for Mrs. Vincent in a way that made me want to do an extra fine job with her house, as if somehow new paint could mask old feelings. Painting her home could help us forget our own problems, deliver us from ourselves. Saint Vincent, I came to call her, made me want to be good, to do good, at least with this one job, no matter what.

At lunch, Mrs. Vincent went inside to escape the heat of the day, while Dave and I walked to the park at the end of her street to eat our sandwiches. We took a picnic table not far from the groups of workers, some still wearing their hard hats or white work jumpers with Boeing embroidered across the chest. We ate fast, washing everything down with a can of warm beer—only one because we were trying to do it right. The sky was a brilliant blue that afternoon as the cottonwoods blew gently in the wind. Some of the workers pitched horseshoes, while others arm wrestled or played a quick game of cards. They seemed to enjoy their routine, as if they knew it would last only as long as the factory kept open. For them, lunch in the park was a sacred act earned from hours of toil. I tried hard not to remember our recent month-long layoff, how in the second week, despite my reservations, I called my father to ask for help with my bills. When he picked up the phone, I could hear his wife in the background asking who was calling. Often, if I called and she answered, she would say he wasn't home and she never gave him my messages. "It's been a while," I said to him, "how are things at the office?" My father, an attorney at the state capital, left my mother when I was sixteen. It had taken years for us to come to the point of conversation and occasional visitation. Sometimes the only way to talk with him was to ask about his work. "Any big cases?"

"A few," he said. "I imagine you're doing well."

"Just great," I said, "never been better."

"Lots of work?"

"Plenty," I told him. "I just called to see how you were doing."

"Good," he said. At that point, to save what little dignity I had, I just couldn't ask for his charity, no matter how much I needed the money or how much he had to give despite his years of lapsed alimony. I quickly made an excuse to end the conversation, hating myself for calling, for knowing I was becoming exactly what he had predicted.

"Just look at that sky," Dave said, finishing his sandwich. "Let's cut out of here, head to the lake."

"We can't," I told him. "We have a job to do."

"That's never stopped us before."

"Let's do it right this time," I said. "If not for the old lady, then for me."

"Easy does it," Dave said, always the voice of reason. "We'll get by."

As the Boeing workers returned to their jobs, we too somehow managed to go back to Mrs. Vincent's walls. Returning on such a nice day took an extraordinary amount of will, more than we ever believed we had in us. We would finish the job, our first in months, making enough dough to get us back on our feet. If not for ourselves, then for St. Vincent, who deserved a good paint job—that much we promised ourselves.

We worked harder than ever that afternoon. From opposite ends, we attacked the eves along the front wall. Dave, as promised, cleared the gutters of debris, and I tried my best to paint perfect edges. With Mrs. Vincent inside, we smoked cigarettes at will, leaving the butts in her newly cleaned gutters. "Tokens of our appreciation," Dave said, as he slapped paint along the high portions of the wall. Everything was going well, and we felt sure that we would finish within the week, that for the first time ever we had estimated the job correctly. To help pass the time, we listened to the paintmobile's radio tuned to a Royals game from Kansas City. With each passing inning, we were that much closer to finishing the first quarter of the house, including the window frames and boxes of eves, each of which needed scraping and sanding. "You know what keeps me going," I told Dave. "In a matter of weeks it'll all be over, Sarah will be back, and we'll find ourselves in a lecture hall instead of on a ladder."

"School never looked so good," he said. "I can't see doing this the rest of my life."

"It's a young man's job," I said. "Too much bending and stooping. Have you ever seen old painters? Think about those guys at the paint shop—hair prematurely gray, eyes with big bags under them, skin like leather."

"It's the fumes," Dave said.

By late afternoon, our first official full day of work in a month, we felt exhausted, like we had painted two, maybe three houses in a day. As we put the final touches on the window frames, Mrs. Vincent re-appeared. She offered us the cookies and doughnuts that had been sitting in the sun since early morning. Not to be rude, I took a cookie, and when she wasn't looking I tossed it to Dave, who placed it in the gutter. When we finished the windows, we loaded up the paintmobile, then promised to be back in the morning.

"Not so fast," she said, the paint brushes and buckets already packed. "You've missed a few spots." We looked at her with surprise as she inspected the wall, going so far as to get down on her hands and knees in the hard dirt along the foundation. She fixed her glasses on the tip of her nose and pointed to a spot along the bottom. "Here," she said, "right here."

"I'll get it tomorrow," I told her.

"And here," she said, pointing to a spot up near the eves.

"Tomorrow," Dave assured her.

"You better get it now," she said, "before you forget."

"We won't forget," we told her.

"Now," she said. Dave looked at me and I looked back at him. For a long moment, we didn't know what to do. We seemed paralyzed by indecision, threatened by the unknown. In a matter of moments, the entire day seemed quickly to slip into another one to forget. If it had been any other job or any other person, or if we had another lined up for the next day, we might have walked away laughing at the old bag, but instead, as if out of reflex or anxiety over our futures, we silently unloaded our brushes and a bucket of paint. While Mrs. Vincent crawled along the ground or pointed towards the roof, we followed slapping paint wherever she wanted. The charade went on for over an hour and continued until she had us scrape the drips from her window panes. When she seemed satisfied, we made our goodbyes, though before we left, she made each of us give her a good hug, as if somehow we had been working for our grandmothers.

On our way home, in the traffic from Boeing's day shift, Dave vowed never to return. "Humiliation," he called it, and he seemed right. That night, before a dinner of macaroni and cheese, we shared a six pack of Pabst. We seemed unable to forget, how well past exhaustion, we followed Mrs. Vincent's orders as if she were running the company herself. "We're finished with her," Dave said. "The nerve of that old hag. And for what, a few lousy dollars? No job matters that much," he said.

"We're screwed," I told him. "Screwed." Our conversation continued that way, beer after beer, until we planned to spray paint her place with graffiti.

While Dave passed out from exhaustion on our tattered couch, I waited for Sarah to call. All day, I had pictured the two of us waking in bed on a lazy Saturday morning, as we had done nearly every weekend during the later half of spring semester. On such mornings after touching her in ways I remembered well into the summer, she would drive us in her convertible to Cattleman's Steak House, charging our food on her father's credit card. Sarah, who was always watching her weight, mostly sipped wine, while I had no problem eating both steaks. I thought that night how in the fall we would start up where we left off, only this time I would finally have some money of my own. That night, however, Sarah didn't call, though it really wasn't her custom to phone too many times during the week as she often worked late.

Even with our hangovers, we returned to Mrs. Vincent's in the morning. "She needs us," I reminded Dave, who despite his gruffness seemed to have a soft-spot for her. "She could be your grandmother, for Christ's sake." Truth was, I though more about my father that morning than Mrs. Vincent. As we drove past the Boeing factory where cars filled the parking lot, Dave came up with all sorts of reasons not to go back—the lousy pay, Mrs. Vincent's demands, big fish waiting to be caught. It seemed talking about not returning saved us from ourselves, from another job we would never complete. We not only went back that second morning, but the next and the next, just like the men at the factory who turned hard work into easy routine.

Even into our second week, every morning began the same way—St. Vincent's coffee and doughnuts on the fold-out table and the widow, dressed in overalls, seated in her lawn chair. By mid-week it seemed no matter how much we painted the day before, the house continued to grow. Since the original blue often bled through the new heather-grey overnight, each wall needed two coats; the same thing happened with the China-white eves. The gutters too were becoming a hassle, the ones on the north side of the house filled with hard-packed debris from the surrounding elms. And then there was Mrs. Vincent with her endless jabbering and nightly inspections.

"My husband, rest in peace, worked for Boeing. Thirty years," she told us one morning. "He was a good man, though he had a weak heart. He would have been proud of you boys." I wondered if my father would ever feel that way about me.

"We're no role models," Dave told her.

"You're hard workers," she said, as if coaching us to perform to our best, "and he was, too. He really loved this house, approved the blueprints himself."

"It's a fine house," we assured her.

"He built it for me," she said.

"That's a nice story," I told her, making sure to push the paint into every crack as she stood close by.

"He was a tall man, like you, Dave, but big with muscular shoulders and large hands," she said. On the ladder beside me, Dave seemed not to listen, a brush in one hand, a doughnut in the other.

"Every night after work he liked a quart of beer," she said. "I kept it cold for him in the cooler. Did I tell you he built this house for me? Now I'm the only one left," she added. "I always thought I'd be the first to go." She walked along the wall I'd been painting and pointed to the spots she wanted me to brush again. "He did the floors himself. Would you boys like to see the house?" she asked.

In all our days of coming to the job, this was the first time she had invited us inside. It was a hot morning and we appreciated the chance to spend a few moments in the air conditioning. It seemed as if we were crossing over into a new relationship with Mrs. Vincent. I felt I knew more about her than my deceased grandparents. "Make sure to wipe your feet," she told us when we entered through the back door. With its white cabinets and linoleum flooring, the kitchen was bright and clean. There was a small dinette with chrome trim against the wall. The kitchen led to an even brighter dining room with a long mahogany table and a breakfront where she stored her chinaware. It was a lovely room with plenty of windows. The walls were an off-white, which she claimed not to have painted in some seven years. Her home was surprisingly spartan with few decorations other than pictures of her husband, who looked as husky as she described him, and her estranged daughter in her early years, who looked surprisingly like my Sarah with whom I seemed to talk with less and less frequently. Mrs. Vincent toured us from room to room, each space immaculate, as if nobody lived in the house. All floors except for the kitchen were hardwood in need of oiling. The oak boards, which squeaked when we walked across them, reminded me of my father's new home, his big spread in an exclusive Topeka neighborhood with an in-ground pool.

Mrs. Vincent led us back to the kitchen, then asked us sit at the dinette. "You two must be hungry, working so hard this morning," she said.

"We're fine," I told her.

"How about some eggs?"

"Really, we're okay," I said.

"And you, Dave?" she asked.

"Eggs sound good," he said, and I gave him a stiff kick under the table. From her refrigerator, Mrs. Vincent pulled out a carton of eggs. She took a skillet from the cabinet and placed it on the stove.

"Scrambled or up?"

"Scrambled," we told her, and in a small dish, she whipped our eggs with care. She seemed to be performing an old ritual, one she hadn't done in years, though remembered like the way long dormant prairie grasses knew when to sprout again. Her beater tapped against the bowl in a steady rhythm. "These hardwoods haven't been oiled since Mr. Vincent passed away," the old lady told us. "I'd do them but can't on account of my arthritis."

"They do look a little dry," Dave said. "I've heard it's a good thing to do them once a year."

"At least once a year," I added. She put the eggs in the hot skillet. While they sizzled, she toasted a few slices of bread. "The dishes are to the right of the sink," she said. Dave set the table for the three of us and when the food was cooked, Mrs. Vincent served us. We took off our hats and waited for her to sit down to begin the meal. "Please," she said, "let's say a small prayer." Dave and I looked at each other, then bowed our heads out of respect for Mrs. Vincent. "Lord," she said. "Thank you for this meal, for these strong men, and for this bright day. Amen."

"Amen," we said, though neither of us were religious. Our saint, it was clear, believed in us like nobody before, especially my father. She poured us tall glasses of milk, made sure we had plenty of butter for our toast. In the kitchen, we rehearsed a play staged long ago. In the quiet of the house, I could almost hear the heavy footsteps of Mr. Vincent on the hardwood floors, the soft voice of her young daughter, my own family at breakfast.

"There is something we need to ask of you," Dave said as he finished eating. "We're falling behind schedule and we need a favor. We need more money," he told her, catching us all by surprise. "You see," he added, "the money you gave us up front is already gone. We had to use it for supplies. It seems we underestimated the cost."

"We're not the best estimators," I confessed, upset about Dave's transgression.

"We need a bit more so that we can finish the job properly," Dave told her. In confidence, we both knew the job was long from over with still more than half the house to go, the more difficult half, where the bushes butted against the walls and ivy crept across the eves.

"I see," she told us. For a moment, she didn't say another word. She took another bite of her toast. "The house is deceivingly large," she said. We sat quietly, waiting for her to continue. "I will, however, give you half of what I owe you," she said.

"That would be terrific," Dave said.

After finishing the mid-morning meal, we did the dishes for her. While I was surprised at Dave, he did seem to work a miracle by getting us the money. We cleaned each plate with care, wiped each cup, then dried the frying pan. While we were busy washing and drying, Mrs. Vincent took from her cabinets a can of oil soap and two rags. "I would very much appreciate it if, before you return to your painting, you would help oil these floors,"she said.

"No problem," Dave said. "It shouldn't take long." I wanted to kick him again, especially for delaying our progress on the house and taking advantage of Mrs. Vincent for whom I had developed a fondness and regard.

Just like when we painted, Mrs. Vincent supervised the oiling, which took us the rest of the morning and most of the afternoon to complete. On our hands and knees, we worked the oil into the boards from the wall to the middle of the room. In some places, the dry wood, aged and nearly cracked, needed extra oil. Slowly, as the oil penetrated deep into the grain, the dry boards came alive with a fresh glint they hadn't had in years. We crawled from room to room, standing only to move the furniture or to allow the blood to flow back into our knees.

When we finished the floors in the late afternoon, Mrs. Vincent wrote us a check, which we took immediately to the bank to cash. We stood in the long line with the Boeing workers depositing their paychecks. I tried to picture how Mr. Vincent, too, had taken his weekly pay to the bank year after year, the dreams he had for his wife and daughter, ones like my father might have once had for me. "It's not so bad now," Dave said and I had to agree, especially when we counted the cash at the teller's window.

That night, we splurged, grilling steaks and buying an extra twelve-pack of Pabst for good measure. As our steaks sizzled over hot coals, we did nothing but grumble about our achy knees and back, how little progress we had made that day on the house. "We're finished," Dave said. "I'm not going back in the morning. We have most of the money and we're not working for charity. We should have quit a long time ago."

"You don't want to finish."

"Why should we?" he said, his soft spot for her having disappeared with his plans for the fall. "There will be other jobs, other calls."

"Have you forgotten how long it took us to find this one?"

"Proves my point," he said. "There's always something else out there. You're not falling for her old lady act?"

"Who me?" I said.

That evening, while I waited for Sarah to call, I thought about the unfinished house, how we had managed to paint nearly half of it, giving three coats to the problem areas. I knew in painting and sanding those rough boards day after day, we had given Mrs. Vincent our best effort, everything we had, proving ourselves to each other. The old lady had believed in us, in me. It was something I felt good about, especially considering how we had never completed most of our jobs, especially the difficult ones. Like my life itself, everything seemed unfinished. That night, after the last can of Pabst, I vowed if necessary to go back to Mrs. Vincent's by myself, finish the job alone if it took me until Thanksgiving or Christmas.

Despite my promises, we didn't return to the job in the morning. Instead, at Dave's urging, we went fishing at the lake. When our phone rang, we didn't bother to pick it up, though I wanted to believe it might have been Sarah calling. It had been weeks since we talked at any length, but fearing it might have been Mrs. Vincent on the line, we let it go.

The next day and the ones that followed were much the same. After fishing all afternoon and a sixer of Pabst in the evening, we slept in late, sometimes even until lunch. If the phone rang early, and most mornings it rang just after sunrise, we didn't bother answering. Sometimes the calls came one after another, but it didn't matter. With each passing day, I cared less and less about the unfinished work or about Mrs. Vincent. Only when we received our pre-enrollment letters for the fall semester did I realize how quickly the summer had been passing. For stretches at a time, I didn't speak with Sarah, who had told me about a new late-night schedule. I didn't speak with my father either, even when our Vincent money dried up, though I assured my mother I was returning to the college in the fall. We seemed to be sailing along smoothly toward our eventual demise until late one evening, I picked up the ringing phone by mistake.

"I'm Lori Vincent," the caller announced. "Mrs. Vincent's daughter. I'm calling to let you know my mother has suffered a stroke and won't be at the house when you arrive for work in the morning." The news was confusing.

"Mrs. Vincent?"

"My mother," she said.

"Is she all right?"

"It's too early to tell," she said. "She's in the I.C.U. Unconscious. I've just arrived at the house after driving down from Kansas City. I saw your names and number by the phone. The walls in the front look very nice," she said. I wanted to ask her what she thought about the oiled floors or why she hadn't called her mother all those years. "Please don't let this stop you from finishing," she told me. "I'm sure my mother, when she comes around, will be happy to know you're doing a good job."

"I'll tell my partner," I said. "And give our best to your mother." I never felt more phony in all my life, as if I should burn in hell. When I told Dave about the call, I pictured our patron saint, the tubes in her arms, monitors tracking her irregular pulse. I couldn't stop thinking about her, the nurses checking regularly to see if she would awaken.

That night I didn't much feel like eating, didn't bother cooking another pot of Ramen noodles smothered in margarine. I had trouble sleeping, could only think about the half-painted house, the remaining boards which still needed sanding and spackling. I figured her daughter had come from the city to pay her last respects, to settle her conscience. Someday, I knew, I would have to do the same. If she ever regained consciousness, I didn't want to be the one to say we never returned to finish her house.

In the days which followed, Dave and I didn't talk much about Mrs. Vincent or about finishing the job. Each evening when we came back from the lake, I posed as a relative of the family to obtain a report from the nurses on the old lady's condition. With little change, she remained the same. We didn't hear from her daughter, who never bothered calling again to ask where we were. With school only a few weeks away, neither Dave nor I had saved any money for tuition. Soon our rent would be due as well. We tried to drum up new business by stuffing fliers in mailboxes, but nobody responded as if we'd been cursed. It had also been weeks since I had heard from Sarah, though it took even longer to admit to myself I had been dumped. Every night I dreamed about the unfinished house until early one morning I rose to pack the paintmobile with our equipment.

"What are you doing?" Dave asked, waking from the commotion.

"Working," I told him.

"Forget about her," he said.

"I can't. It's something more than her. It's me," I told him. "I have to do it right. Put on your overalls. We're going to finish." Even though he seemed to have given up, when it came down to it, Dave wouldn't let me do it alone.

We loaded the ladders onto the roof of the car, bought new brushes with the last of our money, and made bologna sandwiches with stale bread. With traffic from the Boeing factory and Dave's grumbling, it was just like old times, except

Mrs. Vincent didn't greet us with coffee and doughnuts. The place seemed empty, as if one old lady alone could fill it. The sun rose high in the sky that day, beating down upon us as only it can in a Wichita summer. The ivy was in its fullness along the unfinished east wall, the gutters crammed with decaying leaves, but nothing could stop us. We worked together to clean the gutters, then attacked each board as if Mrs. Vincent herself stood right behind us. Dave inspected my work and I inspected his. We tolerated no shortcuts, no drips or spills. Doing our penance, we worked all morning and all afternoon, stopping only briefly to eat our bologna sandwiches under the shade of a cottonwood. We didn't even smoke, respecting the rules of the job as if we were painting the Sistine Chapel.

We worked that day until late in the evening, until the bologna and bread ran out and our arms felt like limp ropes. We didn't once talk about fishing at the lake, though there were moments when I thought about Sarah Birdsol and what would never be. For Dave, it would be years until he ever came close to saving enough to fulfill his mother's dream, but we continued to do our job. The more we accomplished, the better I felt, like an athlete in training. We painted every night until the sun set, only to return again early the next morning.

Each evening after a hard day's work, I called the hospital to check on Mrs. Vincent's progress. She had finally regained consciousness though had difficulty remembering, and was paralyzed on her right side. Her prognosis, as I had come to expect, was not good. In the days of her difficult recovery, if recovery it could be called, the house began to gleam like no house we had ever painted. All our edges looked sharp. Every frame on every window had the proper coverage. We left no smudges or drips. There was no bleeding of colors, only the pureness of fresh heather-grey and China-white. Though Lori Vincent never bothered to meet us, we knew her mother would approve of our work, even it she never recognized us or her house again.

By the last Friday of July, after laboring for two weeks, we finally finished. On that overcast day as dark storm clouds gathered in the west, we took pictures of the house. Dave stood at the white-washed front door with a paint brush in one hand and a can of Pabst in another, while I snapped a couple of shots. We would send one to Mrs. Vincent at the nursing home where her daughter had placed her, and I would send another to my father. It didn't matter that Mrs. Vincent might no longer remember how her house needed painting and her gutters clearing. It didn't matter that we would get nothing for finishing—no tip, no thanks, no check for what was still owed us. Neither Dave nor I would be able to afford classes in the fall, though on that day we finished, it just didn't matter. For once, we were the best. Even as a warm rain began to fall over us, the house sparkled, the unclogged gutters draining the roof the way blood flows through clear veins.

# Alluvial Deposits

## Percival Everett

People are just naturally *hopeful*, a term my grandfather used to tell me was more than occasionally interchangeable with *stupid.* So hopeful were people attempting to tame the arid plains of the west they believed that rainfall would be divinely moved to increase with their coming, that rain followed the plow. Law was at one time you had to plant one quarter of your section in timber, the thinking being that trees increased rainfall. Of course the timber stands did nothing to make the land wetter and served mainly to provide activity for settlers when crops would not grow, that being clearing fallen trees, the steady, powerful wind being the only predictable meteorological event of the great basin and plains.

Indians accepted the natural condition of things and so were nomadic, going to where water, food and agreeable climate promised to be. The settlers, refining and reaffirming the American character, preferred to sit in one place waiting for nature to change. To sit still for so long required food. To raise food, they needed land. Since 160 acres of western land could support only five cows, they needed more land. More land, more cows. More cows, more money. More money, more land. More land by hook or crook, usually by adhering to the letter and not the spirit of the law. More land, more cows, more people, no water.

There I was, driving through southern Utah, as dry as it was a hundred years ago, but having benefited from the ambitious efforts of polygamists to irrigate anything flat. A remarkable job, but canals and ditches don't *make* water. And if you pump it out of the ground faster than it fills, then the aquifer soon becomes almost empty, or as the *hopeful* like to say, "not very full at all." I'd driven from Colorado to do some contract work for the Utah Department of Agriculture and the Fish and Game Commision, to perform flow projection analyses on a couple of creeks. For all the anxiety over water and too little water and no water, all the complaining and worrying, not many people want to be hydrologists.

In order to carry out my first business at the confluence of Talbert and Rocky Creeks I had to get the signature of a woman named Emma Bickers, permission to cross her property to get to where I needed to be. The woman lived at the bottom of the mountain in the town of Dotson. She had been sent the form requesting her signature by Fish and Game, but it had been mailed back unsigned. To save time, I would ask her to sign the form and then finish my work in *hopefully* two days.

* * *

I pulled into a gas station and stepped out to fill my tanks. A skinny fellow with wild red hair watched me from the diesel pump, folding a stick of gum into his mouth. The afternoon sun was bright but the air was pretty cold, the wind steady.

"You ain't from around here," he said.

"Pretty good," I said. "Was it my Colorado tags or the fact that you've never seen me before that tipped you off?" I put the nozzle into my front tank.

"Nice truck," he said.

"Thanks, I like it." He didn't say anything. I moved to my rear tank and continued to pump gas. "Maybe you could tell me where Red Clay Road is."

"Keep on out this road here, pass the motel, pass the Sears catalog store, two streets on the left." He folded another stick of gum into his mouth. "What you want over there?"

"Nothing. I was just wondering where it was. Such a pretty name for a road. Red Clay."

"You're a funny guy."

"That's me." I finished with the gas, replaced the nozzle and then gave him thirty-five dollars. "Gas is high around here."

"Always going up."

"Well, thanks." I climbed in behind the wheel and he walked to my window. "What is it?" I asked.

"Yeah, this is a nice truck."

I nodded, started my engine and drove away.

Dotson was a small town without threat of becoming a city. The nearby molybdenum mine which had spurred the growth of the town had died and taken the downtown and all promise of prosperity with it. The main drag was not a row of boarded up storefronts, but it was close. For reasons too familiar and too tiresome to discuss I was a great source of interest as I idled at the town's only traffic signal. I followed the gas station man's directions to Red Clay Road and turned the only way I could.

I parked and walked the twenty-yard dirt path to the front door where I gave a solid but polite knock. A woman yelled for me to come in and so I did. I was met by a fluffy, purring white cat and reached down to pet it. The chill of the April air outside was lost as I found myself growing uncomfortable in my coat. The heater or a fire was roaring somewhere. An old woman of medium height and an angular face appeared at the end of the hall and she stared at me as if I were naked. I stood up from the cat and said,

"Are you Mrs. Bickers?"

She just stared.

"I thought I heard someone say come in."

"Well, you can just get on back out." She took a half-step toward me.

"Ma'am, I'm from the State Department of Agriculture and the Fish—"

She stopped me with her staring and I began to understand what was going on.

"Okay." I backed through the doorway and onto the porch. She was at the door now. "Ma'am I need your signature on this—"

But she slammed the door and managed to squeeze the word *nigger* through the last, skinniest gap.

I sighed and walked back to my truck.

I don't get mad too much anymore over shit like that. It doesn't make me happy, but it doesn't usually make me mad. It doesn't do any good to get mad at a tornado or a striking snake; you just stay clear. But I couldn't really stay clear. I needed her signature, probably especially now. Who knew how many misshapen offspring she might have roaming that blasted mountain with no more elk to hunt. My next stop would have to be the sheriff's office to see if I could get some help obtaining the woman's scrawl.

* * *

As much as I love the West, the character of its contentious dealings with the rest of the country has been defined by a few rather than the many. The few being a self-serving, hypocritical lot who complain about the damn welfare babies of the cities and take huge subsidies to not plant crops and make near free use of public lands to raise cattle where, if there were a god, no cattle would ever be found. But westerners, perhaps a function of living in such a harsh landscape, perhaps a function of living in such isolation and distant interdepedence, stick together and so, blindly, the desires of the few become the needs of the many.

A man with one section and five sickly cows is a cattleman just the same as a man with four-thousand head and a lease on a hundred-thousand acres of BLM land. But damn it's a pretty place.

* * *

I drove back to the main street with the intention of returning to the gas station and asking where the sheriff's office was, but I spotted it on my way. I parked in a diagonal space and walked up the concrete steps and inside. The deputy was a big man, even sitting, and he watched me coming toward his desk.

"What can I do you for?" he asked.

"I need some assistance." I produced my papers from the Department of Ag and Fish and Game. "I'm supposed to go up and perform some tests on Rocky and Talbert Creeks. I've got to get Emma Bicker's signature on this piece of paper so I can take my readings and go home."

"So, go get it. Her address is right here."

"I tried. It seems she has a bit of a problem with my complexion."

The deputy observed my complexion. "Yeah, I can see. I think you've got a pimple coming on." He laughed.

I didn't, though I appreciated his attempt at humor and his demonstration of something other than sheer amazement that I was there.

He picked up the phone and dialed. "Mrs. Bickers? This is Deputy Harvey... Ma'am?... Yes, he's fine...Ma'am, I've got a fella here from Fish and Game who needs you to sign a paper...Yes, ma'am, that would be him...Well, yes, but I think it won't hurt for you to sign...Just going to check the water in the creeks...Yes, ma'am...Yes, ma'am...I reckon, they'll get a court order and he'll get to go up there anyway...Yes, ma'am." The deputy hung up and looked at me.

"Well?"

"She said she'll sign it, but you can't come in."

* * *

I stepped into the air. It was nearly four and I was hungry. There was a restaurant across the street and so I left my truck where it was and went in and sat at the counter. There were a couple of men sitting at a booth in the back. They gave me a quick look and returned to their conversation. The menu was written on poster boards over the shelves on the wall facing me.

"Coffee?" the waitress asked. She was a pie-faced young woman with noticeable, but not heavily applied make-up. She held her blond ponytail in her hand at her shoulder while she poured me a cup. "Know what you want?"

"You serve breakfast all day like the sign says?"

"All day long, every day," the waitress said.

"Are the hotcakes good?"

"They're okay," she said. Then, quietly, "I wouldn't eat them."

"Eggs and bacon?"

She nodded. "Toast or biscuit?"

"Toast?"

She nodded. "I'll bring you some hashbrowns, too."

"Thank you, ma'am."

She moved to the window and stuck the ticket on the wheel, then talked to me from the coffee machine where she seemed to be counting filters. "Visiting or just passing through?"

"I'm working for Fish and Game, doing some work up mountain."

"What kind of work?"

"Checking the streams, that's all."

"We used to go up that mountain all the time when I was a kid. My daddy taught me to fish there." She came back over and wiped the counter near me. "It was good fishing then."

"What about now?"

"I don't know really. I hear tell it's not good like it used to be." She looked over at the men in the booth. "You all right back there?"

"Fine," one of them said.

"You don't go up there anymore, eh?" I asked.

"Nobody does, really," she said.

"Why's that?"

She shrugged.

A hand reached through the window and tapped the bell, then put a plate down. The waitress stepped over, grabbed it and brought it to me. "You want ketchup or anything?"

"Tabasco?"

She gave it to me.

A couple of young men came in and sat at the opposite end of the counter. "Hey, Polly," one of them said.

"Hey, Dillard." She slid along the counter toward them.

She and the men ignored me while I ate and I liked that just fine. I finished, paid the tab and left a generous tip, figuring I'd be eating there again.

* * *

Emma Bickers' house looked no more inviting than it had earlier. I walked the dirt path to the porch and before I could knock two loud pops hurt my ears and I could feel the door move though I wasn't touching it. I looked at the glass high on the door and saw the small holes. I ran back to my truck, keeping low, my heart skipping. I fumbled with my keys, finally got my engine going and kicked up dust as I sped away. I don't like being shot at, always have a really bad reaction to it. I don't get scared as much as I get really mad. I stayed hunched in my seat until I was well on the main road again.

* * *

I parked in the same space and burst into the sheriff's office. The sheriff was standing beside the deputy and they turned to observe me. I was fit to be tied. "That old lady is crazy as hell and I want her arrested."

"What happened?" the sheriff asked.

"That nut shot at me. I hadn't even knocked on the door and she fired two shots."

"Slow down," the sheriff said. "Who are you and who shot at you?"

"This is the guy from Fish and Game I told you about," the deputy said.

"Mrs. Bickers shot at you?" the sheriff asked.

"I don't know for sure. I was on the other side of the door and when the shooting started I took off. I didn't see if anyone opened the door once I was running."

"Harvey, call over to that old biddy's house and find out what the hell is going on," the sheriff said. Then to me, "Are you all right?"

"I'm not shot."

"Well, that's a good thing." He seemed even-tempered, but of course he hadn't been the target. He ran a hand through his graying hair and watched the deputy hang up the phone.

"No answer," Harvey said.

"Why don't you ride on out there and see what in hell's the matter?" the sheriff said to Harvey. "And take that gun away from her before she shoots somebody I give a damn about."

"I'm going with him," I said.

"I don't think that's a good idea, Mr.—"

"Hawks," I said.

"Mr. Hawks. Let Harvey get things unravelled."

The sheriff was reasonable in his request, but I was hot. "Listen, all I want is this paper signed so I can do my damn job."

"Let Harvey take the form and get it signed."

"No, I want to watch her sign it. I want her to see me watching her sign it. I'm going with Harvey."

The sheriff sighed. "I don't see why you don't trespass on her land and get it over with."

"With all due respect, sheriff, greetings around here are somewhat unpredictable and I would prefer to keep things as simple and clean as possible." I wasn't backing down.

"I see your point. Harvey, see to it that Mr. Hawks doesn't get killed."

"I'll do my best," Harvey said.

The sheriff looked out the window. "Wait a second. It's too dark to go messing around over there tonight. If she can't see you, Harvey, she might shoot again." The sheriff looked at me. "You gonna press charges?"

"Probably not. Not if she signs this form and not if I get to see her do it."

The sheriff glanced at Harvey and blew out a breath. "Harvey will pick you up in the morning from the motel across the street. How's that?"

I nodded.

The sheriff walked away, shaking his head, saying, "I hate this fuckin' job. I want to shoot every idiot who voted for me."

Harvey sat at his desk. "I guess I'll see you in the morning then."

* * *

I checked into the motel which was like any motel anywhere, the same room, the same bed, the same synthetic blanket, the same television with cable and the same fat clerk in slippers, holding a scruffy cat with a terrier standing in the doorway behind him.

I threw myself onto the bed, switched on the television and settled on CNN. I must have fallen asleep fairly quickly, because I couldn't recall any of the so-called news when I was awakened by a crash. Then there was shouting. A man's voice, booming, not so much angry as frustrated.

"I'm telling you it's not my fault," the man said.

I couldn't hear the response.

"Her tire was flat and I offered to change it. When I turned around she had her shirt off."

There was another crash. Then a silence.

"I'm sorry if you think that, but I didn't have any interest in her," he said.

Silence.

"I did *not* know her!"

"__"

"That's not true!"

"__"

"Lord Christ, Muriel! Have you lost your mind! Now, honey, you put that down. Muriel!"

A door slammed. I went to the window and peeked out. A bearded man wearing jeans and no shirt was standing in the parking lot, under a bright lamp, looking at the door. His shoulders fixed in a shrug. The woman was out of the room too, her back to me, a parka covering what I took to be her naked body; an assumption I made observing her bare feet and legs. She was waving a large and nasty hunting knife.

"Now, Muriel!"

The woman said nothing. She stowed the knife under her arm to free her hands for signing something to the man, then pulled her hair away from her head and let it fall. I of course had no idea what she was saying, but the tone of her signing was clear.

"Quiet down, honey."

"__"

"That's just not true," he said. "Muriel, she's fat. For chrissakes, she was gigantic. And ugly. I was just changing her tire."

But apparently Muriel didn't think she was fat and ugly enough because she threw the knife at the man and marched into the room, slamming the door. The man picked up the blade which had bounced to a stop well in front of him. He saw me watching and offered a half-smile as if embarrassed.

I left the window and stepped into the shower.

* * *

Though I had studied water most of my adult life, I could never quite believe the fact that there is never really any *new* water. Water falls, drains, flows, evaporates, condenses, falls. The same water, different states. The thought can be unsettling, given what we do to water, what we rinse with it, what we put into it. The tailing ponds of the mine up on Blood Mountain were dug into rock, but still the water leeched into the ground, finding the tributaries, finding the creeks, rivers, reservoirs, pastures, spigots.

* * *

As I dried with a painfully thin towel I discovered I was again hungry, realized that I should have ordered the hotcakes after all, because, though they might have been bad, I would at least still be full. It was not gnawing, belly-stinging hunger, but worse, it was boredom hunger, the kind of hunger that can make a thrity-eight year old man fat. But when you're bored in Dotson, Utah with the Cartoon Network, Larry King and the people in the next room, you either eat or drink. I decided to eat.

I went to the same restaurant with my heart set on hotcakes. The place was busier, as it was supper time. There were *three* men in the booth in the back. I again sat at the counter. Young Polly had been replaced by what she was bound to become, a forty-year old, wasp-waisted woman made up to hide what years of wearing too much makeup had done.

"Coffee, hon."

I looked into the tired eyes. The coffee pot was in her mit and she was staring right through me, but the "hon" was sincere, however frequently used. I turned my cup over and said, "Please."

"Any idea yet?" she asked.

"I hear the hotcakes are pretty good. I'll have a short stack."

"Coming up."

I heard the bell on the door and felt a blast of chilly air and before I knew it there was someone seated to the right of me at the counter. It was the bearded man from the parking lot. He had on a tee shirt now, but still no jacket.

"Cold as hell out there," he said, slapping his arms and blowing into his hands. He had a tattoo on his arm of a moon smoking a cigar with the caption: *"Bad Moon Raising.*"

He caught me staring at his tattoo. I said, "Shouldn't that say—"

He stopped me. "I know, I know. Pissed me off when I found out." He studied his arm for a second. "My girlfriend, Muriel, told me. She laughed at me. You ever been laughed at by a deaf person? And then she called me a—" He made a sign over the countertop.

"What's that mean?"

"I can't say it; but it's offensive." He made the sign again.

"None of that language in here," the waitress said, coming at us with the coffee. "Turn your cup over, Tim. I ain't got all night."

Tim did as she asked and smiled at her while she poured. "Why don't you and me run away, Hortense."

"So I can have that crazy girlfriend of yours track me down like an animal?" Hortense asked.

Tim shook his head.

"You live in the motel?" I asked.

"House burned down," Tim said and sipped his coffee. "Staying there until we can get back in." He called down to Hortense. "Tell Johnny to slap me on a grilled cheese."

"Grilled cheese!" Hortense called back into the kicthen.

"I heard the son of a bitch," Johnny said.

"Colorful place, eh?" Tim asked, offering his smile to me.

"Slightly."

"What are you doing here? Forest Service?"

I looked at him. "Why do you say that?"

The waitress brought my hotcakes and stepped away.

He looked me up and down. "Give me a break. Khakis, double pocket shirt with the flaps, lace-up boots. Halfway-intelligent eyes. You're black."

"Lot of black guys in the Forest Service?" I asked.

"Don't know, but black people don't generally show up in Dotson." He put some sugar in his coffee.

"Anyway, I'm from Fish and Game," I said.

"Same difference." He grabbed a napkin from the dispenser and fiddled with it. "Sorry about all the commotion earlier. So, what are you doing here? Counting elk, deer. Redneck poachers?"

"Looking at water, that's all. I'm a hydrologist." I offered my hand. "My name is Robert Hawks."

"Tim Giddy, pleased to meet you."

"So, what do you do, Tim?"

"Everything. I chop wood, build sheds, drive heavy machinery. But there ain't no more heavy machine around here. No building."

"Why's that?"

"You ain't looked real close at your map. There is one road that leads into Dotson and it don't go nowhere else. It leads out of town for a few miles on the other side and turns into an old mining road. This town was built for the mine and the mine is dead." Tim's sandwich arrived and he took a quick bite, wiped his lips with his napkin, talked while he got the food situated in his mouth. "We're a dead town, mister."

"Rest in peace," I said.

Tim laughed loudly and called attention from the three men in the booth. "That's funny. Rest in peace. I like you. You're all right. Rest in peace." He took another bite. "So, we got a water problem or something? Our wells drying up?"

"No, nothing like that. I'm just here to measure the flow of the creeks. Nothing special."

"We sure had enough snow this year," Tim said.

I nodded.

"You know, Muriel's awright. She's just a little high spirited." Tim polished off the last bite of the first half of his sandwich.

I watched him chew. "High spirited," I repeated his words and considered them. "She looked like she wanted to kill you."

"Aw, that little ol' knife? She didn't mean nothing by that." Tim got Hortense's attention and pointed to his empty cup. "I just wish I knew what the hell she was signing at least half the time. She gets to going so fast."

"Well, Tim, it was a pleasure meeting you, but I need some rest." I put money on the tab and slid it to Hortense while she filled Tim's cup. "Maybe I'll see you again."

"G'night."

I put myself to sleep as I always did, by imagining myself on a stream, fishing. That night I was on the Madison, fishing a stretch of pocket water that no one human had ever seen before. It was about six in the evening in early August, a slight breeze, not too hot. There was no hatch activity and so I was fishing terrestrials off the far bank. I was letting cinnamon ants fall off the weeds into the water. I would cast, let the ant drift and pull it back before it could get to a fat eighteen inch brown I could see in the shallows. I wanted the fly to float to him just right. I casted again and again, until finally there was no drag, the ant simply floated at the end of the tippet with no sign of the slightest disturbance to the water behind it. The fat trout rose, gave the ant a looking over and ate it. I let him sink with it a few inches and then I set the hook.

* * *

It was windy and cold the next morning. A light snow had fallen during the night and left everything lightly dusted. I rode with the deputy in his 4X4 rig and my attention was immediately fixed on the radar unit between us. It did not look as high-tech as I had imagined. There were a couple of dinosaur stickers on the housing.

"I've never seen a radar thing before," I said.

"To tell the truth, it doesn't see much action around here."

"Not on the way to anywhere, eh?"

"Not that. We just don't care how fast people drive."

I nodded and turned to the window as we veered onto Red Clay Road.

Harvey looked at me a couple of times and asked, finally, "Are you going to wait in the car?"

"Hell no."

"I appreciate guts as much as the next guy, but I don't much want to get shot at either."

"Okay, I'll hang back a few steps."

"Aw, man." He stopped the rig in the same place I had parked. "Please wait in the car."

But I was getting out.

As promised I walked three steps behind him up to the door. He knocked, then knocked again. The door opened and we both jumped. It was the old lady.

"Give me the paper," Mrs. Bickers said.

"I'm going to have to come inside and talk to you, Mrs. Bickers," the deputy said. "You shouldn't be shooting at people. You could have killed Mr. Hawks here."

The old woman cut a glance at me. "I didn't know it was him I was shooting at."

I stepped into the house after the deputy. The house was freezing.

"You see, ma'am, that there is the problem," Harvey said. "It could have been me at the door or the postman. You could have killed somebody. Why were you shooting anyway?"

"I got scared," she said.

Harvey slapped his arms together. "What's wrong with your heat? Your fire go out?"

"I reckon."

"You got any coffee, Mrs. Bickers?" Harvey was looking around the hall and into the adjacent rooms as if for something.

I held off making any noise like I wanted to leave, but I didn't want to linger there. I wondered why he wanted coffee.

"Could you make us some coffee?" he asked.

"I guess so," she said. She gave me a hard look. We followed her into the kitchen. "You can sit there at the table." She turned on an electric burner beneath a kettle. "All I got is instant."

"That fine," Harvey said. "Ain't that fine, Mr. Hawks?"

"Fine," I said.

"I'm going have to take your pistol, Mrs. Bickers," Harvey said, matter-of-factly. He slipped in the line so casually I had a new appreciation of him. He was smarter than I had thought and I felt small for having let my preconceptions get the better of me. The woman complained with her expression and Harvey went on. "Like I said, Mrs. Bickers, that could have been anybody at the door. Mr. Hawks here wasn't trying to break in or nothing, he was just doing his job. While we're on the subject." Harvey looked to me and put his hand out and I gave him the form I needed signed. He flattened the paper on the table, took a pen from his breast pocket and held it in the air for the old woman. "Right there, ma'am."

Mrs. Bickers took the pen and scratched her name at the bottom of the page. I didn't get the satisfaction from watching her sign that I had imagined. She had the eyes of a cornered animal. I felt sorry for the woman, alone in this cold house, scared of noises, scared of me. Then I felt stupid for giving a damn.

While he folded the paper Harvey said, "Now, if you could get me that gun." He handed me the form, then looked over at the woodstove, sitting on uneven bricks on the warped linoleum. "Where is the gun, ma'am?"

"It's in my bedroom. I sleep with it."

"I'm going to have to take it," he repeated. "While you're getting it, I'll bring in some wood for your stove."

Mrs. Bickers stared at me for a couple of seconds and then left the room. I had a passing thought she might come back with the pistol and shoot me. She went to her bedroom, returned and put the gun on the table in front of me. A .22 target pistol. I watched her pour water into two cups, then measure spoonfuls of powdered coffee.

Harvey came in with the wood. "I swear it feels like its going to let loose with a real storm." He stomped his boots clean on the rug inside the door. He put the logs down and came back to the table, looked at the pistol. "Mercy, Mrs. Bickers, how do you even lift that thing, much less fire it?"

"I do just fine. Here's the coffee." She put the mugs on the table. "You drink, I'll start the fire." She knelt by the stove and began to twist up sheets of newspaper from a plastic crate.

The deputy and I sat and took a couple of sips of the coffee. Finally, Harvey picked up the pistol and popped out the clip, put it in his shirt pocket. "You got any other guns, ma'am?"

"No."

"Just asking."

"I've got to get to work," I said.

"Okay, Mrs. Bickers, we'll be leaving now. Thanks for your cooperation and the coffee and your time."

The woman nodded and followed close behind us toward the front door. We were on the porch, the door was shut. Mrs. Bickers on the other side.

# Turn the Radio to a Gospel Station

## Jeanne Bryner

Every night here at Riverbend General it's the same stuff over and over. Babies grab their mamas' hot curling irons from the dresser or root around grandmas' purses. They swaller pain pills like baby shower mints or suck down blood pressure tablets which can stop a heart. Young girls, who haven't got their period for three months, find out they're in the family way, then act surprised. Pretty women from Preston County show up with black eyes *from falling down.* Men squirm and wiggle and sweat with chest pain.

Maybe you don't know it but there are tubes for every hole in the body. And if the doctor takes a notion, he cuts another hole, makes a new place for a tube. Laws, I never seen so much trouble in one spot as this here 'mergency room. The supervisor put me here to clean since Thelma had her back surgery. I surely hope Thelma's coming along. This is no place for a God-fearing woman to work. No sir.

Merle, one of the dayturn girls, told me our lobby has bulletproof glass around the girls who register the sick ones. "Why we need that kind of glass in a hospital?" I asked her. She said, "Wait a week or two, you'll see how folks get when their babies are puking and their legs are broke and they call the whole family in for a death. They're mad but they don't know who to hit. They're hurting, not just the burned skin or the bleeding places but deep, deep inside. Sometimes, they march over to the dead one, grab her face, and yell *Why? Why? Why*? 'Course the dead ain't got no answer. They just lay there getting bluer and stiffer and colder in those thin cotton gowns. Sometimes, a preacher comes, and sometimes, that helps. Sometimes, can't nothing help. Take that grandma who had those little boys in her car. She left them for not more than two minutes to fetch her mail. One of those little fellers got the car in gear and drove it straight into her pond. Firemen came with axes and chains. They broke windows and winched the station wagon back to the yard's dry place. Firemen said them little fellers was pounding with their fists and yelling until the pond water swallered them like minnies. The grandma, she was right there screaming in her orange polyester pants, telling the firemen to hurry up and save her daughter's babies. Our nurses and doctor worked and worked on those soggy towhead boys, but the Lord done took them angels home. Their daddy and mama came then. Behind the curtain, I saw Twila and Gail, crying over them angels when they was pulling out needles and tubes. Twila and Gail, 'bout the youngest nurses on second shift. I saw they was gentle when they washed and combed and wrapped those sweet babies in blankets and finally, handed them to their mama. They sent me to Labor and Delivery to fetch a rocking chair. It was maple, and though it did not seem heavy, I was plum out of breath after hurrying and pushing it from the elevators. Their mama rocked and cried and rocked and sang them a lullaby. Her arms holding death like that, just singing soft and low. Their daddy was all leaned over them, stroking their faces and saying their names, *Timmy and Tommy*. Me, I was on the other side of the curtain, kept shoving gloves into a box and pulled trash in the next room. My nose ran just like a faucet while I heared them twin names being wrote in the holy book. When the doctor told her those little boys was dead, the grandma done fainted and cut her head. She had to get herself sewed up. Her heart was blew apart like an old tire. I saw it in her eyes."

"Sorrow makes 'em crazy," Merle went on, "and with all the cutbacks, they took away our security guard. I liked curly Burl. He was good with the drunks and crazies. Something about seeing a uniform and a shiny badge, I figure."

Merle showed me this job. She spins a good story and wrings a mean mop. She's been here ten years longer than me. She knows dirt about the big shots' wives and the maintenance men. Once, on midnight, she caught a doctor with two women in the laundry (a girl from the kitchen and one from the lab). Naked. All of them. Sickness. A body just got to keep her head down and squeeze dirty water from the mop night after night.

Most of our nurses are good girls: clean shoes, shiny hair, pressed uniforms. But there's a couple who won't give patients a call light. I hear them snickering 'bout it by the station. I seen an old lady press her buzzer, then wait and wait for the nurse to come. Finally, the old lady pooped in her hand. When the nurse walked around the curtain, the old lady gave it a sling. 'Course the old lady, she wasn't right in her head, but the nurse she was surprised about poop hitting her just like that and madder than a mule with a burr in his ear. After they washed her and changed her sheets, the nurses tied the old lady up, strapped her down, and gave her a shot. Then, the old lady laid there moaning about Mamie Eisenhower making corncob jelly. I don't figure she even knows she's in Brier County. No. I don't 'spose she knows she's on this planet. No sir. I don't believe half the folks here even know they're walking straight up.

In the broom closet, there's a list of my **What To Dos** on a yellow paper. Every day, I know what to clean, stock, dust, and when to strip and wax floors. Dusting is everyday. Mopping is dayturn's job and night's if we get time. I do it here like I do at home. I mop whenever mud and slop gets tracked. Blood is everybody's business. Not one drop is to stay on the floor. Not one. Dirty needles are 'sposed to go in red containers with lids. Thelma's daughter got the jaundice from a needle when she was pulling trash. Somebody messed up. Then her daughter got real sick, turned yellow as a buttercup. Now, she has heart trouble. Thelma's daughter is twenty-eight. Her body is more like seventy. Thelma moved her and the grandkids in. That's how Thelma hurt her back. Too much lifting. See, that's how things happen. This job don't pay much, and Thelma's daughter was part time. No benefits. No insurance. She has bills and two kids and an ex-husband who don't care spit about holding a job or paying support. Thelma is not a young woman, but it's her daughter. Blood is a big deal.

Nurses and orderlies get in a hurry, get sloppy, and some people are just plain lazy. They wouldn't let nasty Band-Aids or sticky tissues stay on their kitchen floors, but they make no never mind to missing the trash cans, and hardly ever bend down to pick up a missed throws. They aren't children and I'm not their mama. Still, I'd like to twist their ears and tell them what for, but it's none of my put.

Nobody tells me much. One Tuesday, I went to clean a room and found a woman in a white coat cutting eyes out of a dead man's head. I dropped to my knees, all weak and sweaty, the whole room twirlin'. Nobody tells me nothing. I'm just going from room to room trying to get my work done before the Sup walks around with her clipboard, and the next thing I know, nurses have smelling salts to my nose because I saw an eyeball cut loose from a body like a red radish pulled from the garden. Lordy, it makes a body plum afraid to pull the curtains back. Another night, I started into the dirty utility room to dump my mop water and saw a little baby floating in a green-lid jar. Little feller wasn't much longer than a pencil, tiniest fingers and toes I ever did see. In a cereal bowl, I could have bathed him. I could have. There was a label on the jar, and an orderly snatched him from the counter and stuffed him inside a lunch sack just like he was a hunk of cornbread. After I saw that little baby, who was not a pickle, but a person in a jar, labeled and all, I had a notion to dump my bucket over and watch the water rush every which way, make everybody just stand still for a minute, maybe turn the radio to a gospel station.

The nurses rushed his mama to surgery bleeding like a river. 'Course she didn't see her baby boy like I did. I saw him clean down to his baby toes. I saw he was a boy and that he had a boy's heart to hurry up and run too soon into this crazy world. I wasn't nosing around. Tending to my work is all. Getting me some clean water and more solution. 'Course it stops a body to see something precious. So, I straightened my glasses and looked him over good. I did not pick him up. I am not allowed to do such things.

Once, when I worked Labor and Delivery and it was a full moon, the nurses were short handed, they let me help with feeding. They said to wash up real good, put on gloves and a yellow gown and come into the nursery. When you hold a new baby, the way they smell, better than fresh-baked bread, all lotiony and powdery, a body can't help but feel close to God, 'cause maybe He is right there in your arms. Labor and Delivery is a good floor to work. All the girls want that floor.

In this here 'mergency room, no telling what a body'll find. Liable to be somebody's brain or arm floating in a room one day. It wouldn't surprise me.

Nurses wrap fingers and thumbs in wet gauze like they're sausage links and put them on ice before men are shipped out to big city hospitals. Not one hand surgeon in Brier County. My friend's husband, Cole, lost a thumb once, and they fastened it back. A team of surgeons used microscopes. They say it's finer stitching than tatting lace or quilting. The surgeons' eyes get real, real tired. In Brier County, we know what we can fix on a man and what we can not. That's why we voted for a tax and made a landing pad for helicopters. There is something quieting about seeing a pilot and his starched white shirt. Helicopter noise makes us pay attention to another person's bad luck. When the helicopter lands and takes off, everybody in the waiting room gawks out the window. The blades' wind bends our trees in the parking lot and stirs up a heap of dust for me near the big doors. Folks track it in. No way to stop that. I just mop again.

When a table saw steals part of a man, he gets gray and soaking wet with sweat. Women, they always do better with pain. Ask any nurse. I reckon we're just used to it. I've been in this hospital over fifteen years. Never saw a woman faint from a shot. No sir.

My supervisor wanted an old war-horse for 'mergency when Thelma hurt her back. So, I was bumped to nights. There's no union. Eight months I've been working here, and only two nurses know my name, Cora and June, the midnight girls. The other nurses look straight through me when they carry their shots and enemas and thermometers. Like I said, they couldn't hit a bathtub with a soup can, so they never worry about hitting a trash can with IV bags or dirty Kleenex or bloody bandages. They care less about the stuff that falls on this floor. They like coffee and sweet rolls and potato chips in the side room. They like joking with the doctors and medics.

Doctors all look the same to me: white lab coats, starched shirts, and silky ties which look like slippery tongues. Before they come on duty, it's like somebody pulls a string on their backs. They ask the same questions the same way and half the time, don't even lay a hand on the sick ones. By the gallons every night, lab girls take blood. After second shift, stray needles are everywhere. I find them stuck in mattresses, under pillows, and on the floor. I report it to the charge nurse. I'm 'sposed to do that. She takes up for her nurses. *They're busy. It was a bad patient, a bad shift, a hard IV start. You didn't get stuck, well, then what's the big deal?* I would like to drive her to Wagon Run Road, take her to Thelma's house. She could meet Thelma's daughter, feel that swolled belly under the gown, hear her coughing and spitting into Kleenex, and touch her ankles puffed up like water balloons.

The tan x-ray machine is more like a robot than anything I've ever seen. The techs roll it from one bed to another and take pictures. They yell *x-ray* and step way back like something's gonna fly off and hit them. Lord, I hope that x-ray stuff don't harm this old body of mine. Half the time, I never hear them yell, but I see nurses and doctors run plenty of times. Must mean something bad. I asked my supervisor. She said, "Just do your work, Lucy. Mind that your beds are shiny and the floors are clean. Tend to your business. They'll tell you if anything needs telling."

What's she care about me? She's up there in her office sitting in a twirly chair, calling out girls to cover report offs, and reading dirty books. We've seen them in her drawers with the Bon-Bons. She has blood pressure trouble and sugar. What's she care about me and the stuff that x-ray machine shoots at this old body? Shoot, she don't care one bit. No sir. Tonight, I'm gonna ask Cora and June 'bout that x-ray stuff. They gave me a piece of pizza last week and sent a get well card to Thelma. They'll tell me what's what with the x-ray machine. They done told me why the bulletproof glass. Said some crazy man came into a hospital in Preston County and shot the nurse, a registry girl, and two patients in the waiting room. Shot 'em dead, then turned the gun on himself.

More than fifteen years here, no wonder I got me a little heart troubles. When I get to hurting and pop a Nitro, Cora and June let me take a rest in the family room. I put my feet up and sit a spell. Cora and June don't wear makeup, and they won't take a cussin', not from patients or doctors. They don't make a fuss about Ellie Lance sitting in the lobby after Saturday bingo to wait for the late, late movie. Ellie brings her own popcorn and soda. Her TV hasn't worked since Earl died in '87. When Sonny Crawford shows up half crocked in his army fatigues shivering snow and needing a place to sleep, Cora and June give him coffee, three blankets, and put him in a corner chair.

Once, when I was mopping my side of the station, a doctor stopped his writing and asked me, "Do you like your job?"

Mind you, it's three in the morning, my feet and back are on fire with aching. Somebody plugged the lobby toilet with a bloody Kotex. We have sixteen patients, an ambulance on the way, and Cora's waiting to discharge a squalling baby. She needs to give his mama what the doctor's writing. I look over my shoulder, nothing but the blanket warmer and the clock, so I know for sure he is talking to me. I straightened myself, pushed a gray hair from my face, and said, "I like my job fine." Cora winked at me. Then, I marched my cart into the lobby where spilled cocoa messed up a stack of **LIFE** magazines and a dirty diaper's stuck under a chair and the toilet's full of trouble, fixing to flood my floors.

# One Version of the Story

## Phillip Sterling

The first time Richardson comes in, me and Bruce are backed against a red S-15 Jimmy, drinking coffee and shooting the breeze about the Cowboy-Steeler game. We're just hanging there, gabbing, when this buckskin tan '76 Century Custom wheels in at a good clip, swings around, and lurches to a stop, smack in front of the double doors, as if it was meant for the showroom—if the Jimmy we were leaning on wasn't in its place. A witch of frigid air raced the guy in the door.

Right away I'm struck by what he's wearing—or what he's not, actually—no overcoat or nothing, just a plain brownish-gray suit, and it's only about twenty outside. Still, he's dressed pretty snazzy, with the right kind of tie, and I decide at the get-go that he could turn out to be a good mark. Fact is, he's coming hard, like he knows what he's in for. That's usually a good sign.

Of course, Bruce catches the scent same as I do. I see him roll his eyes—he means for me to see—like we both know the guy's only going to be a bother and Bruce is sorry our little chat's interrupted. But I know better. When it comes to sales, Bruce is a carnivore. He knows wounded prey when he smells it, and so he begins to sidle towards the guy right off, even while he's still blabbing to me about the game, because January's been slower than usual, and old Bruce is a pressure-point, always sizing up prospects with his right brain while figuring commission with his left. I'm sure he is pushing to get a jump on Sales Master of the Model Year, since I'd beaten him out the last two seasons. But just as Bruce moves full stride toward the guy, waving off my smart-aleck come-back, Lucy pages him for an urgent on line two, and I get to belly-up for the sale.

That's when I first notice the guy's a little anxious. He never really stands still the whole time we talk. He's maybe five-ten or eleven and a little paunchy in the gut. His suitcoat's unbuttoned, and his white shirt pulls kind of wrinkly at the waistband of his pants, just about where his solid tie points. I guess mid-thirties, from the gray owl-tufts at the temples. All of a sudden, I'm beginning to have doubts about my prospects, like maybe I've overestimated him. Fact is, he's looking sort of lackey—like he doesn't want our eyes to meet. He stares out the window as we talk.

Still, I'm thinking *upgrade,* maybe a Regal. But before I can even slip him one of my cards or pop a wintergreen Certs in my mouth, he's asking if we have anything with four doors, says he's looking for something with four doors.

"Well, you have quite a choice," I begin, lifting my voice to that friendly twang I was told helps sway the just-lookings into sixty-month payments. I sweep the air with my arm, figuring to bat his gaze out the west window and into the front lot, where dozens of our fastest movers gleam like enamel candy. But no sooner do I start to list our latest models and best options when he cuts me short.

"Four doors," he says. "It's for my wife."

I'm thinking: *Hot damn.* I can't believe my luck. Seems like I had him pegged right all along. It just so happened we *did* have something with four doors, a unit we'd taken in on a dealer trade—from Indiana, I think. It was a white Cutlass Supreme sedan with aqua blue interior—pretty dull, actually—and Bruce and me had a hefty side bet going as to who could unload it first. I mean, activity on that unit was like zero—so bad that Danny, our service manager, had been using it as a short-term loaner. Except for the one hick whose sheepdog upchucked on the backseat, it hadn't been driven much, maybe two thousand on the odometer.

I figure maybe I can still pass it off as a demonstrator or factory program vehicle, and so I begin to describe it to the guy—"Walt Richardson," he says his name is. But again he stops me. Again he asks me if it has four doors. Again I tell him it does. Next thing I know, he's reaching into his suitcoat and pulls out from his inside left breastpocket one of those checkbook-sized wallets serious players so like to carry and begins to thumb through it. I can see that it's fat with bills—three, four-digit bills, new ones—like he'd just stopped at NBD and gotten some. He says that if the price is right, he'd pay cash.

About then I begin to wonder if the Cutlass was still parked beside the service door, like the last time I'd seen it, or if it had been loaned out, or if it was even cleaned up enough for us to take it for a test drive. So I tell Richardson that if he can wait I'd have it brung around, though it'd be a matter of some minutes, since I'd have to hang dealer tags and such—figuring the guys could maybe clean it up a little on the way. He says, "Never mind. Just give me your best price."

I admit, I had trouble believing it myself. I'd been hustling cars for about twenty-three years--the first seven with American Motors, the rest with GM. But never had I recalled such an awesome sale in January. Mostly January's slow—lookers with too little Christmas money. Probably why I remember this one so well. When I ask him about a trade, he nods toward the Buick. So I help him to a cup of coffee—two creams—settle him in my cubicle, and slip on my parka. Then me and Bob, our Sales Manager, go out to appraise his car.

Like I said, I couldn't believe my luck. The Century was in good condition, with many of the more popular options—auto and air, power sunroof, a V-6. And it was clean. Fact is, it looked like Richardson had just come back from a car wash, though I don't know of any that might have been open in that weather. Even so, the mud flaps dripped icicles of what looked like soapy water. Except for a screwed up headlight and some slight damage to the right front bumper, which looked like someone had taken an indirect hit on a garage door or a deer, the car had good resale potential.

We took a chance, since Richardson acted kind of eager, and underbid the book price of the Buick a good grand—given the damage, I said. Then I knocked off just a couple percent from the Cutlass sticker. I figured it would be a place to start, and we could bargain to terms. But Richardson surprised me. He said he'd take it.

Okay, I was a little suspicious then. I mean, the guy didn't even flinch when I said it was a demonstrator. He said again that it didn't really matter—as long as it had four doors—it was going to be his wife's car. And so if it didn't matter to him, it surely didn't matter to me. I was about to make a good week's commission on the sale—and so soon after Christmas—that I didn't press him for *why*'s. I just sold him the car.

Out of habit, I dallied a few minutes in Bob's office—listening to him brag to me about his cruise to the Caribbean over the holidays—while he initialled the deal. When I get back to my cubicle and congratulate Richardson on the deal, he pulls out the wallet and starts counting out bills on my blotter. About then, Bruce saunters in with a set of keys for me—not that I need them, of course; it's just so he can nosey up on how the deal's going. I admit, I was feeling pretty good by then. So I ask Bruce to see if service can prep the Cutlass right away. Well, Bruce's face turns sort of metallic and his eyes bug out. He knows it's going to cost him. Thinking then that I might be able to pour a little alcohol on Bruce's wound, I mention undercoating to Richardson, and sure enough he just flips out a couple more hundreds to the pile. Bruce about keels over.

Within an hour, Richardson drives the Cutlass home.

We ended up unloading the buckskin-colored Buick at auction. We had made such a good trade that it wasn't really worth our time or effort to fix it up enough to put it on the lot. It was in great shape for an auction bid, though, and we did well on it.

After that, Richardson became a regular. Every couple years or so, he'd come and trade what he had on something new. Of course, he wised up some over the years—each time I had to work him a little harder—but it was never *real* work; each time I knew he'd be an easy sway. The only difference was his wife. Except for that first time, when he'd come in alone, his wife came with him, and she always drove. *Mary*, I think, or some other plain name. A small, quiet woman. Had she come in alone, I would have guessed her to be unmarriable. She never interfered much in our deals, never appeared to care, in spite of Richardson's repeated insistence: "It's for my wife." What sparked the marriage is beyond me. Waiting with them in my office for paperwork, I imagined countless hours of dull glances cast about their familyroom, a routine so engaging as to be numb.

At Christmas each year, Richardson would send me a card thanking me for the calendar our office sent to him.

Then, about three years ago, six months after I sold him a silver Calais, he came back alone. He said he was sorry, but he needed to return the car, if it was still possible. If we couldn't buy it back, he said, he'd understand, but he wondered if I knew anyone that would be willing to accept it as a gift. At first, I thought he was pulling my leg. He'd never appeared to have been unhappy before. I assumed it had something to do with his wife, since she had not come with him. I wondered if she may not have been able to look disappointment in the eye. I assured him that we could fix whatever the problem was.

He sort of laughed. He said there was nothing wrong with the vehicle. He just didn't need it anymore. It was his wife's car, after all, and now that she had left him, he didn't want it. He didn't want anything to do with it. In fact, he said, bringing the car over was the first time he had driven in years, and he wasn't about to drive it back. He didn't any longer have a license. He would call a taxi to take him home.

Obviously, I had to check with Bob on that one. We didn't have a buy-back policy, though I think at the time the Ford dealers were advertising one. Bob considered that, I think, when he gave me the go-ahead—since Richardson was a regular—if he'd negotiate on the first year's depreciation and if there was nothing wrong with the car. We went out together to see. Another surprise! The Calais still had the paper floor mats we'd put in when we'd sold it to Richardson six months before, and the odometer barely registered three hundred miles. To top it off, when we offered ten percent under depreciation, Richardson said "Fine."

I should have known then, of course. I should have been more suspicious, more wary. I should have recognized the warning: "Fine" is not something a salesman often hears; like "easy," it's a word that rarely exists in auto deals.

It was shortly after that, as we were waiting for the paperwork to clear, that Richardson began to tell me all about his New Year's celebration eleven years before. He said he needed to tell me because he didn't think we'd ever see each other again and because it had been bothering him for a long time. Because I'd been so nice to him, so helpful. He said he thought I'd understand.

He couldn't remember driving home that New Year's Eve, he said. They'd been to a party—friends of his wife's. At first he'd felt uncomfortable; normally such events didn't set well with him. However, it being New Year's and all, he'd warmed to the occasion with a few drinks. Quite a few. So many, in fact, he didn't want to leave when his wife insisted they go, and he'd stayed at the party long after she'd gotten a ride home.

He assumed that he had driven himself back to their house. But he couldn't remember. And that's why it bothered him so much when he saw the damage to the right front bumper of that buckskin tan Century Custom on the day after New Year's.

He was on his way to work, he said, walking around the front of the car to open the garage door, when he noticed the broken headlight and a slight dent in the hood. When he looked closer, he saw what appeared to be dried blood on the grille and a scrap of fuzzy material, like from a winter coat—he was convinced that it was clothing—caught in the plastic trim near the fenderwall. Could he have been in an accident and not remember? he asked.

Before I could answer, he said, "Apparently so." He had panicked then, cleaned up the car as best he could, and he'd never told his wife. A week later he'd traded it for the white Cutlass.

As he told his story, I began to feel cold, like when Bob turns on the air conditioning too early in the spring. I wondered if it was the coffee—I'd been drinking more than usual that week—or if I hadn't had enough for breakfast. But it wasn't hunger or caffiene; it wasn't in my stomach. It seemed to be centered in a place in my body that I didn't know was there. It was a feeling I'd never felt before. A feeling of disbelief, perhaps. Or uncertainty. I didn't want to accept as truth what he was telling me. Richardson had always impressed me as too conservative, too wimpy to have been blind drunk—out of control—even on New Year's Eve. He'd always impressed me as a kind of shy, maybe even pussy-whipped, man.

On the other hand, when I thought about it, before that moment he'd never really shared very much about his personal life. Maybe I just didn't know any better. It was then that I noticed how much he'd aged since that January day when he'd first pulled up to the double doors. He looked sickly, thin and undernourished. What little hair he had left was nearly white; he appeared fifteen years older than what he probably was. It was then that I recalled how oddly he had acted at our initial meeting. And it was just then when I glanced at my reflection in the small mirror near the door and for the first time, perhaps, didn't want to face the person I saw.

I started to ask him if he'd ever found out for sure if there'd been an accident—but he interrupted my question with a wave of his hand. He told me that for days he had watched the newspaper and the TV for information; there hadn't been any. He had called the hospitals for word of unexplained homicides or injuries. There were none. He even gave himself up to the police—admitted to a hit-and-run—but they had no record of any and wouldn't believe him. He said he began to wonder if he had ever actually hit anything or not. The car *had* been damaged, hadn't it?

When his lengthy pause begged a response, I said it *had*, if I remembered correctly.

He'd stopped drinking after that. And within the next couple years, he gave up driving. When he drove, he couldn't keep his mind on it. Every dead animal on the shoulder of the road brought a bad taste to his mouth; every child waiting for a school bus grinned at him like a skeleton. He began to have trouble keeping to his job, and he lost it. He began to have trouble at every job he tried. He sought therapy, even hypnosis, but nothing helped. He had such terrible dreams that he wouldn't go to sleep for days; then, exhausted, he'd sleep for days without dreaming. And now, finally, his wife, fed up with it all, had left him. It was over. And he couldn't blame her.

I had grown pretty uncomfortable with Richardson by then, even though it did kind of explain why he had acted so strange that first day and why the cars were always his wife's and why she had come with him each time. But what I couldn't understand was why he was telling it all to *me*. It had nothing to do with me. It was not my problem. Yet, I began to feel a little weird, a little nervous, sort of out of sync with the rest of the world. Like I was beginning to lose a certain advantage, a bit of control. I began to fear that Richardson was more deliberate than he appeared—that he was hatching some foul plot that included me—and that it had something to do with me selling him a car, a car I had intentionally misrepresented. I tried not to think about it. After all, that was a salesman's job, wasn't it? My livelihood?

I wanted him gone. As far away as possible. As soon as possible. I got on the horn to Lucy and begged her to hurry the paperwork. We bought back the Calais that very afternoon.

That's the last time I saw Walt Richardson, though I think of him occasionally. I mean, imagine living with the guilt of covering up a crime that may never have taken place. Or imagine living all your life in the fear of having done something that you knew you'd regret your whole life without ever knowing for sure that you did it. The thought scares me, sometimes to the point of affecting my confidence. I've even lost sleep over it. And while I'd like to blame Richardson for that—or the story itself, even though I know it's not mine—placing blame doesn't help. I can't seem to shake it off; it's a burr to my occupation.

There are times when I am driving past children playing by the road and I begin to feel dizzy, so dizzy that I know I should pull over—and yet, I'm afraid that if I do, I will run into something that I'm not seeing. And there are times I'm just about to close a deal when I break out in a cold sweat. I feel like an accomplice to a crime. At those times, I have to excuse myself, seek some fresh air, walk away from the cheesy smells of new leather and car polish. For a moment, at least, I need to get away from it, the commission I don't rightly deserve.

# Layoff

## Jeff Vande Zande

The rumor around town was that this layoff was going to last a long time. Old men talked about it in the supermarket, the sporting goods store, the liquor stores. Although it was spring, men talked about the iron ore mines and the layoff as though it were winter. Paul Wolfe waited behind them in lines at fast food restaurants, and their words suggested a blizzard coming down out of Canada, crossing Lake Superior, and shutting down the whole town. He remembered one layoff from his childhood, his father talking about how friends and relatives were moving below the bridge to find work in Grand Rapids or Saginaw. Some had gone as far as Detroit, others out-of-state altogether. That layoff had lasted three years. This one they said was going to be longer.

Paul was still surprised when his supervisor called him into the office and told him he had to send him home.

"How long before I get called back?" he asked.

"Wouldn't hurt to look for other work while you're riding out the wait."

"You think I'll be back within the year?"

"Hard to say," he said, standing and walking Paul toward the door. "They're going to call back the guys with seniority first." The supervisor's voice was heavy and tired.

* * *

Walking towards his car across acres of parking lot, Paul could hear the robins that had recently returned. Their sounds usually cheered him, would send him into reveries of fishing trips and long camping weekends. Now he hated the birds. On the drive home he thought of all the things he had bought on credit: a house, a car, furniture, a bedroom set, a stereo. Slowly paying them off over months, he had always thought of these things as his. Now he realized they weren't. He thought of his wife and his kids. Though he tried to fight them, the tears slid down his cheeks.

* * *

For the first six months he collected unemployment and looked for work. During the second month of the layoff, he drove down the lakeshore to check on the status of his application at one of the power plants where he'd heard there was an opening. When he arrived, the head of human resources told him that they'd lost his application, but he could fill out another one. Angry, Paul drove home. Waking the next morning with no new prospects, he drove back to the power plant and filled out another application. His wife began to encourage him to apply for jobs out-of-state.

* * *

Most mornings Paul would drink coffee while Sandy would get Katy ready for kindergarten. He closed the morning paper. "Same damn jobs as yesterday," he reported.

Sandy waited in front of the microwave, didn't say anything. When it beeped, she removed a bowl of hot cereal and walked it over to Michael's highchair. Paul watched his wife.

* * *

Just last night they lay in bed together, and he remembered how cold the space had felt between them. And he thought that he couldn't hold her to comfort her (and himself) because she had never really wanted this. She had always wanted to move out of the Upper Peninsula to a big city where things were happening. And though he really didn't want to, they had planned on moving to Minneapolis. Then Katy was born. When Katy was about one year old, Paul's dad got him a job at the mines, which meant good money and stability. He never knew how Sandy felt about the job—he just took it because that's what he assumed a father should do. They had never really talked about their hardships but instead tiptoed through weeks of polite silences that, like aspirin, masked their pain more than healed it.

"I'm cold," she had said, but he'd only rolled over, thinking that somehow her words were simply a reproach to his new habit of turning the thermostat down at night.

* * *

For the most part the kitchen was quiet—the clink of Katy's spoon in her bowl, Michael's little rebellious whines. Through the vents Paul heard the furnace. The blower wheel dragged, screeched and then finally picked up momentum; he could tell that the motor was dying.

"It's snowing," Katy squealed. She jumped up from her seat and pushed the curtain back.

Paul looked out the window and could see the lazy flakes floating down. It reminded him of Christmas, and he opened the paper again to see if he had overlooked anything.

"They go away when they touch the grass," Katy said, her voice disappointed.

"You'll have plenty of snow soon enough," Sandy said. "Now eat up, the bus will be here soon."

Katy sat down again and ate a few bites while her mother watched. Sandy smiled at her. Michael began to cry, and she wiped his face with a small washcloth. Suddenly, Paul stood and wrestled the entire newspaper down into a tight ball and then shoved it into the wastebasket. Everyone including the baby looked at him. Conscious of himself, Paul opened the refrigerator and bent down to look inside.

"My cousin had ten years in, and he hasn't been called back yet," Sandy announced.

When Paul closed the refrigerator the bottles in the door shelves rattled around.

"We have to do something soon," she said. Her back was to him; Michael was finally eating.

"Some of these jobs I can get don't pay what I made at the mines," he said after a few seconds.

She nodded and kept feeding Michael.

* * *

Paul walked Katy out to the bus stop. She tried to catch a snowflake, told him that she wanted to take one to school.

That night another couple stopped by and haggled a hundred dollars off the price of their sofa and recliner.

* * *

By the next Monday the ground had frozen and snow covered the lawn. Paul walked Katy to the bus stop. The children called to her and she ran ahead.

Ignoring Paul, the children talked about sledding and snowmen and the upcoming holidays. Paul noticed one girl standing separate from the rest, closer to the blacktop. Tall, she looked older, maybe in third or fourth grade. He watched her staring down the road. The way she stood suggested that she knew something that the other children didn't or had decided that what they did know was childish. After a few minutes she tensed and then turned quickly to look down the street. Seeing other kids straggling out of their driveways making their way leisurely, she yelled, "The bus!" When they began to run she seemed satisfied and turned to watch the road again.

Paul leaned forward and could see the dim headlights coming toward them. Though he didn't want this world to end he could see that it was already dissolving. The children began to shrug their book bags into place and pick up their lunch buckets. They didn't speak, but drifted one behind the other into a little line, the tallest girl in front.

"Bye Katy, I love you. Have a good day at school," Paul said, his voice rising into sweetness.

"I love you too, Daddy."

The bus moaned to a stop in front of them, and the door sighed open. The children began to march up the stairs and file back to find their seats. The driver nodded to Paul and then scanned the children in his overhead mirror. When he was satisfied, he worked the clutch and gas, and the bus grunted its way up through the gears and then dropped out of sight over a hill.

Paul walked home cutting a path over the snowy sidewalk. He hoped to have some kind of work before the holidays. He had heard that some out-of-work miners, especially those that had been through the last layoff, were driving over to Iron Mountain, a small town about two hours away. The press operators had been on strike at the Iron Mountain Gazette for the past year, and the newspaper owners were offering anyone who'd cross the line twelve dollars an hour. Paul thought about going, but he heard the way the men in town talked about the scabs. They called them thieves, and now and again Paul overheard groups of men talking about individual scabs, saying, "I know where he lives." Unknown assailants jumped one man in his driveway late at night, but he swore to reporters from his hospital bed in Marquette that he'd only been visiting relatives in Iron Mountain. Windows had been smashed out of other houses, and one car was drenched in gasoline and set on fire. Paul was frightened by the situation but in some ways felt he'd never have to get into it. Unlike many miners, he had other skills to fall back on—he was certified in both HV/AC repair and welding. He felt pretty sure that he would find work. *Still, I'd cross a line if I had to* he thought.

* * *

The next Monday another two inches had accumulated on the ground. The back screen door rattled, and Paul looked out the window as a squall whipped snow across their yard. A small voice droned through the radio speaker listing the few cancellations for the morning—church events mostly.

"This ain't bad enough to cancel school," Paul announced. He circled a job in the newspaper. A local chain hotel was hiring a maintenance worker—starting pay was six dollars an hour. He also glanced through the real estate section to see what apartments were available. Seeing the same advertisements he closed the paper and watched Sandy feed Michael. He felt the heaviness that had settled between them. They didn't talk beyond common courtesies—hadn't made love in weeks.

Later while he was helping Katy into her winter coat, Paul heard the telephone ring. Michael jumped from a small nap he had fallen into in his highchair. Sandy answered the phone and then nodded to Paul, her face tinged with a slight smile,

"It's for *Paul Wolfe*," she whispered.

He took the phone, could feel his heart thumping through his ribs.

"Hello?"

"Hello, Paul? This is Martin Rose of Gren&Dell Incorporated in Milwaukee. You sent us an application a couple months back, and we have some openings now. You're a welder, right?"

"Yeah, I'm certified." He heard his own voice rising, becoming almost childlike. Sandy stared at him from across the room, her hand closed over Katy's.

"Good, can you come down this Friday for an interview?"

"I think so." Paul's voice was hesitant. Milwaukee was a five-hour drive.

"We're starting guys at fourteen bucks an hour, and we pay overtime."

"I can be there."

The man told him where to make reservations and to call him as soon as he arrived on Friday. When Paul hung up the phone he danced Sandy around the room.

* * *

Katy missed her bus, so they bundled up Michael and drove to the school together. Paul was excited, and the rear end of the car fishtailed around corners.

"Careful Paul, not too fast," Sandy said.

"Oh, we're fine. Just gotta turn the wheel into the slides." He pumped the brakes and came to a stop at one of the three traffic lights in town.

"I think it would be fun to live in a big city—so much to do," Sandy said.

"Milwaukee's good size."

"We could go to some concerts..." Her voice trailed off and she unbuckled her seatbelt. Quietly, she turned around and checked on Michael in his car seat.

"I don't have it yet," Paul said, his eyes fixed on the snowy road.

"How far is Negaunee from Milwaukee?" Sandy asked as she buckled herself back in.

"About five hours."

Paul noticed that she was quiet the rest of the way to the school and then home.

* * *

That night they found each other lying in the darkness and celebrated with skin and mouths. Afterwards they cooled quietly in silence. He wanted to ask her how she really felt about possibly moving, but he thought he might disturb their perfect evening. *Better not to bring it up* he thought.

* * *

Sandwiched between two letters from collection agencies, a Gren&Dell brochure arrived with Thursday's mail. Standing by the mailbox, Paul examined the cover. About fifty employees were posed outside of the company headquarters in Madison. They struck Paul as clean people—standing straight, smiling, each with the index finger of their right hands held out in front of them to let everyone know that Gren&Dell was number one. In the background the mirrored window of the building reflected their backs, suggesting that they were only whole people because the company was behind them. He read the caption below: "Gren&Dell Inc.—helping you dig in to your future." Later, when Paul was reading through the brochure at the kitchen table, he saw a picture of the welding line where the earth-moving machines filed by. On the same page someone (probably a secretary at Gren&Dell) had pasted a sticky note with an arrow pointing to one of the welders on the line. Above the arrow was written "you!"

* * *

He left early on Friday morning. Coming into Wisconsin he watched the trees fade away into acres of farmland. The tops of cut corn stalks peeked up through the snow like stubble. To either side of him and ahead he could look out for miles. Then, nearing Green Bay he saw the fields rise into overpasses and factories.

* * *

As the interstate wound around the city, Paul noticed exits that looked familiar to him, and he remembered family vacations from his boyhood. Every January his father had always taken the family to Green Bay for a little getaway —a chance to swim in a pool and eat in restaurants. Though his mother had wanted to save enough to go to Florida at least once, his father insisted on the yearly trip into Wisconsin, which always drained their meager vacation account.

Paul could picture his mother sitting by the pool with her sad eyes. And his father came to mind, too. Always going into the sauna, or into the whirlpool, or diving into the deep end—despite the posted signs. This, after the three and a half-hour drive of his father pointing out the same tourist traps and his mother sighing. He remembered that his parents never really had spoken on car trips (or any other time), but instead just looked out their separate windows. When Paul turned sixteen his parents did begin to talk more than they ever had—sometimes yelling.

His mother now lived in Duluth with her second husband. His father, still living in Negaunee, would be leaving for his winter trip to Green Bay in about a month.

Paul wondered if he and Sandy talked enough. He decided he would call her as soon as he got to the motel and ask her if she really even wanted to move to Milwaukee. *If she doesn't, we won't* he thought, but somewhere in the seventy miles between Green Bay and Milwaukee the impulse to call her faded away.

* * *

As Paul drove into Milwaukee the snow vanished, and everything became brick, steel, and asphalt. Hundreds of road signs overwhelmed him and he had a difficult time following the directions to the motel. He nearly missed one exit when a man dragging a sled full of mufflers down the interstate's shoulder distracted him. As he pulled into the motel's parking lot, he was still thinking about him. He wondered if the man were homeless.

* * *

Paul set his suitcase down in his motel room and picked up the phone. He dialed a number from a slip of paper in his wallet.

"Yeah?" said a tired voice on the other end. It was not the same person he had spoken to earlier in the week. This voice was not as friendly.

"Yes, hi. This is Paul Wolfe. I got an interview today."

"Hold on." Paul could hear the man shuffling through some papers.

"I don't have you down here."

"I'm not down?" Paul had trouble taking a breath, could feel his lungs constricting.

"No. What were you coming in for?"

"Welding." His voice was high, and he tried to clear his throat.

"Are you in Milwaukee?"

"Yes."

For a few seconds Paul heard nothing.

"All right, get here by one thirty."

"Where?" Again his voice was timid.

"Jesus, didn't they tell you anything? Take I-43 out of Milwaukee and follow it to Highway 83. Stay on 83 for ten or fifteen miles, and you'll see us on the left. You can't miss it. Just look for the Gren&Dell cars."

Paul scrambled for pen and paper and wrote down the directions. "Got it."

"All right." The man hung up.

Though at first he started to worry, he soon shrugged off the incident for what it was—a paperwork mistake. Someone had misplaced him. He had seen it happen many times at the mines—lost vacation requests, delayed pay raises, deceased spouses left on insurance policies. These were common occurrences. He looked in the mirror, cinched up his tie, and walked out to his car.

* * *

Although traffic on the interstate wasn't heavy he still felt crowded by the many eighteen wheelers passing him. Cars eventually began to honk at him, and he noticed that he was only going fifty miles an hour. As he sped up to seventy, he missed his exit. He had to drive three miles before he could find another exit and get back on the interstate in the other direction. Glancing down he saw that it was already after one o'clock.

* * *

Without a layer of snow over them, the fields on Highway 83 struck Paul as sad and barren. The overcast sky ran all the way down to the horizon. On the edges of black fields crouched tilted barns and houses with abandoned cars rusting around them.

Ahead, Paul spotted a small cloud of dust on the right shoulder of the highway, which slowly became a teenager on a dirt bike. He began to wonder if he was on the right road; he couldn't imagine that a Gren&Dell plant was out in the middle of farm country. He decided he would signal for the rider to stop, ask him if he was on the right highway but, barely slowing, the kid dropped his right leg, leaned into a sharp turn, and raised a ribbon of dust as he sped down a gravel driveway.

*Where the hell am I?* Paul thought. He drove for a few more miles, haunted by the feeling that he should turn around, go back to the motel, start over. But he had nowhere to go from here, no other directions. He had this one road which he wasn't even sure anymore was Highway 83. Slowing, he looked for road signs, but the shoulders were bare, nothing to see except miles of telephone wires.

Just before he was about to turn around and backtrack to see if he had missed any obvious driveways, he finally saw a white building coming up on the left side of the road. Four white station wagons with Gren&Dell painted on the front doors were parked around it. He pulled into the driveway and parked near the back of the lot next to a black truck with Indiana plates. His heartbeat finally slowed.

* * *

Opening the door to the warehouse Paul immediately made eye contact with a bearded man across the room who indicated with a snap of his head that he should sit down in the chair next to the door. The bearded man was standing next to another man, both in white shirts, and they were watching a small forklift stacking boxes. The driver was smooth and handled his loads with precision. After five minutes, he saw the bearded man signaling for the forklift driver to cut the engine and get out. The driver, dressed in jeans and a camouflage jacket, followed the other two men to a picnic table about ten feet from Paul. The bearded man set down what looked like an application onto a neatly stacked pile. His mouth moved, and the man in the camouflage jacket nodded.

After about a minute, the man in the camouflage jacket started towards the door. Paul smiled at him and spotted the dull gray remainder of a black eye above his left cheek.

The man with the beard walked over soon after. "You the one thirty?"

"Yeah, I'm Paul Wolfe," he said, standing. They shook hands.

"What do you do?"

"Welder," Paul said. He looked at the pile of applications in the neat stack. "Are there still positions left?"

"If there's nothing left in welding we can get you in somewhere else." He walked towards the picnic table and Paul followed. He could feel heat spreading throughout his forehead.

"This is going to go kind of fast, we got a lot of guys to hire by Monday."

Paul nodded and felt a little relieved that the interview would be brief.

A balding man sat at the picnic table, a laptop computer open in front of him. He looked up at Paul and then pointed to a box full of applications. "Find yours. They're pretty close to alphabetical."

"His name's Paul Wolfe," the man with the beard said, then turned and walked across the warehouse floor and disappeared behind a wall.

Paul went down to the W's but couldn't find his application. Anxious, he began to sort through the papers one by one starting from the top. He felt a drop of sweat roll down the side of his ribs.

"What's your social security number?" the balding man asked.

Paul recited it as he searched a second time through the applications and could hear the man keying the numbers in.

Another man walked over, a man Paul hadn't seen before. "How many after him?" he asked, motioning to Paul as he pulled a bench out so he could sit.

Paul recognized the man's voice from the phone call in the motel.

The balding man stopped and looked at the clipboard. "About fourteen," he reported.

The new man exhaled loudly.

"Found it," Paul said, relieved. He could see the bearded man walking back towards him.

"Found it? Good." He took the application from Paul's hand and gave it to the balding man who nodded slightly. "Follow me," he said.

Paul followed him to the other side of the warehouse. Behind the wall he saw a small welding station. Pieces of steel were scattered across the floor, but he noticed that a few pieces had been set in vises near a welding table.

"Put that gear on," the bearded man said, his hand pointing to a box under the table. His words were demanding, but his voice was soft.

Paul slipped a heavy leather apron over his head, tightened a mask on his brow, and pulled the thick gloves over his hands. They were damp inside.

The bearded man saw that he was ready. "All right, I made four different seams—ones you'd typically find on the line. Weld them together."

Paul looked over the seams. None looked too difficult, just a few tight corners. Snapping his neck, he flipped the mask down over his face, and everything darkened to a small rectangle. For a few seconds he could only see the silhouette of the steel, but then he pulled the trigger, and his eyes began to follow the bright spot of the arc as it slid down the seams. Between welds he checked his work, trying to be fast but accurate. For the last weld he kneeled to get at a tricky corner. Flipping his mask up he saw that the bearded man was already checking the other welds.

"I can clean them up a bit," Paul said. He looked around for a steel brush.

"No, they look fine."

He took off the gloves, and the man extended his hand down to him. Paul could feel tension and torque in his palm and fingers and knew that the man wanted more than to congratulate him; he was trying to pull him to his feet. He let his body relax, began to rise, and then slipped out of the sweaty grip. His head cracked against the bottom of a vise. Ignoring the hot pain, he scrambled to his feet.

"You all right?"

Paul nodded. His head throbbed.

Walking back toward the picnic table, he saw that the other men were chuckling, and he wondered if they had seen. Another man in jeans and a blaze orange hunting shirt was hunched over the box of applications. He wasn't chuckling.

The bearded man set Paul's application on the neatly stacked pile. "We'll need you to start Monday at six," he said. He shook his hand one last time and then walked over near the new man. "Finding your application all right?"

Paul couldn't hear the other man's answer—only the murmur of words.

"We'll do your W-4 information Monday, " the balding man at the laptop said without looking up.

"Do I come here?" Paul asked.

"No." The man looked up. His face wrinkled as he thought for a moment. "Do you still have your brochure?"

He nodded. He could picture it on the bedside table back in the motel.

"Okay, map on the back will take you to our downtown plant."

"All right, I'll see you Monday then," Paul said. He began to walk toward the door.

"Hey?"

Paul turned and saw the balding man looking at him seriously. "When you get there, just drive through the gates. We'll be looking for your car. Red Cavalier, right?"

Paul nodded, guessing that they had tight security.

"Good, see you Monday then." The man turned back to his screen.

* * *

When he arrived back at his motel he called Sandy and told her the good news. Then he explained his plan. He would stay in the motel for the week and start the new job. During the evenings he would look for a decent apartment, something they could live in until their old house sold and they could look for another. During the week she should have her brothers help her pack up the house so he could drive back the following weekend and move the whole family down.

She started to cry.

"What's wrong, honey?" he asked. He hadn't heard her cry in years.

"It's just so much . . . so fast," she said in between shaking breaths. "I mean . . . it's almost the holidays . . . my family's up here . . . your dad."

"Now I shouldn't take the job? Why the hell did I drive all the way down here?" He could hear the frustration in his own voice and tried to keep it from rising into anger.

"No, you have to take it . . . I know that. It's just a lot to think about. I'll be okay—I just need to adjust." Her voice shook less.

He told her that he could stay in Milwaukee during the week and come home on the weekends, at least until after the holidays.

"No, I'll be okay. I just need to think about everything for awhile," she said.

He told her he'd call again on Sunday. As he hung up he felt he should have kept talking with her. *She'll figure this out for herself* he finally decided.

* * *

He spent Saturday looking for an apartment. Confident, he circled eight prospects in the newspaper. Although he reached six of the landlords by phone he was only able to get to three of his scheduled showings. Driving through the city confused him: the one-way streets, the chaos of signs, the streets without signs. Of the apartments he did get to, two were too small. After seeing the third, which turned out to be an efficiency, he drove back to the motel. He decided that he had all week to look for apartments.

* * *

On Sunday he called home and spoke with Sandy. She told him she felt better about moving and said her brothers were coming on Tuesday to help her begin packing up the house.

"I won't mind moving out of this town," she told him. "I bet there are a lot of colleges and universities around Milwaukee. I could take a few courses."

"I didn't know you still thought about going back to school."

"I enjoyed the few classes I took before Katy was born," she said.

Paul was happy for her, although he thought her voice still sounded quiet and sad. After about a half hour he told her that he would call again on Wednesday. She wished him luck with the job.

* * *

Driving into the buildings of the downtown the next morning reminded him of the time he had fished the gorge, where the Ontonagon River is flanked on either side by two hundred foot cliffs. The river he was in now, however, bubbled with flashing brake lights, and the windows of early morning offices shined in the cliff faces. *Jesus, does everyone in Wisconsin come into Milwaukee for work?* he wondered. According to the back of the brochure, the Gren&Dell plant was on fifth, and Paul had only jerked his way to tenth by 5:40. By the time he finally crossed Sixth Street, he looked at his dashboard and saw the green 6:05 glowing back at him. Five minutes late on his first day.

He slammed his fist into the dashboard, regretting it before it even landed. His index finger split open at the knuckle. Looking up from the small bead of blood, he saw the Gren&Dell plant and he could tell something near the entrance wasn't right. His mind focused the details slowly. *Ah Christ* he thought. A crowd of people was standing in front of the gate, and police cars were parked near the high fence that ran along the sidewalk. *This can't be a strike.* The driver in front of him slammed on his brakes, and Paul just barely kept from rear-ending him. Two cars up, another driver had his signal on to turn into the crowd of people, and Paul saw that it was the black truck from his interview on Friday.

In front of the gate to the plant about fifty angry strikers shook signs and shouted. In the parking lot beyond the strikers, Paul could see white Gren&Dell cars and, beyond that, men in white shirts were moving about in a small eddy near the canopy of the plant. *Those bastards didn't even tell me* Paul thought. He then thought of his family and knew he had to cross the line. There was nothing for him back in Negaunee except minimum wage or waiting out the months—maybe years—of the layoff. If he didn't drive through the gates and take this job, it might be a long time before he and his family could live in a house again. They had grown used to the things that come with a good job—a nice television, newer clothes, two cars, vacations. A good job had helped shape he and Sandy into the people they were, and he wasn't sure that the people they would become without a good job would still want to be together. That's what scared him the most, he wasn't sure who he was anymore. For months he'd felt uprooted, torn from his name; everything he believed himself to be left him when he punched out from the mines that last time back in the spring. The sudden anonymity had fueled his rush to find another good job as soon as possible. More than anything he was afraid of the changes not having a good job would bring. *If I don't take this I could lose everything*, he thought.

The black truck rolled slowly towards the open gates, and the strikers yelled into the windshield. Paul watched their individual faces break out of the surface of the mob like whitecaps on Lake Superior. He had seen these faces before, though none of these men had ever probably been to Neguanee. These were the faces he'd always seen at company softball games, on the edges of parades, or scattered down beaches surrounded by their children. Most of them were good men, and Paul realized that they were angry because they, like him, were becoming less who they were with each scab that slipped by.

A fire barrel on the sidewalk was still throwing up flames, and Paul pictured the men who had stood around it through the cold overnight shift of the strike. Their wives, he imagined, had driven thermoses of coffee and soup to them. Their children, like his own, were in school, unsuspecting, waiting for Christmas. *These guys are the same as me*, he realized.

The bearded man from his interview ran out a few yards from under the canopy and spoke into a walkie-talkie. Suddenly, the police near the gate formed a line like a breakwall and began to push the strikers back, and their desperate, yelling faces disappeared behind the uniforms. Punching the gas, the driver of the black truck drove the rest of the way through the gates, but not before a brick arced up out of the mob.

As the brick shattered the rear window out of the black truck, Paul thought of his wife. *She cried* he suddenly remembered. When he had told her that Gren&Dell had hired him, she had cried. That she had later stopped crying, and had even said that she wanted to move, didn't matter to him. Her first reaction had not been relief or excitement, but sadness. Her crying was probably the most honest gesture either of them had made in months, maybe years.

The cars in front of him began to lurch forward, past the plant, and Paul knew he had to decide whether or not to drive through the gates. As he looked at the men he began to feel guilt—a heavy burn in his spine. Everything these men understood themselves to be was at risk, and Paul felt sorry for them and their families. He also felt the danger in the air; somebody was going to get hurt today. *Courses?* he thought. *If Sandy had wanted to take courses, she could have done that at the college back home.* He didn't know what his wife was thinking, and he decided he couldn't drive through the gates until he did.

* * *

As Paul drove past the plant he kept his eyes straight ahead, and the strikers ignored him. Two blocks down the road he pulled into a gas station and realized that his entire body was shaking. Inside, Paul handed the cashier the last of his bills. The teenager sighed, but cracked open a few rolls of quarters and counted out twelve dollars worth. Paul closed his fist around the money and then walked across the parking lot where he huddled into the small shelter of a telephone booth. Setting the coins in stacks across the top of the phone he thought about how he would start the conversation. Down the street he could see another car rolling slowly up to the gates. Two police officers were trying to pull a striker off of the hood. Paul dropped the first few quarters in and dialed before he really knew what he was going to say. After the first ring he decided he was simply going to talk with his wife honestly. He wanted to tell her how afraid he felt—of everything. He wanted to tell her that he didn't know what he was doing and that he needed her help. He felt the warmth from his tears. Looking down the street he saw a striker holding his right arm and a police officer waving a nightstick in his face.

# Expression of Our People

## Daniel Chacón

This huge white guy walked into the cafeteria, followed by a cloud of dust and feathers. This guy was enormous, fat and tall, shoulders as wide as a VW Bug. He walked fast, as if he was going to a fight that he knew he would win. Then he just stopped and looked around. It was seven, lunchtime for the swing shift, so the place was full and everybody seemed to be watching him, probably hoping he wouldn't sit next to them. He had long dirty blonde hair in a ponytail, and his plump face, scrunched up, scrutinizing, made it seem as if he were looking for an enemy. He caught me looking at him and walked over to my table, where I sat alone. He sat right across from me, bringing this nasty stench with him. From a brown paper bag he pulled out three sandwiches wrapped in waxed paper, a fat chunk of homemade cake with yellow frosting, and two cans of soda.

I was eating one of those frozen burritos you buy from the machines, "green burrito" it said on the wrapping, but it wasn't green and the tortilla tasted like typing paper.

He looked like one of those big white guys who rides a Harley Davidson, and he had a tattoo on his neck, "ESF," and I had no idea what it meant. He had other tattoos, little green crosses, between his thumbs and fingers. We didn't say anything, we just ate, and when the buzzer went off, we got up and went our separate ways.

After that day, every time this big fuck slammed into the building, he looked around for me and sat by me. I wasn't hard to spot, because everyone at the plant was either Mexican or Sikh, real Indians, with turbans and the whole bit, and they spoke in their own languages. My hair was long, almost to my butt, which during lunch I took out of the hair net and let fall free. So he sat by me and started eating. After a while, I got used to the smell. One day, as he was chewing a fat homemade burrito—and for this guy one bite was half the burrito—he looked at me, his brows furled, like he was suspicious of me. "You an Indian"—he said.

"Apache," I said.

"Peacock," he said.

"What the fuck is that?" I said.

"My name, asshole," he said.

A few days later, I was eating one of those egg salad sandwiches from the machine, the kind that are cut in two triangles and taste too sweet, like they sprinkled sugar on it. The bread was soggy, so I was a little irritated to begin with when Peacock, spooning chili from a Tupperware bowl into his mouth and chewing on a fat slab of meat, said, "I'm Navajo."

"That's pretty damn interesting," I said.

He slammed his hand on the table. "What the hell do you mean by that?" he said. His eyes looked threateningly into mine.

I hadn't been living in Fresno for too long, which as far as I could tell was one big city of poverty and violence, but I knew what it meant to guys like him if I lowered my head or averted my gaze, so I stared into his eyes. "What I mean, white boy," I said, "is I don't care how Indian you think you are."

He stood up, slapped his wide palms on the tabletop and bent over toward me. "Fuck you!" he yelled, loud enough so everyone looked over at us, probably hoping to see me slaughtered.

"My dad was full blood," he said. "Lived on the rez."

"Sit down, whitey," I said.

He plopped in his seat, dust rising up around him, and he pointed a fat finger at me. He wore a wedding ring, a tight gold band. "You know what you are?" he said, looking at the name tag sewed onto my work overalls. "Sanchez," he said, in three syllables, as if the name revealed some shameful secret about me. "You know what you are, Sanchez? Redder than thou. You're fucking redder than thou."

I didn't bother telling him that the name tag was already sewed on the uniform when I started working for the plant and that my last name was Carter. Freddy Carter.

My job was cutting the multi-colored entrails from dead chickens that came by hanging upside down on shackles. I was from Arizona, but I had moved to Fresno to live with my brother, who had gone to school here and who worked for a non-profit job-training program for the poor. His wife had a better job, at least she made more than he did, so they invited me to come, and since I wasn't doing anything on the rez but watching my life go by, reflected on the backs of cockroaches, I took them up on the offer. The first few weeks they tried to talk me into going to the community college, because I was smart, they said, but I wasn't interested. I read newspapers and watched TV for a couple of months, and at night I stared at my ceiling or went out in the backyard to hang out with the dogs, who were always fighting each other unless I was there between them, petting them equally on their dumb-looking heads. Then one night my brother came into the little windowless room where I lived, sat on my cot and told me I needed to start working. He was a job counselor, so I could be working the next day. He held before me a deck of cards, each one printed with a low-paying, non-skilled job. I think he figured hard work would make me want to go to school. "Take your pick," he said, fanning out the cards like a Las Vegas dealer.

"What's that one?" I said, pointing randomly.

He read it. "Chicken plant," he said. "You want to kill chickens, Freddy?"

"Sign me up," I said.

As the lady from the personnel office showed me my locker, she started talking to me in Spanish. "I ain't Mexican," I said.

"Ok," she said, throwing me the overalls. "I believe you."

One day Peacock came into the cafeteria without lunch from home. He stood across from me and fished in his pockets for some coins, which he counted to himself, his lips moving like he had to concentrate real hard. "What you eating there?" he said.

It was a frozen pizza turnover, which tasted like shit, because the sauce was sour, like rotten liver paste. "Haute cuisine," I said.

"How much?"

"A dollar fifty."

He counted, then looked around at the machines and went to get one.

The following day, payday, he followed me to the car. I didn't see him, but I felt his presence, like a shadow behind my back. He walked up to the passenger door.

"What?" I said.

"Let's go get a beer," he said.

I got in and unlocked the passenger's door. He brought the smell with him. As we drove through the city, we didn't talk, but just let the streetlights and neon blur by us. It was about midnight and things were crazy, kids driving around in their cars, prostitutes hanging around the phone booths of 7-11, fourteen-year-old gang bangers walking like men along the dark sidewalks.

"This your car?" he said.

"My brother's," I said.

"Looks like a rez car," he said, meaning it was all beat up.

Peacock tuned radio stations in and out until he found a song he liked, a country western tune. He snapped his fingers. "This music gets me in touch with my white side," he said.

We passed a little bar in a wooden building, "The Silver Spike." In front was a lit up sign on trailer wheels that said "Live Country Music" and "Drink Specials."

"Let's go there," he said. "Hang out with the cowboys."

I pulled into the gravel lot. "Are you sure about this?" I said.

"You scared, Pancho?"

"Not of them," I said. "Of myself. You've never seen me drunk," I said.

"Let's go party," he said.

"Seriously, man, you don't know what I'm like." I could have told him stories. I could have shown him scars. "And I ain't drank in a long time. Things could get weird. Especially in a place like this with all the rednecks."

"Don't worry," he said. "I got your back."

We got out and walked through the gravel, the sound of tiny bones crunching beneath our feet. At the wooden door, beyond which we could hear muffled music, we looked at each other. Peacock nodded. I nodded back. He pulled open the door.

Of course, Peacock was a big fuck, so although some of the cowboys looked at us like they was wondering what the hell we were doing there, they looked away when he stared at them. One tall cowboy in a white hat and with a moustache didn't look away. He looked like the Marlboro Man, standing by the bar, his thumbs in the waist of his belt, fingers pointing toward the bulge in his tight jeans. He wore a leather western vest and a cowboy shirt. He looked at us, his eyes squinted, and he looked around at other people, too, as if wondering if there would be trouble. I figured he was the manager or the owner because he kept telling people who worked there what to do. After a while, he quit watching us. It was a good thing Peacock didn't see him, because there might have been trouble, although the drunker I got the more the Marlboro Man irritated me. He walked around the place like he was at a dude ranch and we were his cattle. I felt like smashing his nose.

But what I saw next made me forget that I wanted to fight. Or who I saw next.

She was serving cocktails.

"Damn," I said.

She was clearly a Native, long black hair, black eyes, her facial features sharp and strong. She was wearing real tight jeans and a T-shirt a few sizes too small. She was a cocktail waitress. "Damn," I said. I turned to Peacock. "You like Indian girls?" I said.

"I got me a girl," he said. And then he looked at his beer bottle, as if it were whispering something to him.

The girl was at the bar now, where the waitresses order their drinks, her back toward us. I mean, she looked damn good from behind, kind of like if you just walked into the place and that was all you saw of her, you'd know that on the other side of her, she would be just as good, because if not, something's wrong with the world. I was drunk.

"I'll be back," I said to Peacock, who didn't seem to hear me but was still looking at his bottle.

So I walked up behind her and stood right next to her, her profile so close, and her face so beautiful, so native. She was waiting for the bartender, some skinny nerdy guy with a cowboy hat, so she could give him her order. "Hey," I said, "what tribe are you?"

This seemed to surprise her. She looked me up and down and said, "You made me forget my order." She seemed like she was trying to appear pissed, but I think she was flirting. "Now let's see," she said, still looking at me, counting on her fingers, "three buds, two lights, a bourbon seven, a screwdriver."

"Well, I've been living in this town for four months and I ain't seen many other skins until tonight, until you."

"I'm trying to remember my order," she said.

"Freddy," I said.

"Freddy," she said, like she was chastising a child, "Emily's trying to remember her order."

I figured she slipped in her name on purpose.

The bartender came, leaned over toward her, and she told him her order. As he made them, she relaxed and looked over at me. "What are you?" she said.

"Apache," I said.

"I'm Sioux," she said.

I laughed.

"What's so funny?"

"You're lying, Emily," I said. "You ain't no Sioux."

And then I walked back to the table, where Peacock had a shot of tequila waiting for me. "Fuck it," he said, as I sat. "Let's get drunk," he said.

*"Get* drunk?" I said.

I didn't even look at Emily the rest of the night and even danced with a couple of cowgirls. One of them, a voluptuous girl in tight jeans and with a bunch of blonde hair that smelled like cigarette smoke and that was stiff with hairspray, kept running her sweaty fingers through my hair, saying how beautiful it was. From certain angles she wasn't all that bad-looking, but when she invited me to sit with her, I said no thanks and went back to the table where Peacock was so drunk he swayed from side to side as he sat in his chair.

Then Emily came to our table, her arms crossed like she was mad at me. "What do you mean I'm a liar?" she said. "How dare you!"

"You ain't no Sioux," I said.

"Are not," she corrected.

"What kind of Sioux are you?" I said.

"What kind?" she said. "What kind of question is that? I'm Sioux, a Sioux Sioux."

"From where?" I said.

"Uh, Oregon," she said.

"You don't know shit about the Sioux," I said.

She put her hands on her hips (she was fucking beautiful). "And you do I suppose."

"I know all kinds of things," I said.

"Like what?"

Then the band announced last call and said they'd only do one more song. "I ain't got time to tell you all the things I know," I said. "Better give me your phone number."

"Ha! You think I give out my number that easy?" Then her boss, the Marlboro Man, tapped her on the shoulder. He put his hand on her waist and pulled her a bit closer, and with the rim of his white cowboy hat, he pointed toward her tables, meaning get back to work. After she left, he stood there and looked at me, his thumbs still in his belt, and I was about to tell him to get the fuck out of my face, but he walked away. I felt like punching him, just because he was so arrogant and it would probably make me feel real good. On our way out of the club, Peacock was singing out loud and slapping cowboys on the back, saying "What's up, Pardner?" Emily came up behind me and slipped a piece of paper in my palm.

"If you turn out to be a psycho," she said. "I swear I'll never forgive you."

I was still drunk when I got home—even after I went to Fat Burger with Peacock and almost got in a fight with some black guys until some cops pulled into the parking lot. I didn't even think about it when I picked up the phone and dialed Emily's number. It was four a.m.

"I knew it," she said, "you're a psycho."

We talked for hours, as I walked around the kitchen, until the sun rose over the fence and lit up the dirt floor of my brother's backyard. I could see the dogs, of different breeds, sleeping on opposite sides. She told me she didn't know anything about her tribe because her adopted parents were white, so she never got to know anything about her true family.

"Who knows," she said, "You could be my brother."

"Don't say that," I said, "that's sick."

"Why's that sick?" she said.

As I was cutting guts off the chickens, Peacock slammed into the work area. He was a live-hanger, one of the workers that pulled the reluctant chickens from the cages when they were still alive and fighting, and that was a real dirty job, so he wasn't allowed in our part of the plant. Everyone was watching him walk toward me. The foreman saw him and he started asking Peacock what the hell's going on here, but Peacock didn't stop. He was coming right at me. By the time he reached me there were three foremen behind him, all of them looking nervous, hoping this big guy wasn't going to go crazy and start killing people.

Peacock stopped where I was working. "What happened?" he said. "I don't remember a thing about last night."

"We ended up at Fat Burger," I said. "You slept in the car most of the time."

I looked at the foremen and they were looking at me like they were pleading with me to get this giant out of here.

"Peacock," I said. "Why don't you go back to work. We'll talk at lunch."

He turned around. He looked at the foremen and they looked scared.

Peacock suddenly screamed, *Ahhhhhhh!*, so close to them and so loudly that they closed their eyes and scrunched up their faces as if they were in a sandstorm. Then he laughed at them. Then he winked at me and left.

"What's wrong with him?" one of the foremen asked me.

"He's crazy," another one said.

"He's freaking out," I said. "He needs to be around his people."

"What you mean? White people?"

"No, me."

"You're not white," the foreman said.

"Neither is he," I said.

At lunchtime Peacock hung out by the vending machines until he found things he wanted, and then he came back with an armful of packaged food, which he dumped on the table. He sat down, unwrapped the first thing, and gobbled it up.

"What happened?" I said. "How come you haven't been bringing your own lunch?"

He shook his head, as if the subject was off-limits.

Suddenly, this Mexican, thinking I was Mexican, came up to me and started speaking Spanish, but I didn't know what the hell he was saying. I was about to tell him he was wasting his time, but Peacock surprised the shit out of me. He started talking in Spanish, fast too, like he had been speaking it all his life, pointing to something by the door, explaining something to the Mexican, who kept nodding his head saying, *"Claro, claro."*

When the guy, left, Peacock opened another package of food and started eating again.

"Where the hell did you learn that?" I said.

He shrugged his shoulders and ate.

I looked at the tattoo on his neck. "What does that mean?" I said. "ESF."

"Something from my past," he said.

"A gang?" I said.

"What is this, an interview?"

"Ok, what do you want to talk about?"

"Last night. Did we get in a fight?"

"No," I said.

"Let's go back tonight," he said. "Maybe we'll have better luck."

I had thought by the end of our phone conversation, that Emily was interested in me.

"Come on in tomorrow night and I'll buy you a drink," she had said.

"*A* drink?" I said.

Maybe I was feeling the effects of the booze, but it bothered me to see her flirt with other tables of guys, just like she was flirting with me and Peacock, and

I wondered if she begged them to come to the bar too. This was probably her way of making good money, like she said she made. Peacock was too drunk to know what was going on. Every time she came to the table, he tipped her a dollar.

"We need another shot," Peacock now said. "Where's Emily?" he said. She was across the bar, bending down over some table where two cowboys were sitting drinking long necks and looking down her blouse probably. Peacock stood up and yelled like a cowboy. He was louder than the band and they looked kind of pissed that he would take their attention away.

"Emily!" he screamed. She and the cowboys looked at Peacock, and she gave him a mean look.

So she walked toward us like she was about ready to scold us. She was wearing real tight shorts, her leg muscles flexing, tense, hard, with each step. When she reached our table, she looked at me—not Peacock—like I messed up real bad or something.

"Freddy," she said, "I got to talk to you."

"What?" I said.

"In private. I'll meet you in the back room."

"Another round," Peacock blurted out, like he was throwing up or something.

"I'll get you some coffee," she said.

"Fuck that," he said. "I want some booze, baby."

He was half-conscious.

"Emily'll bring some coffee," I said.

I saw her going through the curtains to the back room, so I followed her and went in there too. We were in one of those extra rooms that they opened up if it got real busy. It was dark inside, and she was sitting at a little bar table, her legs crossed. I sat down. I thought she was going to scold me about Peacock, but she said, "I want to go out with you. But I want to pay for everything. Would you feel threatened by that?"

"Hell no," I said.

"Well, I just wanted to make sure."

"Fine with me."

"I really liked talking with you the other night, Freddy."

"Me too," I said.

This moment was so nice and tender, but I was so drunk, so of course I had to say something stupid. "Are we going to sleep together?" I said.

"What the hell's that got to do with it?" she asked.

"I really want to sleep with you," I said.

"Remember what I said," she said. "No psychos."

Just then a tall man with a cowboy hat filled the entrance, blocking the light coming in from the bar. The Marlboro Man. "Don't you have tables?" he asked. His voice was deep and slow.

"Sure, boss," Emily said. She told me we'd talk later, and then she walked up to the boss, but he didn't get out of her way so she could pass. He looked at me. "Your friend looks like he had a few too many," he said.

"Maybe we'll have a few more," I said.

He grinned, slowly nodded his head, then he looked at Emily. "No more for the big guy," he told Emily. Then he turned around and walked out. Emily followed him, without looking at me.

I waited for the Marlboro Man in the parking lot. The place emptied out, people stood by their cars for a while, and some couples made out. "You going to kick his ass?" asked Peacock.

"Either that or I'm going to dance with him," I said. "I ain't decided yet."

I was drunk enough and unreasonable enough that I would have messed with him, hadn't Emily walked out of the bar and seen me. She walked over to my window, and thinking that I was waiting for her, she said, "You guys want to go get some coffee?"

One weekend we drove to the coast, to Carmel, in Emily's Tercel. It was dark by the time we got there and we didn't much enjoy walking around and looking in the little shops and walking past the restaurants and coffee houses because there was just a bunch of rich people hanging around spending money. We looked through the window of a Native American shop. We saw blankets and jewelry and traditional headgear, things that native people made, costing a thousand times more than what it cost to make.

"How do you feel about that?" Emily asked.

"Well, I don't mind that it's so expensive. These people can afford it. What bothers me is the way the owners of these places exploit the native crafts people."

"You're pretty smart," she said. "I mean, I wouldn't have gone out with you, Freddy, if you were just handsome."

"You think I'm handsome?"

"Oh stop it," she said. "You should go to school. You can start at Fresno City College."

"Why would I go to school? It's just white shit anyway."

"Oh, come on, you're too smart to believe that. I'm doing all right in social work. I'm learning a lot about how to help people. It's important."

"*Our* people don't need social workers. We need guns."

"What?"

"No, I don't mean that. It's just the universities are the training grounds for white leaders. It's a waste of time. I don't want to train to be white."

"Well, I think you could get what you want from it," she said. "I've taken Native American Studies classes that were pretty straight forward from a Native perspective."

"If you want a Native perspective, go to the rez," I said. "Hey, look," I said, pointing between two buildings. Two walruses, wet and black, were sitting on the rocks, their coats reflecting light and water, waves slapping against the rocks. "Let's go check it out."

We sat for a while listening to the ocean, and then she said. "I think you're right—to an extent—about school. It's very white, all these theories and histories. But you know something? You're all I have that's not white. Funny, huh? And I'm full-blooded...something...some tribe. I mean, I must be full-blooded: look at me."

We spent the night in a motel in Salinas. We took a walk to Taco Bell late that night where a bunch of white teenagers were hanging out by their pick-ups, and we drank iced tea in silence.

When we got back to the motel, we went to bed, and Emily told me she really did like me a lot, but she sure wished I would do something with my life other than kill chickens. "You'd make a good lawyer," she said. "You can be very persuasive."

"I like killing chickens," I said. She put her arms around me, breathed warm breath into my ear. "I like you, Freddy."

Monday a foremen pulled me off the line and said I was needed outside because Peacock was going crazy.

"He's tearing the heads off the fucking chickens," he said.

By the time I got to the brick room where the live-hangers worked, Peacock was sitting on a pile of dead chickens, blood all over himself. If the hangers pulled a dead chicken off the truck, they would throw it into a pile in the corner. That's where Peacock was sitting. He didn't kill all those chickens himself.

"Hey," he said when he saw me. "Grab a chicken and sit down."

I sat next to him. We sat for a while without words.

Then I said, "What's up?"

"She went back to Mexico," he said. "She hates everything about this country."

"Why don't you go with her?" I said.

"Wasn't invited," he said.

The foreman peeked his skinny head from behind the door and Peacock grabbed a headless chicken and hurled it at him. The foremen's mouth opened wide, and he disappeared.

"You better quit this shit," I said after a few minutes.

"How come?"

"White people can't handle it when we express ourselves."

Emily had lived all her life in LA. with her adopted parents, but as soon as she could manage it, when she was 18, she packed the '74 Datsun B210 she had bought by working after school, and she drove out of the city and just kept driving north, through the mountains, gliding down into the yellow sea of the valley, and then flat driving for hundreds of miles past fields and farms until she got to Fresno, one hundred square miles of urban sprawl. She had stayed in Fresno once before when she was a child. Her foster mom's sister lived there and they had stayed the night on their way to vacation in Yosemite when Emily was a child. Her aunt lived on a narrow street with leafy trees, forming a tunnel, and Emily liked Fresno and her aunt very much, a high school teacher who lived alone. Her house was full of books, books everywhere, even in boxes in the garage. Emily liked the neighborhood. She chose Fresno. Now she was working on her master's in social work and she owned her own house.

She was looking through a window of her house at the apple tree on the lawn. "My boss hates me. I know he does," she said "I mean, lately."

I walked up next to her and looked out the window, too.

"Sounds like he's getting nervous suddenly that you know who you are for once in your life."

"What do you mean by that?" she asked.

"You're Indian now, of course he's going to hate you. Cowboys and Indians, get it?"

"I was Native American before I met you," she said.

"Yeah, but now you're an Indian," I said.

"You're crazy," she said.

"I'm serious. White people don't mind you looking Indian, but don't act it."

"You're being a bit over zealous, Freddy. Meaning you're..."

"I know what over zealous means, Emily."

"I'm sorry," she said. "Mr. Beauchamp used to really like me. We used to. . .Oh, I guess it doesn't matter."

"You used to what?" I said.

"Never mind," she said. "It's irrelevant."

"What's irrelevant? Tell me what you're talking about."

She turned around, the sun sitting on her shoulders like a little pet. "Nothing. I shouldn't have said anything."

"You're hiding something," I said.

"I don't want to talk about this." She walked away.

"You dated the Marlboro Man, didn't you? You fucking dated him."

"Don't talk to me like that."

"Did you sleep with him?"

"How dare you even ask," she said. "Have I ever asked who you slept with?"

"Fine," I said. "Don't tell me about your affair with John Wayne."

I looked at the apple tree, the street, the neighbor's small homes—and more trees up and down the street. Yellow leafs covered lawns, sidewalks, and some parked cars.

I put my arms around her. "You got nice trees in this neighborhood," I said. "I think I'm falling in love with...With your neighborhood."

She turned around. "You know, I got this house for such a good price," she said. "In LA this place would go for hundreds of thousands. I'm serious." She turned around and looked out the window. "But I guess this is supposed to be a bad neighborhood, huh? I mean, I guess it is one—although no one's tried to bother me. The neighbors I've met are good people. Sometimes I hear gun shots at night. But that's pretty normal, I guess. I mean, for living in a city, huh? I mean, for Fresno."

"Sure, neighbors kill each other all the time."

"May sound crazy," she said. "But I like this city. I'm never going to leave it."

"You found your homeland," I said.

"What about you, Freddy?"

"What about me?"

"You scare me," she said.

"Scare you?"

"Where are you going with your life?"

I was sitting in the cafeteria eating something Emily made. She cooked a few meals a week and took them to work and school as lunch, so she could save money by not eating out every day, and lately she had been giving me food to take too. When I told her I had nothing to save for, she assured me that I did, that I had a future that she was convinced was inevitable and dynamic, that I was too smart to not some day see the importance of an education. Today I had some sort of hamburger casserole, and it was pretty damn good compared to all that frozen shit I used to eat everyday.

As I ate, I kept looking toward the entrance, waiting for Peacock, expecting him to come in. It was almost halfway into lunch and he hadn't appeared. People were finished eating and were leaving the cafeteria, going outside to smoke. Suddenly, an argument broke out on the other side of the cafeteria, but I couldn't tell what it was about because they were yelling at each other in Spanish, waving their arms close to each other's faces. Then one charged the other, pushing him back and they were fighting. The people sitting with them didn't do anything, they just watched. It was slow, each of the men trying to land a punch, and then stepping back to see if they had done any damage. It was as if they didn't really want to fight, but what else was there to do? They had no more words, not enough to express the deepness of their feelings. So the Mexicans articulated themselves, dancing in slow motion as their friends watched. Then a Sikh man in an off-white turban walked up to one of the guys, gently put his hands on his shoulders and led him away, speaking to him softly in the ear, like a father cooing his child. The other Mexican stormed out of the building.

I called Emily before lunch was over. "Freddy?" she said, surprised to hear from me.

"Yeah. What are you doing?" I said.

"Studying. Is something wrong?"

"No. I just called to say something."

"What is it, Freddy?"

"Well, see Emily. You know I'm in love with you, right? I mean, that's pretty obvious, isn't it?"

"Oh, Freddy, that's nice. Really, that's nice."

She said it like she meant it, not like she was brushing me off.

"I can't wait to see you," I said. "I'll come over right after work."

"Can't tonight. Sorry, baby. Tomorrow, okay, Freddy?"

"I thought we were going to..."

"My boss called. He wants me tonight. Sorry."

"He wants you, huh?"

"Don't start, Freddy."

He was already drunk when I got to the car after work. As I drove toward The Silver Spike, he handed me a bottle of tequila, half empty, and I took some gulps, waiting, waiting for the feeling to rise from the warmth in my stomach to the buzzing in my head. Peacock was irritating me, slurring about how tonight he was going to kick some ass. What bothered me was the way he emphasized his words by slapping his palms on the dashboard. What bothered me was that his wedding ring was off, and all that was left of it was a band of white skin, lighter than the rest of the finger. What bothered me were his eyes, because no matter what he was saying or doing, they were sad. I was quiet. I gulped tequila. The more he talked, the angrier I got. At him. At the Marlboro Man. I drank more. My eyes focused on the road ahead of me.

"Those fuckers fired me," he said. "Slapping his palms on the dashboard. Those fucks."

"What the hell did you expect, stupid? You were pulling heads off the chickens."

"It's a fucking chicken plant," he said. "That's what we do."

"Would you shut the hell up," I said.

He looked at me, swayed in drunkenness, closed one eye and scrutinized me with the other. "Are you talking to me?"

I took a big swig from the bottle. "No shit."

Then he yelled, poking his chest with his fat finger, making a thumping sound. "Me? You're talking like that to me?"

I could see the Marlboro man in my head, putting his hand on Emily's waist, sliding it down further and further. I took another gulp.

"I'll kick your ass," Peacock said to me.

"Fuck you," I said, driving closer and closer to the Silver Spike. "I'd like to see you try it."

# Double Shift

## Daniel Coshnear

Ruby shouts, "Don't damn you touch me!" and shoves through the screen door and onto the back porch where fellow residents puff on cigarettes around a white painted picnic table sticky from spilled coffee, smeared with ashes. Ruby abhors smoke. One of her fears is that she'll get cancer from other people's exhalations. She continues out into the yard and the flood light triggered by the motion detector catches her slapping herself on the cheeks. It's her fourth tantrum today.

Back through the screen door, through the kitchen where Gordon scrubs the plastic juice pitcher for the third time before putting it into the dishwasher, past the cubby where residents can make or receive phone calls until ten thirty is the office, a boxy room with two desks, four tall file cabinets, a threadbare plaid sofa and a humming photocopy machine. The office is airless and tends to retain the dinner smell longer even than the kitchen. Tonight it stinks heavy like the kielbasa and steamed cabbage Carl cooked. Trish is brushing her hair and searching a desktop for a black pen to complete her charting. She'll put a note in the Comm. Log about Ruby's behavior and a recommendation for a med eval. It's a few minutes after eleven and she's waiting for relief.

Johnson, short for Mike Johnson, works as an on-call relief counselor for a large social service agency with four group homes. The Open Door serves as a sixty day shelter for homeless folks with mental illness. The Bugel House is for teens referred by the California Youth Authority. Burger House is for adults with mild to moderate retardation. Johnson fills in most often at the Burger House. The Path is the home for men and women with dual diagnoses—substance abuse and mental illness. Each of the homes has its own staff and management, its own rules and jargon. Johnson rarely works at The Path because it is a long drive from his home. He will take a double shift if he is called, then the drive seems worthwhile. But, Johnson dreads the double shift at The Path. He is driving not too fast down 101 toward Cotati, looking for the moon and feeling acid rise in his throat. He is about to clock in for a sixteen hour gig.

Johnson has been with The Agency for seven years. Many times he has wanted to call the main office and tell Patricia, Vicky, Karin to erase his name from the relief list. He's angry about the seven fifty an hour and he's bored, more than bored, sickened, depressed, by the way The Agency treats its clients, especially at The Path. The staff there are so damn self-righteous, so full of themselves. A poorly understood mission and a little authority adds up to ugly treatment. He might have taken a regular position at any one of the houses, a few years back there'd been plenty offers, but as he tells it, 'I'm freer this way, I can make my own schedule.' In fact, he works more hours for less pay than most full-timers. He'll tell you, 'At least I don't have a boss,' and in a sense it is true, but in another sense, he has many bosses and less say-so than the greenest of case managers. If pushed, Johnson will say that he's an artist, which means he's an outsider. This work is supplemental income. His real job is as a back-up singer and song-writer for an R&B band called Johnny Bourgeois and The Means of Production. Subtracting the expenses from the revenues of his show business, he has earned one hundred and ten dollars in four years.

Johnson straightens to six feet out of his Corona Hatchback. He has to lift up on the door when he closes it, reminder of a brush with a telephone pole on a wet winter night. That was the last night he'd spent with his fiancee, four years back. She'd pushed him to articulate his career choices. He'd driven home alone angry, feeling reckless. Losing grip, spinning out, it was the end of something, the beginning of something else. As he lifts up, he clutches his lower back.

"Hey Ruby," he says. He saunters to the stairs, the porch. "You ok?" Ruby moves into the shadow of a diseased Willow. "Come see me later, if you want," he says. Ruby shakes her head, a pale smile. Joy shifts her weight and he can hear her thighs unstick from the picnic bench. She squeezes out a Pall Mall and rubs her tobacco-brown fingernail with the yellow thumb and forefinger of the opposite hand.

"You're back."

"I was in the neighborhood," Johnson says. "Figured I'd stop in and earn a living."

"What a day it's been," Joy wags her head.

"A shitty day," says Javier through the screen door.

"I'll come and get the dope after pass-on," Johnson says.

"Don't say dope," Paulie giggles. Paulie's new, eighteen, the youngest of the twelve residents. He wears a goatee like Johnson, a tattoo on his wrist like Johnson, and he wants to be a musician. He rooms with Phil, which is unfortunate, but everyone says Paulie's got the stuff, the right attitude for recovery. Some of the staff hope that Paulie will be a "positive influence" on Phil.

"Sorry," Johnson says. "I mean scoop."

"Hey Gordon," Johnson says. Gordon is bent over reading the instructions on the box of dishwasher soap.

"You're late," Trish says to Johnson. "I guess it doesn't matter, I'm not finished charting yet."

"Just leave yourself a space and do it tomorrow." Johnson takes up the badly warped guitar from the rec. cabinet on his way into the office. "I'm serious. Get out of here. I heard it was a shitty day."

"It was."

"Go have a couple stiff ones."

"Funny." Trish like most of the workers at The Path is in recovery. "I want to go sit in a hottub."

"Do it." Johnson picks blues chords, nothing fancy. "Go get soaked."

"No, I should finish up."

"Do it," Johnson sings, "get out of here, the moon is big and the night is clear."

Trish presses her cuticles hard against her lower lip. Her eyes swim across the ceiling. "Quickly," she says, she screws the cap on a plastic bottle of diet cola and nestles it in her handbag, "a couple things you should know. Ruby's having intense mood swings. I think they should up her Lithium or something."

"Surprise."

"Phil's on blackout." Blackout is twenty-four hours without visitors, phone calls, television, without permission to leave the premises. Three blackouts equals expulsion—in Phil's case, a police escort to the lock-down at Atascadero.

"Surprise. What'd he do?"

"At morning check-in, you know, he never wants to say how he feels. That's all he's got to do, say how he feels and what's his goal for the day."

"Maybe his goal is *not* to say how he feels."

"Maybe, but that's rules Johnson."

"So he got blackout? You're tough."

Trish thinks. "He said, 'This is pissing me off.'"

"So what's wrong with that?"

"He said, 'My goal for today is to kick some punk ass.'"

Johnson plucks the g-string. "Seems appropriate."

"It's not. It's not appropriate." Trish lugs a pair of big black binders from the desk toward the standing file, but Johnson blocks her way. He takes the binders out of her hands.

"Go. Rest." She blows a puff of air that makes her bangs fly up, then leaves. She stops at the screen door.

"You know, it's different for you. You're not around here all the time."

"What are they paying you?" Johnson asks.

There's a pause. He doesn't expect an answer. He scans the top pages of the med file to see that everyone has received evening doses. "It'll be nine fifty with the increase, not enough."

"What increase?"

"Oh. I guess you're not in on that. I guess it's only for full-timers."

"Fuck. You're kidding me."

"You subs'll be next, I'm sure." The door slams.

Johnson pulls a drawer from the desk and fills his palm with Tums. He says "Fuck" eleven times while he crunches, his mouth full of white paste. He puts the guitar back in the rec. cabinet and as he walks through the kitchen he says, "Wash your ears, Gordon, while you're at it." He finds an edge of bench on the picnic table and sits, straddling. He rolls a smoke. "Shitty day, eh?" He looks at Javier. "I thought you guys were heading out to Salmon Creek."

"It would've been," Joy answers, "but something with the van."

"It wasn't the van," Javier says. "It was cause of Phil." He pulls up hard on his jeans which are hanging below his butt and they fall back below his butt. "It was cause of Phil wouldn't go and they didn't have no other staff to sit here with him."

"Sounds like Phil's just settling in." Johnson says. Only the crickets respond. "It takes time," he adds.

"I didn't want to go anyway," Paulie says. "Not with this sunburn." He reveals a pink, fleshy bicep from under his sleeve.

"I wanted to go," Ruby walks up on the porch and into the house. "Get out of here and get some fresh air for a change."

The thing about Ruby, Johnson realizes as he converts the sofa in the office into a bed, is that she's kind of cute when she's not pouting. She looks like the lover from years gone by, pale as paper with henna red hair, even pouts like her. He spreads a sleeping bag across the coarse cushions, but he doesn't lie down. He takes up the guitar again:

*I'm blazing through the twilight*
*Pleading that the sun don't set*
*Ruby of the red highlights*
*I'm not ready for the darkness yet*

First staff arrives at eight a.m. Dawn. Johnson hasn't met her yet. At nine thirty, Trish. At ten, Bruce. The manager, Ted Braddock, will arrive at eleven with an over-dressed salad bar lunch in a white bag, loud greetings and hearty laughter. Ted Braddock is one of few black men in The Agency, the only in management. He's an addict. He used to sing the blues. He's known as a no-bullshit guy and Johnson has to keep mindful of certain facts to dislike him.

Ted and Johnson first met at Sonoma State University. They took a class together called The Therapeutic Relationship and enrolled in another called The Social Work Matrix, but Braddock dropped that one in favor of Mental Health Administration. They went through The Agency's orientation together. They had a common interest, music, and what seemed like a shared suspicion for The Agency's lack of regard for clients' rights and dignity. When Braddock was promoted to management a year ago, Johnson put a note in his box: *You're smooth, buddy. I'm glad it's you. This agency needs a little soul.* And Braddock left a note for Johnson, folded, stapled in the relief box: *Time to get with the program, Mike.*

It is the responsibility of the overnight staff, Johnson in this case, to see that all residents are up, dressed and medicated by eight. Chores are done between eight and eight-thirty. Check-in is at eight-forty. The day is plotted thus with short breaks between groups, exercise, chores and meals, lots of short breaks for bitching and smoking.

Johnson had difficulty drifting to sleep. He leafed through the charts and found nothing out of the ordinary. He took an extra minute to read Phil's psychosocial. The man was first incarcerated in 1972 at the age of twelve. He's been in and out of institutions ever since, except for a time of five years when he worked as a motorcycle mechanic in East Palo Alto. Reports to have been clean and sober during that period, until his girlfriend was killed in a crash, relapsed. When Johnson finally nodded off, he was awakened by Gordon who needed his Albuterol inhaler, a wracking hacking cough. Then there was a wrong number. Soon after came the grinding gears and wheezing hydraulics of the garbage truck just outside the window. At seven-forty-five Johnson fell into a sweet dream, first swimming, then flying through shades of blue. He felt as if he was being drawn toward a bolt of light. He was startled awake by pounding at the office door.

"Morning," he wipes his eyes.

"It sure is." An officious young woman with an enormous handbag pushes through and leaves a short line of residents waiting in the doorway. "I'm Dawn," she says. "I'm new."

"Jeez, what time is it?" He holds his head low, pinching the bridge of his nose as he makes his way to the bathroom. When he returns Dawn is administering pills to Paulie. She is textbook thorough, double-checking the names and numbers on the packets against the listings in the file binder. It will take all day at this rate. "I can do this," Johnson says.

"Oh," says Dawn, "I'll go and wake up the others, I guess." She puts her big handbag under the desk. "I'm kind of excited," she says. "It's my first full shift, groups and all."

"I'm Johnson. I'm not too excited yet, but I'll see what I can do." She tilts her head, puzzled, then a sudden smile.

"Next," calls Johnson. Joy steps up with a glass of orange juice in her hand. "What'll it be, mam, a Serzone Screwdriver?"

"Make it a double," she laughs.

"You shouldn't joke like that," Gordon says from the doorway. He laughs.

"It's all one big joke around here," Ruby standing behind him.

"I forget," Johnson says, "you people in recovery don't have any sense of —" he stops because he sees Ruby making a white knuckle fist. "I'm sorry," he says. "I forget."

The line is five long. Others drift into the kitchen and mill around the toaster, the microwave and the two refrigerators. Dawn returns. "Well everyone's up, except the guy in room six." She looks at a chalkboard on the wall, "Phil."

"Phil likes to sleep," Javier says. Javier has a habit of touching women in inappropriate ways. His hygiene is exceptionally poor, his pants are always falling and some of his fellow residents, particularly the women, find him repulsive. Now he leans from his position in the med line to examine Dawn's backside. Johnson's examination is more subtle. He watches and waits to see how Dawn will react. She squares up, faces Javier.

"Well, he'd better get up or he's going to get blackout," she says with stunning authority. *Yep*, Johnson thinks, *she'll fit in.*

Javier doesn't back down easily. "Phil's already on blackout," he says.

"Well then," Dawn looks at Johnson.

"Well then," Johnson says, "we'll have to bust a cap in his lazy ass."

Javier laughs and Dawn makes herself busy moving papers from one desk to another. She can't know what she's putting where or why, but the thump of the heavy stacks seems to satisfy some need.

"Look," Johnson says, "as soon as I finish with the meds I'll fill you in on the routine." His voice is soft, vaguely apologetic.

She pulls the orientation packet she'd been given by Braddock out of her handbag and holds it up. "I know all about the routine," she says.

Johnson and Dawn make the rounds, check the chores. Johnson gives a perfunctory glance and a thumbs up. He doesn't like this part of his role. He doesn't like to feel that he's treating adults like children.

Dawn is a stickler, but she lavishes praise on a job well-finished. She finds dust on a bureau, a scrap of paper on the carpet, a strand of hair on the toilet seat. She gives Gordon a hug for his spotless kitchen. The performance of the residents is a reflection on her, um, professionality. Johnson feels the acid rising again. Has he contributed to this? "Look," he offers, "maybe I kid around too much. I hope you didn't feel that I was undermining you."

"You weren't *undermining* me," Dawn says. "I know what I'm doing. I know what these people have been through." It's apparent she's been working herself up to this. "I've been there."

"Yeah," says Johnson. "I don't doubt you."

"They need structure and they need compassion."

"They need respect, too." Johnson says.

"They earn respect," Dawn says.

Johnson is rarely left speechless. Dawn is circling the halls, clipboard in hand and calling residents for Check-in.

Residents lumber in and lounge on the sofas in the dark living room. Everyone knows to avoid the soiled cushions and broken springs. Johnson sinks deep into the last seat available. In a moment of quiet he scans the faces in the room. Can it be that everyone looks like Johnny Cash? He blinks. He decides he didn't get enough sleep. Dawn wheels a chair out from the office. With her pen in the air she counts the number present. "We're missing one," she says.

"Phil," says Javier.

"Go ahead and do The Serenity Prayer without me." Johnson digs himself out. "I'll get Phil." He takes a brief detour out to the back porch for a couple of drags on an unfinished butt, then he taps on Phil's door. "Yo man, it's group."

No response.

Johnson inches open the door and sees Phil, shirtless, sitting on his bed. He is large, but not muscular. He looks as if he might have been very strong once, probably did the weights thing in prison. Now, with big fleshy shoulders hunched and belly folded over the top of his jeans, he resembles a sagging buffalo. He raises his eyes without lifting his big head.

"It's check-in time, Phil. A chance to let us know how you feel."

"I don't feel like it," Phil says.

"That's a start."

"I'm not like the rest of these assholes." He scratches his chest. One hand finds a gray t-shirt in his wrinkled bedspread. "Judge ordered me here."

"Yeah, I know. You're not the first."

"I'm just saying I don't buy this bullshit, somebody riding my ass every minute of the day."

Johnson nods sympathy. He sees that Phil is slowly complying and he wants to be careful not to tick the big man off. "There's a lot of bullshit," Johnson says, "but hell, look at your alternatives."

The shirt comes down over Phil's head. Slowly, stiffly he makes his way to the door, then with a ribald three-packs-of-filterless-a-day laugh he says, "I'd get drunk with you."

Phil falls into the seat Johnson had occupied. Johnson sits cross-legged on the floor. Aloud, Carl falters through a passage from the Big Book. Is it Step Two, or Three; the one about the Higher Power. Many in the room could recite the passage in their sleep, but all refrain because it is Carl's turn.

"I got a question." Phil says.

"Please wait," says Dawn. Carl drones on until Phil interrupts again.

"Who are you?"

"Wait," she says, she straightens in her chair, "Carl is not finished." Carl takes up the book again and struggles through another half-sentence.

"My question is," counter clock-wise, Phil meets every eye in the room, comes to rest on Johnson, "is this Higher Power higher than the cops?" Johnson grimaces, shakes his head.

Dawn says, "One more disruption from you and there will be consequences."

Javier perks up, "He's already on blackout. Whadya gonna do?"

"Double blackout," Paulie says cheerfully.

"I'm gonna kick some punk ass," Phil tries to rise out of his seat, but it's difficult and he's halted by Johnson's quiet pronouncement.

"You're out of line, Phil. Cool down." Johnson looks at Dawn and he's afraid what she might say and what consequences might follow. "Let's get onto the goals thing. I think we're running late anyway," he says. The screen door bangs, it must be Trish already. "Kick it off, Carl."

"I want to call my sponsor."

"Good," says Johnson. "Joy?"

"I want to call my sponsor, too."

"Ok, Angela?" says Dawn. She smiles enormous.

"I'm starting a diet today. I'm going to look irresistible in my new one-piece." Angela does a little shimmy with her shoulders, a grin for Francis.

"Very good, wonderful." Dawn slides forward on her seat. "How about you, Francis?"

"I'm going to have to take a cold shower," he says. Everyone laughs. Johnson breathes relief. "No," Francis adds, "I guess I'm going to think about getting in shape, too. Summer's here."

"Ruby? What's your goal today, Ruby?"

"Same as yesterday. I just want to hold it together."

"Good," Dawn says, "Dorsey?"

"I got an appointment with SSI. And I'm going to get myself a sponsor."

"Wonderful. Lou?"

Lou is new and still frightened of speaking in the group. His lower jaw moves but no words come. "Do you want us to come back to you, Lou?" Johnson asks.

"You must have some goal?" Dawn says, a tone that makes Johnson's teeth hurt. Phil sits back in his hole, closes his eyes.

After a very long pause, "Express myself," Lou manages.

"Good," says Dawn. "Very good. Kit?"

"I'm going shopping, some boots I saw in the newspaper."

"Marvelous. Javier?"

"Well," Javier leers at Francis, then Paulie, "I'm looking forward to getting to know, you know, the new staff." There's some snickering, an awkward pause.

"O-kay," Dawn says, her voice rising. "Gordon?"

"I have a lot of laundry to do."

"And how about you Phil?" All eyes turn to Phil, whose eyes are closed.

Trish pokes her head through the doorway from the office into the living room. “Morning everyone,” she says. She gives Dawn a warm smile. “Don’t let me interrupt.”

“Phil?” says Dawn.

“Nothing,” Phil growls.

Johnson stands, slaps his legs, “Well,” he says.

“You can do better than that,” Dawn says.

Phil thrusts his big head and shoulders forward, puts his elbows on his knees. He makes his eyes wide and glares at Dawn. “I want to get a twelve pack of Miller Genuine Draft, an eightball, and I want to find my fucking brother who stole my fucking Harley—”

“All right,” Trish says very loudly. She walks to the center of the room. “Phil you get blackout. Meeting is finished.”

The three staff take seats in the office for pass-on. Trish pulls the door shut. “He’s out of here,” she huffs. “I’ve had it with him.”

“He’s not at all interested in recovery,” Dawn says.

“You just met him,” Johnson says. “How can you know?”

“No Johnson, no. Dawn’s right. And you’re not helping.”

Five, six, seven years ago Johnson had strong convictions about helping people. He read all he could find on social group theory and he had a broad vision, change on many levels. Words like *advocacy* and *empowerment* used to stir something. *Recovery* was a complex and provocative idea in a society that promotes illness in so many ways. Johnson used to dream of creating a real treatment community with real self-esteem building through real work based upon real goals. Maybe Braddock had sold out or maybe he was the one that dared to be real, but Johnson simply soured and Trish *was* right—he wasn’t helping. Occasionally a resident here or there would serve to rekindle some of the old spirit. Ruby stirred feelings of tenderness, pity. Phil, this whole thing with Phil, has made Johnson angry.

“Look,” Johnson says, “he’s not out of here. That’s only two blackouts, right?”

“He’s out of here as soon as Ted says so,” Trish says.

“Well, maybe I’ll talk to Ted,” Johnson says. “I will.” But he has no intention of talking to Braddock. The two haven’t exchanged more than hello in months. In their last conversation Ted had advanced an opinion about the new Robert Cray album and when Johnson disagreed, the manager countered with a such a tone of authority. Not only was he the boss, but now the bastard thinks he knows more about blues. There was no way Johnson would willingly request Braddock’s support on a treatment issue.

“You can bet I’m going to talk to him, too,” Trish says.

“Me too,” Dawn says.

Some residents grab snacks, one makes a rush for the phone, several return to their rooms to finish dressing, and the others assume their relaxation posts. In fifteen minutes there will be exercise. Joy, Francis, Angela, Paulie and Javier surround the table on the porch, their smoke turning white in the dull white sky. Ruby paces on a thin brick walkway between the parking lot and a field of dandelion grass. Just beyond is a patio, next to it a vegetable garden which has yet to be turned. Phil sits and smokes on the patio. Johnson feels a rush of energy, a sudden breathlessness, warmth in his cheeks—it's an idea, a very big idea that keeps expanding. He returns to the office. He can hear Dawn speaking in a confidential voice, and if there could have been any doubt, the way she smiles when he enters makes it clear she was speaking about him. He doesn't care. "Excuse me," he says. "Trish, where're the keys for the shed?"

"I sure don't know. Why?"

"I'll tell you why."

"Tell me."

"Cause I want to turn the garden."

Trish picks up a heavy wad of metal from the desktop. She rolls it in her hand. "It's got to be one of these." She tosses.

Johnson shakes the keys, tambourine percussion. He's buzzing from his idea. "Listen," he says, "Let me run the House Relations Group. I'm going to get Phil to contribute."

"It's too late, Johnson. My mind's made up."

"Just wait and see." The two women look dully at Johnson. "He'll surprise you. I promise."

Trish shrugs, looks at Dawn. Johnson bounds through the kitchen out to the porch. He overhears Bruce speaking to Paulie, something about, "Let go, Let God," and something about, "recovery is hard work," and he thinks there might be a contradiction but he doesn't want to get sidetracked. "Morning Bruce." His idea is growing, growing, beyond words. "How you doing there, Ruby?" He fears it will slip away from him like this morning's dream. Nervously, he tries key after key in the shed's lock. It's as much about treatment as it is about art. It's about respect and it's about love. A key turns and in the dark moist of the shed, smell of rust and potting soil, he finds a spade. "It's about Phil's recovery and my own," he whispers to himself.

Johnson chooses a corner of earth ten feet from where Phil sits hunched, puffing smoke, and he sinks his shovel head three quarters into the gravelly dirt. "Miller Genuine Draft," he grunts, "for me it's always been an icy Bud." Phil looks up. "Especially after a hard day's work."

"Bud tastes like water," Phil says. He laughs, "Not like I'd turn one down right now."

"To each his own," says Johnson. He turns the shovel and chops. "My old lady," he says—he'd never referred to his fiancee this way—"used to keep a garden. I used to bust my ass out there in the sun, for her, you know, because she loved it."

"Got another one of them rollies?" Phil says. "I'm out of smokes." Johnson tosses his pouch.

"You can roll 'em, can't you?"

"Shit yeah. You learn something in the joint."

"Yeah, well," Johnson says, "at least you learned something."

"I learned plenty, believe me."

"Yeah?"

Here comes Dawn, again with the clipboard. "Come on you guys, it's exercise time," she calls.

"You want to do knee bends?" Johnson whispers to Phil.

"Fuck no."

Johnson quickly grabs a metal rake from the shed. "Phil's going to help me," he says.

"I'm not sure," Dawn holds the clipboard in two hands at her waist. "I guess that'd be ok." She waddles back into the house.

"So what else did you learn in prison?"

"Give me that shovel," Phil says. He puts his cigarette on the edge of an aluminum pie plate ashtray. With a Harley starting kick he sinks the spade deep in the dirt. "You can't bend over the way you're doing it, unless you want to ruin your back." Johnson watches. "And if you think about it, you're better off hosing the ground before you start turning your dirt. Not too much though, cause you don't want clumps." Johnson nods.

"I'll get the hose." Johnson sprays while Phil digs. With every turn of the shovel, Phil proffers a piece of wisdom about proper care of the soil and efficient methods of weeding, but he surprises Johnson when he says, "So what happened with you and your, um, girlfriend?"

"I blew it," Johnson says. Now he surprises himself. "I was too fucking selfish."

Phil flashes a look of recognition, suspicion. He lets the shovel fall in the dirt. He returns to his seat and his smoke. "Selfish is the only way to be," he says. "Any other way is stupid."

Ted Braddock rolls into the lot, shiny blue Camry. This is not what Johnson wanted, not at all. The windshield glares. There is an authoritative crunch from the emergency break. Braddock shifts his white lunch bag from left hand to right so he can look at his watch. "Morning fellas," he's up onto the porch, "Time for exercise, isn't it Phil?" and into the house. Johnson suddenly feels very tired. He'll find a way to pass the remaining hours of work because he always does, but it will be dreadful.

"I've got to take a leak," he says. He leaves Phil puffing on the patio.

The regular staff gather in the office, talk of car payments and hottubs and Dawn's got an endless story about her veterinarian, her laughter loud enough to match Braddock's. Johnson is outside paging through the sports section. He's trying to tune out the banter, mostly Paulie defending his manhood. "I don't care where he's been or how big he is, if he comes near me I'm gonna kick his ass." And Joy, peacemaker, "Maybe you'll get a room switch as soon as someone moves out." And savvy Javier, "Phil'll be the one to go. They ain't gonna put up with that."

Johnson imagines several things to say to Paulie, how the kid might reexamine his response, how it seems to fit a pattern. He might get the kid to think and speak realistically about what he'll do with his anger, and what his anger will do to him. This is a therapeutic opportunity, Johnson remembers, but what he feels most of all is sleepy. *God grant me the wisdom...* he thinks, because nothing I say or do is going to make a damn bit of difference.

Dawn calls, "Group." She looks at the clipboard in her hand. "Step Study." She tells Johnson that Trish is going to let her run this one, that he can sit in if he likes. "No," he says, "I'd prefer not to." And thus goes the late morning and early afternoon: Johnson turns over some dirt until he's bored with it; he makes himself a bologna sandwich on white bread; he rolls and smokes seven cigarettes; he completes the *New York Times* and the *Press Democrat* crosswords; he plays horseshoes with Carl; he avoids Ted at all turns, except when he must go to the office to take charts out of the cabinet. Ted surprises Johnson with an enthusiastic, "How you doing, Mike?' And Johnson mumbles back, "How you doing?"

"Have you heard the latest John Lee Hooker? Takes me back." Braddock is working his plastic fork through a pile of chick-peas.

"No," says Johnson. "Not yet." He carries the heavy binders to the picnic table where he can leisurely scribble what he's observed.

It is nearly three o'clock when again Dawn calls "Group!" from the screen door. "Look lively!" The residents trudge in. Johnson holds the door and follows Phil, the last. "Look lively!" Phil says. Trish is already in the living room. "Go ahead, it's your show," she says to Johnson.

"What?" he says. "Forget it," he says. "Let Dawn do it."

"It's yours. You asked for it," Trish says, "but wait just a minute because Ted wants to sit in."

It's a full house, minus Bruce who files paper and takes calls in the office. Johnson takes the tall chair on wheels, Trish beside him. Though it's meant to be a circle, he feels very much in the center. Phil sits deep in the sofa, a tight squeeze between Ruby and Joy. He puts his head in his hands, eyes down.

"Welcome to House Relations," Johnson says. It is indisputably the most unpleasant of the groups, worse even than Addictions Awareness. It's a bickering session about dirty dishes left in the sinks and refrigerators. Nothing ever improves as a result. "If it's okay with the higher powers," Johnson nods in the direction of Braddock seated on a folding chair by the office door, "I'd like to abandon the usual format. Rather than go around the circle and have everyone say what gets his goat, let's do it like a conversation. Someone starts and others join in when they have something to say."

"That's all right with me," Braddock shrugs, "so long as everyone says something."

"I like it this way better," Javier says.

"Good, now who's got what?" Johnson looks at the sliver of light cutting through the blinds across Paulie's neck and face. After a long silence Braddock looks up at the clock on the wall behind Johnson.

"I don't like people touching me when I don't want to be touched," Ruby says very quietly. She's hugging her thin arms around her knees in front of her chest.

"Neither do I," Angela says.

"Sometimes I like a hug," Joy looks thoughtful, "but I don't like people coming up from behind and putting their hands on me. It gives me the creeps."

"I don't do hugs," Phil says.

"Let's back up," Johnson faces Ruby. "Do you want to say who's touching you, or would you rather not say?"

"He knows who he is."

"Anyone else?" He looks at Angela, then Joy. It's a moot point because most heads have turned to Javier.

"Javier, is there anything you want to say?" Johnson's voice is soft, unaccusing.

"I don't mean anything by it. Where I come from people touch people all the time. It's just being friendly." There is another moment of quiet while the room considers this.

"It doesn't seem that it's being taken as a sign of friendship," Johnson says.

"It's not that bad," Joy says, so long as he doesn't come up from behind."

"You might sometimes accept an embrace from Javier? If you can see it coming, that is."

"Sure," Joy says. "Javier is my friend. But I also know what Ruby is talking about."

Ruby puts her feet on the floor and her hands in her lap. A tear runs from her eye. "I get lonely, too," she says. She's present and she's long ago. Now she twists her hair around two fingers. "Maybe I know how you feel, Javier. I'm just not ready to be touched. I had too much of that, you know, when I didn't want it." Her eyes flash to the carpet and rise slowly back up to Javier.

"I hear you," Javier says, and he does and everyone knows it because you can't not hear Ruby on the occasions when she opens up. What could possibly come next? Johnson is stunned.

"Thank you," Johnson says. "Do we want to go deeper with this, or do we want to move on?"

"I said I don't do hugs," Phil says, still with head in hands and eyes ground in the carpet.

"I see," Johnson says. What he sees is a trap. A work of sabotage. He sees Phil in one of a million angry moments vindicating Trish's distrust, Dawn's superiority and Braddock's self-serving perpetuation of the status quo. He feels like a fool, but he must proceed. "And has that been a problem for you here? Hugs?"

"No," Phil says.

"Well then, the floor is open."

"I used to hug," Phil says. He lifts his big buffalo head until his eyes find Johnson, "I remember a time when I cared about things like gardens." Very tentatively his gaze turns the circle until it settles on Paulie, "and staying sober, though it was always fucking hard. I used to think that everything mattered, especially keeping my bike tuned and keeping my friends. I used to have friends."

Again Johnson is stunned. Paulie breaks the silence. "What happened?"

"I don't talk about that," Phil says. "Not yet, kid."

"Some day, maybe," Johnson suggests.

"Yeah, maybe."

"I get angry," Javier says, "when I feel like something's been taken away from me. Something that was mine."

"Like what?" Ruby asks.

"Like my family in Mexico," he says. "They can't come here. And if I go there, I can't get the money to pay for the medicine I need."

"I don't think I've ever seen you angry, Javier. You must have some way of expressing it," says Johnson.

The room considers. Trish taps Johnson's elbow and whispers in his ear, "I think we're getting away from House Relations."

"It's my show," Johnson whispers back.

And Phil says, "I get you," to Javier, "about something being taken away. There's always some bastards—"

Ruby cuts in, "Stolen."

And Johnson says, "Forfeited." He doesn't mean to look at Ted Braddock when he asks, "Can you ever get *it* back?"

Kit and Angela try to speak at the same time and after embarrassed laughter they both persist. Braddock pulls his chair into the circle to listen closely, perhaps to speak, but he'll have to wait his turn because it's Johnson's show, Johnson back-up singer, Johnson song writer, Johnson blues man, he's never heard the notes so precisely, and on it goes, his show, without a single reference to dirty dishes in sinks or refrigerators, just one sweet, sad, honest riff laid down upon another and another. Johnson's long shift is almost finished, and yet it seems he's just started.

# Clack, Clack, Clack

## Bernadette Murphy

I knit. Let's just get that little confession out of the way right now. I got injured on the job and then followed doctor's orders. That's all. I didn't expect it to turn out this way, but then, who ever does? I'm a plumber by trade and frankly, sick of the jokes—butt-crack routines, roto-rooter gags. After thirty some-odd years, I've heard them all. People make fun of us, our hands in the sewer and heads in the toilet, but face it, you'd be lost without us.

So there I am, stuck in the crawlspace under Mrs. McLaughlin's weather-beaten Cape Cod place, working with these corroded three-quarter-inch galvanized pipes that burst during that last big freeze. I'm cold and rushed and not in any great shape, but I'm damn well going to do it right. Another ten minutes and it'll be done, it's the last call for the day, and I can go home and take a hot shower, change into something clean and warm, get away from the shaggy smell of mildew. There's just this tiny elbow joint I need to replace. It won't budge.

The day's been about two hours and one job too long. I curse the piece of metal for making my life miserable, blame my headache on the god-forsaken coldness and wonder how I got into this profession in the first place. I'd kill for a Thermos of hot coffee, a shot of Jack Daniel's, even the heater in the Bronco and the way it blasts against my work boots. The cold seeps through my jeans, inching its way over my chest through the gap between my belt and undershirt. The damp tickles my belly so that even with my down-lined flannel shirt, I'm achy and annoyed.

I warm the joint with my hands, rubbing the metal for a full three minutes, the friction making my palms itch and my forearms tired. It doesn't work. I consider going out to the truck for the torch, but can't be bothered. I use a towel, blowing into the baby bunting I've made for the joint, trying to warm it with my body heat. Come on. Here you go. Come on.

It won't give.

I have the wrench hooked on at a right angle and my entire body weight pressing against it, and still, two-hundred-sixty pounds of me isn't enough to move it. Nothing. It's not going. I take a swipe at the joint with the pipe wrench, and snap! there goes the wrist. It flops, like a dead fish, broken clean in two.

You'd think it would be pretty straightforward, wouldn't you? An x-ray, a few weeks in a cast, some time to catch up on re-runs of Sister Wendy's Renaissance Art. Yes, I have disability insurance, but it wasn't that simple. One cast, another, and then surgery. Week after week dragging on. Then months. Annie's bugging me to get back to it; she's tired of having me underfoot. The kids call to ask how I'm doing; they want me to say everything's back to normal, but nothing feels like it's back to normal. It isn't *my* fault. I'd gladly start plumbing again if my wrist would do its job.

Wandering around the house, I pick up a book or a magazine and try to read, but can't seem to sit still. Without my hands, busy at work, I'm useless. I miss the way my fingers knew what they were doing and got to it, independent of my mind. When my hands are working well, it's like I'm a lone onlooker watching an expert magician performs his show. *And now, ladies and gentlemen, fingers will execute a feat of terrifying complexity with a U-joint, plumbing tape and two washers...* Without that daily magic, I'm lost. Exhausted all the time, thinking too much. I have to keep reminding myself: rehashing old decisions doesn't change anything, just tires me out with this hamster cage of a brain. I need work.

Finally, two surgeries and a slew of casts later, the arm's free, but I can barely move it. Can't hold a pen too well, never mind a drain snake. The doctor sends me to physical therapy to exercise my small motor skills. And that's where they get me.

The physical therapist says that the exercises she'll show me will help, but that there's one thing that'll get me back to work in no time. The knitting. It strengthens the tiny muscles in the hands and wrists I need to do my job. Of course I'm embarrassed at first. What, me: a knitter? But it's doctor's orders, and so I get Annie to work with me.

She sits me down on the tired beige couch and hands me a hank of wool —grey, like it's just come off the sheep, and meaty. Her leftovers. The pair of needles she's dug out are wooden and oversized, like a kid's set of beginner crayons, easy to grasp. They look ungainly compared to her slender silver needles, but feel solid in my grip. With her freckled hands on top of mine, she helps me cast on the ten bulky knots I need to get started. Once they're in place, she resumes her own knitting, delicate and peach-colored. I'm to follow her dainty motions with my thick fingers, thick wool, thick needles. Everything in the room, from the coffee table's scattered collection of *Time* magazine to the antimacassar-draped television—even Helen the parrot—is watching.

"Keep the yarn in your right hand and let the left hand just guide you." Annie demonstrates with sharp, cold movements that remind me of the knife-edge crease in my army trousers—*what was I thinking when I joined up?*— progressing so quickly I can't tell what she's done. When she pulls the stitch off the needle, she looks pleased to see the end of it, as if she's shown the wool who's boss. I try to mimic her and get tangled.

"No, you're splitting the stitch. Can't you see!" A strand of wiry hair escapes her tentacle braid. I undo what I've done and try again. Poor Annie.

She's got that resigned look, like she's having to teach four-year-olds how to read Greek, putting a smile on a completely impossible task. It's the same way she smiled at me when I bought her this house. Sure, it wasn't exactly what she'd wanted, but it was solid investment, something to be proud of. She never saw it that way.

"Wind the yarn around the needle clockwise. Knit the stitch as it presents itself." Her hands perform a triple backflip with a twist from within the gauzy skein burrowed in her lap. "Then slip the new stitch off that needle. Just like that."

I imitate her movement, trying to get the flow of it; it's not wholly unlike learning to tie your shoes. I imagine Mrs. Farmer, my kindergarten teacher, standing next to Annie, watching my stubby fingers fumble with the laces. My palms sweat, trying to get it right. After a few botched attempts, miraculously, a loop of yarn slips off the needle cleanly.

"That's it. You made a stitch! Now do another." Annie stops her work to hover, her breath whistling in my ear as I slide my needle into the next stitch. "There you go," she says. "Clockwise… don't let your hand come off the needle… around and off… "

I'm getting the hang of it. I do a few more. And then a whole row.

"You won't tell anyone about this, will you?" I ask.

"Next stitch, keep the needle to the back." Annie's fingers hammer through her yarn, executing crisp, rigid moves.

"The guys at The Nest, the kids…?" Clumsily, I mirror her and then stop for a moment. "It's physical therapy. You wouldn't want me blabbing about your bladder infections?"

"Don't worry, hon." Her eyes are intent on her work, strangling peach cobwebs. "I wouldn't embarrass you like that." She looks over to see how I'm getting on. "Watch what you're doing there, your stitches are bunching up," she corrects.

A week later, I'm starting to fly. I'm not as fast or smooth as Annie, but I'm moving well. I relax in my easy chair, feeling the needles as an extension of my fingers. My hands let loose and my mind darts along, skimming over thoughts, playing tag with itself. My shoulders ease up, the belt on my jeans gives way, I feel breath filling my lungs.

Most nights, we sit in the living room, Annie on the couch, me in the easy chair, my bottle of Guinness an arm's reach away. As much as I thought Annie liked knitting, she seems to prefer crossword puzzles from the newspaper. Often, I end up knitting alone.

My wrist is getting stronger and finally, my needlework looks presentable. I can make uniform stitches, smooth edges. A few weeks later, I can even do a respectable cable. So I keep at it, first a scarf for those winter nights when I get called to check on someone's malfunctioning water heater and they're all inside nice and warm and I'm stuck in the freezing parts of the house. I use a navy Shetland and alternate the rows with the sheep-grey wool Annie first gave me. The scarf looks damn sharp when I'm done and matches my favorite sweatshirt. Then I make one of those Irish fishing sweaters in a bulky oatmeal wool. Raglan sleeves, wide neck. It's warm and fits better than anything Annie's ever made.

By now, the wrist is feeling great, full range of motion, lots of strength. The physical therapist and the doctor, too, say I don't need to knit any longer. My knitting has knit my bones back together and I'm off the hook.

"I'll finish the green cardigan you were working on, so as not to waste the wool," Annie offers when I tell her the good news. "Be sure to put all my needles back in their cases. I hate when they get mixed up."

I put the extra needles back, but place the green cardigan-in-progress next to my easy chair for when I come home from work.

My first day back on the job goes well, the wrist is a bit awkward, especially in the cold. A few hours into the day, though, the joint seems to remember how it used to work and kicks in, cleaning out drains, inserting washers, using the snake. All day long, as my hands work themselves among the pipes, my head is filled with ideas for sweaters. I imagine intricate Fair Isles with variegated color schemes in olive green, deep plum and charcoal. Traditional Arans, knit with thick, lanolin-rich unbleached wool, shaped generously through the shoulders and chest. And this one ski sweater, a mind-boggling Norwegian so layered with color and stitch complexity that figuring it out is like putting together a jigsaw puzzle the size of a baseball diamond.

Not that I've ever gone skiing.

Overall, it's a good day. Until I come home. Annie has dinner on the table and my cardigan on her needles.

Today I'm working at the Kazen's house, the big fancy place near the apple orchard, installing a reverse-osmosis drinking-water filter, along with a replacement water softening system. The installation isn't going off well, pipe threads aren't matching up, parts are missing, it's a fiasco. I jerryrig the configurations to make it work. It's like changing a v-neck into a crew. No big deal. A few extra stitches here, decrease a little there. Finally, I adjust the water softening system and go into the Kazen's house to present the bill. It's good to be inside, out of the drafty garage, away from the finger-numbing pipes.

"So why charge me for labor on the softening system when it was *you* that installed the last one and it didn't work?" Dr. Kazen's voice is accusing and gruff. He always tries to argue his way out of my invoices, even though he agrees to the amount up-front. "And it says here three hours of labor," he continues, "and you couldn't have been at it more than two and a half."

Normally, I'd have had it. I charged him less than I should have because I knew he'd argue about the softening system. I warned him last year that if he bought the off-brand system he wanted, I'd install it, but no guarantees. And here he is, still at it. Last time he did this, I fought back, raising my voice, wrangling him into paying at least 70 percent of what we'd agreed on, then stomping down the driveway with "cheap bastard" under my breath, kicking his privet hedge along the way. I'd told Annie I'd never work for him again and I meant it. Until he called last week, offering to pay cash, off-the-books. Annie wouldn't have to know, and I could use the money to order the custom-dyed merino I'd been eyeing.

"O.K, then." I shrug at Dr. Kazen. "What do you think would be a fair amount?" My voice is softer than normal. "I comp'd you the filters, I paid the shipping for the special pipes. Why don't you tell me what you're willing to pay."

My approach throws him, though to be honest, it isn't a premeditated tactic. I just don't want to do this any longer. Give me my money and let me go home. My knitting's waiting and I want to be warm again. He looks at me like he doesn't know who I am, but doesn't argue back, just pulls out a wallet and counts out twenties, paying me 90 percent of the invoice.

The heater in the Bronco hits its stride after a few miles. My fingers thaw out, stinging at first and then turning pink and limber. I tap the steering wheel along with the opening music to NPR's All Things Considered. Just a few more hours...

I wait until Annie watches the late news in bed and falls asleep with my cardigan, at-rest now, in her lap. It's been weeks and she's still on the right shoulder. She's making the sleeves too narrow and the arms too long. I can tell from here but I'm not going to say anything. Her reading glasses tilt sloppily at the end of her nose. Turning off the bedside light, I lean to kiss her onionskin cheek and then change my mind.

She's been asking about my moods lately, the way I seem distracted. I can't explain what's wrong except to wonder about all the years I've gone to work, doing jobs that I never wanted in the first place to give her this life, to be a good husband. When I was in college and she got pregnant with James, I didn't complain. Just quit school, said goodbye to my high-school love Grace, joined the army, got a steady paycheck. Annie set-up housekeeping near her sister Michelle's place, here in Littlerock just off Highway 138. You know that painting by David Hockney of Highway 138—the road to Vegas? Go left about two miles and you'll find my home.

Tonight, like every night now, I sneak downstairs. It's cold this late, the smell of pork chops and jacket potatoes linger in the rooms, emptied of heat as the night has progressed. I can almost hear the sounds of the kids still clomping across the hardwood floors. I squirrel my knitting bag from behind the microwave cart and take my place in the easy chair, wondering why no one ever asked what *I* wanted.

It wasn't much, really. To study architecture. Be the one to draw the plumbing fixtures onto the blueprints, not install the things. Maybe live close enough to LA to go to a museum once in a while. Here, the California Poppy Reserve, which is just a windblown swath of chaparral and sage that blooms for maybe three weeks out of the year, is the closest thing we have to a cultural establishment.

"Once the baby's born, we'll figure a way," Annie'd said. "With the GI Bill, it shouldn't be hard."

"We'll have to move back to the city," I reminded her. "Rents'll be higher and there'll be books and tuition…"

"We'll manage."

I was half-done with my tour when James was born; my life would soon resume.

And then she was pregnant again. We'd never discussed it, but I assumed she knew that more children meant—well, never mind what it meant. We had a brother and then a sister for James. Annie wanted proper furniture and a house, here, of all places, here, where she had friends and her sister and I had—shit—I had the plumbing business that I started to buy her the house in the first place.

Now, all I have are these nights, this quiet I wrap myself in, holding on for all I'm worth. It's the only time my jaw relaxes. I want to stay here, now, in this very moment when everything's shaded golden and the night is holding its breath with a kind of silent resignation and there isn't a sound except the clack, clack, clack of my wooden needles sliding through the strong, nearly unbreakable wool. In this dusky quarter-light, my hands weaving effortlessly, I remember the man I used to be. Before Annie. Before the army, the kids, the house, the plumbing. I hardly recognize the person I see. He's unbearably young, startled by my investigation like I've caught him red-handed with life.

The wool I'm using was ordered from a yarn-by-mail catalog, delivered to my new P.O. box. It's an Icelandic worsted: Prussian Blue, Tibetan Gold and Indian Garnet. The color names roll around in my mouth, foreign places I'll only touch this way. Sometimes, when I hold the hanks and concentrate, I can almost feel the heat of the sheep they came from. If there's such a thing as free-range sheep, I hope this wool is from them.

Tonight, I'm working on a lap throw that'll keep me warm on these nights when I'd rather knit then sleep. I keep my patterns, the extra knitting supplies and sketches for future projects out in the garage workshop, tucked behind the tablesaw. Not that I want to keep secrets from Annie. It's just…

This is mine.

For once, I have something that's mine.

I dream infinite designs, picturing every type of sweater I could possibly create, each made to fit a different person than the one I've become. These imagined sweaters line up in my mind as shadowy brothers—endless versions of the me I might have been—surrounding my needles as I work. One by one, I'll make them all. I knit and purl, cast on, cast off. I could keep going all night long, and very well might.

It may be late, too late to matter, but I can't stop. I have to knit one more row, and then another. One for the architect I'll never be. One for the young man who still aches for Grace even as Annie sleeps next to him. One for the plumber who should have demanded college. One for the Littlerock homeowner who wishes he'd hit Highway 138 years ago. One for the good husband who can't get warm. One for this old guy who finally, finally, has a sweater that fits. Another. And another. And another. I have to keep at it. If I stop, I'm afraid I might unravel.

# The Habit of Despair

## Gary Eller

The M.P.s were clean and quick and they had their papers right. The fine southern accents, carried for the fragments of communication required in the course of their work, must have added a sting to Vernal's outlook. They came through the green and white storm door of the double-wide with its plywood add-on, and there in front of those pee-smelling and puffy-faced kids, announced that he, Private Vernal Gene Frew, also known as Vernal Eugene Olson, was under arrest for desertion from the United States Army.

Vernal lay flat on the couch by the wall where he'd tacked his seal skin, and across the room from the new TV he'd bought with the bonus money I gave him. He was strained from finger-wording his way through the Coho story in *Field and Stream*, but to accommodate the M.P.s he raised his arms while they put cuffs on his wrists, and lifted his feet while they slipped irons around his ankles. Then they stood him up, and one on each side, walked him out to the car, commandeered from the island police department just for the occasion.

I knew Vernal well enough. I gave him a job after my friend Sid gave me a job running the hardware. I guess since Sid was acquainted with me from the old days he expected that I'd be drunk half the time and less able to think up ways to steal from him like his other managers had. He was partly right.

Sid insisted his life was headed for grander purposes than stove bolts and hollow point shells, and he wanted time to concentrate on finding those purposes. The store was the only hardware on the island. The first thing I did was figure out what items we sold that we had monopolies on, then I had the clerks mark them all up twenty percent. Sid thought I was a genius.

I'd been there maybe four weeks and was still swollen with authority and good feelings when I met Vernal Frew. I was in the back when he came in. I watched him as he approached, walking straight-spined the way a shorter person will, but halting and careful, like he expected someone might leap out from the Thermos display and give him a good scare.

"Y'all har-rin?" he asked.

Vernal had a bad eye—it wandered, curious and solitary—making it harder to pay attention enough to understand him. "What's that?" I said.

"Help," he said. "Y'all need help? Um lookin' for work."

By then the commotion of his wife and kids caught up to him. There were four children, all with black mop-head hair, though only one or two were Vernal's. The baby, lighter-skinned than the others, was in its mother's arms. Vernal introduced them all, including the baby, playing a finger under its fat chin. But I only caught his wife's name, Wanda. She was an Eskimo from St. Lawrence Island, and had the straight black hair and perfect skin common to Indians and Eskimos. She lowered her chin and smiled toward the floor when Vernal pronounced her name.

As it turned out my sporting goods man had just given his notice. I asked Vernal if he knew anything about guns.

"Bin farn 'em all my life," he said.

I took a hunch, figuring he was pressed hard for a job, and I hired him cheap. It was a good choice. Vernal moved a lot of merchandise for us. Eskimos in from the villages liked him, and trusted him. They called him Bernal.

"Where's Bernal?" they'd ask, leaning over the handgun case, palms flat on the glass. Vernal would hear them and come out of the back room, happy to get away from the puzzle of invoices and stock cards.

"If it ain't Joe Tommy," he'd say. "Didn't know y'all was in town. Did you get you a moose? I heard tell the salmon are runnin' in Shishmaref."

They knew Vernal had married an Eskimo, and even if she wasn't highly thought of, they realized that marriage and his lack of book learning would hold him to the country. They liked that he said he was from Tea Hook, West Virginia, because it sounded so far away and because the place seemed like it might have something to do with the Civil War. He'd also gathered some local fame from a time he'd been a hero when his seal hunting party became stranded. But mostly they liked the benefit of his expertise with guns and the easy way he handled them.

"Now that would make you a quality piece," Vernal would say if he noticed a customer eyeing a particular hunting rifle, such as an average-priced Mossberg. "But first let me show you this here one, just in case you had in mind to go after seal." Then he'd reach for a Wetherby or even a Sako, knowing full well that seal was exactly what the customer had in mind.

Vernal would never hand the gun over directly. Instead he'd hold it just out of reach, delicately, sighting down the barrel, polishing the stock with his handkerchief, all the time talking up the virtues of that rifle—its accuracy, its range, its power. Only when his customer was primed would Vernal place the gun in the person's hands, holding it so it had to be received just above the trigger guard where the balance felt best.

Things worked. Sales went up, Sid stayed away. I felt enough in control that I started spending late afternoons at the Board of Trade bar. I noticed Wanda come in now and then with two or three girl friends. They'd take a table near the juke box and listen to Ferlin Huskey tunes. They talked a little, danced gently, smoked Kool cigarettes from one another's packs, and in an hour sipped maybe a third of a beer each. It was all harmless. They dropped their kids off at one of their many relatives just to be with other adults in an adult world for a while. It was less than the equivalent of a tea party in other places.

I might smile and wave to Wanda, keeping it proper and polite. She was Eskimo, I was white, and her husband was hired help. But one afternoon I was a little juiced, and though I knew it was off base, I asked her to dance. She looked at me like I'd called her a name.

"Me? I can't," she said. And she stared at the floor while I stood there with one arm stuck out, feeling foolish.

I should have let it go then, but there's always that mystery between men and women. It doesn't have to do with race or age or married, or rich or poor. They don't have to speak the same language. It doesn't even have to do with lust. There is a curiosity involved, and it includes both people, and the tiniest thing—just a glance is all—gets it going. And like many a habit, once the thing starts, it carries itself.

Not that there was any denying my interest. I caught the air of something in Wanda—a pleasurable spirit and smokey attractiveness. Her friends had the appearance of Eskimos, short and middle-thickened, like they were getting ready for winter. But Wanda was pinch-waisted and light. In her blue jeans she looked fit and ready, like a Montana cowgirl at a rodeo. And she had a way of tossing that tress of dark hair back over her shoulder as if it were a handful of troubles.

My luck started slipping when Sid got into one of his spells of interest in the store and found my microwave order—a mistake, I admit, since most of the outlying villages didn't yet have electricity. A couple days later the mail included a memo Sid sent from home, advising that purchase orders for high ticket appliances must hereafter be authorized by him. He signed his full name to the memo, middle initial included.

Vernal lived with Wanda and all those kids in a double-wide back of the gravel pit. I could see the place from the airport road. A propane tank leaned against the far end, its copper line coiling in through the corner of a window. Strips of loose plastic flapped in the wind against the plywood add-on. Vernal was drawing a hundred and forty a week before deductions. They were probably getting food stamps, and with Wanda being Eskimo they likely qualified for a little aid of this and that kind. Getting by, if you can call it that.

I let Gertie in the office know to bump Vernal up ten bucks a week, and when Sid learned of that I got another memo in the mail. When it came I made a draw slip for a hundred dollars which I covered by under-ringing the Evinrud that Jack Kanalak paid me cash for. I tucked the hundred in Vernal's shirt pocket behind his pack of Lucky Strikes. Tears came to the man's eyes. He took my hand in both of his. "I'm mighty grateful," he said.

By then I knew that I wasn't about to be retired from Sid's hardware with a pension and a party, so I figured I better help myself to some moving money. The department with the highest volume was sporting goods, and the department head with the least amount of business sense was Vernal. A good combination. I started to skim from his register, ten or twenty at a time, just to see what would happen. I figured to up it to a hundred a day come hunting season.

After a few days—time enough for word of my generosity to pass from Vernal to his wife—I spotted Wanda at the Board of Trade and sent a round of Old Style to her table. I waited a few minutes before I walked over.

"Wanda, that's a pretty sweater you got on," I said. "New, ain't it?" I reached for her elbow. "Feel a little more like dancing today?"

I've never liked dancing. But when I pulled Wanda against my chest and tucked her arm under my own to begin the slow two-step, which was all I knew, I felt some of what people must dance for. I shuffled to the left, one step, then another, then a step back. Wanda followed. This was a woman who'd given birth four times in not many more years, but she was as light as a broom. She danced with me, stepping with me, giving me my way across and back the little wooden dance floor, while through the window the thin northern sun trickled in to mix with the stink of the beer and the smoke.

I found myself wondering about those four kids and their fathers, how many fathers were involved, and how many times it took to conceive the babies, and if they'd been goals of lovemaking or just some kind of accident. Wanda didn't talk. She would never let me know what she was thinking—love or hate. That was her way of defending herself, but I was working against it, drawing that resistance out of her and plugging it with curiosity. The song ended and Wanda stopped moving. I held on to her.

"Can I come see you sometime?" I said. She looked at the floor. I think she saw me in a new arrangement, like the way you might look at a relative that's just come into money—or maybe it was that big TV that I knew Vernal had put the hundred bucks down on.

"When?"

"Oh, on a nice afternoon, maybe when the kids are down for their naps. And when everything's good and slow."

She moved her foot back and forth on the floor as if to grind out a cigarette. Then she gave the toe of my boot a little tap, then another. "Vernal, he likes you," she said.

"Vernal's a good man."

"He's glad you hired him on. Working at the hardware."

"Can I come see you tomorrow then?"

"No, not tomorrow," she said, and she walked away.

I waited several days. The barge shipment came in on a Thursday. I marked the invoices with my grease pencil and set Vernal and the high school kids to shelving and pricing it all. Then I washed my hands real good and picked up a couple packs of Kools.

I left the Blazer parked out on the road, though anyone that came along could spot it and make the connection if they had the bent to look for those things. The four-year old, sleepy looking in a raggedy Seattle Mariners T-shirt answered my knock. I smiled. Wanda appeared behind him.

"Charlie, get back to bed," she said. I stepped inside. As Wanda herded Charlie to the back room I took my coat off. The TV already had a purple gob of jam or jelly smeared along one corner of the screen. The arm to a doll and a couple of fishing magazines were on the floor. Tacked to the wall over the couch was what I figured to be a trophy-size seal skin, all stiff-haired and mottled.

Wanda came down the hall, tossing her hair over her shoulder. She stopped at the corner where the hallway turns to the kitchen, listening for the kids' voices and the thumps they made jumping from the bed to the floor. Finally there was silence.

When I kissed her, her mouth was wide and ready. I put a hand on her breast and worked it until my fingers felt the nipple respond through the fabric of her blouse. I undressed her from the top down. In the manner of a first-time lover she seemed not to know if I wanted her to help. I twisted her bra off and she was naked and beautiful. I pulled her to the floor, not wanting to move from that corner and put the good mood at risk. Only when I was in her, braced for leverage against Vernal's new jam-stained TV, did Wanda break out of her shyness enough to make a sound.

The next time I came by we made love in front of the baby. The kid giggled and cooed, and so did the mother. All of it served to excite me and by the time we finished we'd writhed and slithered from one corner of that dirty rug to the other. After we lit up our Kools I asked Wanda about the seal skin.

Vernal had shot it, she said. He was real proud because he got it at the end of a hunting trip he'd taken with Wanda's two brothers and her father. They were in the long boat, had engine trouble, and drifted away from shore. They made a landing after two days, but it was foggy and they dared not move. They ran out of food the second day ashore, and were down to four rounds of ammunition. The three Eskimos had a conference and decided that Vernal should be the one to take the gun with the four bullets and look for game. It was an honor on top of the great responsibility, and it was with one of those bullets that he got the seal.

We'd been lying on the floor, and I heard a stirring from the back bedroom. One of the older kids was waking up.

"That's a thing to take pride in," I said. "Where'd he learn to shoot so good?"

"In the army, I guess." Wanda's hands were behind her back as she concentrated on fastening her bra.

"I didn't know he was in the army," I said. I'd been in the service myself, and I was sure I'd have noticed if Vernal had listed it on his application.

"Could be I'm wrong and it was somewhere else," Wanda said. "Men don't tell me all that's on their mind."

I pulled Vernal's application. There was a space with several lines for military service in which Vernal had written in little slanted letters a single word: none.

That afternoon I pinned Wanda between my hips and the kitchen floor of the double-wide, and she wrapped her dark legs around me while the baby spit and squawked in the high chair three feet away. Then she told me about Vernal. He'd even changed his last name. He carried hope they'd never find him so far from West Virginia. It had been several years now, and he was just beginning to think that maybe they didn't care anymore, and that it might be forgotten after all. He'd never done much wrong except walk away. He even left his dress boots behind, in place beneath his cot and all spit-polished for inspection.

Wanda begged me not to let on to Vernal that I knew. "Don't worry," I said. "If you can't bank on me you're in real trouble." And I kissed her on the lips.

Three days later she told me not to come back for a while.

"You feel guilty?" I asked.

She laughed. "You whites, you're so stupid. This with you and me is nothing. The Eskimo way, the old ways, they got no—what do you call it—monogamy. That's your idea."

"Then why?"

"You can't see it." And she looked away, as always, avoiding my face. "I like dancing. You'll never take me where we could dance."

"Sure I will," I said.

Wanda put a fresh cigarette between her lips, and struck a match, but stared at its flame without lighting the cigarette. "I got four babies. By the time they're gone I'll be like my mother. Always cold. Coughing all the time in the night. The things I got right now is those kids, the new TV, and to dance with Vernal."

I stayed away a long time. Now, I watched her in the B.O.T. bar and knowing she'd been available made it all the worse. It was unfair—I'd gone the hard miles of conquest, making pretending unnecessary. The only obligation we had left that was hooked to any truth was to please each other. I wanted her available again. I watched and listened while Ferlin Huskey sang and Wanda danced.

Vernal asked to talk to me away from the store, and I spent an edgy two hours at the B.O.T. waiting for him. I decided if he confronted me I'd deny it, now that it was more or less over.

Vernal ordered a can of beer, any brand, no glass. I ordered an Old Style for myself and paid for both.

"It's about my gun sales," Vernal said, his bad eye scanning my face. "I figure somethin's off. Last weekend there wasn't but twenty-one hundred in the cash register. I sold more than that in deer rifles."

Deer rifles, I thought. I wanted to cry with joy. Still. "Are you sure?" I said.

"As I'm settin' here."

I listened, watching that nervous eye, trying to read everything. But the rest of his face showed nothing. Trying to find meaning in it was like plumbing the expressions of a goat. I thanked him for coming forward, and asked him to please not say much while I looked into the situation on my own.

The next day I made the call to Fort Richardson. They pushed me along a command chain of five different people, and I kept telling the same story. In between, they called me back twice, asking for more details. In a few days, a man in a suit came in the store, looked around, and was gone on the evening flight. He was there just long enough for me to know.

The Aleutian fog blew in the day they arrested Vernal. The plane couldn't get out directly so they took him to the city jail to wait.

I'd been a little out of sorts so I started drinking around eleven, nipping from a bottle I kept in my file drawer. By the middle of the afternoon I was bleary and mixed-up from what daylight and alcohol do to the system, and I got a notion that I wanted to see Vernal before they flew him away for good.

The M.P.s at first would hear none of it. But the store had helped out with the police department fund raising, and the chief told them I was all right. They said I could have five minutes, and I had to stand six feet away from the prisoner.

Vernal was in a cell alone, down the corridor from where they housed the drunks, the pot heads and the wife beaters. They let all of them have radios, and the radios blared with the same tunes you had to pay for in the Board of Trade. Vernal shook his head when he saw me, as if he'd just had a piece of bad luck.

I spoke first. "Vernal, I'm sorry about this. But don't worry, they'll soon get it cleared up in your favor." I knew there was zero chance of that, but I had to say something.

"No, no," he said. "Wasn't none of your doin'."

I'd sobered up a little, and was starting to feel uncomfortable. The other prisoners turned their radios down, and I felt like everyone was listening to me. I asked Vernal if he needed anything. He shook his head.

I told him the job would still be his when this was all over. He smiled at that and shook his head again, as if it was a shame I couldn't seem to understand the serious nature of what had happened. It was warm in there, and I started to sweat, and I was tired. Vernal stood there, a hand on each of two thick bars, staring at me with that one direct eye while the other looked up, down, here and there. I was unsatisfied with the visit, and with myself. I could think of no more to say, and I wanted nothing but to leave. I reached to shake hands, but remembered the six foot rule, and changed the shake into a little wave.

"Eddie?" he said.

"Yeah Vernal?"

"I just wanted to let you know I liked working for y'all."

"Don't mention it," I said.

"I'll tell you, Eddie," he said. "I never had a job I liked 'til you gimme that one. I love to think of the way them old boys looked at me when I'd hand them a firearm, all bright and smelling of oil and gun bluing. They figured I really knew what I was talking about, didn't they Eddie?"

"And you did, too," I said.

"Eddie?"

"Yeah?"

Vernal licked his lips, searching for more words, more ways to express his laid-open feelings—but he'd exceeded his limits. "I'm just tickled to know ya'," he said.

The weather broke that evening and the plane took off. I drove over to the double-wide, and Wanda let me in. Vernal's magazine was still on the floor, open to a photo of an Oklahoma Chevy dealer straining to hold his salmon to the camera. It was probably the picture Vernal was looking at when the M.P.s crashed in. Now he was 27,000 feet in the air and on his way to fifteen years of hard labor.

The tension of everything brewed a sexual hunger in me that wasn't to be put off. I nudged Wanda toward the hallway, past those black-haired kids watching TV. But Wanda wouldn't be nudged. The more I pushed, the more she stood her ground.

"What's wrong?" I said. I knew it wasn't the kids, and I was pretty sure she wasn't all that choked up about Vernal.

"I was just thinking I'd like to dance," she said. "Dance me back to the bedroom."

The kids were watching a show with background rock music that jangled the whole place. I did my best, bumping my hip into Wanda's crotch, following the beat, sliding along the ridges of the paneling to the bedroom.

"Vernal, he could dance," Wanda said. "Even at the Legion Hall with that concrete floor—he made it feel like the carpet at the Captain Cook Hotel."

We made love on her bed, on Vernal's bed. Then I stood up to put my clothes on. Wanda just lay there, with her legs parted a little, stroking the top curve of one breast where she said it stung a little, from my teeth.

"You turned him in, didn't you?" she said.

I fiddled with my clothes, shaking them out. "What was that?"

"You told on Vernal." Her chin was angled down, like she was searching for something on her breast.

"Goddamn," I said. "How could you even think that—for one thing he was the best gun salesman I ever saw. And for another, I like him. A whole hell of a lot more than you do, probably."

I was pleased with the last thought, and I let it hang in the air so it would be there and ready to bump into her own arguments. She stopped rubbing her breast and looked at me.

"You know something, Eddie," she said. "You're an asshole and I wouldn't give you a bullet if I had a bucketful of them."

She lay there and I felt her dark eyes burn into my back as I pulled on my shirt and my pants, then my socks and boots. And while I dressed I thought about Vernal.

There was something in him that I'd been reaching to when I saw him in jail. It was in his face, and in his eyes. His expression had things to say, ideas too complicated for his words. His face offered a recognition, a granting that he did know who he was, and where he was going, even if it was nowhere. It was a taking up of the habit again, the habit of despair. It wasn't just acceptance, it was that he was glad to have that acceptance. He was already serving those fifteen years, and Wanda and the babies and his job and the TV were all just stops along the way. Vernal was a guy who had to grab his happiness fifteen minutes at a time, and even then he lived knowing that his pitiful bit of joy could be gone, just like that.

That's all he'd get in his life, but then I realized—why the hell should I care—it could have been me, and no one told either of us we deserved any better.

The kids were still watching their show when I came out of the bedroom. For a minute I stood there in front of Vernal's seal skin, watching the kids and the TV, but I was anxious to leave—I didn't care to be there when Wanda came out.

But before I left I went to the kitchen and found an old dishrag that I doused in warm water. I came back to the TV and worked on that purple jam stain until the screen looked as bright and clean as when Vernal first saw it. Then I tossed the rag back toward the kitchen sink, picked up Vernal's magazine from the floor, and closed the storm door behind me.

# Stopping In Grace

## Jill Hochman

I like to tell the story about how Joseph Jacob was conceived. I know I m supposed to be ashamed, but I m not.

"Mary Jo, not again!" Cindy and Darlene would squint down at me, warning.

"Aww," I tell them with a twitch of my apron and a flick of my hand that I swear makes me look stern and somehow glamorous all at the same time. "Ain't nothin so private you can't tell a stranger." My customers like my sass and they lean closer, practically straining out of their booths. Not that much exciting goes on near Starr Diner, so even a little gossip gets these folks going. But, Cindy and Darlene, they get mad either because I get more tips or because, well, to be honest, they each have at least a cameo, if not a supporting role in the story I'm about to tell.

* * *

We've all been working at Starr Diner for about twelve years now, ever since we graduated from high school. Cindy Sue, well, she graduated the year before me, but originally she was engaged to marry Tommy Bell, at least until his football scholarship came through. She visited him once. Though the way she tells it, she was practically an honorable member of some high-class sorority out at Penn State. It was all bull and didn't matter anyway because by November of his freshman year Tommy Bell wrote a Dear Cindy. So by Christmas of '81, Cindy was a pink apron trainee at Starr Diner instead of preparing to be Mrs. Cindy Sue Bell. When I started six months later, Cindy was an institution, a fixture in Starr Diner, only she didn't know yet.

"I'm just savin' money to move to Hollywood. I mean it's practically a done deal," Cindy assured me as she patted her bangs to make sure they still arced over her forehead and hadn't yet succumbed to the grease in the air. "Don't you worry, honey," she told me, "before you know it, this will all be yours." She laughed and tapped my shoulder.

But Cindy Sue never moved on to Hollywood; as a matter of fact, the only time she ever left Starr was to work at a new joint down the road, the Dixie. Cindy Sue stormed in one July day and scrapped her pink polyester dress right across the serving counter. Starr's air-conditioner had been busted approximately 36 working hours by then, and we were all wilting. Mr. Starr was covering for our sick cook at the time Cindy announced her departure. "I'm goin' to Dixie," she declared as she turned in her uniform. "Down Dixie we get to wear sequins—none of this dusty rose..." She poked a finger under the skirt of her uniform, There's air-conditionin,' and and, well..." She looked back at Darlene and me and the customers who were picking at their dried up eggs and perusing the murky depths of their coffee cups, "and, and none of y'all," she stuttered and stomped out of Starr's.

She wasn't gone much longer than the air conditioner though before she slunk back in and asked Ray Starr for her job back. She never mentioned that the Dixie got run out of town, something about the Dixie and ill-repute. And Cindy would have been out of a job and all. None of us were allowed to mention how she'd worked there. We were just supposed to forget the big old scene she made that day she walked out and the day she came back snuffling with puffy pink eyes to talk "in private" with Ray. Instead we just had to put up with her strutting around like the doily on her head was some kind of a tiara. Her new walk must have been something she picked up down at Dixie.

But I've gotten off track, and I still haven't even gotten to Darlene. And in some ways, Darlene was the interesting one. Darlene had thick, curly, brown hair that took two fat bands before it'd stay out of her face. She was littler than me and Cindy, and her round-eyed tortoise shell glasses made her look like a baby coon staring out of its nest. Cindy and I kind of squabbled at first over who would get to take care of her, but in the end she was mine, mostly because, like Cindy said, the two of us were so beyond a make-over.

Darlene played the piano and the violin. Not that I know much about it, but I heard she was very talented. Sometimes on a slow day, I'd catch her contemplating her long white fingers, smoothing down each finger, rubbing each joint. Other times, she'd be kneading the air with her fingers, pushing away at an invisible keyboard or strings. Darlene's zoning spells enraged Cindy, and she'd stomp over to Darlene's silent symphony banging a fork or a plate or clattering cups together and shout, "How you like that music, Darlene?" Cindy always insisted that Darlene's talent was an excuse to get out of work, mostly because whenever a dishwasher called off one of us would get stuck doing dishes, never Darlene because the water was bad for her hands. Cindy'd slam back to the kitchen and lean over my shoulder, "Miss Sacred-Finger's playing air piano again. Can you hear it way back here? Mmmnnn..." Cindy'd cock her head like she was listening. "That Beethoven's ninth or tenth? Hmmmm..." I don't know why it bothered Cindy so much though because I was the one who always got stuck doing the dishes. Didn't really matter to me either because the nights that I filled in for washers we had to split our tips three ways even. There was less rush in the back anyway, and I could daydream, holding each plate flat under the suds, I'd pretend I was panning for gold instead of scraping dried ketchup and grease off the dishes.

Ray Starr always said that I had a good attitude, a positive work ethic, but the way I see it, all that really meant was that I got to do more work than Darlene and Cindy. Between all the primping and switching Cindy did and the way Darlene tapped out time instead of writing on a notepad when she took an order, I think I was probably the most popular waitress at Starr's, at least like I said before, I got the most tips. I'm pretty straight-forward, an uncomplicated type of person. The only art I had was maybe for conversation—not like I'd win any speech making competitions, but I could tell a story that makes people laugh, keeps them occupied when the grill overheats or the deep frier gets behind on the fries. I never planned working at Starr as a rest stop between two places, never planned anything really. Saves on disappointment that way. Just work and sleep, a little eating, a little laughing in between. That's the way we kept on Cindy Sue, Darlene, and me. At least that's how it was until Tyler Perkins came to town.

First day Tyler came into Starr, Cindy Sue got his table by rights, by rights meaning she had first dibs on men anywhere from 20 to 35. So even though Tyler sat in my territory, Cindy strutted across Starr's to slap his menu down on his paper placemat. The laminated edge of the menu cracked the table top like a whip, and Tyler whistled up at Cindy. "Whew, not so bad stoppin' in Grace now, Larry, is it?" Cindy smiled and pulled her pencil from behind her ear, flicking loose a few tendrils of her summer time bleach job. Seemed like the whole diner waited for that one curl to stop its slow motion spring before everyone breathed again. "What'll it be, boys?" Cindy emphasized the *boys* and made sure to pay more attention to Tyler's boothmate, a closer to middle-aged paunchy man with a stained baby blue tee and a drooping tool belt.

"Ha, BOYS...Cindy Sue," Tyler squinted at Cindy's name tag. "These here," he jerked his head at his buddy. "These here, are certified men. Maybe you girls don't recognize that yet but you will."

But that all went down before we knew Tyler was Tyler. Back then he was just a man in tight blue jeans and a close fitting white tee.

"Hmmm..." Cindy snorted at me that day, after Tyler and his mate had wiped their plates clean, eaten every crumb, practically licked up the salt from their fries, swirling their potato wedges through their ketchup until only a thin trace remained. Tyler had clacked his coffee mug down, sighed, and stretching his belt for more room, tapped a cigarette out on the table. By the time Cindy went back to refill their coffee mugs, Tyler and his partner were sprawled, feet propped up, belts loosened, dropping ashes on the floor.

"Didn't your momma never teach you how to behave in public?" Cindy interrupted their reverie.

Tyler sat up and looked deep into Cindy's eyes, shot her a glance like live sparks. "Momma, there's a few things I could teach you." He leaned close, close enough to whisper a few things, and Cindy blushed redder than I've ever seen. She left me to pick up the bill, but by then Tyler was already gone, only his partner remained.

Cindy came to work the next day with a triple roll in the waistband of her skirt, her hair curled around her face, her ponytail sculpted into an intricate fan, her lipstick bright red, and her eyes blackened so dark that the blue of her iris was electric, the light at the end of a deep tunnel. She looked exactly the way she had back at Grace Central High when she was cheering on the Bears. She licked her lips carefully, trying not to eat off any of their color. "Uh, hey, Mary Jo. Those construction working guys come back, make sure you let me get the table." I watched Cindy's eyes dart toward the door all that day. But Tyler and his partner didn't show.

Didn't show up for another week. By then we'd all forgotten about them at least me and Darlene had. It was funny how Tyler just sauntered into Darlene's half of Starr's, and she didn't think anything of waiting on him since Cindy Sue was in the bathroom or something and couldn't be found.

Regardless, I guess that day caused some bad blood between Darlene and Cindy, at least more than before. When Cindy finally emerged from wherever she was hiding, she caught the tail end of a conversation that went something like, "Everything OK? Can I get you anything else?" from Darlene to Tyler who was poking at his paper placemat, a sketchy map of the town of Grace, with his fork saying, "Yeah, actually, Darlene, this here map has all of the highpoints of Grace labeled quite clear, but it don't have nothin' about this here's where Darlene Dumas lives." Tyler traced his finger across the dotted line of Fairbanks Ave. to the big star of Starr's Diner. He looked straight up at Darlene, right into her brown eyes and said, "Think you can help me out. Maybe give me directions?" Darlene abruptly ended a silent rendition of Handel's *Water Music*.

She had no time to answer before Cindy Sue shouldered her out of the way and attempted to greet Tyler in a nonchalant manner that came out both squeezed and extra loud. "Hi, Tyler, What's that you say you were lookin' for?"

"Well, Cindy Sue," he replied completely unruffled, "I was just askin' your friend here about some cultural high points in this here Grace. Turns out she's an established musician."

Cindy snorted and muttered, loud enough for all of us to hear, "established my ass. Imagine that an established musician." It wasn't until Darlene and I both drifted into the kitchen to replenish our salt and pepper shakers that we realized that Tyler had never told one of us his name, at least not while he was in Starr. Cindy didn't wander off in the afternoons anymore after that. She was always close enough by to make sure she got Tyler's table.

"So, uh," Darlene approached Cindy Sue after close one Sunday night. "You gonna make Monday movie night this week?" Sunday was my day off, so the exchange that followed was related to me over the phone Sunday night.

"Something's definitely up," Darlene informed me. Neither of us spoke for at least a minute, and I could hear the slippery hum of rosin' being dragged across a bow. The sound was unique but familiar, made me cringe. I'd always imagined violin bows as a thin ribbon, a solid piece, but Darlene had let me examine one, so I could see the individual hairs that went into the bow. Darlene broke her own silence, "I mean, this is her week to pick. God forbid we don't get our monthly dose of shiny fairy tales." Last week we'd seen *Home Alone*, my choice. I was rooting for *Alladin* this time around, but it was Cindy Sue's turn, and she'd probably pick something with Sharon Stone or Tom Cruise in it, lots of nudity and happy endings. See, back then, every Monday was movie night, our version of girl's night out: Monday Movie Madness at the Plex on Main Street. Two dollar adult admission on Mondays, so we pooled our tip money and paid for the movie popcorn, one large soda each, a pack of Good-N-Plenties for me, licorice for Cindy and Junior Mints for Darlene. We swopped boxes during the movie, so we each got some of everything.

After the movie, we usually gathered in Cindy Sue's over-her-parents' garage-apartment. While Cindy Sue twined thick hunks of her hair into spongy pink curlers and applied a ghostly mask of cold cream to her face, Darlene and I made coffee. By ten our feet were curled under our bodies and we gossiped, weren't waitresses anymore, just girls. Waiting tables gives us an edge on gossip. Something about a woman with a frilly apron and a pot of joe makes people want to gab. So we found out who was cheating on who, who was expecting, and who flunked out of Grace Com U. All that Grace gossip combined with the traumas of our own lives kept us talking most of the night.

Monday nights had become important to us, and no matter how much Cindy resented Darlene's silent violin and no matter how angry I'd get when Cindy disappeared just around the time when Miss Caroll, notorious for not tipping, or Mr. Slate, "Miss, I ordered eggs LIGHTLY boiled and Miss, my toast is a LITTLE underdone," wandered in, on Monday nights the three of us were friends, counted on each other.

Cindy Sue had already missed one Monday night, and Darlene and I had gone without her, but Darlene had fallen asleep, left me to eat all her Junior Mints. I'd ended up wishing that I'd gotten licorice instead of Good-N-Plenties.

So it was Cindy who originally broke things up that summer. By July, she'd become a zombie. And though neither Darlene or I could be certain what was wrong with her, she slipped up now and then, made comments like, "Tyler said Ray should get that ceilin' replaced. The damp sittin' up there'll cause electrical problems," or "Tyler's about ready to start dry wallin' the Baker's place. Good thing cause he got jobs lined up all summer."

But the big explosion, the one that divided our threesome irrevocably, at least for the summer, occurred on Cindy Sue's day off, a Tuesday afternoon. Tyler wandered back into Darlene's half of Starr. I saw him come in, and I felt the bottom fall out of my stomach. Maybe that was the first time I realized where

Cindy Sue was every Monday night. Darlene had let me pick our movies for the past two weeks. But that Tuesday when I saw Darlene drop her invisible violin, just let it clatter right there on the floor, so even I could hear it fall, I suddenly realized that I knew that I was losing Darlene too. I felt like a kid who'd just found out that all that stuff he'd learned about in Health Class was what his parents had been doing all along.

I watched as Darlene darted to the restroom, bobbing through the door and bobbing back out with her hair straightened and her glasses off. Somehow, I guess by leaning on the edges of tables around her, she navigated herself back to Tyler's booth.

"Well, well," Tyler began when Darlene got back to him. "Where they been hidin' you, woman?"

I heard Darlene giggle, and I looked away, but later I noticed Darlene tracing a line across Tyler's map. She etched a tiny heart, tapping her pen on it for emphasis. Tyler smiled, folded the paper placemat into quarters and stood up to shove it into his pocket. I figured where Darlene's line had lead to: 19 Grant Street. Darlene lived over Harvey's Hardware Store. Harvey liked having Darlene live over his store; he used to joke about hanging a sign in the window: Live Music Monday at noon,Tues. and Wed. 8-10 pm., Thurs. and Fri. 6-8pm. Darlene's practice hours. The whole store vibrated when Darlene thumped away on the piano, rattled the display case and kept communication to a minimum. Harvey smiled, called his store the only hardware store in town with culture. I guess living over the hardware store turned out pretty good for Darlene too, seeing how Tyler just kept happening to stop by needing a saw blade, some extra nails, a spackling brush

One day Darlene just splurted out, "Ya'll know Tyler listens to opera? He says it's painting music. I know he don't seem like the type, but go figure. I didn t know nothin' about opera 'til he told me."

Cindy's eyes narrowed, and she stormed into the kitchen, slammed a few dishes down and charged back through the swinging doors. That's when I remembered that Cindy'd said something earlier, something like "Tyler's workin' lot of overtime the past week. Fell asleep by 8:30 the other night."

There weren't any more movie nights at all after the big opera blow out. First Monday, I went by myself, but I gave that up fast. Not much use when there wasn't anyone to talk to after. The only talk that was going on at Starr's was not pleasant.

So after about three weeks, Tyler stopped showing up around Starr again. And I have to admit that it was kind of funny watching Darlene and Cindy trying to figure out what was going on. Cindy started it after a week of silence, "Tyler tell ya there's some Beethoven special on PBS tonight? Seein' that you're both all into classical music now." Cindy studied Darlene's profile, reading her out. But Darlene didn't look up from the dishes she was stacking, "Yeah, sure, uh huh," She stood up from the table, no sign of emotion evident except for a small push at the heavy frame of her glasses, a furtive gesture that made her eyes look heavenward and sent a chiseled tumbler toppling from the precarious balancing act she'd constructed on her tray. The glass hit the ground and shattered. Cindy made her exit, smirking with satisfaction, while Darlene stood, the rest of the dishes still rattling. She handed me her dishes and ran for the bathroom. I ended up getting the dustpan and sweeping up the carnage. Cindy strutted around me, flicking at her curls and twitching like a peacock who'd just won a stand-off. So much for little-Miss-Know-It-All, so much for little Miss Culture.

It was hard to ignore Darlene s puffy eyes and her foggy smudged lenses when she finally came out to wait tables. It was looking like a clear sweep victory for Cindy Sue. Harvey had confided in me earlier, told me that Darlene had gone from the soft pleas and tripping *Ein Klein Nacht Musick* to the sombre moan of the *Symphony Fantastique*. "It's like the hardware store's some spook show, run by the blasted Adam's Family, for Crips Sake!" he told me.

But I personally suspected things weren't so good on the Cindy Sue front either. She'd cornered me in the back of Starr and demanded to know what Darlene had told me. I shrugged, told her Darlene was fine, thank you for asking. That's when Cindy leaned real close and hissed, "Mary Jo, you can't keep walkin' the line, sooner or later you gotta pick a side." Cindy slapped down the wet rag that hung around her shoulders so hard I could feel the wind right down my whole left side.

I never really thought I'd have to actually pick sides, but when the time came I did. And it wasn't the side I was expecting to take.

Tyler wasn't so stupid. After two months of Starr Diner lunches, he was laying low. Didn't stop Cindy Sue and Darlene from shooting to attention every time a battered white pick-up pulled into the lot. Didn't stop their ears from perking every time they heard heavy exhaust, a door slam extra loud, or a work belt jingling. Two weeks of dishes dropped for unexplained reasons, orders written half way and then forgotten, coffee cups left unrefilled....Got so I was everybody's waitress. It was a relief to work the six to nine shift by myself. Darlene and Cindy hung their aprons at the time clock, not touching or looking at each other as they looped the aprons and checked their cards. Darlene walked out first, Bye, ya, Mary Jo, stress on the Mary Jo. Cindy Sue hung back, her eyes scrunched up, mouthing an ugly exaggerated Mary Jo behind Darlene's back. I watched Cindy Sue begin the desperate process of smoking her first post-work cigarette. First patting each pocket in her skirt, rustling the pack open, shaking the cigarette out, lifting it to her lips, puffing out her cheeks, then the second pat down for a lighter, a click, her cheeks sinking in for the first puff, relaxed lean backwards, remove cigarette, blow and cough.

"When'd you start smoking again?" I couldn't help asking.

"Mmmm..." Cindy shrugged, "recently." She left and there was silence, the lingering smell of her smoke, a few coffee stragglers, either alone or gesturing madly at each other, their cups only props.

Only a half hour had passed when I saw the truck pull in, heard the fender scraping metallic on a cinder block in the lot. I heard the door open, heard the jingle of the workbelt as Tyler removed it, saw him sling it back into the seat, saw him curse silently to himself, heard the car door slam. I shut my eyes and stood there waiting for him to come in, ease into his booth.

He was exhausted. I saw that when I brought his coffee out. He'd lost the edge, the cynicism, he usually brought into Starr with him. "Lo, there," he said barely looking up. I took his order: burger with lettuce, tom, BBQ sauce on the side, two orders of fries, extra salt, and a milk. Now and then when I whisked past him filling up someone else's coffee, I glanced over, saw him dunk his burger into the little cup of sauce he'd asked for, then take a bite. He got three coffee refills before I decided to give him one of the cinnamon rolls we still had left in the case. By that time, I'd noticed him watching me as I rustled past.

"Mary Jo," he called, once the diner was practically cleared. "Hey, Mary Jo, can't you sit your ass down a minute and give a guy some attention?"

I laughed, mostly from the ache that was rising up from my arches, climbing the backs of my legs and nestling into my lower back. "I sit down," I told him, "I might never get up again."

He nodded, "Yeah, you might be right."

Nine-thirty, some days it can't come soon enough. I hustled that night. The diner had emptied early, so I filled the straws and napkins, collected the ash trays and wiped tables.

Tyler must have been waiting, maybe sleeping in his truck, but when I came out, he sat up and leaned out the window of his truck. "Mary Jo, I come to take you home. Get off them feet already, girl." Somedays you're so near beat it shows through your eyes, your skin, even your hair, hangs funny. Tyler must have seen it, recognized something kindred.

That night we lay in the bed of his truck and watched for shooting stars. "Missed the meteor showers in August," he told me. But it was only September, one of those nights so clear the air feels endless and sharp, clusters in your bones, just enough so you want another person for extra heat. We talked, starting with work and moving back, moving to the things that make a person who they are. For Tyler it was traveling, how the scenery changes the further down the road you go. "Ain't got much baggage," he told me, "'cept what's in my head."

We kept right on, me and Tyler, pointing out stars to each other, trying to glimpse what trail might be left from one we'd missed. We looked for so long I can't remember how I ended up looking into his eyes instead of the sky, even how he ended up on top of me at all. By then he'd spread a blanket over us, balled up his jacket to put behind my head. He just held on until I whispered, "missed another one." And he had, the brightest star I'd ever seen gliding right over his shoulder.

It was getting late by then so we went to bed, folded ourselves into my single somehow, and we slept. Woke up to Tyler holding my feet, running his fingers along the arches. I watched him pondering the lines and veins. He cupped my heels and rubbed my calves. He waited and I didn't respond, pretended to still be asleep; he kissed the bottom of my foot, the part that dips between the heel and the toes. I figured right then that he could see my whole life mapped out on the sole of my feet. Whoever'd thought up palm reading had gotten it all wrong, cause your life, it's all there in your feet.

I got to lie there after he left. Lie there and smell him in my bed, the downy scent of his hair, soft and baby fine, buzzed close, though he told me it used to be long, the smell of his cigarettes, and the smell of his skin.

I didn't slip up like Cindy Sue or Darlene. I never mentioned Tyler's name, not once, even when they called me panicky late at night, trying to get me to admit that I knew which one of them Tyler was staying with. Nope, didn't mention his name to them, not once, even when he was beside me, trailing his fingers across my back or rolling my hair between his fingers, while I was on the phone with one of them. Never tested Darlene or Cindy at work to see if he'd been with one of them. But I guess I didn't have to, cause every night he'd be with me.

The day he wasn't there any more, I knew he was gone. I knew it like I knew the taste of his skin, or the way the red dragon on his right arm, right where his flesh was slightly raised, felt against my palm. Guess most people would've cried, got angry or something, but I just took off my shoes, unlaced them, and rubbed my own feet.

By then it was November. Cindy Sue and Darlene had just about given up walking past the Baker's house just to see how far along it was. By then I think they both knew that Tyler wasn't with either of them anymore. I even walked into Starr and saw them sharing an ashtray, rehashing some episode of *Melrose Place*.

So it didn't seem strange when Darlene, on her way to grab her apron one morning, said, "Harvey told me Tyler closed out his account, paid up. The Baker house is done, and Tyler told Harvey that he's going back North, got some work in Ohio."

Cindy Sue was tying on her apron. I couldn't see her face because she was kind of bent over and taking one last draw from her cigarette.

That was pretty much it for Tyler though, and the following Monday we were all back at the Plex again like nothing had happened. But that night at Cindy's, I announced that I was expecting.

Course it was a big mystery to everyone, the baby and all. But when it comes down to it, that's it, the story of how Joseph Jacob was conceived. He wasn't born until June, exactly a year after Tyler made his way through Grace.

Cindy Sue and Darlene threw a baby shower for me, just a few of our friends from Starr.

Everybody expected me to be real ashamed or mad or, at least, something. Cindy Sue and Darlene were all for tracking Tyler down, whether to make me an honest woman or for them to have one more night with him, I'm still not sure. I knew those two were whispering about me behind my back, saying that I should have known better, and what could you expect from me after all.

When it comes to Tyler, though, I don't have any regrets. I figure one day my son will ask me who his Daddy is, and when he does, I'll take him out late August and tell him to look at the stars, try to catch one moving. I'll tell him about Tyler and how one night Tyler threw me a star and I caught it, held on tight, and watched it grow because that's the way things really happened.

I guess Cindy Sue and Darlene really started to bond when they decided to quit smoking together, smoking being bad for the baby. Darlene got contacts and even let Cindy cut her hair. And Cindy Sue, well, from what Darlene tells me, her piano lessons are coming along.

Joseph Jacob is a fine boy, growing up good, maybe because he's Starr Diner's pet. It's usually just the four of us now: Cindy Sue, Darlene, me, and, of course, little JJ strapped securely across one of our chests.

# Holy Water

## R Yañez

Apolonio had passed the courtyard of the Hillcrest Nursing Home many times before, but today was the first time he stopped and entered.

In the courtyard's center, there was a cement fountain with a statue of an angel-faced boy. He carried a pitcher from where water once poured. The fountain was not working, and judging from the boy's chipped limbs and the condition of the round base—drowned with leaves and dirt—it had been abandoned for some time.

Taking a break from his third daily visit with his wife, the retired plumber studied the figure in the fountain. "Qué lástima," he mumbled and imagined a happier boy if water would only come out of his jarra.

He went back inside the disinfectant-smelling hallway that led out to the courtyard. He passed storage closets full of sheets and towels and rooms eighty-two through eighty-six, two hospital beds to each room, and entered the room near the building's main entrance.

The first thing he heard was Mrs. Mercedes calling for Eva. Esta mujer está loca, he thought. He wasn't being mean. It's just that he knew from personal experience what this El Paso Rest Community could do to one's mind. He wanted to go over next to the Mexican woman and tell her that Eva, her only daughter, had left hours ago after feeding her lunch, but decided he'd better not or risk having to hear many questions for which he didn't have answers.

In the other side of the room, his wife slept or so it seemed. It was hard to tell since she hadn't spoken or moved voluntarily for many months now.

He examined a face he better recognized in yellowed photographs and gripped his wife's small, well-lotioned hands. He rubbed her fingers like the physical therapist had shown him. Pressing knuckles and squeezing joints, he shut his eyes and prayed the rosary from where he'd left off before walking out into the courtyard.

*Dios te salve, María*
*llena eres de gracia,*
*el Señor es contigo,*
*bendita tu eres entre todas las mujeres . . .*

When he opened his eyes, it was dark outside the room's only window. Reaching in his pocket, he sorted through loose change, aspirins, and screws until he retrieved a watch with a busted band. He realized that evening mass at Cristo Rey was already under way. If he hurried to San José, he could catch the late mass, but he decided to pray another rosary at home instead. He'd be up a little after dawn and after feeding the gatitos—some his and others strays from around La Loma—morning mass would put him back on schedule.

Before he left, he made sure his wife was tucked well under the sheets and blanket he'd brought that first night she was transported to the nursing home from the hospital. Hope it doesn't get too cold, he thought as he put dirty tissues, his Spanish *Reader's Digest*, and an empty mason jar in a Big 8 Supermarket bag.

Trying to make as little noise as possible, he inched his way toward the door. No luck. Mrs. Mercedes's opened her glazed eyes, and she called for Eva once again: "Venga mijita, ayúdame. Andale, no seas mala." She repeated this several times, while managing to bravely raise one of her puny arms in his direction. "Eva, hija . . . ayúdame." Her voice was a scratchy phonograph.

He knew she'd keep up if he didn't do something to comfort the woman. From his shirt pocket, he pulled out his black rosary and placed it in the woman's palm. As if she were a baby and the string of blessed beads a pacifier, Mrs. Mercedes's otherwise-blank face grew what appeared to be a smile.

He decided that if he wanted his wife to get some sleep tonight her roommate would need to be quiet. He left the rosary that Padre Islas had given him after his wife's stroke. The business-like nursing staff would remove the rosary in the morning among their changing of soiled sheets and sponge bath. They wouldn't care if the lonely woman cried for Eva, or God, for that matter, he thought. Mrs. Mercedes was one body among the hundred-plus at the nursing home, so they would stick something in her mouth if she made too much of a fuss. He never forgot his fear of the morning he'd found Mrs. Mercedes gagged with a sock.

In a way he didn't fully understand, he was glad that his wife couldn't speak. Or else she'd also be victimized by nurses who confessed that they worked long hours and were underpaid.

The nursing home's superintendent, Mrs. Hennessey, appeared very surprised when he offered to fix the courtyard's fountain. She said they'd always meant to get it repaired but never had the funds. He told her he would take care of everything. Most of the materials, he already had.

After getting her blessings, he went to his truck. He always carried his plumbing tools in the back. "Nunca sabes cuando va haber un trabajito," he'd told his grandson many times. Along with his wooden toolbox, he got a flashlight and dragged a rooter that he used for clearing out drains. "La Víbora Negra," his grandson named the long, metal coil.

In his worn army-green overalls, he crouched over—his shrunken size held together by a life of labor—and put his bare hands into the pipe leading out behind the nursing home. From the way it felt, the fountain's drain hadn't been cleaned in a long while. And if his experience with the plumbing of other, newly-built buildings was any sign, he knew that the cheapest materials had been used. He'd rely on his twenty-eight years with El Paso County Maintenance to finish the task.

He felt good to be working on the fountain. Finally, after what seemed like a lifetime of witnessing his wife's demise, he faced something he could fix. The longer he strained clearing the pipes, replacing all the corroded fittings, and hauling heavy tubing from the back of his truck, the more absorbed he became in his work.

Padre Islas would ask him at Sunday mass why he hadn't joined him recently for a cup of coffee, not knowing that one of his most loyal parishioners had taken a vow outside of church. As a compromise, Apolonio had taken to saying his daily rosary while he worked. The time passed quicker. He found that handling crescents and pliers, turning the pipes and fittings, was like rolling rosary beads with his fingertips. He was most at peace when his hands were working.

After another dawn-to-dusk day of work under El Paso's sun, he went home somewhat satisfied. Tired and achy, he didn't look in on his wife before he left the nursing home. While his thoughts were of her on his drive home, completing the work on the fountain was his immediate priority. First thing in the morning, he would drive to I & M Plumbing for some more materials. The store was out of the way, but he thought that he would enjoy the drive down North Loop Road to Alameda Street. And seeing an old friend even more.

Manuel, his partner from his days with El Paso County Maintenance, always had the right supplies for any trabajitos he took on. Having contact with someone who didn't feel sorry for him, he decided, would also do him good.

Before he went to sleep that night, unlike other nights, he didn't ask God why He hadn't just taken his wife that Sunday afternoon rather than prolong her ascent. After praying on his knees before his dresser—lit velas rested next to a faded print of La Virgen—he fell asleep and dreamt the boy from the fountain came to La Loma.

The laborer welcomed the visitor in his adobe home. He drank when the boy offered him water from his clay pitcher. The boy then went over and gave water to a woman in a hospital bed. Apolonio first thought it was his wife, but when he hurried over to her, he realized it was Mrs. Mercedes. She stood after drinking the water and walked off with the boy.

Apolonio was content on sleeping that night—not feeling too alone—and for quite some time after, he awoke without being thirsty for answers.

He listened to Manuel speak of a trabajito he had done for his compadre's son. The way his old friend explained it the kitchen sink would continue to leak no matter what he did.

"I'm a good plumber, tú sabes eso," Manuel said, "but when they don't pay me . . . pos, I replace the washer y me voy."

Apolonio smiled and drank from his cup of coffee, which Manuel had served him although he'd said no thanks.

"Next time he calls, I'll just say my arthritis is acting up." Apolonio shared in Manuel's laughter.

Every few minutes a customer would come to the counter and pay for some materials. If they didn't know what it was they needed or where to find it, Manuel would help them. But only after making a fuss about having to put down the pan de huevo he was enjoying with a cup of coffee, his third since Apolonio's arrival.

I & M Plumbing was one of the few places left in El Paso that had everything you needed if you were a plumber—out of necessity or because you couldn't afford to pay a certified one, like Apolonio and Manuel. Yes, other stores had recently opened nearby and were bigger and more modern, and maybe even cheaper, but these flashier stores made you wait up to a week for some things you needed right away. Like the model of water heater a man was describing to Manuel.

"I don't have it here but come back tomorrow y te lo tengo listo." Manuel winked as if to assure the man he'd come to the right place.

"Really, is there an extra charge for that?" the customer asked.

"Cómo qué extra charge?" Manuel pursed his lips. "Oiga, joven, just come back." He wrote down the man's name and the water heater's model number.

"Thank you. My family's been taking cold showers for two days."

"And if you need a good plumber to put it in, this is your man." Manuel patted Apolonio on the shoulder. "He's the best I know. Next to me."

The three men grinned.

The customer said thanks but that he would try to install the water heater himself. Apolonio was embarrassed by his friend's flattery but silently agreed that he was one of the two best plumbers he knew.

Manuel took out a notepad and phoned the person who could get the water heater he needed. Apolonio didn't keep a notepad with names and phone numbers anymore, but he, too, knew from who and where in the border city he could get what he needed for any trabajito. That's why he was here today visiting Manuel. Well, at least, that's what he'd told his friend, who he hadn't seen since around the time of his wife's stroke.

"¿Miraste los Dodgers?" Apolonio asked Manuel after he got off the phone.

"No. When they play?"

"El otro día."

"¿Quién les jugaron?"

"Los Padres, no, los Giants. Dodgers won, seis a dos."

Silence filled the next moments. Apolonio liked that they didn't have to talk all the time. This silence—unlike the one with his wife—was comforting.

"Polo, ven, te quiero 'señar algo." The two men walked out from behind the front counter to the sales area. In front of rows of bins filled with pipe fittings of all sizes, PVC and brass, was a display: King Speed Rooter—"Gets The Job Done Fast."

"Look at this." The price posted was $299.99. "¿Quién va tener tanto dinero?"

Apolonio pulled on the metal coil and stroked the chrome casing of the electronic rooter. If he had one of these, he thought, he could finish unclogging the fountain's drain in no time. The manual rooter he was using was doing the job, but he had to take frequent breaks because his arms, especially around his shoulders, tired from cranking it. Ever since he started fixing the fountain, he had to rub Ben-Gay on himself before he went to bed.

"'sta suave. But too much money." Apolonio stood back and admired the King Speed Rooter, certain it was a better machine than the ones hooked up to his wife.

"The salesman who brought it in told me to put it here, right as you walk in the store," Manuel said. "If it doesn't sell by the end of the month, he said he'd take it back. He gave me some free washers, fittings, and this calendar."

He took the calendar off the near wall and showed it to Apolonio. A blonde woman in only overalls was posed among assorted colors of sinks, bathtubs, and commodes. Apolonio put his hand under his cap and scratched his balding head. When they'd worked together at the County Coliseum, Manuel decorated the tool room with pictures from magazines he thought the other workers would like—women in bikinis, Ford pick-ups, Carlos Palomino, Fernando Valenzuela.

"Casados," was what the supervisor used to call them. In their marriage, Apolonio was the worker and Manuel the thinker.

Apolonio had always been thankful that Manuel had taught him patience. When they'd met, right after he came out of the Service, his approach to every job was finish it as fast as you can. He felt proud when he did twice as much as other plumbers and his superiors, like Lieutenant Jarvis at Fort Bliss, praised him for it.

"It's no good if you do it fast and you have to go back and do it again in a few months," Manuel had told Apolonio on their first job together, installing the urinals at Western Playland Amusement Park. He learned to listen, take his time, and eventually it worked out to where they would always be partners. Twenty-five years, second only to his forty-three-year marriage.

Behind the counter, they finished their coffees and watched customers enter the store. The retired plumbers would scrutinize the materials people purchased after they left the store. Nothing was as good as it used to be, they agreed.

"When are we going?" Manuel made a drinking motion with his hand, a big grin on his face.

"Cuando quieras." Apolonio didn't like lying to his oldest friend. He knew that he couldn't go drinking like they used to every payday, and he didn't know how to say this without sounding like less than the man he once was. Anyway, his friend wasn't supposed to drink anymore. After his operation a few years ago, the doctors told him to stop drinking and smoking. From the full ashtray near the coffee machine, Apolonio guessed that his friend had said to hell with the doctors' instructions.

"I could use a cervezita right now." Manuel took a long swallow of coffee from his "Viva Las Vegas" mug. Apolonio wondered what his friend kept cool inside the refrigerator in the back room.

They talked about their children. Manuel had always been jealous of Apolonio because he had only one, a son. In Manuel's own words, he'd been cursed with bad luck—four girls. The oldest was a dancer in Nevada, the next oldest was married to un Americano and lived way on the other side of town, and the other two attended the local college. After Apolonio told his friend that he didn't see his son much anymore, his friend joked that he wished his two youngest would go on and get married and leave him alone.

"I know when they want something. They call me 'Papi' and put their arms around me and tickle my stomach." Manuel went into an adjacent bathroom, left the door open, and kept talking. "They don't like sharing a car, but that's all I can get them. I told them one could drive my truck.'Yonque' they call it. ¿Lo crees?"

Apolonio found it almost unbelievable that Manuel could still be driving the truck he'd had since before they started working together. It *was* a piece of junk, and he'd told him many times before.

"Comprate otra."

"¿Polo, 'stas loco? Esa troquita es mi sweetheart—together forever." Manuel walked from the bathroom to a window. The body of the Ford truck was more rust than blue paint, the hubcaps had been stolen, and cardboard was taped over a broken window. The only thing that had kept it from completely falling apart all these years, Apolonio thought, was the rosary hanging from the rearview mirror.

Shaking his head, he remembered Manuel was as dedicated to Iliana, his wife. After she died about fifteen years ago, work was the only thing that Manuel seemed to care about. Often, Apolonio would get home late because his partner wanted to answer another call, or after clocking out early, he convinced him to go over the Zaragoza Bridge for a few beers. Apolonio never had to explain his lateness to his wife. She said his best friend needed his company now more than ever.

Apolonio told Manuel that he had to go. The drive to the nursing home was a long one, and he wanted to see if the hose and valves were right for the fountain. Manuel assured him that they were, but if not, he'd be here tomorrow —"Como siempre."

The soon-to-be widower took comfort in this. And he didn't feel guilty anymore that he'd skipped his morning visit with his wife. I & M Plumbing was the one place that had what he needed.

A few days passed before news of the working fountain made its way to every room of the nursing home. No longer were the residents satisfied with being placed in front of a talk-and-game-show-happy TV set in the facility's lobby. Even ones that couldn't—or wouldn't speak—somehow managed to communicate to the nurses that they'd rather be outside in the courtyard. Mrs. Mercedes, for one, had Eva wheel her out every morning and evening to see the fountain, or else the mother refused to eat.

The courtyard's centerpiece was not the only thing that had been resurrected. Encouraged by Apolonio's success, Mrs. Hennessey put some staff people to work on the landscape: Flowers from the nursing home's front lawn were transplanted, plump bushes were trimmed into matching shapes, and, in a few weeks, the grass would be alive again with color.

Inside the faded-blue walls of room eighty-nine, Apolonio only hoped that his wife could imagine the courtyard from his simple descriptions in Spanish. But many doctors were positive that she couldn't hear or see anything and, if she did, she most likely didn't understand it. The stroke, along with her already weak heart and chronic diabetes, had completely wrecked most of her brain. When Apolonio tried to speak with her or get her to move a hand or a foot, he considered a blink a cruel settlement.

To make it easier for Apolonio to understand, a member of the hospital staff had tried to explain his wife's condition in terms he might recognize. The male nurse told him in Spanish that his wife suffered a stroke, which is like when a machine short-circuits.

Staring at his wife's lifeless face, he remembered thinking back then at the hospital that if the stroke she'd suffered was like a machine breaking down, then there must be someone who could provide repair. Doctors are like electricians and mechanics and plumbers, he thought, they can fix whatever's broken. The following months changed how his own mind understood and registered things. His wife's physical state was more than a trabajito.

He placed a new box of tissues and a mason jar on the table next to her bed. After he opened the jar, he put his fingers in the holy water and made the sign of the cross on his wife's forehead, then did the same for himself.

Wanting to pray a rosary before he visited the courtyard, he searched his pockets. He remembered that he never got his rosary back from Mrs. Mercedes. All he had in his pockets were some fittings that he'd replaced on the fountain. Rather than throw them out, he was taking them home, where he had buckets of brass and copper materials among an altar of sinks and commodes in his cuartito, a decrepit tool shed.

Sitting down on a corner of his wife's bed, he shut his eyes and began a rosary. He winced as he prayed. The sharp edges of the metal stung and creased his fingertips.

# Hawk

## Rachael Perry

Farley is not opposed to the silence, he feels it, he breathes it in. Morning silence, sparrows, gulls, jays, shoulders of water curving toward the shore, crisp breezes, stiff, the kind that make his throat raw. A silence that is not silence at all, more like the sounds of anticipation and hope.

Farley will follow this Tuesday like he follows the others. He wakes without an alarm, his eyes peel open to hushed pinks and yellows that wave across the water on the other side of his screened-in porch. A normal, quiet Tuesday. He pulls himself from the thin sofa cushion, vertebrae by vertebrae, curls his stiff muscles and joints. Matted brown fur, raggedy, stuffs itself in his direction, under his palm, tail thumps against the floor. Morning, girl, he says to his dog.

A quick shower, a quick shave, Farley stops in front of the laundry hamper, unsure which flannel to pluck from it. Two to choose from—a green plaid and a blue-red plaid. It takes him longer than it should to swipe up the green one, and he admits that perhaps this Tuesday might be a little different. A little, he admits, and he drops the green one, switches it for the blue-red plaid, and then switches again. New job to start today, roughing in what will be the Collins place, working alone, mostly. Farley is busy this time of year, people rush to dig and pour basements, to fix roofs, and that suits him just fine. Though his phone does not seem to quit in the evenings and requests filter through the lumberyard, work for him, people who hear how he does not take breaks, how he does not curse, how he can raise a wall by himself, how he packs his own lunches and says "please" and "thank you" softly with almost no voice at all—opportunities to make the money that will help him through winter when jobs are scarce—Farley lunged at the Collins job. Without knowing the specifics. Without knowing the pay. Without *looking* like he lunged at the Collins job, he hopes.

He tosses down the green plaid again. Straightens his back, stretches, tall, tall, as tall as he can, steps in front of the oval mirror swinging over his bathroom sink, gold-threaded olive. Farley wants his blue-red plaid to make his thick skin rugged, his bland thin hair smooth, touchable, the slouch in his neck, the slouch to the right side that makes strangers question whether he understands what they say when they speak to him, he wants the blue-red plaid to make that look gone.

He will see her today. Friend. The Collins place is only a half-mile away from Friend.

Farley shuffles to the kitchen, bare feet skimming across cracked, wood-paneled floors. Two eggs over easy, three pieces of toast, unbuttered, two for him and one for Mae, who perches on a rickety wooden chair at the round table, ready, her tail bumping back and forth across its spokes. After breakfast, he wipes the plate with a dishcloth, scrubs the pan, places each in the plastic rack next to the sink so as to be dry by suppertime.

He flips his flat feet into wool socks, straps up his boots. Not today, girl, he says, you can't come today. Mae flops down in the center of the kitchen, watches him leave.

Farley starts up his van—it takes two attempts—and hunches over his steering wheel, gripping it tightly. He knows he should putter to the lumberyard, pick up the supplies he will need before he can start the job. On other normal Tuesdays, this is what he would do. He pictures Friend, corn-stalk hair dragged back by a denim headband, round cheeks pushing at her smile, the biggest smile, pink trousers rolled up once to keep out of the mud, and he cannot resist the possibility that she might be walking her cat around this time. Maybe he will say something to her, pull his van up next to Friend and the cat, lean elbow out of window, notice flushed face, puffs of breath, mention the cat's jewel-studded leash, the cat's fluffy tail. Maybe he will say something this time. Farley unlatches the top button on his blue-red plaid, decides to set off for the site first.

Spins the wheel to the right, foot on gas, Farley heads toward Friend. The trail away from his house is a patchwork of pale sun and shade, beyond the pines a spongy sapphire that begins white around the edges, in the distance, and turns into sky somewhere above the treetops. The pines give way at the end of his road to towering birches, soldiers and soldiers of them, head-heavy, flaking white bark. Birches that cast diagonal shadows, dark arrows pointing him at Friend.

Farley feels this Tuesday, smells a fresh dust clank among his hammers and his saws. He clears his throat, in distinct beats of two, *a-hem*, then four, *a-hem-hmm-hmm*, practices what he might declare to Friend. *I have wanted to say hello ... You have great teeth ... Perhaps we can spoon each other watermelon, wild watermelons grow near my house ... I walk my dog on a leash, too, sometimes ...* Farley practices all of these lines and more, practices them so much that he almost does not catch a crimson rip across the sky above his van and to the north, a hawk tearing through his line of vision. He slows his van to a crawl, sucks in his breath, gapes at this creature, this hawk, which clutches a wriggling snake and shoots from one set of birches to another. What magic, Farley has never seen anything like it, what beauty. He loosens his grip on the wheel, two of his tires spill off the road, onto the gravel. Farley jerks the van back on the road and loses sight of the hawk.

A story like this, Farley thinks, only happens to people who are alone.

And then: his left eye catches it, the prey-bird plunges toward him. The other direction, it was just going the other direction. He pushes on the gas, feels this hawk, which must be as big as his torso at least, diving at his van, at his open window, at him. He does not know if he should ram the pedal against the floor, if he should slam on the brakes, and before he decides, a thump, only wings, feathers, a stony-beak, and a snake, a snake slithering around his lap, onto his crotch, down his legs. Farley swaps at the snake, large, unbelievably larger than when it was wriggling in the sky, spatters blood. Still driving, he has not thought to stop, Farley kicks it near the door, there is a foothold near the door, and the snake slumps over, unmoving. The *thump*. Once the snake stops, Farley remembers the thump. He pulls his van over. Steps out.

The hawk, he expected, would be crumpled, too. It is not. It stands, wings rest at its sides, astonishing feathers, shimmery coppers, brown-ashes, striking splatches of white, gnarly claws as big as Farley's own hands. Straddles a dotted-yellow line that runs down the only paved road in town. Marble-eyes swoop in on Farley, seem to change colors. Mustard-gold. Blink. Russet. Blink.

And here Farley is, twenty feet away from that hawk—magnificent, he thinks—with sticky snake blood on his pants and on his hands and on the side of his van, not knowing what to do next. The hawk does not move. Farley does not move. Magnificent, again. Magnificent. Magnificent.

The hawk opens its wings and flies away.

Farley remains. Alone. An empty road with an empty place where a hawk was just standing, looking at him. And too late for Friend's walk. He returns to the van, gently picks up the snake with both hands, rests it on his passenger seat and drives to the lumberyard.

Two dusty pick-ups and a rusty station wagon fill the parking lot. Farley stops next to the station wagon, goes into the store. To the right of the door, cylinders of glue stacked in pillars. White buckets of drywall compound fashioned into a pyramid. The man behind the counter, stout, a wreath of bushy gray running around his head, fleshy lips, glances up from scribbling across a customer's yellow form to greet Farley.

Instead: God bless America, boy. What has happened to you? The customer, a man wearing suspenders that Farley does not recognize, gawks.

Farley wonders if it is that obvious, if there is something about him that makes it obvious. He looks down at the blood on his hands.

A hawk, Big Joe, Farley says. A hawk was flying, and he gave me a snake.

A who did what? The man behind the counter asks.

A hawk, Big Joe. I even have the snake still, Farley says, dashes to his van, returns, both palms up, with the four-foot garter. Look. Blood on my pants. Snake blood right here and right there. Farley points to the stripes of brown that look fresher than the other earthtone splashes on his workpants. Steps forward, curls the snake around a stack of fat orange pencils next to the cash register.

Hawks have the most precise eyesight in the animal kingdom, suspenders drawls. He just gave you the snake.

Just gave it right to me. Just dropped it into my van's window. Look. Go look if you need to. There's some blood on the van, too.

Big Joe laughs, a rotund laugh, full, a laugh that bounces around the room. I would not have believed it for a minute. Laughs. Not for a minute, Farley. Pauses. No, not Farley anymore. Big Joe raps his fist against the counter. Now we call you Hawk.

Hawk. Aside from short-term interest rates and the pumpkin festival, they do not talk about anything else. They talk about Hawk in the typical places: in the diner between gusts of smoke and pecan rolls, in line at the grocery while ringing up frozen dinners and exchanging crumpled coupons, in the barbershop, using spiritual, muted tones, pushing baby strollers and stretching necks toward the tall birch branches. They notice that Hawk changes, his face is rugged, his neck is straight, they invite him to brunches and offer him zucchinis from their gardens. They ask each other questions like *Would you rather shake hands with Hawk or the President of the United States?* and *How much would you sell the snake for?*

At the fast-food restaurant over coffee, black, and cheese danish:

Darn near tore his head off is what it did, the old man says, juts his forehead forward for emphasis, nods, throws up his eyebrows. Claws like nothing you've ever seen, thick and leathery, bigger than my arms, the old man holds up two raggedy paws, or yours.

You don't say, the old man's listener says, a plump old woman who wears a red-polka dot handkerchief over translucent hair, slurps coffee swiftly and smacks lips together three times.

They say Hawk grabbed those claws, soft and gentle-like, held his other hand over the beak, drove with his knees until he could move that rattler out of biting distance, then pulled over, checked the bird for broken bones and set it free. They say he set it free, even though it tried to kill him. Now that's something.

I'll be darned, the old woman says.

At the post office:

You didn't hear this from me, a skinny woman slaps stamps on first-class packages, looks from side-to-side at empty boxes, but you will not believe who got back together.

You don't mean? asks the customer, auburn hair curling over wide eyes.

Yes. Skinny scarecrow-legs crosses one over the other. Slaps a stamp. Smooths.

But how?

They say he was there, in the lumberyard, when Hawk went in that first time. Slap. Smooth. He stole one of those big pencils, the one Hawk used to fill out his little request form, he shoved that pencil in his suspenders and went straight home. Used it to write letters to her, a letter every day for one week and then two weeks. Every day. Told her that bowling night isn't the same and that he misses her meatloaf and lovemaking. That's all it took. Those letters with that pencil.

That pencil helped him with the lovemaking.

You better believe it did.

At the lumberyard:

You have got to be kidding me. A man with a molten face leans in on Big Joe.

No, sir. Big Joe shakes his head. Five thousand. I can pick it up tomorrow.

And all you did was play Hawk's numbers?

I tried to get him to listen, Big Joe says, I tried to tell him that he needed to play the lottery or something with luck like his. No. He refused. Over and over again, he said he *could not do that*—just like that— *I can not do that. It would not be right.* He even got mad at me for saying so, grabbed his snake and stormed off. I watched him drive away. Decided to write down his license plate number for the daily three …

Five thousand just like that?

Five thousand just like that.

At the laundromat:

Darn near hauled that van up with its immense claws, the old man says, palms out and thrust forward, crinkly fingers stretch open. Could have been one of those dinosaur birds from one of those darn movies, it could have, wingspan as long as Hawk's whole front bumper. And he drives a van. That is a long dinosaur-bird wing is what that is.

You don't say, the old man's listener says, an old woman whose scrawny elbows shake the card-table as she adjusts the bobby-pins in her black bun and applies coral lipstick.

They say Hawk talked it down, the dinosaur bird, nice and gentle-like. Just like I taught him. I coached that boy in the Little League when he was eight years old—I knew then that there was not another kid could have handled the pressure of second base like that Hawk did—and before each game I pulled Hawk aside and I said, Farley (Farley was his name back then), Farley, there will come a time when you'll need to be the hero, son. Can you be a hero? And he said, Yes sir. Isn't that something.

I'll be darned, the old woman says.

Farley knows what they say, hears it under the questions they ask. Seventeen offers to buy the snake, three offers to trade for it, two attempts to steal it. (Early on, the hardware store donated a safe-deposit box to him if he would agree to wear their toolbelt. He has locked the snake up ever since.) Requests for him to touch the bellies of pregnant women, speak to the sick at the nursing home. He shakes his head, no, replies "please" and "thank you" with almost no voice at all.

No, he will not take their money. No, he will not kiss their children. No, he will not guess the future.

No, he will not tell the story again.

After a while, the police are forced to trace the Collins yard with yellow tape, command that people do not cross it, for their own safety, and that they do not use flashbulbs while Farley splits two-by-fours, thumps across plywood floors. They leave candles and helium balloons, tissues of red-ribboned wildflowers, cards and prayer etchings scotch-taped to nearby birches.

Farley tries to ignore them. The acoustic guitars and campfire songs and stringed-renditions of Psalms make that difficult. During the Fifth Psalm, Farley glances up and notices purple gingham slacks and a loose blouse, creamy, ruffled. Purple gingham. Friend. She is not walking her cat. She is walking toward Farley.

Hello, Friend says.

Farley is quiet. Anything but Hawk, he thinks, no more Hawk. And then: I walk my dog on a leash, too, sometimes.

Is it true what they say, Friend asks, does not let him compliment the cat's jewel-studded leash or her teeth.

Wild watermelons grow near my house, Farley says, slouches his neck further to the right. Wild watermelons.

They say you have magic. That you're Hawk. That you have powers, Friend says.

Farley backpedals away from Friend with deliberate, unhurried steps. She is not smiling the biggest smile, she does not have flushed cheeks.

I have wanted to say hello to you for a long time, he says, and rushes to his van.

An unwanted convoy. A rainbow of faded Pintos, Volkswagen vans, Chevettes take less than three minutes to form. Stretch two miles behind Farley. He races home. Tries to think. Is alone to think. The cars track closely. Confidently. Farley feels that they are there. And wants to think. And wants to go home. And wants to be alone. Left alone. Chase. Farley is chased. He skids into his driveway. Glides through the front door. Unbuttons shirt. He feels them. His pursuers. He feels their eyes on him. Peels off shoes and socks. Steps out of pants. Stalked. There is nowhere for him to go. Fumbles with safe-deposit box. Pulls out snake. Car doors slam. He hears them. Ties snake around his neck. Skin flakes. Walks through the living room. He walks now. Breathes deeply. He is in his underwear and he walks. A crowd outside his porch. Hungry eyes. Claws. He walks by them. He is in his underwear and he walks toward the lake. Toes. Ankles. Icy. They hound him. Shins. Knees. Glacial. He splashes forward. Hips. Belly-button. Shoulders. Neck. He flails his arms. Treads water.

No one is behind him. Farley turns around, stares, gapes at the swarm of people on the beach.

No more, he shouts, his voice is a megaphone. No more stories. No more snakes.

Farley unwinds the snake from his neck and flings it. It coils and bends, twists poetically, winds a flip-flopping arc in the air, end over end, and plops into the water.

A loud gasp, throats and throats of gasps, and then silence. Farley thinks he hears a child cry. People turn heads, look at one another, shuffle feet.

What the town worried about seconds before the end of it all: how to handle the wrath of God, or the wraths of gods, or the stink of spirits, or the haunting of ghosts, or the devil's shadow, or the trees swiping, or the broken bones, or the deers marching, or the break-ups, or the blue gills strutting out of the lake and slapping people around with sharp fins and tails, or, really, whatever it was that Hawk's refusal might bring upon them.

Farley fears he might freeze, treading water, waiting for these people to go. Faint mutters emerge, snatches of disbelief strengthen. He has the snake but he can't even walk on water. Did you see his shabby underwear. That's not a rattler.

One by one the voices trail off, strip the on-lookers away.

Patches of blue jeans and corduroys and khakis disappear until all Farley sees is purple gingham.

# Square

## Bret Comar

Mrs. Simmons is standing down by the lake when I pull in. She looks in my direction for a second, then turns back to the house we're building. It's at the stage where it looks like a bunch of boards tacked together, like the first good breeze will blow it over. Fifty yards further on, the ground drops to Lake Michigan. Whitecaps all the way to the horizon.

Roger and Jamie are loitering around the muddy lot, pretending to work. Jamie walks over and leans into the door of my truck.

"She was here when I got here," he tells me. "She knows about the plumbing."

"You talked to her?"

"One or two words." Jamie glances over his shoulder at Mrs. Simmons. He doesn't take customer complaints seriously, but he knows how to look like he does.

I punch the cigarette lighter in and take out a cigarette. I've had a headache since waking up, which is a particular bitch because I didn't drink last night. I tried, but drinking when I've got things on my mind makes me feel like an alcoholic.

"The plumbing," I say.

Jamie nods. "She ain't happy."

The cigarette lighter pops. I pull it out, but don't light up. Theresa, my wife, doesn't approve of smoking. It's dangerous, she says, not "unhealthy" or "bad for you"—dangerous. *Dawn-ger-urz*—six years in Michigan she never lost her accent. The coils cool from orange to gray.

"I'll talk to her."

"Wait for Tucker, man." Jamie grins at me. "You'll just piss her off more."

I push the door open against his weight. He takes the cigarette I have decided not to smoke and shrugs. You're the boss, the shrug says, which I'm not.

Mrs. Simmons watches me cross the lot.

"Good morning," I say.

She blinks, a fifty-year old woman with a girl's haircut, short, bangs swept back.

"Morning," she says.

It sounds more like a fact, like she might as well have said *Morning, Northern Michigan, March, fifty degrees at 7:30 in the morning.* Like that, I wish I'd waited for Tucker.

"You drive all the way up from Detroit?" I ask.

"Bloomfield Hills," she corrects me. "Nobody lives in the city."

"Long drive."

"Yes. Five hours. I hope I won't have to make it often." She turns to what will eventually be a 4,500 square foot summer-home. "Explain to me what's wrong."

I tell her about how the plumbing we laid in the cement floor isn't going to work. We miscalculated the grade so now the pipes aren't at enough of a pitch to drain properly.

"It's not a problem," I finish. "We'll just put it in the walls."

This is the wrong thing to say.

"Really?" she says. "Then why did my husband and I decide to pay twice as much to have the plumbing in the floor? Remind me of the advantages again."

"It's a little quieter," I admit.

"And aren't the pipes safer in the foundation?"

Tucker must have told her this. It's half true. The plumbing is safer embedded in the floor if you expect someone to drive a bulldozer through your house.

"In some ways," I say.

"What ways?"

"Well, if there's ever a problem, it's easier to get to it if it's in a wall than if it's in the floor."

"Why didn't anyone tell me that before?"

She waits for an answer. I want to tell her not to worry about it, that we're going to make mistakes and that she'll be happier not knowing about them. She'd take it as an insult, though, and no better answer occurs to me because I'm thinking about the call I'll have to make to Theresa tonight.

Mrs. Simmons is about to say something when Tucker's four-by-four pulls in. Tucker climbs out, talks to Jamie for a second, then starts across the lot towards Mrs. Simmons and me, stepping over ditches filled with brown water from last night's rain. Smiling.

Twenty minutes later, Mrs. Simmons is nodding like she agrees with the whole world, like now everything makes sense. When he's done with her, Tucker comes over and steadies a sill plate I'm fastening to the top of the garage foundation. The plate doesn't need to be steadied.

"Nod your head a little and look sorry," he winks at me. "I told Leona that I'd talk with you."

Mrs. Simmons has moved out of view, but I can hear her clearly. She is talking with Chris, a college kid who went to high school with Tucker and who works part time doing no-brain stuff like moving lumber and pounding nails. He's a philosophy major, and he's always telling me what a great job I have. It's so real.

"I called her about the plumbing last night," Tucker says. "It's better to own up to these things than to let people find out on their own."

Tucker is twenty-four, eight years younger than me. He started a lawn service when he was thirteen, then branched out into snow-removal. We've got no shortage of snow here, and by the time he was seventeen, he had a dozen trucks working Charlevoix County. I don't know how many he has now, but you see them in Traverse City all the way up to the Mackinac Bridge. A few years ago, when he won the Michigan Young Entrepreneur Award, one of the Detroit papers ran a big story on him. I've known him since he bought my father's contracting business three years earlier. It was a small-time operation—sheds, additions, a cottage every now and then—but Tucker's building it up. He has five crews, and now we build summer homes for rich people from Detroit and Chicago. Besides the contracting firm, Tucker also owns a brick yard. The bricks have some special quality. He exports them to the Netherlands.

He doesn't know much of anything about building houses, just enough to talk to customers. He jokes with the crew that he couldn't build a cabin out of Lincoln Logs.

Over by what's going to be the sunroom, Mrs. Simmons says something to Chris.

"She's okay?" I ask.

"She will be." Tucker laughs. "She's pretty strong-minded. All the way up from Bloomfield Hills on the spur of the moment."

Tucker glances at her. He's about five-nine, and he's got the most bowed legs I've ever seen. Jamie is always asking him where he hid the horse he must've ridden in on.

He looks up. I don't know at what. "I hope I've got that much initiative when I'm her age."

"What'd you say to her?"

"I told her that in some ways it's better to have the plumbing in the walls. In case anything goes wrong with it."

I drive a nail through the last tie-down. "That's what I told her."

Tucker thinks this is funny. Like I've asked him a question, he says, "Yeah, but, Mitch, you've got to believe what you say."

"It's so much safer in the floor," I say.

Tucker laughs. "Well, isn't it?"

The papers are still sitting on the kitchen table when I get home. They came yesterday from the Ninth District Court of Traverse County. I have to sign a couple of places to make the divorce official. I can't see where it matters. In the fall, Theresa took Jim and moved back to her father's dairy farm in Quebec. Papers or not, you can't get more divorced than that.

Theresa's been waiting for them, though, so after a hamburger, I take the phone out to the front stoop and punch in the number, which I know by heart. My lot sits next to Kovac's U-pick-em blueberry farm. The berries have not come in yet, but Kovac's dog Buster—a German shepherd big enough to tow my trailer—is patrolling the rows. I whistle, and he comes over and sits next to me while I pet him. It's warm for March, but there's a steady breeze and before long I'm fighting shivers.

After four or five rings, someone picks up the phone.

"*Allo*?" It's a man's voice, but not Theresa's father's.

"*Je voudrais parler avec Theresa*," I say. I've memorized the phrase. It's like one word to me, like abracadabra, but it works. A few seconds later, Theresa comes on the line.

"Mitch?" She pronounces it *Meetch.*

"Yeah," I say. "Hi, T."

"Hi." Her father's house has only one phone, so I know she is standing in the kitchen, probably looking out the window, probably at cows.

"Jimmy is in bed," she says. Her voice doesn't give anything away.

"It's all right," I say. The news relieves me. Since moving to Quebec, Jimmy lapses into French every now and then when he's talking to me. It's like having a conversation with some little foreign kid I've never met. "I called to talk to you."

Right away she's happy. "The papers have come?"

I stand up and walk over the edge of the lot. Buster trails along. The phone crackles.

"You're awfully anxious for a Catholic girl. Isn't the Pope going to kick you out of the club for this?"

"He will forgive me, I think. A Methodist wedding doesn't count."

"Sure it does. To a Methodist."

"Are you a Methodist now?"

"No."

"No," she repeats. "And you're not Baptist or Lutheran or Episcopalian and your congressman is a thief."

"Senator," I say.

"And the rich get richer, and Babe Ruth had syphilis, and, and, and." She takes a deep breath, to brake herself. "I can't talk now."

I think of the voice that answered the phone.

"You got company, T?"

She gives the answer I deserve. "At least I waited."

"What's his name?" I ask. "Pierre or Jean-Claude? Does he carry a hockey stick everywhere he goes?"

"Mitch," she says—and this time it sounds like *Mitch*. You see these foreign people on t.v. who start jabbering away in their own language when they get mad. Theresa is just the opposite. The madder she gets, the more American she sounds.

"Have the papers come?" she asks.

The phone hisses. I am standing next to a line of blueberry bushes that borders my yard. In three months the rows will be packed with tourists and summer residents filling buckets berry by berry. I touch one of the bushes and Buster barks. A second later, the floodlights mounted on Kovac's roof come on and Kovac himself appears at the front door. He looks my way, and tells Buster "Okay." Buster wags his tail, a happy bureaucrat.

"They came," I tell Theresa.

She sighs. "You always make things so difficult," she says, and from her accent, you'd almost think that she'd grown up in Petoskey.

She's right. I feel guilty again about never learning French.

"What's the weather like there?" I try to ask the question the way Tucker would ask it.

"Cold. We had snow today."

"You're the only person I know who lives further north than me. You and Jim."

She says, "So?"

"So nothing. It's strange when you think about it. That you can always go further north."

"No." It's a French "no." She's calmer. "Eventually you are going south."

Around quitting time the next day, Tucker shows up at the job site. We drive to a bar outside Petoskey, a roadside place made of cinderblock that doesn't have a name so far as I know. The trees are still bare, and the roads aren't busy the way they will be in a few weeks when tourists start arriving. The sky is clear in every direction, pale spring blue.

At the bar, Tucker orders a couple of beers, which we take to a pool table in the back. It's not quite level, and the felt is torn in places. The table's condition throws my game off, but Tucker can barely hold a cue, and in the first game he's cleared only two stripes when I sink the eight.

"You know what I've decided about you, Mitch?" Tucker asks. "That you must think a lot. Because you sure don't talk much."

"I never learned how to keep talking when there's nothing to say."

"Oh," Tucker smiles, making fun of himself. "I find there's always something to say."

As Tucker racks the balls for another game, I tell him that my divorce papers came.

"Congratulations," he says.

I raise my beer to him.

"I got to tell you, Mitch, I always envied you being married."

"You must enjoy stubbing your toe."

"Depends what I stub it on." He puts enough chalk on his cue to write the Bible with. "And if you stubbed your toe, it wasn't Theresa you stubbed it on. I forget her name, but it wasn't Theresa."

"Once," I say. Two stripes drop on my break.

"Once," Tucker repeats. "If you ask me—and I know you didn't—an affair is an affair."

"It wasn't an affair."

"So what was it?"

I line up my next shot, sighting down the cue stick, to the cue ball, to the beer-stained felt.

"An excuse. That's what Theresa called it."

Tucker hums like he doesn't believe me, but it's true. Whatever went wrong between me and Theresa didn't go wrong in a loud way; no yelling, no big fights. But when it did go wrong, you couldn't miss it. Looking back, the marriage didn't have a chance. I couldn't list all the reasons why—I'd gotten her pregnant, she was nineteen, six years younger than me, her family was too far away. She never liked that we lived in a mobile home. "A carpenter in a mobile home," she'd say, then she'd toss something French at me which I eventually began to translate *How can such a thing possibly be?* When she brought up the idea of divorce, it made more sense than the marriage ever did.

"I plan on getting married someday," Tucker says. "Some woman who gets turned on by bow-legged men. Having half a dozen kids who ignore me."

"Well, Tucker," I say. "On your golden anniversary I'll be first in line to ask you for advice."

Tucker grins as I sink the eight ball. "Am I full of shit?" he asks.

A few weeks later, the divorce is official. The envelope comes on a Monday. I open it up, look at Theresa's signature on the papers, and then put them in a drawer with my birth certificate, my journeyman's card, and a fourteen-year-old report card from one of the two semesters—the good one—I went to Michigan State.

The next morning, I'm up on the roof building a dormer. Roger and Jamie are nearby putting down shingles. Jamie is talking about a television special that was on the night before. He and Roger watch a lot of TV. Roger used to say he didn't mind paying his cable bill because he got his money's worth out of it. That was before he got pulled over again for drunk driving and ended up in a halfway house. Now he gets around on a little motor scooter that doesn't require a license to drive. Loaded with Roger's two hundred and thirty pounds, it can manage—maybe—twenty-five miles an hour on level road. Cramped onto it, knees bent halfway to his chest, he looks like a straggler from a clown parade.

To judge by his most frequent complaints, the greatest hardship about the halfway house is that it has only one television, which all the residents have to share. He refers to his housemates as "them fucking guys."

I didn't watch the show Jamie is talking about, but I'd seen advertisements. It was an end-of-the-world thing. In the previews, a serious voice asks whether we are on the brink of Armageddon while these old-time drawings of hell and devils and shots of mushroom clouds flash on the screen. At the end, an academic type comes on. "All the prophets agree on one point," he says in a tone like he's a scientist and these are the facts. "Time is running short."

I look out over Lake Michigan. It's busier every day. A dozen or so sailboats creep along the horizon. I don't believe all the Armageddon stuff, but we're definitely on the brink of tourist season. These are the first sailboats I've seen since getting divorced, I think. This is the first open water I've seen since getting divorced. I expect to get over this.

Theresa was working at the Grand Hotel on Mackinac island when we first started going out. The hotel had moved her from waitress to maid when none of the customers could understand her English. Northern Michigan was supposed to be a temporary stop for her, a working vacation before she started doing whatever it was she was going to do for the rest of her life. I don't think she ever had any firm plans. She'd just gotten tired of living on a dairy farm in Quebec. Then, like a lot of people I've known who've left small towns and come back, she began to wonder what she'd expected to find.

She didn't expect to find a husband. I met her through a friend who captained a charter boat on the island. My father still owned the contracting business, and though he didn't like it, I had no trouble getting time off to go visit her. Two or three times a week, I'd make the half hour drive to Mackinac City, then ferry over to the island. The place didn't offer much in the way of entertainment. It doesn't allow cars, and there's no place to drive anyway. Other than the Grand Hotel, the island has a few bars, some souvenir stores, and I don't know how many fudge shops. When Theresa wasn't working, we'd go to the bar or swim. Mostly we stayed in her room, though I had to sneak in since she wasn't supposed to have visitors. We'd lie in her bed for hours having conversations that should have taken fifteen minutes. Theresa has this theory that we ended up getting married because each of us could hardly understand what the other one was saying. We could think whatever we wanted. She could get into the kitchen, so we ate pretty well.

A lumber truck backfires down in the yard. Jamie is still considering interpretations of various prophecies. He wonders whether Kennedy or Martin Luther King was the great man that one of the prophets predicted would be killed by thunder from the sky. The show doesn't have him convinced, but he's troubled.

"Freaky, freaky," he says. "It gets you to thinking."

He asks if Roger saw the show. Roger spits over the edge of the roof.

"No," he says bitterly. "I wanted to, but them fucking guys had to watch the Oscars."

After the problem with the plumbing, Mrs. Simmons makes a point of driving up to check our progress—once a week at first, then more often. By the time tourist season is in full swing, she is staying at a Holiday Inn in Harbor Springs three or four nights a week. It's a hundred and seventy-five dollars per, and whenever something doesn't meet her expectations she threatens to make Tucker pay it. Most of the time she just hangs around and makes everyone edgy. Tucker is the only one who can talk to her. She has a sharp voice that carries, and I'll hear her complaining across the lot, clear as a bell. I never hear what Tucker says, but Mrs. Simmons usually ends up nodding and letting him lead her around the property, taking his arm as they step over ditches or go up unfinished steps.

She asks lots of questions, but almost never catches real faults. You have to use tools to see the real faults. That's the thing about tools—they show mistakes. You work with them enough, you realize nothing's perfect. Everything's a little off. A simple balance—what that'll tell you, that bubble. You're better off not knowing. Or a tile floor. You aim to lay tiles within a sixty-fourth of a true ninety degree angle. Theoretically it should be perfect. It should be 00 tolerance--straight. But it never is. No matter how careful you are, sometimes you finish and find out you're only within a sixteenth. Roger and Jamie have the attitudes. They'll discover some slight imperfection—a shaggy angle, maybe, a wavering in a line of shingles, or maybe the transit shows a little variation in floor level.

"Good enough," Roger will say. "We ain't building a fucking piano."

On my birthday in June, I go down to Traverse City with a woman I've been introduced to who manages a swimsuit store that's only open during the summer. It's a date, but it feels more like a veteran's reunion. She's recently divorced too, and because we both try to avoid the topic, the conversation keeps dying out. I got used to it pretty quick when Theresa and Jim moved to Quebec, but it's harder to adjust to the divorce. I wouldn't have thought so, but the papers make a difference.

"I used to have pride," she tells me at one point in the evening. The remark comes out of nowhere. We're sitting in a bar halfway between Traverse City and Petoskey. We'd both decided we needed to drink more. "It wasn't that I was just choosy. It was more like I was sure that I'd end up with the guy I'd always imagined. Not anymore. Now I'll go out with just about anyone."

She takes a slug of beer, and looks at me, glassy-eyed. "Don't take that wrong."

I'm drunk. What she says doesn't hurt my feelings, but I pretend it does because I know the conversation will die out again if I tell her I know what she means.

"What's the right way to take it?"

"Oh, I'm no catch either," she says. "I've still got my body, but I'm neurotic. No one has to tell me. I know. After a while I start to drive people crazy."

"You do have your body," I say because it's something to say.

"I work out. Selling swimsuits keeps you motivated." She signals the waiter. After he's taken her order for another beer, she appraises me. "Are you—as they say—in the mood, Mitch?"

Truthfully, I don't know if I am in the mood, but it feels like there's a part I have to play. "It's been nine months."

"Well, Doug, don't think you're going to break the streak tonight. I'm celibate."

"Who's Doug?"

"What?" She gives me a look like she doesn't know what I'm talking about.

"You just called me Doug."

"I did?" She sounds disappointed in herself, but shrugs it off. "Oh, you don't mind being Doug for the night, do you?" She reaches across the table and puts her hand on mine. "Come on, be a sport."

"Sure," I say. We've been sitting here too long. My beer has gotten warm. "Why are you celibate?"

"Because it lets me focus on the important things. Sex is a distraction."

"That's the best thing about it," I say. "What are the important things?"

"Well," she sips her beer, "I'll admit I don't know yet. It's only been a week."

One Friday in early July, Mrs. Simmons is waiting at the site when I pull in. Instead of greeting her, I sit in the truck, pretending to look over a set of plans, glancing up at the house occasionally. We have the front half-sided, cedar-shakes up to the second floor, bare sheathing from there to the roof. All day yesterday, Jamie kept joking that the house was going topless.

After a minute or two, Mrs. Simmons makes her way toward me. I see her out of the corner of my eye, but I don't look up until she taps on the window.

"Morning," I say.

Her eyes narrow. "Follow me."

Without waiting, she turns away and starts across the lot. I follow her to a skid of cinder blocks at the back of the house. Laying in the mud is a turd. There's no denying that it is a human turd. Next to it is a sweat sock that someone put to emergency use.

"What's this?" she asks.

The answer is so obvious it makes me think that I don't understand the question. I shake my head.

"Who's responsible?" Her voice is calm, but her earrings quiver.

"Look," I say, glancing around. There are houses on both sides of the site, the lake in front and the road in back. "Whoever it was, he didn't have many options."

"What about the woods?"

The woods border the road. They are perhaps fifty yards away. To someone up on the roof, they could look like a long ways off.

"Some of the guys drink a lot of coffee," I say.

She makes eye contact and maintains it. After a few seconds it occurs to me that she has made up her mind to wait for me to look away, so I do.

"Well, it's a perfect metaphor for this project," she says, turning to go. "Whoever it was could have at least cleaned up after himself."

Later in the afternoon she comes back with Tucker. She leads him to the cinder blocks, but by then I've gotten rid of the metaphor. They stand at the spot for a while, then begin walking around the site together, examining the house. At one point I hear Tucker tell her to keep her eyes open for someone wearing only one sock.

That night, I call Theresa, but she's out. Jim answers the phone. We talk about school for a while. I listen for any trace of a French accent in his words, but he still sounds like any kid born and raised in Michigan. According to Theresa, he speaks French as well as he does English. Visiting Quebec for a week once, I bumped the rear end of some farmer's pick-up. Jim was with me, and he had to translate while the farmer cursed me out.

"How's Mom?" I eventually ask.

"The same," he tells me, bored but patient.

"Exactly the same? Isn't her hair longer." Theresa had told me she was letting it grow out.

"It's long," Jim says.

"Is it still brown?"

"Uh huh."

"How about her eyes? Are they still brown?"

"Of course," he says. His tone tells me that my question is dumb.

"How do you say that in French? Brown."

He says a word and suddenly sounds like some French kid I've never met. I try to repeat the word.

"No, Daddy." He says the word again, emphasizing the pronunciation.

"Is she still pretty?" I ask.

"Yes," he says, matter-of-factly.

I want to ask him if I could still almost completely encircle her waist with my hands, if the mole under her left shoulder blade is still there, if she still whispers in her sleep, if her lower left front tooth still tilts a little to the side.

"Does she still hum while she's making dinner?" I ask.

"Oh," Jim starts, and by a distance that comes into his voice, I know that something else has gotten his attention. Maybe a cow wandering through the kitchen.

"No," he says. "She sings."

In September, a miracle happens. We finish the Simmons job, and Mrs. Simmons is happy with it, or at least satisfied. I'm there when Tucker takes her on the final inspection—a kind of joke since she has basically supervised construction over the last month. There have been signs that she might like the place—a compliment on the spiral staircase, a nod at the cabinet work—but just two days before, she noticed a drywall seam on a vaulted ceiling twenty-five feet in the air and wondered out loud what else she would find after we had all "washed our hands of the place."

As we tour the house, though, she smiles. It looks good the way new things can look good, when the gleam hides small mistakes that will seem obvious later—a post that interferes with the view of the lake from the dining room, a transom window that should be four or five inches lower. Right now, the brass trim around the fireplace shines in the evening sun. The interior still smells like new wood. The balcony offers a view to the horizon. We finish in the living room, standing in front of peaked windows that look out over Lake Michigan.

Mrs. Simmons takes a deep breath. "So we made it."

"You didn't doubt it?" Tucker teases.

"I think we both did."

She looks at me when she says this. Surprised, I only nod.

"I know I wasn't easy to get along with," she says.

"A house is a big investment," Tucker says. "You should be picky."

"I had to learn to keep re-adjusting my expectations. I guess you do with this kind of project."

This sounds like something Tucker has told her. It's true, but the way she puts it, it sounds like a pitch.

"It was a big job all right," Tucker agrees.

"My husband," she says. "He doesn't believe in adjusting."

"Nothing wrong with that," Tucker says.

She turns back to the window. We all do. The sun is setting behind the lake, shining on the polished oak floor.

Mrs. Simmons sighs. I don't think she's talking to anyone when she says, "He's a surgeon."

After saying goodbye to Mrs. Simmons, Tucker and I drive to the party that Tucker always throws for the crew after we finish a job. This has been our biggest single job to date, and the party reflects it. Rather than the VFW or the Petoskey Community Hall, Tucker has rented the banquet room of the Harbor

Springs Yacht Club. Little Traverse Bay is busy, speedboats pulling skiers, catamarans, sailboards. The water glitters. We eat from a buffet of barbecued chicken and spare ribs. There is an open bar, which Tucker watches to make sure Roger avoids. None of us except Tucker belongs to the club, and we stand out in the crowd. It makes me feel like a crasher. We sit on the balcony overlooking the harbor and drink and as a joke send beers to people watching us.

After the party breaks up, Tucker and I stop at the site of the next job. The lot sits above a small ravine. It's late. You can't see much, but we park and stare into the dark, listening to the Tigers play the Mariners out west. It used to feel good finishing a big job, and tonight I remember the feeling. I haven't seen the plans to this new place yet, and I ask Tucker what it's going to be.

"An A-frame," he tells me. "Simple. You'll have it framed in a few days."

"A fresh start."

"Not a bad ending, either."

"Better than I would've guessed," I admit.

We're quiet for a minute. The Tigers leave two on at the end of seven. While everyone in Seattle is stretching, Tucker asks, "Do you want them back, Mitch?"

"Who?"

"Jim. Theresa."

Normally, I wouldn't want to discuss the topic with Tucker, but tonight, I give it some thought. Theresa and Jim back here, or me in Quebec.

"Not much chance of that."

"You know something I've learned?" Tucker asks. "Sometimes you've just got to look at things and say, 'This is not a problem. One way or another, I can handle this.'"

He looks at me for a response, but I don't give him one. He cracks open a beer.

"When I was fifteen, I started doing snow-removal. It was a big thing for me at the time. A good truck, a plow—all that costs. I took practically every penny I'd made from the lawn service the first two summers and put it into snow equipment. It wasn't a problem getting customers. I was only fourteen, though, so I had to get my brother to drive the truck. It worked pretty well for a few weeks. He'd plow driveways while I shoveled walks or whatever.

"Then all of a sudden he gets sick of waking up in the middle of the night when it snows and he quits on me. I can't find anyone else to drive, so what do I do?"

"You drive yourself."

"Right," he nods. "My first day out, a county deputy caught me—Janke. Know him?"

"Of him." Janke has pulled Roger over two of the three times he's been caught driving under the influence.

"Yeah, well, he got me, but he didn't bring me home. You know why? Because it had snowed about eight inches the night before, and he needed his driveway plowed. That's where he caught me, in his driveway. I was halfway finished when he came out and asked me where my brother was. I told him, and he asked me if I was sure I knew how to handle the truck, and I said yes. He said, okay, but to stay off the main roads and not to come into town. And so that's what I did, though every now and then I'd sneak in for salt or sand or a new shovel. That's how it is—once you get in a little bit, you can usually get in a little more."

He has turned fully toward me. He is glowing in the dashlight. "If you want them back, you can get them back."

I finish my beer. "I can't give her what she wants."

Instead of asking me what she wanted—a question I'd have no trouble answering—Tucker starts the truck.

"It doesn't matter what she wants," he says. "The key is making her want what you can give."

Twenty minutes later we're on the Mackinac Bridge, heading north. During the day, the bridge is busy with tourists crossing it for no reason other than that it is the longest suspension bridge in the world. They drive the five miles to the Upper Peninsula, turn around and drive back. This time of the night, the bridge is nearly empty. Lake Michigan is black beneath us. It's windy. Gusts shove the truck so that Tucker has to fight to stay centered in the lane.

"It's eighteen hours," I say. "We could make it to New York city faster."

"We'll drive in shifts," Tucker says, darting his eyes toward the railing. The bridge makes him nervous. "Be back Sunday afternoon."

"What would you have done if you'd gotten into an accident?" I ask. "With the plow."

"I don't know. Something." His knuckles whiten on the steering wheel as a gust of wind rocks the truck. "You remember that car got blown over the railing last year? What was it? An Escort or an Accord or something?" He shakes his head. "If that's not a reason for buying a big car, I don't know what is."

He gets tired after a couple hours but won't admit it. Every now and then, I have to take the steering wheel to keep the truck from drifting off the road. After going through customs at Sault Ste. Marie, we stop at a service area to switch seats. Tucker digs a blanket out of the back and wraps himself in it.

"What are you going to tell her?" he asks me.

"I'll ask if she wants to try again."

"Okay," Tucker says. He reclines the seat. His eyes close slowly. "But don't just ask her. Tell her why it's a good idea. Be specific. Think of something she'll like to hear." He yawns. "Rehearse it in your head."

I don't answer. Just when I'm sure Tucker has fallen asleep, his eyes open. "You tired?"

I shake my head. I've been awake for almost twenty-four hours, but I feel alert.

Tucker's eyes close again. "It's the best thing for Jim," he says.

I keep driving.The highway is deserted. I can't see in the darkness, but I've made this drive before so I know that Canada doesn't look much different than northern Michigan—the same trees, the same grass, the same rolling hills. Tucker's truck glides past it all at an effortless eighty-five. It's a good truck. It's part of what keeping me going. The ride is so easy that I can't stop. And who knows? That's what I think as I drive. Who knows? Tucker might be right. The possibility keeps me awake all through Ontario. The countryside does not change when we cross into Quebec, but suddenly Canada feels like a foreign country. At a truck stop where I gas up and get coffee, the kid behind the counter has an accent. Back on the highway, I turn on the radio and half of the announcers are speaking French.

I settle on an AM station out of Montreal. All the talk tells me it must be a news station. Now and then a word that I know falls out of the edgeless conversation, sinks in easy as a nail struck dead center. Listening, I remember times with Theresa—she'd be on the phone with her father or reading a story to Jim in French—when the language seemed easy, when it seemed like I could understand exactly what she was saying if I just paid a little more attention. The idea comes to me to memorize a few words to recite for Theresa, for kicks, for good will. On the radio, the announcer pauses for a breath, then begins talking again. I turn up the radio and concentrate on the voices that fill the cab, listening hard for something that sounds right.

# What We Won't Do

**Brock Clarke**

There are no astronauts born and raised in my town. Maybe if there were, I would not have done the following: destroyed one marriage, two friendships, and my wife's confidence in me as a dependable life-partner. Nor would I have turned an innocent barbecue—the kind of peaceful American backyard outing you'd see in a commercial for Ford trucks or the beef industry—into something you'd see in a professional wrestling steel cage match. But I have done these things, and that's because there are no astronauts born and raised in my town. No olympic figure skaters or beauty queens or I-knew-him-then and look-at-him-now quarterbacks either. No returning dignitaries of any kind. I believe that this is a problem for all five thousand of us here in Little Falls, this forgotten chunk of earth in upstate New York. We could all use a good parade, a fund raiser, something where we could stand to the side and lie about the ways and degrees in which we violated the famous in our youth. Who we fucked standing up, who we beat the absolute-living-hell out of, who we out-drank and then left laid out in their own vomit. All we want is the chance to do violence to our old classmates' bodies and to their reputations. Maybe tear down their *Welcome Home* banners.

Other towns have their opportunities. I went to a parade in Herkimer last year. A soap opera star home for Fourth of July. He was a big, good-looking guy with a California tan. His name is Chip and you've seen him. He's as famous as famous gets. As Chip eased by on the town's favorite-son convertible, an old boy in front of me said, "A goddamned queer. Remember? Remember him and Boyle outside the art room?"

"Remember?" his buddy said in gleeful mock outrage. "I was there to beat the shit out of the both of them."

By God, that's what we need. Someone to hate from great distances of time and space and social circles. A politician, someone who wants to be one, anything.

As it stands, we're left with each other. This is what I'm here to tell you downstaters and outsiders who have your pick of scapegoats and enemies and hated rising stars. Up here, we don't have those kinds of choices. We're stuck wounding the people we know in all the familiar, vicious ways. It's not something we can help.

I am also here to tell you that we hurt each other so badly because of our jobs, because of who does what, for how much and for how long. Me, I'm a school teacher. Ninth grade English, to be exact. My wife, Sabrina, is a dental hygienist, a hard job I'm sure, and one I don't like to think about. The reason is, once a year Sabrina makes me come in for a cleaning and she's a changed person in that room, I swear. She wears a protective mask, a face-length visor. I tell her she looks like a welder in that thing and that is exactly the way she acts: like a person possessed by the charm of dangerous machinery. The fact that she lives in people's mouths just complicates things. Her sort of oral violence doesn't sit well with me, necessary or not.

"Open up," she tells me while I'm in the chair. "Spit." These are commands, not requests. What kind of way is that for two married people to talk? That's not the way it works at home, believe it, but at work anything goes.

"Your mouth is a disaster," Sabrina says.

"That's an awful thing to say," I tell her.

"I'm just doing my job," she claims, and I believe she is right. You see what I mean? You see how work can ruin people? You see why we need someone with a world, a job beyond the scope of our own, someone who will come home and let us feel up their livelihood and smile and wave and pretend that they don't know it's happening?

It takes two whole weeks after a routine cleaning for my wife and me to be in love again.

I'm telling you all this because of what happened two weeks ago, Friday, July 29, when we had people over to dinner, and when my ideas about work turned from theory to practice to disaster. There were four people coming over to our house that night, two couples, people Sabrina and I knew pretty well. Michael and Celene were and are doctors, one a pathologist and one an obstetrician. And then Sid and Lori: ex-high school math teacher and real-estate agent, respectively. Sid quit teaching two years ago, citing burn-out, and hasn't found another job since. Sid also drinks, heavily, although Lori does not drink at all. She does have a good temper, though, and a nice way of dealing privately with public problems. To be true, I find this quality plenty endearing. Lori is a woman who knows that life, at its core, is embarrassing.

As for Michael and Celene, they don't do much except for work, although they do play tennis. They make a big deal out of this, playing tennis every Saturday morning. It's their quality time, the rock-solid basis to their marriage. They're not afraid to publicize it.

Sabrina is neutral about which couple she likes better, but I prefer Sid and Lori, something she can't understand.

"Why do you have to like one more than the other?" she says. "What is your thing with having favorites?"

"It's not that I have to like one more than the other. I just do. I just happen to like Sid and Lori better. There is no compulsion involved here. And I like Sid the best out of everyone. That doesn't make it a political choice."

"But you're a teacher," she says. "You're supposed to be neutral."

I laugh at that one every time. "There is a kid is my lower-level section," I tell her. "Every time I turn around to the board, he punches the girl next to him in the side of the head. He hits her with a closed fist. How neutral should I feel about that little asshole?"

Still, I like Michael and Celene fine. "They're both perfectly nice people," I told Sabrina the night before they came over for dinner.

And it's true: they are perfectly nice people. But it is also true that I had been in a bad way in the days and weeks leading up to that dinner. For one, it was my summer vacation, and I'd been doing some drinking. This doesn't make me much different from most people; it's just that my summer vacation lasts the whole summer and not a week or two weeks or anything remotely human like that. No surprise, this is also when I start thinking about the people I know, about what they do for a living and what they don't do. This kind of speculation helps pass incredible amounts of time, especially in late July, the belly of my vacation, when a life of leisure wears thin in places you can't begin to imagine.

"Listen to this jerk-off," my working friends always say when I complain about all my free time. Around mid-July they become consumed with the thought of their week-long August vacations and their neglected Criscraft outboards and their Lake Placid time-shares and their rural white-boy *Field and Stream* dreams of the good life. They listen to me complaining and spin off into some new lower middle-class orbit of righteousness. "Three months of vacation and he's bitching. What kind of job is it you have anyway? You call what you do *work*? And it's people like me who are paying your salary. I pay taxes. You're fired."

And so on. My out-of-work friends, like Sid, have no such complaints. They're just happy to have someone around in the middle of the day, someone they can call at noon on a Tuesday and ask, "What's going on?" and someone who will answer, "Nothing." My out-of-work friends have almost no interest in putting me on the defensive. They're ecstatic that they're not alone for once, that someone isn't shitting on them with their salt-of-the-earth routine.

What I'm saying is that I was in a truly susceptible frame of mind the day of our dinner party. I could make excuses and say that the dinner was a matter of bad timing, that if it had been a week later everything would have been fine. I could say that July is just a bad month for me, flat out, with its surplus of free time and beer and heat. That I'm just not a July person. In fact, I have said these things. I have also said, "I'm sorry," repeatedly. To this, Sabrina responds, "Don't be a goddamn liar, Gerald."

There is no good comeback to this. I *am* sorry, but it's also true that I am, on occasion, a liar. It is my lying that started all our troubles, a fact that makes Sabrina's request so difficult to ignore.

Anyway, the six of us sat down at our backyard picnic table that night, and all was fine at first—the shish kabob was good, the conversation friendly—and we were into our second bottle of wine and having an early go at drunkenness when Michael asked Sid: "So, how's the job search going?"

Sid was chewing a piece a meat and finished chewing before saying to Michael: "Nothing new, nothing big."

"That's really too bad. It's unbelievable, really. What kind of things are you looking for?"

"Well, I'm looking at different things. What I'd really like to do is work with my hands. You know, something that will keep me busy, make me tired. A good tired, is what I'm saying, not just a mental tired."

The truth was that Sid wasn't looking at all and Michael should have known that. He should have known by the way Sid spoke that this wasn't a conversation that interested him. Work or talking about work, particularly his own, wasn't high on his list of things to do. And it's not that Michael was a bastard about the whole thing. He was just a little dense, which is not as bad as being mean-spirited, but is just as dangerous.

"Really?" Michael said. He seemed interested now. He dropped the fork he'd been holding and raised his glass of wine to his mouth. "What kind of work are you thinking about, exactly? I mean there are all kinds of things you might do."

"I've got an eye out for carpentry jobs. I've done some general construction and that wasn't so bad. I could do that. But carpentry is the way I think I'll go."

That was as good a place to end the conversation as any. Sid set it up that way and we all saw it, I think, except for Michael. He had an eye-shine that said: "I'd like to help you." He wasn't in any mood to be subtle. He was busy being philanthropic.

"So where are you looking? I mean, what kind of channels are you going through?" Michael clearly directed these questions at Sid, but it was Lori who answered.

"You know, Sid and I decided that we're too old to go rushing into things. I mean, Jesus we're not that old, but we are particular. We can wait out the good jobs. I get the inside track on all the contracting and development news through my office. The big and the small stuff. Something will come up, and there isn't much use thinking about it until it does."

There was a pause and Sabrina took the opportunity with both fists.

"Would anyone like more food? Wine? Celene, you look like you could use a little more."

Celene did want a little more wine and said so. In fact, everyone wanted some. This was as pure a diversionary tactic as I've ever seen and for a few seconds it worked. Those few seconds were the crucial time. I probably should have said something. Something to move the conversation. As the host, that was my job. I should have been a neutralizing force. But why just me? Why not anyone else? We all gave Michael another chance to push things too far.

"You know, there is something to be said about patience," Michael went on. "Patience is a good thing. But on the other hand, sometimes you have to go out and get things. You can't just wait for them. Sometimes that's the worst thing you can do."

Michael's voice had changed slightly. It sounded like he had a job and wanted to know why anybody couldn't get one. I heard it and I'm sure Sid heard it too, both of us being sensitive to these types of things. Sabrina claimed later that she didn't hear, but she did think that Michael was pushing things a little too far. This means she heard, and could admit to it only in code.

And maybe Michael himself knew that he had pushed things too far, because he gave a little embarrassed laugh and said: "Well, you could always go back to teaching. That's not exactly backbreaking work anyway, is it."

This was clearly a joke. I knew that. But still, I got myself into a little fit of resentment and said: "Wait a minute."

"Come on, Gerald," Sabrina said. "I've heard you say the exact same thing."

And I have, it's true. I've often said that we teachers don't *work*, exactly. What we do is plan, budget. We section off the day into seven, fifty minute periods. We take ten periods of material and turn it into fifteen. For instance, I can stretch out *Julius Caesar* for eleven periods. That's five hundred and fifty minutes, not counting attendance, which I tend to drag out like an acceptance speech. Five hundred and fifty minutes may be more than *Julius Caesar* needs, but it is a testament to my ability to make things—time, literature—work for me.

I wouldn't say I work, then; I would say I do a kind of simple math for a living. I am a mostly well-intentioned, highly educated bean counter. Nonetheless, I didn't like Michael joking about my job one bit, no matter how true the joke was. So I turned against him somewhat, and even found myself *hating* Michael a little, when Sid took a sip of wine and asked, "So, Michael, who was that you were with the other day when I saw you?"

"Who was who?"

"That woman you were with the other day. You were coming out of the hospital with her and I waved, but you didn't see me."

Which was a lie. I know it was a lie because Sid would never have waved to Michael. He doesn't know him well enough; in fact, Sid and Michael only knew each other through me, and weren't really friends at all. In Sid's mind, they didn't have that kind of relationship, the kind where you would flag someone down from great distances. Michael, not operating by these rules of social reservation, couldn't have known that, but I did. I knew Sid wasn't anywhere near the hospital and I knew he didn't see Michael there, companion or not.

"I'm not sure when you're talking about," Michael said.

"It was the other day. I think it was Tuesday, although it might have been Wednesday. I think she might have been another doctor."

"Why do you say that? Was she wearing a lab coat or something?"

"She may have, but I'm not too sure. I can remember just thinking that she looked like a doctor, if that makes any sense."

It was obvious that Sid was having a good time at this point, but the conversation hadn't gone far enough to make the rest of us uncomfortable. At this moment, we just wanted to know where it was all going and how it was going to be resolved. There is intrigue in unraveling these mysteries of mutual acquaintances, and we waited for them to arrive at the right name, the right place and time.

I shouldn't use the word "we" so easily. Celene was probably already uncomfortable. She knew where this might be going. Her face said that this was old, familiar territory.

"Maybe it was Lynn Karpath," Celene said, turning to her husband.

"No, I don't think it was Dr. Karpath. I haven't seen her lately. Or in a while, for that matter." Michael's voice was jerky, like it was caught on something. It was a small thing but we all could hear it. He asked for more wine and Sabrina poured him some.

Celene looked away from her husband and over at Sid. She asked him, "This woman. Did she have blonde hair?"

"Yes, she did."

"Was she my height, maybe a little taller?"

"A little taller. Yeah, I think that's right. Not too much taller though. Maybe an inch." Sid thought about it for a second. "Two inches at most," he said.

"It sounds like Lynn Karpath to me," Celene said.

"Well, it must be her then. I'm glad we figured this out." I looked over at Sid. He didn't seem like he was having fun anymore. He looked serious, like he was willing to take things where they shouldn't go.

Michael and Celene were sitting next to each other on one bench, Sid and Lori doing the same on the opposite side of the table. Sabrina and I sat at the ends in white plastic chairs. Michael turned all the way around to face Celene, his legs straddling the bench. In a deadly serious voice he said, "Celene, I don't care what Sid says he saw. I wasn't walking with Lynn Karpath. If it was her he saw, then it wasn't me she was walking with. If it was me, it wasn't her."

If you've ever heard someone tell the truth, you would know that Michael was telling it at that moment. His voice was clear, each consonant, each vowel sure of its own purity. It was a kind of voice you wouldn't challenge if you were at all interested in honesty.

"You know, Michael, I think I saw you with someone like that the other day too. It wasn't exactly in front of the hospital, but it was near there."

I don't know exactly why I said it, and the reasons I have probably aren't good enough to mention. I should have just let them settle it. It should have stayed something between Sid and Michael and Michael and Celene. Let's just say I don't know why I did it. Let's just say it slipped, and that I would take it back if retraction were still a possibility. If that isn't good enough, let's just say I felt like I was involved already. Staying out of it didn't seem to be an option.

Without moving, Michael looked at me and said, "You know you are a fucking liar. You've got to know that. There can't be any doubt in your mind that you are a conscienceless fucking liar."

With that, Sid came over the table at Michael. It was something he had been waiting to do, although I suspect that Sid doesn't really hate Michael, doesn't even dislike him. The circumstances were right. There were strange, unspoken things going between the three of us, forces that made us do what we did. I'd like to think that things were beyond our control, although Sabrina claims that this is so much garbage, and I have to admit that she's probably right.

By the time I got in there to break it up, Sid was kneeling on table and he had Michael bent over backwards. Michael's legs were stuck somehow underneath the bench. In that position, Sid was obviously getting the better of it. He had all the advantages of leverage and gravity. When I tried to separate them, I somehow got caught up in the flaying limbs, the push-and-pull of things, and we all fell to the ground. I threw a few punches while we were there on the grass, and got hit by a few. The blows were soft-sounding, muffled, as if we weren't really hitting each other but plastic dolls made to look like us. The women were yelling, but other than that, noise seemed to have lost its ability to have any real effect upon the three of us.

We stopped fighting when Michael got hold of a salad bowl and hit Sid over the head with it. The bowl was ceramic and it shattered on impact, but not before making an unmistakable sound. The sound was loud, a resounding crack. It was a sound that tells you when a fight is about to become something irreversible, something settled not by mutual consent but by hospitals, lawyers, by the people who love you and their life-long grudges.

I lay there for a second and watched everyone get their things together and leave. Sid was bleeding badly from his forehead. It was something he should have gone to the hospital for, but I have no way of knowing if he did. We haven't talked to or seen each other since. I think we're afraid to see each other, as if seeing each other might be a kind of confession in itself. He and Lori left, and Michael and Celene followed them a minute later. Michael somehow remembered to take the casserole dish they had brought over. It might be the only intact thing they left with that night. I don't know. I haven't spoken to any of them and that's too bad. They are all decent people, as far as decency goes.

Sabrina and I sat outside for a while that night. The sun went down while we sat there and the air turned cool, too cool for what we were wearing. Sabrina got up once to get sweatshirts for both of us and ice for my right eye, which was swelling from the fight. When she went inside and when she came back out the motion light came on, spooking me like it always does. I remember looking up into that light and watching the bugs swarm there, diving into and in front of the bulb's eye. I wondered how they managed to get there so quickly, if they waited there in the dark for hours, just for the chance to do what they were supposed to. Those bugs were opportunists. God knows what they wanted from that light or why they wanted it, but at the very least they were in the right positions to get at it first.

What happens when one bug gets what another one doesn't? I wondered that night. What happens then? I suspect I already know the answer. It isn't what you would call a taxing question.

That night, we sat there in the dark for three hours before we finally went to bed. This was before Sabrina began to blame me for that night, before she bothered to figure out how and why things happened as they did. As I applied ice to my eye, she sat there with her hand on my leg. She moved the hand a couple of times, and once she wiped her face as if she were crying, but mostly we just sat there, watching and listening to our backyard negotiate its sleep with the nighttime.

I remember asking myself that night: What can you count on? It seemed like an important question and I thought about for it a long time. What matters? I thought, listing the things that people normally rely upon: their jobs, their friends, their cars and their connections. I wanted to do away with all of that, to rid myself of all the lousy things of this world. I wanted to reduce life to its bare bones. What do you really need? Ultimately, I decided on Sabrina's hand. It was heavy on my leg, unmoving, and its weight was reassuring. It reminded me of how the best things in this life are supposed to be simple. What else do I need besides this hand on my leg? I asked myself. What else is there?

Sabrina moved the hand, obviously, put it right in her pocket. I suppose she got cold; or maybe she just moved beyond sad, into the place where you break down emotions in terms of who made them public property. Whatever, the hand was moved. I asked Sabrina to put it back on my leg and she did, but it wasn't the same, and when she stuffed her hand back in her pocket a few minutes later, I didn't object.

We sat for a while longer that night, not touching, not speaking, until finally Sabrina asked, "Why can't we be better people? What won't we do to hurt each other?" She didn't look at me, like she was addressing the sky, the house, the motion light, but it was clear whose questions they were to answer.

Those two questions have stayed with me. It's August now, only three weeks until school begins, and there are still no parades scheduled, no rich-and-famous coming home just to place themselves at our collective mercy. No clear shot at someone who is above the fray. And other than that, I still haven't come up with the answers to Sabrina's questions. But I want to be a better person, I do, and so I will keep trying to find those answers. Besides, I don't have much to do until school starts in September anyway—and as everyone knows, being a teacher isn't exactly backbreaking work in the first place—and so even if I haven't found the answers when school begins, I will keep trying.

## — Biographical Statements —

**Jeanne Bryner** was born in Pennsylvania, and then raised in an Ohio mill town. A writer of family and work, she seeks in her prose and poetry to "document the lives of women, children, and men whose names are part of a great American silence: ordinary people." At twenty-five, she studied the art and science of nursing; ten years later, she returned to college to find her voice as a writer. A graduate of Trumbull Memorial Hospital School of Nursing and Kent State University's Honors College, she works as an emergency room nurse and teaches creative writing. Jeanne Bryner is the recipient of fellowships from Bucknell University, the Wick Poetry Program at Kent State University, and the Ohio Arts Council in 1997. Her poetry has been adapted for the stage and performed in Ohio, West Virginia, Texas, Kentucky, New York, and California. Jeanne has two books in print: *Breathless* (Kent State University Press, 1995) and *Blind Horse: Poems* (Bottom Dog Press, 1999).

**Bonnie Jo Campbell** has worked as an egg-sorter, a coffee girl, a typist, a microfilmer, a newspaper keyliner, a museum guard, a math teacher, and English professor, a bicycle tour leader in Russia and Eastern Europe, and a snow cone butcher with the Ringling Bros and Barnum & Bailey Circus. Bonnie's collection *Women & Other Animals* won the 1998 Associated Writing Programs Award for short fiction. Her story "The Smallest Man in the World" will appear in the 2000 Pushcart Anthology. Campbell is finishing "The Barn," a novel set on the banks of the Kalamazoo River.

**Daniel Chacón** has held jobs ranging from walnut picker to dish washer. He earned a master's degree in English from Fresno State and a Masters in Fine Arts from the University of Oregon where he taught composition. He now teaches full-time in the MFA program at the University of Texas at El Paso and "marvels at how gentle my work is compared to pouring hot tar on a roof like my brother or working like my father until he was too bent to work anymore." His stories have appeared in *The Bilingual Review, The Americas Review, Quartely West, The Colorado Review ZYZZYVA*, and *In the Grove*. His first book, *Chicano Chicanery* (Arte Público Press, 2000) is a collection of stories, and he is currently working on a novel called *Joey Molina!*

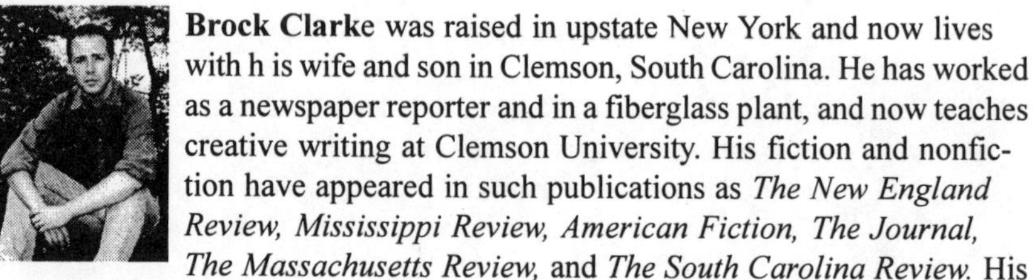

**Brock Clarke** was raised in upstate New York and now lives with h is wife and son in Clemson, South Carolina. He has worked as a newspaper reporter and in a fiberglass plant, and now teaches creative writing at Clemson University. His fiction and nonfiction have appeared in such publications as *The New England Review, Mississippi Review, American Fiction, The Journal, The Massachusetts Review,* and *The South Carolina Review.* His short story collection, *What We Won't Do,* has been awarded the 2000 Mary McCarthy Prize in Short Fiction and will be published by Sarabande Books in 2001.

**Bret Comar** has painted houses, sold bicycles, pumped gas, delivered pizza and taught freshman composition. He is now part owner of a paint contracting and construction business. "My feelings toward work have changed over the years, from not caring for it to finding in it a sense of satisfaction that has increased in more or less direct proportion to the pay." Bret lives in Richland, Michigan with his wife and two daughters. This is his first published short story.

**Daniel Coshnear** lives in Guerneville, California, "under tall trees, across the highway from the Russian River." He works part time night shift at a group home for men and women with mental illnesses and teaches creative writing at San Francisco State University and the University of California's Berkeley Extension. Daniel worked ten years in New York City with mentally retarded adults and prior to that as a housepainter, dishwasher, graveyard grass-cutter and astbestos remover. His unpublished collection of stories is entitled *Jobs & Other Preoccupations.*

**Jim Ray Daniels** was born in Detroit and currently lives in Pittsburgh, where he teaches at Carnegie Mellon University. His other jobs include working as a party store clerk, as a short-order cook, bank bookkeeper, soda jerk, a stockboy in a department store, a janitor, and as an assembly-line worker in an auto plant. His collection of stories, *No Pets*, was published by Bottom Dog Press, 1999. His books of poetry include *Blue Jesus* (Carnegie Mellon, 2000), *Blessing the House* (1997)and *M-80* (1993), both University of Pittsburgh Press; *Punching Out* (Wayne State University Press, 1990) and *Places/ Everyone* (University of Wisconsin Press, 1985). His short story, "No Pets," was turned into an independent feature film directed by Tony Buba in 1994.

**Kathleen De Grave** was born number six of seven children in Kewaunee, Wisconson. Her father was an electrician at a paper mill; her mother ran a small dress shop. Her first job was tending the family grocery store in De Pere, Wisconsin. She has also worked as a cafeteria server, short order cook, dishwasher, canning factory worker, "parent" for troubled girls, Social Security claims adjuster, and English teacher at Pittsburg State University in Kansas. Her two books are *Swindler, Spy, Rebel: The Confidence Woman in 19th-Century America* and the novel, *Company Women* (See Sharp Press 1995).

**Stuart Dybek** lives in Kalamazoo, Michigan where he teaches at Western Michican University. As a youth he worked at labor jobs in construction, washed helicopters, painted buildings, hired out for Man Power (day labor and landscaper). He also worked as a bookkeeper, copywriter, and caseworker for Cook County Department of Public Aid, and yes, on the production line of an ice cream plant. Dybek is the author of three books. His poems, stories, and nonfiction have been widely anthologized and appear regularly in *Harper's, The New Yorker, TriQuarterly,* and *The Iowa Review*. Awards include a Lannan Prize, the PEN/Malamud Award for distinguished achievement in the short story, a Whiting Award, a Guggenheim Fellowship, two National Endowment for the Arts prizes, and three O. Henry Prizes. "Sauerkraut Soup" originally appeared in his *Childhood and other Neighborhoods* (Ecco Press).

**Gary Eller** was raised in North Dakota where he earned a degree in Pharmacy, then a Masters of Fine Arts from the Iowa Writers' Workshop. He worked as a pharmacist in Alaska before returning to the Midwest and was rescued twice from the Alaska wilderness. He is the author of the short story collection *Thin Ice and Other Risks* and is working on a novel set in Alaska and a memoir set in North Dakota. He has published articles on baseball and the craft of writing and the winner of the River City Award in Fiction along with the Fowler Award and a Minnesota Voices Award. He received a Creative Writing Fellowship from the National Endowment for the Arts.

**Percival Everett** grew up in South Carolina, though he considers himself a Westerner. "My first job was carrying hods of bricks at a construction site. It's been downhill from there." He has worked as a musician, a guide, a high school math teacher and coach, and a ranch hand. He has been a novelist for almost twenty years, once worked as a screenwriter, and sells an occasional painting. Everett has taught at the Universities of Kentucky, Notre Dame, Wyoming and California and presently serves as Chair of the Department of English at the University of Southern California. "I live on a small farm outside LA where my wife and I care for dogs, sheep, horses, donkeys, a mule, a cat, and a crow." He is the author of thirteen books, the last four published by Graywolf Press: *Watershed, Big Picture, Frenzy*, and *Glyph*. His new novels, *Modern Art and Grand Canyon, Inc.* will be published by the University Press of New England and Versus Press respectively in 2001.

**John Gilgun's** career as a college teacher lasted for 39 years—1960-1999. "I remember every working day as being exciting, challenging, creative. In 1960, they needed us. There weren't enough college teachers. They took me and I found my vocation." Before finding a teaching position, he had dozens of minimum wage, "no benefits, no hope, no future, dead-end jobs....I was fortunate enough to have been able to spend my entire adult life doing work I loved. Find the work you love and do it. It will save you. It saved me." He is the author of *Everything That Has Been Shall Be Again: The Reincarnation Fables of John Gilgun, Music I Never Dreamed Of, From the Inside Out, The Dooley Poems* and *Your Buddy Misses You*. He has also published over a hundred stories, poems and essays. He has recently retired from Missouri Western College in Saint Joseph, Missouri.

**Philip Heldrich** has been a landscaper, dishwasher, file clerk, bank clerk, grill cook, demolition laborer, pipefitter, painter, data entry operator, day laborer, plant man, tutor, teacher, writer. "I know about calloused hands, dirty hair, and sore backs. I was raised in the City of the Big Shoulders on hot dogs and spaghetti, briefly was a sushi-eating San Diego surfer and Oklahoma beef-eating Cowboy." He now makes his home in the Kansas Flint Hills, where he directs the Creative Writing Program at Emporia State University. His award-winning stories, poems, and essays have appeared in *The North American Review, South Dakota Review, Southwestern American Literature, Seattle Review,* and others. A recipient of the Council on National Literatures Award in Fiction, Co-editor of *Flint Hills Review*, he is the author of *Good Friday* (*Texas Review* Press 2000), winner of the X.J. Kennedy Poetry Prize.

**Jill Hochman** lives in McKeesport, Pennsylvania where she works as a tutor coordinator and professional writing tutor at Penn State. She has had a wide ranging working experience that includes a brief career in the movie business as a ticket taker and concession stand worker, and a management position at a Subway restaurant in White Oak, PA, where many stories, including "Stopping in Grace," found their origins and first audience. As an undergraduate her writing won various awards in Penn State's Honors College and English Department, and she plans to continue her education at the graduate level while continuing to write fiction.

**Kaye Longberg** was born and raised in Grand Rapids, Michigan, and has worked as a waitress, a bartender, and a real estate agent. For a time she worked as a document analyst for a litigation support firm, then answered phones at Amway Corporation. She is married, has a five year old son, and is back at graduate school working on a Master of Fine Arts degree at Western Michigan University. She has published fiction in *So to Speak.*

**Bernadette Murphy's** work history includes stints as a waitress, a bartender, a short-order cook, a professional dancer, a dance instructor, a community relations representative for a large metropolitan hospital, an advertising copywriter, a scriptwriter for industrial films, and a sales representative for a children's book publisher. She also taught fifth grade as a substitute teacher for exactly one day. Bernadette is the mother of three elementary school-aged children, and like her character in "Clack, Clack, Clack," she is a compulsive knitter. She is completing *Venice Street*, a first novel, and makes her living as a literary journalist, book critic, and essayist writing for the *Los Angeles Times, Newsday*, the *San Francisco Chronicle, Book Magazine,* and *St. Anthony Messenger*. She also teaches creative writing at UCLA Extension Writer's Program.

**Rachael Perry**, like her father in his youth, "cannot drive nails without planting hammer blossoms in curving arcs around the wood." She has been a babysitter, a burger flipper, a factory worker, a child caregiver, a flower deliverer, a telemarketer, a gardener, a reporter, an editor, a freelancer, a book reviewer, a volunteer, a website designer, an instructor, and a writer. She calls Michigan home and recently completed a Master of Fine Arts degree from Bowling Green State University where she served as technical editor of *Mid-American Review.* She has had fiction in *New Delta Review, Elysian Fields Quarterly: The Baseball Review* and other magazines.

**Larry Smith** has worked a variety of jobs in the industrial Ohio Valley of his youth: short order cook, playground director, delivery person, dishwasher and waiter, musician, steel mill laborer, and high school English teacher. He is a professor of English and humanities at Bowling Green State University's Firelands College in Huron, Ohio. As poet, fiction writer, essayist, critic, biographer, and editor, Smith has published in a variety of publications including *Missouri Review, Parabola, Ohio Magazine, The Journal, River Teeth, Asheville Poetry Review, Cortland Review* and *Descant*. His *Kenneth Patchen: Rebel Poet in America* biography appeared in 2000 (A Consortium of Small Presses). Larry directs publications at Bottom Dog Press and previously co-edited *Getting By: Stories of Working Lives* and *Writing Work: Writers on Working-Class Writing.* He is working on a memoir, tentatively entitled *Mill Dust.*

**Phillip Sterling** has worked as a union gravedigger, a potato chip delivery man, a lifeguard, a pin factory maintenance person, a cherry picker, a gas jockey, a soda jerk, a children's ride operator (zoo train engineer), and a frozen pie technician. He is currently a Professor of English at Ferris State University in Michigan. Among his awards are a National Endowment for the Arts Fellowship in Poetry, a P.E.N. Syndicated Fiction Award, and two Senior Fulbright Lectureships (Belgium and Poland). His poems, stories, and essays have appeared in such periodicals as *The Paris Review, The Kenyon Review, The Georgia Review, Western Humanities Review*, and *AWP Chronicle.* Sterling's *Mutual Shores*, a collection of poetry, has been published by New Issues Press.

**Jeff Vande Zande** was born and raised in Michigan's Upper Peninsula, then moved to Illinois for graduate school at Eastern Illinois University, and now lives with his wife and son in Lower Michigan where he teaches developmental writing at Delta Community College. He has worked as a fast food employee, an usher, a projectionist, a bass player, a furniture mover, a painter, a janitor, a maintenance engineer, a welder, a gas station attendant, a part-time college instructor, and a university administrator. His work experiences have always shaped his writing experiences. His poetry has appeared in such journals as *College English, Passages North, Green Hills Literary Lantern, Blue Collar Review*, and *Fugue*. He is poetry editor of *The Driftwood Review*. "Layoff" is his first published story.

**Julie Weston** grew up in Kellogg, Idaho, and often writes stories of mining and other work in Idaho. Her research for "Doc" included a trip down into one of the still operating mines near Kellogg. She has practiced law for over thirty years and taught in an adult literacy program. Now semi-retired, she lives and writes in Seattle, Washington, and Hailey, Idaho. Her stories have appeared in such publications as *Sojourner ,the Women's Forum, Rocky Mountain Game & Fish, AIM, Clackamas Literary Review*, and *Fishtrap Anthology*. "Doc" is an excerpt from her novel *Bitterroot*, concerning a labor strike in an Idaho mining town in 1960. She has won awards for her writing and been a fellow at the Vermont Studio Center and the Imnaha Writers' Retreat.

**R Yañez** was born and raised in El Paso, Texas. "On the Border between the first and third world," he learned the value of labor. From the working men and women in his family to the undocumented who crossed the Rio Grande, he witnessed the daily struggle for a better life. And while his hands are relatively free of calluses, his writing seeks to honor generations of trabajadores.

As part of an emerging generation of Chicana/o writers. R Yañez's work has appeared in the Chicano Chapbook Series edited by Gary Soto, *Puerto del Sol, La Revista Calaca*, and *Flyway*. "Holy Water" is part of an unpulished book of stories, *Paso del Norte*. He also assisted in editing *Hayden's Ferry Review* and the *Colorado Review*. Currently he is a Riley Scholar at Colorado College.

**Nancy Zafris** has worked a variety of jobs: as Dayton's first "girl" ice cream scooper at Baskin Robbins, as secretary and waitress, high school English teacher in Brooklyn, university professor, and technical writer of computer software manuals. She was also apprenticed for a year under a master calligrapher in Japan.

She has published short stories in numerous literary magazines including *Antioch Review, Missouri Review, Gettysburg Review*, and *Story Quarterly*. She is the fiction editor *of The Kenyon Review*. Her collection of stories, *The People I Know* received the Flannery O'Connor Award in 1990. She recently returned to her native Ohio after teaching at Masaryk University in Brno, Czech Republic thanks to a Fulbright grant.

## Working Lives Series

Robert Flanagan. *Loving Power: Stories.* 1990
0-933087-17-9 $8.95

*A Red Shadow of Steel Mills: Photos and Poems.* 1991
(Includes Timothy Russell, David Adams, Kip Knott & Richard Hague)
0-933087-18-7 $8.95

Chris Llewellyn. *Steam Dummy* and *Fragments from the Fire: Poems.* 1993
0-933087-29-2 $8.95

David Shevin. *Needles and Needs: Poems.* 1994
0-933087-30-6 $6.95

Larry Smith. *Beyond Rust: Stories.* 1996
0-933087-39-X $9.95

*Getting By: Stories of Working Lives.* 1996
eds. David Shevin & Larry Smith
0-933087-41-1 $10.95

*Human Landscapes: Three Books of Poems* 1997.
(Includes Daniel Smith, Edwina Pendarvis, Philip St. Clair)
0-933087-42-X $10.95

Richard Hague. *Milltown Natural: Essays and Stories from a Life.* 1997
0-933087-44-6 (cloth) $19.95

Maj Ragain. *Burley One Dark Sucker Fired: Poems.* 1998
0-933087-45-4 $9.95

*Brooding the Heartlands: Poets of the Midwest,* ed. M.L. Liebler. 1998
0-933-87-50-0 $9.95

*Writing Work: Writers on Working-Class Writing.*
eds. David Shevin, Larry Smith, Janet Zandy. 1999
0-933087-52-7 $10.95

Jim Ray Daniels. *No Pets: Stories.* 1999
0-933087-54-3 $10.95

Jeanne Bryner. *Blind Horse: Poems.* 1999
0-933087-57-8 $9.95

Naton Leslie. *Moving to Find Work: Poems.* 2000
0-933087-61-6 $9.95

David Kherdian. *The Neighborhood Years: Poems.* 2000
0-933087-62-4 $9.95

*Our Working Lives: Short Stories of People and Work.* 2000
eds. Bonnie Jo Campbell & Larry Smith
0-933087-63-2 $12.95